About t

Valerie Ad
Belfast, comp
in Pharmacy   ... . in Hospital
Pharmacy.

She worked, initially, as a Drug Information pharmacist, then, latterly, in the community.

Fond of travelling, Valerie and her long-suffering husband, have traversed the globe and hope to continue doing so well into their retirement.

For Kathleen Quinn

Acknowledgements

There are many people I'd like to thank for helping me bring this book to print.

First and foremost, my husband, Gordon, and children, Julie, Richard, Katie and Lucy, who offered me ongoing support, advice and encouragement.

Gordon gave up the kitchen table on many occasions, allowing me the time and space to write, and was always ready to listen to my readings. I'm glad for his sake that I've finally something to show for it.

I started writing this book many years ago when attending a creative writing class at Queens University Belfast, working at it on and off as my day job would allow. I count myself very lucky to have had Kathleen Quinn as my tutor. It was she who inspired me to write and keep writing. When Kathleen started a women's writing group and asked me if I'd like to join, I was delighted. Through this group I met Judith, Amanda, Zarina, Catherine, Jane and Elaine. Sadly, for our "Sister Scribes", Kathleen returned to Chicago prior to Covid. Happily, though, the group has continued to flourish. Latterly, we've welcomed our first male participant, Ed, and more recently Claire S and Claire M.

This wonderful group of writers have helped me more than I can adequately express, and they've all become firm friends. I'm fortunate to continue to enjoy their company via Zoom on a weekly basis.

Poolbeg Publishing offered to publish this story but on the condition that I'd write two further stories. The added pressure was something I didn't want, but I am grateful to Poolbeg for providing me with the confidence to self-publish.

I'd also like to thank those who read my appalling first drafts, Hilda and David T. Thanks also to my brother, David, sister-in-law, Carol, and my sister Diane.

My grateful thanks are due to Zarina, for her fastidious editing, as well as her warm and gentle temperament. Zarina, it has been a great pleasure to have worked with you.

Finally, I'm not a historian. Forgive me if you judge that I've over-used my artistic licence to create this story. It's a work of fiction and I hope you enjoy it.

Valerie

Child of Prejudice
by
Valerie Addy

1916

Chapter One

Liam woke to the cock crowing and the sun winking at him. Throwing off the eiderdown and kicking back the blanket, he kneeled up on his bed and held the small square of lace curtain to one side. Peering out at the rolling hills, he spied the white specks of sheep and, far in the distance, the sandstone walls of the Cistercian Monastery.

The smell of bacon frying drifted upstairs and made his mouth water. What a treat! He hadn't expected more than the usual bowl of porridge. Wrestling into his clothes and tugging his boots on, he glanced at his reflection in the mirror. Wearing an old pair of his father's trousers that had been altered to fit him, he imagined himself much older than his ten years. He rubbed his stomach. The thought of the grown-up work he'd be doing that day was giving him butterflies in his tummy.

As he clattered downstairs, he could hear his parents talking.

"Oh, Pat, it's shocking to think those young boys will soon be fighting in some foreign country."

"Ah now, it'll be an awful worry for the family." Daddy crinkled up his newspaper and, folding it, set it on the dresser beside him. "Liam." He looked up and smiled. "All set for ploughing?"

Mammy turned round from the work top. "Have you washed your face and hands, and combed your hair?"

"He'll do all that after his breakfast, Mary. The boy looks fit to eat his own fist if he can't start right away." Daddy got up from the rocking chair and took his place at the table. "The smell of your cooking would drive any man to distraction."

"Away with your nonsense!" Two plates of rashers and soda bread clunked down on the table. Mammy stood with her hands clasped and her eyes sparkling, tapping her brown-laced boots on the stone floor. "Well, eat up!"

Liam pulled a chair out from under the table and plonked himself down, a broad grin on his face.

Mammy hummed Eileen Oge as she reached for the tall jug and poured milk into three enamel mugs.

The grandfather clock struck six.

She took a small sup from one of the mugs. "As soon as you've eaten, I'd like you both up and out for the floor needs scrubbing."

Daddy, whose head was bowed over his food, raised a hand towards her.

Spearing a piece of bacon, Liam stuffed it into his mouth, grease dripping down his chin. He wiped his mouth with his sleeve as he chewed on bacon rind.

Tutting, his mother wagged a playful finger at him, then wrapped a chunk of cheese with slices of brown bread in a cloth. She slid the parcel across the table so that it came to rest in front of him. "You'll need extra rations this morning if you're going to plough those two fields." She returned to humming Eileen Oge, singing out the few words she knew. 'Eileen Oge, there's good fish in the sea, But there's no- one like the pride of Petravore.'

Liam laid his cutlery neatly on the plate with a clink.and smiled. He loved to hear his Mammy singing even though it wasn't tuneful. Thoughts, like field mice scurrying, raced through his head. For the first few hours, his father would have his help alone. Ruari Corvin would join them later, for he'd an interview at the barracks that morning. If Ruari got the job with the police, then he wouldn't be able to work for them anymore. That would mean Daddy would need extra help. Today, he'd prove just how big and strong he was.

"Sit there while I comb your hair." Mammy ran her apron-pocket comb across his head.

He closed his eyes and smelled lavender from her dress. When he felt her soft lips on his scalp, he gently pushed her away, shaking his head.

She stood for a moment looking at him, a softness in her face. Then she lifted the broom from beside the fire. "Now get a move on, the two of you! Sara's coming over later and we're planning a morning together stitching clothes for the orphanage."

Liam giggled as he felt the rushes of the broom swatting him lightly on the legs.

Daddy gave Mammy a peck on her pink cheek. "Maybe you could mend the backside of my britches while you're at it."

She sniffed, shaking her head, her curls dancing. "I'll do no such thing. Sara and I will have too much to occupy us." Mammy's usual smile disappeared. "She must be sick with worry about her boys." She set the broom to the side and pushed a curl back from her face.

"I'm sorry, love. Of course." His father looked sad for a minute before hugging Mammy and kissing her cheek. "Tell Sara we'll keep the boys in our prayers."

While his parents talked, Liam ran a wet cloth over his face. Then, he put his boots on, bending down to tie his laces.

His father slid his lunch into his work bag and opened the door. A smell of grass mixed with farmyard wafted into the kitchen. He strode out and Liam had to run to catch up with him.

"What war were you talking about?" he asked.

"The British against the Huns, Liam." Daddy spun round and waved, at the same time blowing a kiss in the direction of Mammy who was standing at the door. "The Leavy twins have signed up to fight."

"Sammy and Arthur are going to fight! Where?"

"Somewhere far away from Ireland."

"Will you not have to go to war, Daddy?"

His father laughed. "Thank God, I don't have to." He rubbed his hands together, then scratched the back of his neck. "It's not a war for the likes of us to be involved in."

Liam wondered what type of war would be suitable for them to be involved in. Daddy always said that only fools sorted out problems with weapons. All that trouble just passed in Dublin; had those fighting been fools? Anyway, his father was too far ahead to ask, and he had to sprint to fall back into step with him.

When they got to the outhouse, Daddy threw the doors open and hauled the plough outside. "This will be a grand old day," he declared. "Now, no more talk of war. We've our own battle to wage with the soil and I need you to heed what I say."

"Yes, Sir!" Liam saluted.

Once in the field with the horse shackled to the plough, Liam kept his hand on the animal while Daddy struggled to keep the plough in line as it jumped and jarred over the stony ground. Yells from his father urged Liam to hold Bobby tightly while keeping him calm. He patted the horse, feeling the damp hide beneath his hands and the roughness of the twine-like mane moving through his fingers. A pungent horsey smell made his nostrils twitch.

With his shirt sleeves rolled up, Liam could feel sweat on the back of his neck and the heat of the sun strong on his head. He looked up at fluffy white clouds sliding across the sky. Initially, he thought he could see a genie with a lamp, but on studying more carefully, a devil with horns sneered down at him.

"Liam!"

His head shot round.

"You have to concentrate on keeping her steady. We can't be making wavy lines! What sort of ploughman would do that?"

"Sorry!"

Cows in the adjacent field crowded at the fence as though inspecting the ground for perfectly ploughed rows. They jostled and mooed, scaring the magpies that had alighted on the wires close to them. The birds soared upwards, the dark blue of their tails visible, their calls harsh and grating.

After working for another hour, Liam heard his father calling him to stop. He laid the handles of the plough down on the dark brown soil. After patting the horse, his father called him over and held out a handful of oats which he trickled onto Liam's outstretched hand.

Liam curled his fingers over the grains and let the horse have the scent of them. The tickle of the moist mouth on his palm as the oats disappeared made him giggle. He stroked Bobby's mane. "Good boy."

Daddy crooked his finger towards him. "Come here, son."

"Yes, Daddy?"

His father had a wide smile like a crescent moon on his lips. "I'm so very proud of you."

Liam felt the heat of his father's hands on his shoulders. He looked up at him, the stubble round his mouth, his hair black, sleeked back behind his ears. For the first time, Liam could see green flecks in the blue of his daddy's eyes. It made him think of what the colour of the sea might be like. The horse whinnied and Liam felt himself being pulled into a bear hug; his nose pressed against the leather of his father's wrinkled waistcoat.

"Liam, you're a fine lad."

He wriggled free and hoped no-one was watching. He loved his daddy, but he was getting too old to be hugged like that.

"There's lots more to do today." Daddy tousled his hair. "But I just need to go up to the house for a few minutes. I forgot that Mammy had asked me to fix the mangle."

"Can I come too, for I'd like to see what you do?"

"No. I need you to stay here with Bobby. Keep him happy." Daddy raked his thick hair with his fingers. "I won't be long. You take a rest and eat your lunch."

Liam shrugged. "All right. I'll do that."

"And Ruari said he'd be with us after lunch. So, wait until he arrives now, will you?"

His daddy winked at him before heading off up the hill. Liam could hear him whistling as he walked away.

Liam felt good. This day was going really well.

Chapter Two

Sara and Mary had been best friends for as long as Sara could remember. Having grown up on adjacent farms, they had gravitated to one another, meeting as soon as they could squeeze through the hole in the boundary hedge.

Now, although married, and living at opposite ends of the village, they still saw each other at least once weekly.

It was an unusual friendship, as most Protestants and Catholics in Lisowen kept themselves to themselves. Not unfriendly, but with an inch or two of reserve between them.

The two religions had their own churches, their own schools and their favoured pubs. Only when a large event, such as a concert or a play took place, did they share the hall that stood beside the village clock. A large, single-storey, red brick building with a certain air of foreboding, it had formerly been used as a famine hospital. Now, with the local sanitorium in Kilkenny, the whole community had claimed Donnybrook Hall as its own, with the priest and rector deciding when, and for what, it should be used.

Sara passed in front of the hall and stopped to remove a stone from her shoe. As she rubbed her foot, she glanced at the brass plate above the arch-shaped doors, welcoming all who were sick and destitute to enter in. Although the sun shone brightly, she felt chilled. She'd left her husband and sons to finish their breakfast in peace, and knew they'd be talking about the call-up.

She was glad to have an excuse to leave the house. The boys were full of chat about the trip ahead! *A trip to God knows where,* she thought. She sensed that her queasy stomach had more to do with the boys' imminent departure than her present condition.

The walk helped to calm her whirring mind and, after a further twenty minutes or so, she reached the winding lane leading up to the O'Dowd's small farm. Through the straggly brambles, she saw Pat and young Liam ploughing in the field and waved to them. They waved back, and she walked on.

Outside her door, milking the goat, sat Mary. She looked up from the stool that was lost under her plump body. "Ah Sara, take over milking this yoke and I'll put the kettle on."

Sara's mouth curved upwards. "Now, Mary, you know you're the expert. The goat wouldn't like my cold fingers working its teats."

Mary shook her head, her curls falling over her face. "Sara Leavy, you just don't want to get those pretty hands of yours dirty." She laughed. "I know you only too well." Mary shook the last drips of milk from the goat and eased herself up, placing the bucket to one side. The goat chewed at the rope that was securing it.

"I'll take that," Sara took the bucket, a small splash of milk slopping over the side, "and set it out in the press."

Mary patted the goat and waggled its hairy ears. "Would you ever mind filling the kettle, while I put Paddy back in the field?" She brushed the front of her apron. "Ah now, I forgot. Can a woman in your condition still do that?" Mary chuckled as she shook goat hair off the front of her apron and smoothed it with her hand.

Sara waggled her finger at her friend. "If I'm not mistaken, I'm your guest!"

Mary curtsied, and both women laughed.

Untethering the goat, Mary led it towards the iron gate securing the side field, her skirts swishing around her legs.

Once inside the house, Sara crossed to the back door. Opening it, she walked into the small yard and unlatched the press. A strong smell of the rabbit hanging behind the door made her retch. Holding her breath, she set the pail of milk on the shelf, covering it with a large, enamel plate.

Back inside the house, Sara hooked the kettle over the fire. Soon, she heard Mary's familiar tread on the steps. She turned as Mary entered the room and flounced down into the rocker.

"Be a good friend and put a cup of tay in me hand."

Sara tutted. "My goodness but aren't you the demanding one. And me expecting a baby and all! Give me time to make it at least!"

"I'm only teasing. "Mary got up and opened the tea caddy. "Take the weight off your legs and sit down." She spooned two teaspoons of tea leaves into the teapot. "Now tell me how you're managing?"

"To be honest, I'm finding things hard." Sara set her bag to the side of the fire and patted her stomach. "The baby's no problem. Not too long to go now. It's hard to believe after all these years and giving up hope." She dropped her chin to her chest, stray hairs coming loose from her bun. She looked up briefly. "Like yourself."

Mary crossed herself. "God works in mysterious ways. It wasn't meant to be for us." She went to the window and looked out as though searching for the answer. She turned back to Sara. "So, what about the boys?"

Sara swallowed hard. "I'm at my wits end with worry."

"Oh, of course, you would be. What mother wouldn't?"

Sara reached for the cup that Mary set on the table. "You know them so well, Mary. No-one would think they could be twins. Arthur with his dogged determination and my soft Samuel."

Mary smiled. "Sure, manys a time they spent here in this house, playing with Liam. Liam would get Arthur to kick a ball with him and then Samuel would read to him." She topped up their teacups. "Ah, they were grand times."

When they'd drank all the tea in the teapot, both women rooted through the basket of orphanage clothes that needed mending. Sara looked at the unruly mess in dismay. "So much to do!" She held her hands either side of her face. "Well, we might as well get started."

"I think you've enough to be thinking about, Sara, without stitching these."

Mary held up a child's linen pinafore where the pocket had come adrift. "I don't mind doing these myself." She laid the garment back on the pile. "Maybe next time we'll do it together."

Sara pursed her lips, suppressing the urge to cry. "Thank you." She took a small sip of tea. "I'm so scared, Mary. Especially for Samuel. He's just so sensitive. Sure, he wouldn't even kill a fly."

"And what does William say?"

"He's all talk about the glory of fighting for the Empire! For a better world. He tells the boys they'll be heroes."

Mary leaned forward in her chair; her face soft with sympathy. "Now don't get yourself all worked up. Samuel and Arthur need their Mammy to be strong."

Pulling her handbag up onto her lap, Sara blinked back a tear. "I don't feel very strong." Unclipping the bag with a snap, she searched in vain for her handkerchief. "Enough about my boys. I see Liam's helping Pat in the fields today."

Mary pulled a small, clean square of linen from her apron pocket and handed it to her. "We're thinking about telling him tonight." She cleared her throat. "About his real mother."

"So, you think now is the right time?"

"Could there ever be a right time?" Mary pulled at a stray thread on the seam of her apron. "Hopefully he'll accept us and not be too vexed."

"Well, he couldn't have had a better upbringing than with you and Pat."

Through the open window came the noise of boots crunching on the gravel, followed by the thud of toecaps kicking mud off them. Pat strode in.

"Sara – good to see you. How are you keeping?"

Sara nodded. "Thank you, Pat. I'm keeping the best."

Mary gave Pat a little look, her eyebrows raised.

He nodded slowly. "I hear the boys have signed up."

"They have."

"Ah now, God protect them." Pat crossed himself. "Let's hope that war will be finished soon, and they'll be back home, safe and sound."

Sara smiled weakly. "Thanks Pat." She lifted her bag and hooked it over her arm. "I need to be going. There's lots to be doing before they leave."

Mary got up and embraced her friend. Squeezing her eyes tightly shut, Sara allowed her shoulders to slump as she exhaled fully.

"Remember to put on a brave face for your boys' sake." Mary smiled.

"We'll be saying a little prayer for you all." Pat caught her eye and smiled too.

Sara unlatched the door, keeping her back to them. After raising a hand, she called out "Bye," then pulled the door behind her.

***

From outside, the mooing of the cows grew louder. "There's a change in the weather ahead." Pat looked towards the window, then turned to Mary. "Poor woman. I hope Liam never has to fight in a war!"

"Where is he?" Mary dunked the teacups into the enamel basin full of water.

"With Bobby. I've just fixed the mangle, you'll be glad to know." Pat rapped the table lightly with his knuckles. "Better get back out to them. Liam'll be getting restless."

As he opened the door, Pat peered into the distance. The horse was thundering along the bottom of the field with the plough behind him and, attempting to keep up, was Liam, his legs working like tiny pistons.

Ruari Corvin was chasing after them.

Letting out a cry, Pat started to run.

Chapter Three

After his Daddy had left, Liam looked about him. They'd almost ploughed one whole field but there still more to do. What if he worked on instead of taking a break?

"Right, Bobby," he whispered into the horse's ear while stroking its mane. "We'll make a fine furrow or two together."

Liam gave Bobby a sharp slap on the flank.

"That's it!" Liam watched as Bobby and the plough trundled away from him. He ran to catch up, grasping the ends of the plough handles as soon as he could.

The sun blazed down on the back of his neck.

They picked up speed. This was what it felt like to be doing an honest day's work! Soil flew up and hit him in the face. He chuckled. It was the very best of dirt. He loved the way the dark brown earth smacked his eyes and his mouth. He tasted the satisfaction of it, enjoyed the smarting of the specks in his eyes. He felt the dampness beneath his armpits. It was the very best of sweat. It was grown-up perspiration, grown-up effort, grown-up independence.

The plough veered wildly over the ground. What would Daddy say now? On and on they went, Liam clinging white-fisted to the handles. He had to keep hold, no matter what. What a disappointment it would be if Daddy had to take over? No, he would plough a furrow on his own.

He thought he heard a voice from far away, but dismissed it as the workings of the wind. He careered on, his legs running to keep pace with the horse. "Whoa, whoa!"

The plough jammed against a large rock causing the horse to rear. Bobby whinnied and bucked.

"Steady there, boy." Dropping the handles, Liam came to where the plough was stuck. Digging his legs into the ground, he grunted and groaned as he struggled to pull the trapped implement free.

"Come on Bobby – pull!" he muttered through clenched teeth. His exertions were to no avail. After his breathing settled, he whispered 'Sorry,' to the horse before taking his hand back behind his body as far as it could go, and then swinging it hard at the horse's rear. Bobby responded immediately, kicking and neighing. Scrambling to get hold of the plough's handles, Liam tripped over a stone, his breath leaving his body with an oomph. He fell beside the wheel of the plough and caught the hem of his trousers in his foot.

Bobby reared again, this time dragging the plough forward. As Liam kicked to free his toes from the hem, the spinning plough wheel caught, first some threads, then material from his trouser leg. Tugging at the material, he managed to break a few strands, but the remainder wound ever more tightly into the axle of the wheel. Aware that the horse was now moving, Liam used all his strength to try to pull himself away.

He felt fear now. He had to free himself. Fast. His trousers would have to come off. He yanked at his belt.

"Stop. Stop, Bobby!" He was being pulled on his back, thudding and thumping, trying with one hand to undo the belt buckle, while throwing his other hand out towards the plough's handles. The horse gathered speed. Liam was helpless. He was a like a rag doll; his head, his free leg and his back flailing beside the plough, every jolt jarring his body.

Kicking his foot with all his might, he felt the trouser leg wind itself further into the metal work. Heaving himself onto his belly, he was dragged face down; eating dirt, the smell of the damp earth heavy in his nostrils.

Suddenly, he felt an explosion of pain.

There was a noise of grating and splintering.

Someone was yelling at Bobby.

Eventually, the horse came to a standstill.

Then Liam heard Ruari Corvin's voice: "You're safe, Liam. I've got hold of Bobby."

In the distance he heard his father calling out to him. "Liam, Liam!"

He could hear himself crying. He could hear his daddy crying.

He felt himself being carefully lifted up onto his daddy's shoulders.

I was only trying to help. The words formed in his mouth but stayed mute on his lips.

***

Later, much later, he was lying on his bed, his parents peering down at him. Their faces swam, forming strange shapes before him, their voices low and muffled. He lifted his head to see where the stabbing sensation was coming from, struggled to lever himself onto his elbows but sank back in agony.

He howled. He was a fox with its paw caught in a snare.

Mammy was stroking his head. "Shush." Her hand was warm, her fingers soft.

The covers were half over him. One side of him was icy cold, the other burning hot. He pulled at the blankets. They were too heavy and wouldn't shift. Why was one foot hurting so badly? He thrashed about. He wanted out of bed, to shake his legs and rid himself of the horrible pain.

Daddy had his hands on his shoulders. Feeling their heat, he sank back into the pillow and let himself be.

***

Hours or maybe days later, Liam heard the door creak open and footsteps on the wooden floor. He blinked, then opened his eyes. They were there again, Mammy and Daddy, but this time their faces were normal.

He looked at them both. Daddy's dark eyebrows were knit together, Mammy's eyes red-ringed and damp. Daddy looked older. He'd never really studied his Daddy's forehead before. Now the lines were etched deep, his cheeks red and angry. And, although the corners of his mouth were drawn up into a smile, Liam could tell he was worried.

Daddy's fingers stroked the back of his hand. They felt like sandpaper. "That's been a good doze."

Mammy leaned over him. She kissed one cheek lightly, then the other. He smelled lemons on her skin as her curls tickled his nose. He wriggled, wincing when he felt the sharp pain at the bottom of his leg.

"There, there." Mammy helped him prop himself up, bunching the pillows and bolster behind him.

He looked down the bed. One of his legs was partially uncovered, the other tucked cosily into the blankets and eiderdown. The uncovered foot throbbed. What lay under the mountain of bandages? *They must have used half a dozen bandages on my one wee foot,* he thought. It was as big as the football he kicked about in the yard. The sickening stabbing feeling returned when he tried to move the limb.

"What happened?" Liam saw his mammy bite her lip and turn away.

Daddy stood up and went to the window. He undid the latch and hoisted the lower window some inches. Cool air slid into the room. "You had an accident. Ruari saved you from much worse; got the horse under control." He looked away. "You've been sleeping this last week."

"I was ploughing?" Liam looked at his parents for confirmation.

"You were ploughing." Daddy gave a little cough. "And it all got out of control. Luckily, Ruari saw everything and was able to stop Bobby. We owe that lad a lot–"

Daddy didn't seem able to finish what he was saying, instead he pulled out his handkerchief and blew his nose.

After tucking the bedclothes around his shoulders, Mammy brushed his fringe back from his eyes. "Dr O'Neill will be back this afternoon. He came just after you had the accident." She smoothed the covers as though she were ironing the creases from them. "He says, all being well, you'll be back at school before Christmas."

Liam jerked upright, sending a spasm of pain through his body. "Christmas?"

Daddy took the small brass clock from his bedside table and began winding it. "We'll get you back as soon as we can."

Liam allowed his head to hit the pillow. He couldn't believe the fuss they were making. Maybe he had broken a bone. Maybe two? What could keep him off school till Christmas? As he tried to make himself comfortable, he began wondering what lay beneath the bandages, and became fretful.

When the Dr O'Neill visited that afternoon, Liam watched as the bandages were removed. A horrible smell, like rotting food, hit his nose. He gagged, turning his head towards the floor, where the discarded dressings lay. They were wet; stained yellow in part. He looked up as the last bandage was removed. Lying on the sheet was his leg, and at the end of it was something that couldn't possibly be part of him.

"Where's my foot?" He yelled. "Where's my foot?"

"Calm down, young Liam." The doctor looked up at him, his eyes peering from over his spectacles. "It doesn't look good now, but it will heal."

Liam shook his head. Things were very wrong. His foot was the size of an elephant's. It was a frightening colour; dark red and purple, the redness going from his toes to half-way up his leg. He could just about see his horribly swollen toes, some of the nails having disappeared. Was he dreaming? Was this a nightmare? Tears forced their way out of his eyes, dripping onto his nightshirt. How was he going to be fixed? He willed himself to lie still and bit his lip as the doctor dabbed something wet and stingy around his foot. He closed his eyes, not wanting to look anymore and tried to think of playing in the schoolyard with his friends.

After the doctor secured the final bandage, he got up and came round to the head of the bed. "You've been a very lucky boy, Liam."

Liam felt a cold hand placed on his shoulder.

"It could have been worse," Dr O'Neill told him.

"How?"

A strong smell of a medicinal substance oozed from the doctor's clothes. Liam resisted the urge to vomit.

"Well, you might have been killed."

Liam stared back, tight-lipped. What could he say? He wouldn't be able to kick a ball about the schoolyard for a while. Worse still, he wouldn't be able to help Daddy in the fields. The doctor's eyes bored into him. Liam bowed his head to break their stare. Then remembering his manners, he thought to say something. "Thank you," was all he could muster.

"I'll call next week, check that the wound's healing."

Later, Liam heard Dr O'Neill talking in the parlour to his parents. Even with his bedroom door fully open, however, he could only pick up on some of the gobbledygook: surgery...gangrene...infection. When the conversation finally came to an end, Liam was glad to have the doctor leave and Mammy come up to see him.

"Dr O'Neill is pleased that the infection seems to be going. He says you have a strong constitution."

"Is that good?"

"Yes. That's very good. It's not good to have an infection," Mammy had a pack of cards in her hand, "but it's very good to have a strong constitution." She smiled at him as she sorted the cards out on the eiderdown. "Now, why don't we have a game of Happy Families?"

Chapter Four

Sitting beside William in the horse and trap, the boys in uniform behind, Sara watched the bramble hedges speed by, followed by the forbidding walls of the monastery. A monk, hoe in hand, was stooped by the gates, clearing weeds from the drains. He raised a brown-cloaked arm and they all waved back.

They were off to Kilkenny to have the twins' photographs taken. It was a week before their departure and the boys were in great form. Excited. For them, it was going to be a grand adventure. For Sara, a time of perpetual worry. Looking up, she watched as oyster-coloured clouds drifted by. She couldn't bring herself to feel anything other than sadness. Pondering on the prospect of a tidy house, devoid of the noise and disarray of her sons, she wished she could say something to make them stay. But that was impossible. They were going. Her boys were going to war.

Yet, it only seemed like yesterday that she was tying their laces and combing their hair, and tucking them into their beds with a story book. Two smart, young men in khaki uniform, barely finished school. The only small crumb of comfort was that they'd be serving in the same regiment.

Behind her, she could make out a few trivial words from their teasing banter. As the trap rattled over the uneven road, the brothers blathered away incessantly.

They passed a sign almost hidden by the hedgerow: Kilkenny 5 miles. William jiggled the reins, urging the horse to speed up.

"Do you know what? I'm sure Mummy's having another boy. I just get that feeling!" He threw his head back. "Three boys! Ten shillings to each of you, if I'm wrong.

They all laughed, except Sara. Well through her pregnancy, she wished for a girl, for a girl could never be expected to go to war. A girl wouldn't leave her mother to travel far away, perhaps never return. At this thought, her heart began to race, and she turned her mind from her boys to her husband. Thank the Lord that William was not joining up. If she'd ever been grateful for his dedication to teaching, it was now. He would have gone, lied about his age, if it hadn't been for the schoolchildren.

Some time ago, he'd arrived back from school, enthused about how his pupils had performed in their examinations.

"Education is what the children of this island need," he'd told her, his thumbs hooked into his jacket lapels. "Education is the key to pulling the country up by the bootstraps!"

And what about their own boys? Why didn't he want them to further their education? Why hadn't he argued against them going? And why hadn't she demanded that they stay? So much unsaid. She thought of the wives of the church organist and the grocer, already grieving for their husbands.

She should have put her foot down when the boys had first mentioned going to war. There was no conscription in Ireland. No necessity for them to go. Now, as she turned her gaze to the greyness of the road sliding by under the wheels, all she could feel was dread.

She wondered how her husband could sound so cheerful. He was chatting to them now, raising his voice to cover the noise of the wheels on the gravel road.

"It'll be grand fun meeting with the other young lads. Sure, you'll be making friends from all over Ireland. All getting behind the great British Empire."

Sara thought about how they'd be taught to fight. How to kill someone else's children. She stroked her belly and looked out over the side of the trap; her eyes fixed on the horizon, the ground stretching flat and green far beyond them.

There was silence for a while, until William pulled the reins for the horse to stop at a crossroads. Two men on bicycles cycled past, enthusiastically engaged in conversation, their jackets flapping. Neither seemed to have a care in the world.

Arthur, directly behind her, tapped lightly on her back. "Sure, we'll be home before you know it and the war will be done and dusted. All before baby's crawling."

William turned to the boys and winked. "Might take more than a few weeks to beat the Hun." He laughed. "Baby Leavy might be up and walking."

The boys chuckled but Sara stayed mute. What was there to say? She pursed her lips. She felt Arthur's warm breath on her neck as he leaned forward.

He spoke softly into his mother's ear. "Don't worry Ma, Sammy and I will be keeping our heads down. Before you know it, we'll be back in Lisowen."

"Marching down Main Street with all the lads," his brother added, drumming his hands on the side of the trap in mock celebration.

William swatted a bluebottle that had been circling his head. "Not everyone in Ireland will welcome such a parade!"

Feeling her eyes begin to smart, Sara pulled her handkerchief from her sleeve and wiped away a stray tear. Arthur squeezed her shoulder. She laid a hand over his and savoured the feel of it. His hand had a suppleness about it. She clasped it lightly. It would be a while before she could do this again. Stretching across Arthur, she reached out for Samuel's hand. He held her hand between both of his, as though cradling an injured bird before finally releasing his grasp.

A farmer herding sheep caused them to stop. Two barefoot children, wielding birch twigs, danced along beside the animals. Sara envied their jollity.

The farmer called out, waving his flat cap at them as though waving a flag. "Good luck, young men. Wherever they send you."

The boys tipped their caps with their hands, broad smiles on their faces.

"God bless you, sir!" William exclaimed.

Sara could see pride in the brightness of his eyes. After the flock had disappeared into the neighbouring field, William shook the reins and the horse trotted on.

***

A couple of weeks later, Sara opened the door to the postman, a letter stretched out in his boney fingers.

"For you, Missus." He held onto the letter as he looked her up and down. She shivered. His eyes seemed much too seeing, as though he could tell the nature of the undergarments she was wearing. She pulled the letter from his grasp, noticing thick dirt under his fingernails.

"Something from one of your sons?" He cocked his head to the side with a greasy smile.

He was too familiar, the last person she'd want to spend time talking to.

She frowned. "Perhaps."

Instead of walking away, the postman stood, hands on hips, eyebrows raised over dishwater-grey eyes. "Young Liam O'Dowd had a bad accident the other day."

Sara startled. "What happened?" She shoved the letter into her apron pocket. "What sort of accident?"

"You're friendly with the mother, aren't you?"

She nodded, irritated by his nosiness. "Do you know what happened?"

"Something to do with ploughing." He hitched his postbag up over his shoulder and sucked his teeth. "His father told me they might have to amputate."

Sara gasped. "Amputate? Dear Lord! Amputate where?"

The postman admitted he didn't know the full story, but Liam might lose a leg or a foot. He shrugged. "I'll find out more. Tell you next time."

Sara shut the door on him. Odious man! She sat down, feeling faint with the news about Liam. Removing the letter from her pocket, she set it on the table. It bore Sammy's handwriting and was postmarked England.

William had gone that morning at the usual time to open up the school; leaving her at home, supposedly resting.

"And what will you do today, my dear?" he had asked. "Nothing too taxing, I hope."

"I'll write a line or two to the boys," she had replied. "Tell them all our news."

"Be sure and say that I was thinking of them," he'd said before planting a kiss on her cheek and heading out the door.

But her thoughts were now for Liam and Mary. She hadn't seen Mary for a while, what with all the fuss over the boys leaving. She reached for her paper knife, holding the letter in front of her. Sammy's childish script. After opening the letter and scanning it to make sure that the boys were safe, she kissed the bottom of the page where both Samuel and Arthur had signed, and laid it back on the table.

What would Mary be doing now? She'd be stuck in the house, nursing Liam, worried to her wit's end. She wanted to see her, but it was a long walk. William would disapprove. He didn't like her walking too far now. All the way over to the O'Dowd's and back? And on her own? He wouldn't be pleased.

But she was pregnant, not ill. She reached for her hat and coat. She'd be there and back and have her reply written to her sons long before the end of the school day.

**

She stood rapping the door with her knuckle, her breath coming in shallow bursts. Looking down, she noticed a few stray weeds growing beside the front step. *Not like Mary to leave things like that*, she thought, wondering if she could ease herself down to pull them out.

The latch of the door clicked open. Mary, her hair a mess of tangled curls, peered round the corner of the door. A strong smell of disinfectant wafted out from behind her.

"Sara! What are you doing here?"

"I heard about Liam." She handed Mary a bunch of powder-blue hydrangeas she'd hurriedly snipped from the hedge outside her house.

Mary took the flowers, mouthed a Thank you, and opened the door wide. "Come in. Come in." She wagged her finger at Sara. "You should be home with your feet up!"

"Well, I'm here now." Sara stepped inside. The parlour table was strewn with rolls of bandages and jars of ointment. "Where is he?"

"Upstairs sleeping."

"And Pat?"

"At the monastery. Called out on an emergency." Mary set the flowers on the worktop and raised her hands. "Their range has packed in!"

"And Liam. Is it bad?"

Mary bit her lip and heaved her shoulders.

Sara threw her arms around her friend. Mary sank into her embrace, her ample chest rising and falling as she sobbed. Pulling a handkerchief from the cuff of her blouse, she held it to her eyes, then pushed Sara gently away.

"I'll make us some tea."

Sara took in the untidy scene, the unwashed dishes, wet nightclothes and bandages hung over the fire. "No need to do that. I'm not here for tea, just to find out how Liam is."

"His foot is almost destroyed." Mary pushed her handkerchief back up into her sleeve. She lifted the poker off the companion set, holding it so tightly that her knuckles stretched white round the handle. "And you'd be doing me a favour by having a cup of tea with me." She poked the fire viciously until the embers blazed, then hung the kettle over the flames. "The doctor thinks the foot can be saved but that Liam will never be able to walk properly again."

"Oh, that's just awful." Sara looked into the distance, her mind momentarily flitting to her own sons, fit and well. "Thank God, though, that he wasn't killed."

"Thank God, indeed."

Sara agreed to stay for a short while, knowing that Liam would want his mother's attention and that was more important. She sat in her coat at the table, as the teapot and a mug were set beside her.

Mary poured a little milk into the mug. "And what about the boys?"

"They've started training."

"Well, we'll both be worrying together." Mary glanced at the picture of the Pope hanging over the mantlepiece and crossed herself. "And saying extra prayers."

They sat together in silence, sipping from their cups. Every so often, the rafters creaked, the only other sound being the ticking of the mahogany clock.

"Mammy!" Liam's voice called out, suddenly, loud and shrill from upstairs. "Mammy!"

Mary ran to the bottom of the stairs. "I'll bring up some aspirin!" She grabbed a brown envelope of powders from the sideboard.

Sara drained her cup and struggled up from her seat. "I'll go, but I'll come back soon." Rummaging in her pocket for a small paper bag, she set it on the table. "Some boiled sweets. For Liam."

"Thanks." Mary gave a weak smile, her eyes flat and tired. "I'll come to your house, next time."

Sara smiled and nodded. She laid her hand lightly on Mary's arm, then turned and opened the door before clicking it shut behind her.

As Sara walked back, her heart felt heavy with sorrow for Mary and Pat. They'd brought Liam up as their own and he'd turned out so well. He was their precious son and now this horrible thing had happened. Crippled for life. It wasn't fair. Then she thought of her own boys. They would be training, learning how to hold guns and shoot them.

She stopped to catch her breath, leaning on a wooden gate at the side of the road. Halfway home. She looked up at the sky, shutting her eyelids partially to screen out the burning rays. She could feel the baby's kicks inside her. Please God, the war would end before the boys would ever need to use weapons. Please God. She held her hands around her belly as she rested on the gate. She looked skyward again.

Are you listening, God?

Chapter Five

A couple of weeks after his accident, Liam was still yelling out in agony when anyone touched his wounded foot. Every day, Mammy would gently place a scalding bread poultice on his injury, but each time, he'd flinch and clench his teeth. Keeping his eyes averted, he tried to avoid looking at his foot. He'd had too much of a shock the first time he'd seen it, and he would wait till things were well on the mend before having a good inspection.

Finally, the pain began to subside.

"You're a very lucky young man," the doctor said on his third visit. "Your lower leg is healing nicely, so it's here to stay."

Liam looked at the doctor, not understanding but Dr O'Neill just shook the glass thermometer violently making a clicking sound. "And your temperature is normal."

Mammy who was standing by the door with Daddy, smoothed the front of her apron. "That's grand news, now." She came over to Liam and took his hand in hers, rubbing the back of it with her thumb.

"Grand news," Daddy echoed, although his voice sounded far away.

"Did the big bone in my foot break?" Liam asked as the doctor examined each toe, pulling them apart, as though inspecting their cleanliness.

"The bones, Liam. There's over twenty of them, just in your foot."

Liam gathered up courage and looked down. He gasped. His white leg merged into a bloated purple-yellow mess which led to five puffy toes. There was no sign of his ankle bone. Indeed, his foot didn't seem to have healed much at all.

The doctor cleared his throat. "I know it still looks bad, but the bones have to knit together, and that takes time."

Liam felt his eyes tingle. He wouldn't cry. "How will the bones know how to get back together?"

Mammy plumped up the pillows behind his back. "Dr O'Neill hasn't time to answer all your questions. He's a very busy man." She turned her head to the doctor. "But he's happy with the way things are going. Isn't that right, Doctor?"

"I am that." The doctor straightened his tie and took out his pocket watch, which he dangled between his thumb and forefinger. "Unfortunately, young man, the bones in your foot have splintered." He held the watch-face up, glanced at it and slid it back into his breast pocket. "But don't you worry. After you get the calliper, we'll be able to have you up and on your feet again."

Liam looked at his Mammy and then his Daddy. "What's a calliper?"

Both had the corners of their mouths turned upwards, but their eyes wore frowns.

The doctor picked up his bag. "A calliper is a metal device that will help you with walking." He looked Liam. "And I'm sure that's what you want!"

Walk with a calliper? Liam didn't like the sound of it. Some stupid metal thing? If he was to use it, then it would only be for a few days.

After Mammy, Daddy and the doctor had left the room, Liam tried to make out the muffled conversation between them, but with the door almost shut, he soon gave up. He lay back on the bed, replaying the conversation that had just occurred. So, all the bones had broken into splinters. If his daddy splintered a piece of wood that he was working on, he threw it away. What use was splintered bone? Would the splinters not poke out through his skin? His stomach heaved at this thought.

**

Spending his days in bed, Liam played board games with the schoolfriends who drifted in and out. He wished the girls from his class wouldn't call so often. It was fine to have boys call, but the girls wanted to know how he felt. They would often weep at the sight of his bandaged foot, wanting to sit and hold his hand. Their sobbing made him feel like crying too. He hated that.

Ruari Corvin visited too. This time, he came in his new police uniform. Liam had never seen a policeman so close before; his dark-green jacket of the Royal Irish Constabulary, with its black leather belt smelling of newness. Ruari had started training.

"The other lads are great fellows," Ruari had said. "Maybe you'd like to join up in a few years."

Liam didn't think so. "I think I'd rather work here …out on the land," he'd replied.

Ruari had patted the bed with his large hands, smiled and said he'd have to go.

After Ruari's visit, Daddy came in to say what a fine young man that Ruari was, and how he'd miss his help about the farm.

"You've me now," Liam piped up.

His daddy suggested that Liam wait until his foot was healed, then changed the subject to talking about the sow that had just had piglets.

***

Some weeks later, Mammy proposed Liam have his first proper soak in the tin bath in the parlour. He couldn't wait. To sit in warm water, to feel the heat of the fire blazing beside him and then be wrapped in a towel. How he'd missed his regular Saturday bath night! When the last dressing was removed, Liam examined his lower limbs. His good foot had life about it, but his bad foot looked dead. His good foot could move this way and that, but his bad foot refused to move at all. The foot was all wrong. It looked just like a big, unshapely lump of suet with five tiny sausages at its end. And his legs weren't the same size anymore. The good leg was twice the width of the damaged leg. He was all lopsided.

Daddy plonked him in the tub, water splashing out gently over the sides. "It'll be good to get the bog off you now, won't it?" Daddy ruffled his hair.

His mouth quivering, he turned first to his father and then to his mother. "Will my foot never work like a foot again?"

"Sure, aren't you so much better." Mammy's gaze was on the bar of yellow soap that lay in a white saucer on the ground. "And the calliper will make all the difference."

"But how long before I'm really better?"

Mammy rubbed his shoulders, squeezing them tight. "Liam dear…"

"Mammy's right. You're well on the mend." Daddy walked over to the back door and put his hand on the doorknob. "I just need to check on a few things outside."

Liam felt the chill of the autumn night for a few seconds before the door was closed.

His mother washed his back, her hand making lazy circles over his shoulders with a cloth, a lingering smell of carbolic soap in the air. Warm water trickled down his chest. Once or twice, Liam saw her turn her head and wipe her eyes with the back of a wet hand.

When his father returned, he helped him out of the bath and, once dry, carried him up the stairs in a fireman's lift. Dressing him, he eased Liam into the bed, and tickled him gently under the arms, making him squirm and giggle.

"Just because your foot's not what it was, won't stop me teaching you how to fix things." Daddy pulled the bedclothes round Liam's shoulders. "Now don't you fret. Your mammy and daddy will make sure you're all right." He patted Liam's head and turned out the gas lamp. "That's a promise."

Liam lay awake that night, worrying, unable to sleep. This calliper thing, what would it be like? Was it some sort of crutch? After a while, he could hear raised voices. Normally, there was peace and quiet in the evening. His parents were soft-spoken and didn't shout at one another like some of his friends' parents. He'd always thought himself lucky; never to have felt his mother's hands sharp on his legs, or his father's belt wielded across his backside.

But tonight, there was an argument in the parlour. He struggled from his bed to hop out of the room and listen from the landing. He felt the cold of the bannister rail against his belly as he hung over. If they looked up, they would see him looking down at them, but their faces were on each other. He stood on one leg, shivering.

Mammy's hands were gripping the back of a chair. "We should have taken him up to hospital straight after the accident!"

"How much would that have cost?" Daddy's face looked hollow, his cheek bones sunken in the gas light. He said something about an operation being useless. Then his voice grew louder. "Sure, they might have taken his foot off then and there!"

Liam gasped. Taken his foot off? Taken his foot off with what? And why? The doctor had said his foot was getting better. As his mind whirred, he heard snippets of things, talk of Mammy's cousin in America and how he might have helped, and then Daddy saying he was to blame. But Daddy wasn't to blame. Liam knew that. He was the one who'd caused the accident.

Then Mammy was talking. "No Pat. It's not your fault. Some things are God's will."

His parents were hugging, Mammy's head resting on Daddy's chest. He watched them for what seemed like an age. When they eventually let go of one another, they started talking again. He gnawed the knuckle of this thumb as he strained to hear. Their voices were lower now, having lost their harshness.

"He'll cope. We'll help him cope." Mammy was wringing her hands together.

Daddy shrugged his shoulders and said something about being out in the fields, learning about farming.

"There are other jobs, Pat. You can teach him how to mend machinery."

"And how's he going to hobble around, heaving heavy weights about with a gammy leg?' Daddy shook his head and muttered something about himself and finding things difficult. Then, taking a step towards Mammy, he took hold of her hands as though they might have been about to dance. "We will do as Dr O'Neill bids. We will take him to Dublin and get the blasted shoe or device, or whatever it is!"

Had he misheard? Shoe? Shoe? Surely, he would need a pair of shoes. Didn't he have two feet? Chilled to the bone, he hopped painfully back to bed and flung himself on top of it. There, he lay, uncovered, before pulling the eiderdown from both sides to try and cocoon himself in.

***

Some days later, Pat offered to stay home with Liam and let Mary visit Sara. Liam had friends visiting and seemed relatively happy.

"Good days and bad." Mary had hugged Pat as he helped her put her coat on. "But all things work together for good. Isn't that what they say?" She wasn't sure she really believed that sentiment, but Pat liked to say it. He'd like to hear it coming from her, too. They had a certain way with one another that served them both well.

"I'll be working for good while you're gone. Mucking out the pig pen, don't you worry!" He'd shouted to her as she walked off down the path. She was glad to hear him joking again. It had been a while.

***

Sara was outside with a cloth, cleaning the door knocker when she saw Mary approaching. With her large belly indicating the imminent arrival of the baby, Sara waved, happy to see her friend.

Mary's round face was red with exertion, stray curls dancing like springs having escaped from her bun. "I don't know which of us has less puff, you or me," she wheezed, handing Sara a barmbrack from her basket as she caught her breath.

Sara inhaled the aroma of freshly baked bread. "Wonderful. Smells just grand, and still warm too. Let's have a slice, thick with butter." She opened the door for Mary and nodded her head towards the parlour. "I'll put the kettle on."

Sara had been thinking about what she would chat about before Mary arrived. With the baby due, she'd have to give an account, first of herself, and then of the boys at war.

But Sara wanted to know about Liam. From the sound of things, Liam was going to be left crippled, and for Mary and Pat that would be just awful. Liam, the boy who loved to be out kicking a ball or helping his father with some job or other.

As they were drinking their tea, Sara placed her elbows on the table, holding her cup in both hands. "How's Liam getting on?"

Mary shrugged. "I suppose you could say he's on the mend." She took a sip of tea. "And the twins? Have you heard from them?"

"I got this yesterday." Sara took a letter from under the candlestick that stood on the mantlepiece. "Would you like me to read it?"

"Of course!"

Sara took a seat and set the letter out on the table.

Dear Mummy and Daddy,

We are both doing well. There's always great banter among the lads, especially us Irish boys. We've even met a bunch of lads from Dublin, all RCs just out of a school run by priests. They say those priests were so vicious that they don't mind at all being away and going to war. That gave Sammy and myself a right laugh.

Sara looked up at her friend, wondering if she felt a slur on the priesthood, but Mary was grinning. Sara smoothed the creases of the letter with her hand and read on.

And every day, they love sharing their terrible jokes with us. I hope you get to meet them some day. The training's hard but well organised. The food isn't like yours and we can't wait till we're home and you bake us an apple tart. Meanwhile, I'm reading that poetry book by John Bunyan that Daddy gave me. I know that will surprise you for I never was one for poetry. I'm halfway through it. Sammy's waiting for me to finish so that he can read it next. I especially like the line:

"You have not lived today until you have done something for someone who can never repay you."

It makes you think, doesn't it?

Don't you be worrying about us. We're doing the best. Tell Daddy that we're taking all his good advice, and we'll have lots to tell when we get back.

Hope you're keeping well and putting your feet up.

Your affectionate son,

Arthur

Mary took a gulp of tea and set the cup back on the saucer. "Sounds like they're getting on the best."

"Hmm." Sara slid the letter back under the candlestick. The picture of King George, hanging, pride of place, over the mantlepiece, stared down at her. The very King in whose name her sons would fight. She clutched her belly and put a hand out on the table to steady herself. *Not worth getting all upset over a portrait,* she thought.

"Are you all right?" Mary got up to help her back into her seat.

Sara winced. "Just baby kicking. You said Liam's on the mend?"

"Thank God. But we're worried about him. What he'll be able to do and how long we can get him to stay in school."

"Staying on at school's a good idea. He could be a teacher or a doctor, clever boy like him."

"Or a priest." Mary crossed herself.

Sara raised her eyebrows. "Would that please yourself and Pat?"

"I can see you don't think too much of that idea."

"It's just hard for us Protestants to understand." Sara pursed her lips, "How a young man is forbidden to marry or have a family."

Pulling a fleck of thread off her dress, Mary rubbed it between her fingers before throwing it towards the fire. "Studying to be a teacher or doctor would take a lot of money. More than we have. But the priesthood wouldn't cost the same."

Sara couldn't imagine Liam being a priest. All somber, dressed in a black cassock, living alone in a big drafty house. She shifted uncomfortably in her chair.

"I'll get you something to ease your seat." Mary took the cushion off the rocking chair and tucked it behind Sara's back. "For us, it would be a proud day if Liam felt a calling to the church."

"Well, I hope he's able to do whatever he wants when he's older." Sara breathed in and out heavily. She didn't want to further the conversation about the Catholic Church. It wasn't her church. The fire spat out some sparks.

Both women got up. While Sara struggled to stand, placing her hand on the flat of her back, Mary brushed up the small nuggets of hot coal from the floor. Then she opened the lid of the teapot and peered inside. "Why don't I make us another cup?"

"Thanks. I'm parched today." Sara sank back into her seat with a groan. "Baby must be thirsty."

Mary buttered some more brack and placed it on the blue-patterned plate on the table. "I've something to tell you about Pat."

Sara cocked her head to one side.

"He's got some work in the big house close to where he was born in Cork. Just for a couple of weeks, every so often. The money's what we need, what with the doctor calling and everything."

"That's grand news."

When the kettle started whistling, Mary poured fresh water into the teapot, swirled it round and topped up the two cups. "He's working for a Lord and Lady, no less." She lifted a small piece of bread and held it between her thumb and forefinger before biting into it. "His uncle's been there all his life, doing odd jobs, but he's getting on now. Pat's taking the strain off him." She rubbed her fingers, a few crumbs tumbling to the floor. "The lady of the house is very kind, makes sure the workers are well fed and well paid. To tell the truth, getting the blasted calliper is going to cost us a pretty penny, not to mention thinking about Liam's education."

***

A cold realisation dawned in Liam's mind. He would never walk properly again. He would be a cripple, like the man he'd seen returning from the war abroad; on crutches, one trouser leg pinned up at his waist.

The trip to Dublin now filled him with dread. He wasn't visiting a shoe shop, as he had first hoped, but a hospital. A hospital filled with disinfectant smells and starched uniforms and clanging metal devices. When the day came, it was up to Mammy to take him. Daddy was away in Cork for a few days. Mammy's older cousin offered to help get Liam on and off the buses. She had some messages to do in Dublin and, sure, wouldn't it be a grand day out for all of them. They sat swaying gently on the bus as Liam tried hard to concentrate on reading his comic.

Arriving at the hospital, they were directed to the 'Handicapped Patients Department'. There, the doctor produced a strange metal contraption, the whole length of his leg. The calliper. Liam stared in horror.

"Mammy, is there not some other way?" he whispered.

Mammy sat with her hands on her handbag, her hair tucked under her hat, her eyebrows knit in a frown. "Is there any other thing that Liam could use, Doctor?" She held a hand out towards the mangled foot. "Something more… normal?"

The doctor said that maybe a special boot might work.

Liam whispered, "Yes," to Mammy. He could manage a boot. He'd always worn boots.

The boot would have to be made specially for him. Would take a fortnight or so. It would cost more than the calliper. Around five pounds. Liam saw the look on Mammy's face, her eyes wider than normal, her skin pale.

"Of course." Mammy offered to pay some of the money there and then.

The doctor said to wait until she collected the boot. Was she able to come back with Liam in a couple of weeks? Yes? Good. If the boy was to wear the boot, the doctor continued, then he'd need a stick. Another two shillings.

Mammy nodded and thanked the doctor while Liam stayed silent. Inwardly, he vowed there would be no stick. He would walk unaided.

***

Several weeks later, Liam returned to school. Each day, Mammy helped him force his mangled limb into the chasm of the black monstrosity of a boot. The sole was thick and heavy. It smelled like the inside of the cobbler's shop but had the weight of a smoothing iron, clacking horribly each time it struck the ground.

Everyone heard him coming long before they saw him.

The girls would run to carry his schoolbag for him. Most of the boys were kind too, but a few of the older, meaner ones would chant, Lame, lame, Liam, behind his back. Sometimes, one or two would try to trip him up and watch him struggle to get up while they sniggered.

Ruari Corvin's younger brother, Sean, who was soon to leave school, gave two of the bullies a hiding.

"I don't like to see young lads being picked on," he told Liam.

Liam liked the fact that Sean didn't refer to him as a cripple, just a young lad. Sean was a good sort too, just like Ruari.

Daddy had been very sorry to lose Ruari to the police, for Ruari had been a good and loyal worker. "A well brought up young man, Ruari Corvin," he remembered his daddy saying. "The RIC will be all the better for him."

Now, it appeared that Sean was going to follow in Ruari's footsteps. Before his last day at school, he told Liam to call on himself if anyone gave him bother.

Liam said that he'd manage fine.

"Right you are, young Liam." Sean slapped him gently on the back. "But any more trouble…"

"Thanks, now." Liam grinned. Outwardly, he decided that he'd fight his own battles but inwardly was glad to have friends that were watching out for him.

Chapter Six

Arthur and Samuel were doing just fine – according to their letters. Sara would read, then re-read them. Chatty, bright nothings from somewhere foreign. Where could they be, she wondered. France? Belgium? Turkey? What would the weather be like? Lots of rain, like Ireland? She hoped they were getting enough to eat. And was there fighting going on? Her stomach tightened. That question she quickly stuffed to the back of her mind.

She took out Samuel's last letter to read over, once more. Arthur was carving a wooden box for her jewellery and Samuel was writing poetry.

'I've read those John Bunyan poems, and now it's time for myself to have a go. I'll never make a poet, but for sure, it helps to pass the time.'

Good that there's time with nothing happening, she thought. Maybe there is very little fighting. Then she remembered what they'd signed up to do and the newspaper reports that continually listed young men dead or missing.

The other lads like to tease me about my writing, but the banter is all good humoured. Most lads here have some sort of hobby, working with matchsticks, or old bits of metal. We've made a great mate of a lad not far from home, Joseph Murphy from Rathduff. He keeps our spirits up with all his japes. He fashioned a couple of hurls from pieces of wood and taught us how to smack stones high into the sky. And didn't he joke that we'd maybe make the team for next year's league. He said that it would be grand to have two Prods join a team of RCs.

Don't you be worrying about us, Mummy dear.'

But the words seemed too cheerful, too contrived. She could almost sense the missing lines pockmarked with something more sinister.

***

A week later, Baby Richard arrived, adding a burst of sunshine to the coldness of that autumn. Mary called, leaving a crocheted blanket and a linen bonnet she'd embroidered.

Liam was back at school. Pat was up and down to Cork. The work and the money were helping. Sara was glad. It was good that Mary was having a better time and that Liam was able to manage his new boot.

As the baby slept next to her, just two days old, she wrote to the twins to tell them the news:

You have a new brother. He's the dead spit of the both of you when you were born, and no doubt will grow up to be just as handsome.

And the baby was a treasure.

As the weeks went by, he slept well, fed well and seemed to thrive on hugs and kisses. A perfect child. William was so proud – three sons.

***

It was on a frosty morning, when the chimney smoke cut an upward spiral into the vastness of a cold blue sky, that the news came.

She was scrubbing the front steps of the house, looking up every so often to peer into the pram beside her. Richard slept soundly; his cheeks rosy. Tucking his hands under the blankets, she caught a flash of sunlight from the handlebars of an approaching bicycle.

Hearing the crunch of the bicycle wheels on the gravel and the squeak of the axel, she wondered as to why the boy might visit their house. It wasn't the usual nosey postman. A dreadful thought suddenly struck her. She threw the scrubbing brush in the bucket and ran towards the youth.

Dismounting, he took two items from his bag, holding them towards her in his grubby outstretched palm. "Mrs Leavy?"

Snatching the telegrams, she bade him a hurried goodbye. She tore at the seals, scattering flecks of paper on the ground. Her heart pounded. "No, please no!"

Deeply regret to inform you …
Deeply regret to inform you …

William came home that evening to find a cold house. The fire was set but unlit. In the gloom, no glow issued from any of the oil lamps.

She heard the familiar cadence of his boots on the stairs and her name called as she lay on the bed staring at the ceiling. The baby slept beside her, curled under the crook of her arm.

The door of the bedroom creaked open.

"Oh, there you are my love. Are you not well? Is baby ailing?" William struck a match and lit the oil lamp that stood on the tall boy. The smell of paraffin seeped into the room and harsh haloes of light crept eerily along the walls.

Sobbing, Sara pointed to the floor, to the crumpled pieces of paper.

He picked up the telegrams, scoured their contents and slumped into the chair beside her. His face was ashen in the gas light.

"No! Not our boys! It can't be true!" He banged his fist hard against the wall.

The baby startled and cried, puckering up his tiny mouth.

"They're dead! Our boys are dead." Sara suckled the infant as she lay, her face to the wall.

She heard William kick his boots off and felt the bedclothes lift as he climbed in beside her. He reached his arms around her waist.

She felt the cold off him. Shivering, her whole body seemed to scream with discomfort. The baby sucked as she held his tiny head tight to her breast.

After a while, William stirred. "I'll go feed the horse. The horse will need fed." He said the words so flatly and quietly, she didn't recognise his voice.

"Do that," she whispered.

She lay on, then struggled out of bed and placed the baby in the cot. Unaware of the cold of the floorboards, she made her way, barefoot, downstairs.

When William returned, he came to her as she stood in the parlour, peeling potatoes onto a sheet of newspaper. He hugged her fiercely. When she touched his hands, they had a clamminess about them, and she could smell the sourness of his sweat.

Craving words, she waited for him to speak.

But he said nothing.

Chapter Seven

Time ground painfully on. The next weeks felt like months. Bled of colour, empty, save the suckling of the tiny infant, Sara allowed life to carry her forward. Washing, cooking, cleaning, feeding.

Only Mary's visits brought small chinks of light into her life.

"When the spring comes, we'll go walking. We'll take baby and a picnic, and we'll trot on up to Carnspindle with the heat on our faces," Mary had said when making tea one dreary day.

Forcing a smile, Sara had reached for her friend's hand across the table and took strength from the grasp.

Joseph Murphy, who had been on leave when the boys were killed, wrote a long letter to the Leavys, recounting his conversations with their sons. He told of their fondness for their Irish countryside and their hopes for returning to farm the land, growing orchards of plums and apples.

The pain of a stranger telling her about her boys.

Her boys!

Did he know that Samuel liked salt in his porridge and Arthur didn't? Did he know that Samuel could recite the alphabet backwards? Did he know that Arthur, aged nine, broke his arm falling out of a tree?

Sara peered out of the parlour window. The tree was still there, living on as though to spite her. It was misshapen, missing the branch that hit the ground with Arthur astride. Sure, they'd made the trip to Kilkenny Hospital with the boy softly whining, cradling the limp arm and Samuel sitting beside him in the trap patting his back, telling him the doctors would make it all better.

She remembered her annoyance at William's reaction. He hadn't seemed concerned enough, while she worried that the arm might never heal.

"It'll heal. Boys get into these scraps. They recover. You worry too much."

William had told Sara to bite her tongue so that 'be careful' weren't the only words that Arthur heard from her each day. He'd taken her thin shoulders in his large hands before drawing her close in a hug.

"Don't be mollycoddling him," he'd said.

That was several years back, a lifetime ago. Mollycoddling? She mulled the word over. What she would give now to be mollycoddling her sons! She felt a rush of anger spreading upwards through her body. Her heart thumped wildly, and she could feel the stickiness of her palms. Why should her Irish boys have been fighting for a British cause?

But she couldn't voice this to William. In spite of everything, he worshipped the British Empire. It was the same with her Protestant friends. The King ruled over both Britain and Ireland, and that was not to be questioned.

***

William opened his newspaper and showed Sara a picture of John Redmond, the Irish politician. The picture had the headline: Obituary. And below it: John Redmond.

"That's the man who thought he could push through Home Rule," he muttered.

"Well, wouldn't that have been good for Ireland?" Sara soothed the baby's head with gentle strokes of her fingers as he lay under the blankets in the make-shift cot. He snuffled a few times, then closed his eyes.

"I don't think so. Ireland should remain British."

"Sure, aren't you Irish too?"

"Yes, Irish, but with allegiance to the King. We are both Irish and British, Sara." He licked his finger and turned over the page of the newspaper.

She didn't want to argue with him. She kept a lot of things buttoned up inside her now. She could talk with him again, but the conversation had become strange and stilted. The softness had gone. The war had done more than destroy her boys. That bloody war! She pushed her fingers into her palms, digging her nails deep into the skin.

She closed her eyes and pictured the twins, fooling around like two ligs, getting in her way as she peeled potatoes on the table. What was it about war that made them want to go? "For King and Country," they'd said. Did the King know? Did he care? And why hadn't William stopped them. They might have listened to their father. Seen sense. She felt suddenly unsettled, unbalanced, as though she could tip over and fall to the floor.

She took a deep breath in. Funerals. They needed to have funerals. A memorial service wouldn't do them justice.

William looked at her as though she'd lost her mind. "But there's nothing to bury!"

"You think I don't know that?" She stood with her back to the worktop, a dishcloth dripping cold water from her hand. "Maybe they could parcel a few fingers and send them back in the post?"

It was unfair of her, she knew, but she'd spat the words out into the room on purpose. She wanted him punished. Maybe now there'd be a response.

"Sara." He held his hands out towards her in an appeal.

She turned away from him. "We're having a proper send off for our boys." She threw the dishcloth into the basin. Why couldn't he talk to her the way he used to. Before the boys went off? She marched up the stairs, the staccato sound of her boot heels puncturing the silence.

At the top, she paused. She heard him. Gulping. Sniffing. He was crying. Slowly, her breath captured deep within her, she looked over the bannister rail.

He sat, hands pressed hard against his eyes, elbows on the table. His shoulders heaved convulsively.

She exhaled. A thought bubbled up inside her head. It wasn't just her that was hurting. She collapsed, sobbing to the floor, banging her knees on the rough floorboards. The baby's cries echoed their own. They were no different to the hundreds of mothers and fathers and sweethearts the length of the country who had lost someone.

She sobbed, repeating, "God help us," over and over under her breath. Eventually, her chest felt hollow. For her, no more tears would come but her baby cried on. She came down the stairs and lifted him gently into her arms and rocked him. Standing in front of her husband, she caught his gaze through his watery eyes. In that moment, she felt she could almost see into his soul; the cut of it, bruised and flayed.

Baby Richard whimpered. She lowered him into his cot and shushed him until the little eyelids fluttered shut. Returning to William, she helped him out of the seat and on tiptoes nestled her head against his neck.

He stroked her hair. "I was afraid to say anything, afraid of losing my wits. I needed to be strong for you."

"Oh, William. Why would you think like that?"

"Some hurts are best buried. My mother and father believed in the stiff upper lip." He took the photograph from the mantelpiece and looked at his sons. "They were our fine young lads and I'm not going to forget them." He ran his sleeve over the portrait, faint flecks of dust taking flight. "We'll have a funeral that will honour their bravery."

She filled the kettle and hung it over the fire. Lingering by the flames, she let her body feel the warmth.

***

They debated what should go in the coffins. Medals would arrive with personal effects, but this could take months, depending on how the war was progressing. Decisions were required now.

Samuel was easy. Sara had taken the one-armed teddy from the small cast-iron bed and held it to her nose. She thought she could still smell her son, his boy aroma encrusted on the long-since flattened fur. Teddy would go in place of Samuel.

Arthur had never had a teddy or comfort blanket. The first twin to be born, he was walking by ten months. He didn't suck a finger or thumb but beat saucepans with a wooden spoon. William suggested his catapult.

"His catapult?" Sara fought back the urge to disagree.

"It was always sticking out of his coat pocket." William took the catapult in his hands, working the wooden handle softly between finger and thumb. "I don't know how often I told him not to bring it to school."

"I don't know how many times I had to sew his jacket pocket when that silly thing had ripped it."

Sara put her hand out for the catapult and William laid it on her palm. She grasped it, the handle warm to the touch. A little piece of Arty. Opening her fingers she held it up and looked at it. Swivelling it to and fro, she watched the rubber band dance.

Her mind flashed back to all those years ago, when her father had presented Arthur with it for Christmas and the boy's eyes had lit up. He'd thrown his arms around his stunned grandfather, who'd extracted himself from the embrace and shaken Arthur's hand instead.

"Glad you like it." Her father had beamed at Arthur; then winked at her. "Share it with your brother. Boys need to learn how to be warriors." He'd pointed his boney finger at his grandsons. First Arthur, then Samuel. "Can't have the two of you growing up to be cissies."

She'd hated the gift; but she loved her father, so she vowed to keep her feelings hidden. Arthur was warned not to target the sparrows that pecked the crumbs she threw out each day. She didn't want any living creature hurt. So Arthur had set up tin cans in the yard and whiled away hours taking pot shots at them. Samuel showed little interest, preferring to have his head stuck in a book. Arthur was thus allowed free rein with his toy. The catapult would be buried in Arthur's place.

The funerals were the best they could afford. A ham was boiled and lay waiting on the parlour table beside baked breads, ready for those returning after the interment. A carriage, drawn by two gleaming black horses with plumes, arrived to take the two coffins. Relatives and friends followed the procession, their black coats heavy with rain.

On their way back to the Leavy's house, people ruminated in hushed tones on the events unfolding. De Valera, President of Sinn Fein, was pushing for an independent Republic. How that could happen was a contentious issue. The war abroad was a bad business altogether, but they might be heading for another one in their own land. One that was more insidious, with no trenches to mark out who was who.

Chapter Eight

The Great War was over. Over two hundred thousand Irish men had been recruited; thirty-five thousand never returned. For the majority of those that did, there would be no celebration. They would have to keep their nightmares hidden, put on a brave face and hope that they could eke out a future without resorting once more to wearing a uniform of combat.

Many of the veterans, disillusioned with civilian life and unemployed, would return to fight again in the months and years to come.

***

Liam had grown to accept his disability, but in doing so, appeared to have lost something of himself. He couldn't keep the weight on, and his face was thin and gaunt. His boyish enthusiasm was gone and he didn't say much.

"What you'd expect of a lad approaching manhood," Pat had said to Mary. "Don't you see the whiskers taking root round his chin?"

Mary agreed. She thought Liam needed a good feed or two, extra butter with his champ and colcannon. They'd discussed, again, when the time would be right to tell him that he was adopted. Not yet. He needed to be more accepting of his limitations before they could open that conversation. It was a matter of time. For wasn't Pat forever taking Liam out to the shed and getting him to help fix some aul broken yoke of a thing, even when the things that needed fixed were beyond fixing? Pat still harboured hope and encouraged Mary to be hopeful too. Someday, they'd get the old Liam back and then they could tell him.

***

Sara and Mary had been at the Post Office when the postmistress said there was a letter for Sara. Would she take it and save Malachy the postman the bother of riding all the way over on his bike?

"Of course." Sara wondered who would be writing to her. Maybe one of the war widows that she'd made contact with.

Mrs Mullan looked around her. "Now where did I put it?" When she finally located the envelope under a brown paper parcel, she put her hand on top of it. She took a deep breath in and tapped her fingers over the letter as though playing a piano. Her large chest heaved up and down, straining the buttons of her white, ruffed blouse.

Sara could see two short thick black hairs twitching on the end of Mrs Mullan's double chin. She knew what was coming. She gave Mary a tiny nudge, but Mary's mouth was already showing the traces of a smile. It was never easy getting away from the Post Office. Mrs Mullen had an opinion on everything and liked to share it with all and sundry.

"What do you ladies think of Malachy? Terribly failed he is. More meat on a sparrow's ankle than on his two legs put together."

The postmistress looked from Sara to Mary, then sniffed, folding her arms under her chest. "Well, it's his wife that's doing it, and her fondness for the bottle, don't you know? Apparently, she doesn't feed him. I've heard he lives off scraps. And isn't he needed here at the Post Office, strong and able for work, for that other young lig of a postman has gone to seek his fortune in Dublin. And at this time too! What do you think of that, ladies?"

Sara and Mary shook their heads simultaneously.

"Not easy for you, Mrs Mullan." Mary answered, her mouth pulled down at the corners with as much sympathy as she could muster.

"I was right vexed, I was. What with all the army about, suspicious and that. He could be shot out on the road. Well, he'd better watch himself if he does make it to Dublin. And he'll need to find a clean, decent place to live, for that flu from Spain is cutting a right swathe through them. Bodies everywhere." Mrs Mullan leaned forward towards Sara and pointed a finger at her. "I mind it's the dirty houses that's the problem, and, sure, Dublin's full of dirt. For isn't it all the poor articles who share a room? Coughing and spluttering their guts up." She shook her head. "If consumption doesn't get them, those Spanish germs will. Lucky we're alright here in Lisowen." The postmistress stopped to draw breath.

Sara seized her opportunity. "The letter, Mrs Mullan?" She pointed towards the counter, and was briefly tempted to reach across and grab the envelope.

Mrs Mullan lifted the letter and cast her eyes over the handwriting. "It's official looking. Addressed to Mr and Mrs Leavy. Must be important."

Sara searched wildly for something to say. "Probably someone looking for money." From the corner of her eye, she saw Mary stifling a giggle with her handkerchief.

Mrs Mullan looked directly at Sara, her chins jutting forward. "And who in London would be writing to you, Mrs Leavy, for money?"

Mary tapped her foot on the wooden floor. "We have to get back home, the both of us, to get the dinner on. Thanks now, Mrs Mullan, and good day to you."

Sara could see disappointment written all over Mrs Mullan's face. She felt Mary take her elbow and direct her outside, the door ting-a-linging shut behind her.

Mary tittered. "What a busybody!" She put her basket on the ground and straightened her skirt, tugging the material over her puffy knees. "Well, get yourself home and see what it's about. I'll just have to wait till next time to find out who's looking for money from you."

Sara laughed before sliding the envelope to the bottom of her grocery-laden basket and bidding her friend goodbye.

***

William was standing by the door, the sleeping baby in the crook of his arm. He kissed Sara lightly on the cheek and she smelt his hair pomade mixed with the milky smell of the baby.

She hung up her coat and reached inside her basket for the envelope. William took Richard outside. Just for a little dander and to get some air, he said. The legs of the chair creaked as she sat down. There was a heaviness about the envelope, and the handwriting looked official. A sudden thought flashed through her mind. Could it be possible that a mistake had been made? Could the boys have been found alive, in some foreign hospital. Her pulse raced. She used the paper knife to slit open the envelope, pulling the letter out. The thought dissolved as soon as she read the first sentence.

Samuel Leavy had been posthumously awarded the Victoria Cross. As she read on, the weight of the letter seemed to increase in her hands. Reeling backwards on two legs of the chair, she almost tipped over, then steadied herself.

Samuel, her soft, sensitive son, had left his trench on numerous occasions to retrieve the injured from the battlefields. He had even, while terribly wounded, carried a soldier on his back to safety. Through his brave actions, many soldiers' lives had been saved.

The letter had ended by saying how proud Mr. and Mrs. Leavy should feel, knowing the courage and bravery of their son.

Her pride was suddenly replaced with rage. What about Arthur? Wasn't Arthur just as brave? Where was his fancy letter? Arthur was just as precious as Samuel.

William sauntered in, bouncing his little son in his arms. For a moment, she could see something approaching happiness in his face. Sara passed the letter to him in exchange for the baby. His expression changed to one of concern when she said nothing.

He looked for his spectacle case and, after finding it, hooked his glasses over his ears and sat down. After reading the first few lines of the letter, he let out a gasp. He inhaled deeply and read on. His eyes flickered then his lips trembled, when he came to the bottom of the page. Setting the letter on the table, he ran his hands over his face. She looked at him, her eyes misted and, on seeing her tears, he reached for his pocket handkerchief and handed it to her.

"I don't know what I'm feeling about this." William shook his head. "I don't have the words. What I want, and can't have, is for them both to be back."

She stroked his hand as it lay limply on the arm of the rocker. "We have Richard," she said.

He feigned a smile, got up and paced the kitchen, stopping to look at the picture of the boys in their uniforms. He stood there, staring. "I can't go to Kilkenny to collect the medal." He balled his fists. "The Mayor spoke out publicly against the war. He's a dyed-in-the-wool Republican."

"I'll go." Sara took the letter from her husband and smoothed it out on the table. "I want to go."

***

The letter had given a time and place to attend: The Town Hall in Kilkenny. Three pm.

Sara wore a felt bonnet with two red feathers. Lacing up her Sunday boots and pinning her mother's shamrock brooch on the lapel of her green coat, she hugged William and Baby Richard before setting out alone. It was a cold winter's day and she took care to avoid stepping on the icy patches glistening on the road. Most of the journey would be by bus and she was glad, for the winter still had the countryside in its vice-like grip.

As she sat on the bus, she wondered how the ceremony would be conducted.

Would there be several dignitaries present? William had warned her that the event would most likely be short, just long enough to present her with the medal, but not long enough to celebrate the true meaning of Samuel's sacrifice. She felt nervous, not wishing to be noticed, and hoped that she wouldn't be asked to make any kind of a speech. The thought of it made her hands feel clammy within her leather gloves.

On arrival, the Mayor's sharp-faced secretary instructed Sara to wait, before disappearing into the official office. Sara sat in the corridor, the breeze from outside finding its way through the cracks. Chilled, she tugged the lapels of her coat around her neck.

After ten minutes or so, the door to the office opened, the thin nose of the secretary just visible from behind.

"Next."

Sara got up from her seat and smoothed the front of her coat.

"Come along now." The voice was more insistent this time.

Sara approached the room in front of her with trepidation.

A bald man with small eyes and thin lips looked up at her from over his round glasses. In front of him was a large mahogany desk stacked high with untidy towers of pamphlets and papers. Behind him was a picture of Eamon de Valera and beside him stood his stony-faced secretary.

"Mrs Leavy?"

"I am Mrs Leavy."

"I think you are here to collect this." He pulled a small packet from the drawer of his desk. Clutching it in his hand, he opened his fat fingers and flung it across the table towards her. "Now if that's all, I bid you good day."

She placed her hand over the package as it slid to a halt in front of her. Would she say something? Should she? Then, suddenly, something welled up from deep inside her. Anger.

"So that's it?" Her eyes blazing, she looked from one face to the other. "That's all you have to say?" She stared at their faces, then shook her head. There was no response. They seemed caught in time. Frozen, their faces devoid of expression.

"He was my child! My Samuel – my brave boy! Nineteen years of age, with brown hair and a small scar above his left eye." She leaned across the table towards the Mayor. "He had a twin, Arthur, who had fair hair and freckles across his nose. He was every bit as brave!"

"Thank you, Mrs Leavy. The Mayor has work to get on with." The secretary moved to the door and opened it wide, returning to stand beside the bald man.

He shuffled some papers in front of him. "Close the door on your way out please! It's rather cold today, don't you think?"

Picking up the small brown packet, Sara turned swiftly and ran out of the door, leaving it swinging on its hinges.

Shaking, she steadied herself against the cold wall leading out to the street. Never had she spoken to anyone like that before. It wasn't her nature. But this was different. This was about her boys. Her brave boys. Her heart pounding, she walked briskly out of the building, only stopping when well away from the Town Hall.

She caught her breath and opened the packet. Assured of its contents, she secreted it safely into the depths of her handbag. Fixing her hat and face, she squared her shoulders and marched resolutely towards the bus stop and her passage back to Lisowen.

1920

Chapter Nine

On Mondays, Liam walked home alone. That was the day his school friends stayed behind to play football in the schoolyard. They kept asking him to join in, but he could really only do goalie. Even then, the ball was forever speeding past him, and it wasn't fun playing football if he couldn't do it properly.

Two more years at school! How could he stick that? His parents had pleaded with him, and were always going on about schooling and making something of himself. No-one he knew had stayed on past fourteen, and many of his friends would be away soon. In another few months he'd be old enough for the big college in Kilkenny, and he knew his parents were hoping he'd agree to go. His exam marks were always good and his da thought he could learn bookkeeping; maybe work in a factory office. Mam had even mentioned the priesthood. Then he wouldn't be able to get married and joke about like Mam and Da. He screwed up his face at the thought of it.

Why couldn't he be a farmer even with his bad leg? He was managing, in a fashion. A bit slow, mind. As these thoughts weaved their way in and out of his mind, he heard voices shouting:

"Lame, lame Liam!"

As he neared the forge, the chanting got louder. Damn them! He wished for a downpour to send them all running. But looking upwards, he saw only blue sky. He wasn't going to be able to avoid passing them. There they were, sitting together, swinging their legs from the wooden tethering rail on the other side of the road.

As he crossed the entrance of the drive to the parish house, a boy called out, "Come over here, cripple!"

Liam shuffled on, his gaze fixed on the gravel beneath his feet. He smelled cigarette smoke wafting from across the street.

"If you're not coming to see us, then we'll have to come and see you!"

Liam flung his legs out in a vain attempt to gather speed.

A different voice called, "No point in running away. We just want to see what's in that big schoolbag of yours."

The voices were those of Declan, Finn and Padraig. Older boys, who'd just left school and were now working at the forge. He'd seen them recently, on his way home from school, marshalling animals and stoking the fire. He'd heard his parents discussing how Dan O'Toole, the 'lazy' blacksmith, had been left to run the forge on his own. Apparently, years of swilling porter and poitín were to blame for his assistant keeling over, dead, on the straw floor. Since then, Dan's son, Declan, and a couple of his friends had been enlisted to do the heavy work and fill the gap.

Most times, Liam was with his pals and Declan wouldn't bother him. It was when he was on his own that he could be in for trouble. He'd already had a few days of being roughed up. Nothing too bad, so far, just shoved about and names called. The name calling was the worst. Spastic, cretin, cripple. He'd suck in his cheeks and try to close off his ears when they started that carry-on.

He realised that Declan was standing in front of him, blocking his way. A rolled-up cigarette hung from his lips. The two other boys hung back a little. Liam tried to plough through them. Declan held his arms out, goalie style, dancing side to side. His feet made a hard tapping sound on the ground. Finn made a grab for Liam's schoolbag. He undid the leather buckles and peered inside.

"Now look at this! History, geography, algebra. What use is that to anybody? Why aren't you out working like us, cripple?"

Declan beckoned to Finn to give him the bag, then held it upside down. Books tumbled out onto the road.

Liam bent down to pick them up and felt a sharp kick to his backside. Losing his balance, he sprawled flat on his face to the ground.

Declan howled with laughter. "Let's see how he gets up."

Liam felt a jolt of pain through his knees. There was a strong smell of horse manure close to where he lay. Thank God, he hadn't landed on it! He struggled to get up, leaning hard on his hands and his good leg to stand. On the first attempt, he fell back down. The boys jeered.

He blinked violently to hold back the stinging in his eyes. He would not cry. His knees throbbed. In spite of his best efforts, a single tear tracked its way slowly down over one cheek.

Padraig knelt down at Liam's side and shook his head, his big ears waggling. "Want a handkerchief?" He used his clenched fists as wipers for his eyes. "You big baby."

Liam wiped his sleeve across his face, trails of snot catching on the material. "Piss off, elephant ears!"

Padraig stuck out his tongue, stuffing his thumbs in his ears and waggling his fingers.

Finn and Declan bent over, holding their stomachs as they mocked him with their chortles.

Pushing hard on his hands and knees, Liam managed to stand, wincing at the sharpness of the pain. He looked at his grazed knees, a red trickle was making its way down his leg towards his deformed foot. There was an ache in the place where his ankle bone once was, a bigger ache than usual.

He felt like a deer surrounded by wolves; helpless, the pack prowling, playing with their prey. What could he do? If he tried to walk away, they could just as easily knock him over again. He stared past his attackers and out towards the hills. Willow and sycamore trees danced in the breeze.

Declan pointed a finger at him. "Of course, cripples can't do anything useful! Cripples can't make a hay bale, plough a field, shoe a horse."

"Shovel shite," Finn added, to hoots of laughter.

Liam tucked his chin into his neck. He could be a bull, though. A bull that would gore anyone who stood in his way. "Get out of my way!"

As he flailed forwards, Declan, the tallest, caught hold of him by the arm and brought his face so close to Liam's that he could smell the bread and dripping from it.

"You're pathetic." Declan pushed him back so violently that Liam stumbled again. "You should be locked away in the looney bin."

The others laughed.

"He'd fit right in with all those mad people." Padraig slapped him so hard on the back that it knocked the breath out of him.

Declan grabbed him by the collar. "I'm going to do you a favour and make that good foot of yours match that other useless one. When I stamp on it, we'll see how much you squeal."

Liam closed his eyes. This was really going to hurt.

"Hey, you lot! What are you boys up to?" A priest, panting for breath, was running towards them. His black cassock billowed out from him.

Declan released Liam and patted the top of his head. "We were just having a bit of fun, Father."

"Well, it didn't look like fun to me. I saw you all from the upstairs window."

"Ah, no harm done now, Father."

With that, Declan and his friends sloped off in the direction of the forge. As they did so, Dan O'Toole, the blacksmith, came round from the side of the forge. "Why the feck aren't you getting on with the job I gave you?" He cuffed his son on the ear, then touched his cap in recognition of the priest. Finn and Padraig slunk behind Declan, keeping well away from the blacksmith.

Father Flaherty nodded at Dan then took Liam by the shoulders fixing him with his dark eyes. "Are you alright now, Liam?"

The smell of incense from the cleric's clothes tickled Liam's nose. "I'm fine, Father."

The priest looked from Liam's scratched knees to the books strewn in front of him. "They've no wit, at all." He shook his head. "Boys can be cruel without knowing. Most times, they don't even know how to be dealing with themselves."

Liam wondered what that meant. In his mind, Declan and pals were just plain nasty.

The priest helped Liam gather his books together and put them back in his schoolbag. "Not fair on you, though."

Liam shrugged. "I'm alright now, Father." He didn't want the priest's concern, and he didn't want to be late home. There'd be questions asked.

The priest pinned his eyes on Liam's face. "Do you want to come into the parish house for a drink of milk?"

"Thank you, Father, but I'd best be getting home" Liam hoisted his schoolbag onto his shoulders. "I've a few chores to help my da with before supper."

"Of course. But my door is always open."

Liam nodded to the priest and turned away from him. He listened for the sound of the priest's feet crunching back towards the parish house but heard none. He turned round. The priest was standing on the pavement looking at him. The cleric raised a hand and Liam waved back. It wasn't nice to be stared at. What was Father Flaherty thinking, watching him like that? He didn't need more pity. But he'd been kind and saved him from a real hiding. If he was to tell his mother – and he didn't plan to – she would say that Father Flaherty was something of a guardian angel. She worshipped the priest and always blessed herself when his name was mentioned. Anyway, he wouldn't be calling up at the parish house any time soon, asking for help. Going to mass with his parents was enough to be doing.

He limped on down the road. As he passed the Protestant church, he saw his mother's friend, Sara, with some other women on their knees weeding the flower beds. Sunlight glinted off the names that had been carved into the brass plate affixed to the newly-erected monument to the war. Arthur and Sammy's names were on it. It was sad that they'd been killed. They'd been nice to him all those years ago, and played with him even though he was so much younger. Arthur had even let him use his catapult to try to shoot Sammy.

He hoped Sara hadn't seen him. He'd be really late home if he had to speak to her.

Too late.

"Hello, Liam." Sara left her trowel sticking in the clay and went to greet him. She rubbed the soil from her hands on her apron. "It's a bit late for you to be passing at this time, isn't it?

Liam hung his head. "No, not really."

"Hmm." Sara looked at his bloody knee. "Did you fall?"

"I stumbled, but I'm fine, thanks."

She tilted her head to one side and studied his face. "You should wash that graze when you get home. Get the gravel out. Well, your Mammy will tell you the same thing when she sees it." She fished in her apron pocket for a paper-clad toffee and gave it to him. "For after your tea. And tell your Mammy I'll call by tomorrow."

Liam, relieved to have extracted himself so lightly, and happy to be the proud recipient of a piece of toffee, felt that the rest of his journey home had been somewhat eased. Next Monday, he'd take the longer way home from school, by the river.

His mother met him as she carried a basket of freshly dried clothes into the house. "What happened to your knee?"

"I took a tumble." He opened his bag and put his books out on the table. "It's nothing." Several loose pages floated to the floor.

His mother picked a book up that had lost its cover. "What happened here?" Another page fell from the book. "Has someone been throwing these around?"

Liam shrugged.

She pulled him close to her. "Oh, Liam."

He struggled out of her grasp. "I'm fine, Mam. It's only horseplay."

He watched his mother as she let him go, a concerned look on her face.

"As long as you're all right."

"I am. You don't need to fuss."

His mam didn't look convinced, but busied herself at the fire, stirring the pot of vegetable broth hanging over it with a large wooden spoon.

Liam went to the tin jug and poured himself a glass of water. His hand shook as he filled the glass. Water slopped over his hand. He wasn't sure which was worse, the bullying or his mother's pity.

"I'm going upstairs, Mam." He could feel his mother's eyes on him. "Don't look at me like that. I'm fine. Really." He didn't want her to worry. He didn't want anyone to worry about him. There was a baby on the way and that was enough for Mam to be thinking about. He drank the water with loud gulps, put the glass on the drainer and heaved himself up the stairs.

Lying on his bed, he grimaced as the day's events played out before his eyes. He wished his parents had thought of another name for him. It would have been grand to have taken his father's name. But Lame Liam! He rolled the letters round his tongue and spat phlegm out onto a handkerchief.

And why couldn't he have gone to hospital all those years ago? Why didn't his parents ask for a lend of money? There were enough money lenders in Lisowen. The hospital would have fixed him. Operations fixed people. But Mam talked about God's will. So, why had God decided that he shouldn't walk like everyone else? He rolled round and buried his head in the pillow.

Chapter Ten

Mary had news for Sara. She'd been bursting to tell her but been afraid to say. A baby! Pat and herself were to have a baby. After all the previous miscarriages she'd suffered, the doctor had confirmed that all was well. Would Sara forgive her for keeping it to herself? Just for a while, until everything seemed certain.

Sara hugged her friend. She understood. She remembered the delight when told that she was to have a baby once more. Mary had been through some terrible years and deserved some happiness. Sara's mind flitted momentarily back to her twins, their freckled beaming faces, but brought herself quickly back to the present and Mary's parlour. It was a Saturday and William had taken Richard on the bus to Kilkenny to buy some books. Liam was at a friend's house playing chess and Pat was working in Cork for a few days.

Mary patted her stomach. "I'm surprised you didn't ask me about my big belly."

Sara sucked in her cheeks and stifled a smile. "I just thought you must have been getting through an awful lot of potatoes."

"Ah, you did, did you?" Mary scowled, then her face broke into a wide grin.

"Well, it's great that you're keeping so well." Sara glanced at the newspaper lying on the table. She shook her head. "Another police barracks burned to the ground and two policemen shot."

Mary nodded. "I know." She let her breath out with a long sigh. "Pat's worried about his cousin in the RIC. The Cork people have turned against them and some of the shop keepers won't even serve them."

"That's horrible."

"It is. But it'll be worse with those soldiers from England helping the police." Mary took several skeins of wool from the bottom of her wicker basket, laying them out on the kitchen table. "A ragbag lot of hooligans; the Black and Tans." Finding one of the ends of wool, she twiddled it between her fingers. "Pat says it'll only lead to more trouble. His cousin doesn't want to be working with British soldiers, but he's little choice if he's to put meat on the table. Then, Pat says, there'll be more violence before Ireland is ever ruled by the Irish."

"Well, I hope not." Sara felt uncomfortable. She hated this unrest. The whole situation in Ireland worried her. Frightened her even. She forced a smile and took a skein of wool from the table, laying it over her lap. "Am I right in thinking that you'd like me to help you get this wool in order?" She held her hands up, a strand of wool pinched between her thumb and forefinger.

Mary smiled widely and looped the wool back and forth around Sara's outstretched hands. "What does William think?" She cocked her head to one side. "You know, about things going on?"

Sara thought of what William had told her. Home Rule was dead and that was a good thing as it would have meant Ireland being controlled by the Pope. Imagine that? Paying their taxes to a foreign false idol? No, thank you. The counties at the top of Ireland would never accept Sinn Fein governing them and would revolt. The Leavys were British and would remain so.

She chose instead to say: "William thinks that our family might be safer up north."

"No!"

"Don't worry Mary. It won't happen. He'd have to lead me kicking and screaming to get me past Beggarstown. He knows that."

"But there's no danger to you."

"I know. It's all bluff and bluster."

After all the wool had been neatly wound into three large balls, Mary placed them carefully back into the basket where she kept her needlework.

The kettle was hung over the fire and both women sat either side of it. Mary rocked gently; Sara sat upright.

"How's Liam?" Sara asked.

"He doesn't say much when he comes in from school." Mary spooned tea leaves into the white teapot, then poured boiling water over them. "But he often looks dishevelled, as though he's been in a fight." She stirred the tea. "I really hope he isn't being picked on."

Sara unhooked two teacups from the dresser and set them on the table. "I hate the thought of anyone being cruel to your Liam. Especially after everything he's been through."

"Well, children can be little villains. Our Donal was teased mercilessly because of his stutter." Mary sighed and crossed herself. "God rest his soul." She poured tea for both of them. "Pat says we mustn't treat Liam differently but it's so very hard for me."

Sara shrugged. "Everything about being a parent is difficult." She added a little milk and blew on the rim of her cup before lifting it to her lips.

Shunting the last few pieces of coal from the scuttle onto the fire, Mary said she'd fetch more coal from the shed. The tick-tock of the clock filled the room, the warm glow of the fire lighting up the stern-faced Pope hanging above the mantelpiece.

As she sipped her tea, Sara studied his picture. How could such a cross-looking man be revered by so many people? Protestants thought it all akin to idolatry, a mortal sin to put faith in any living person other than God.

When Mary teetered into the kitchen, laden down with two buckets of coal, she caught Sara staring at the photograph. "I know from the way you're looking at him that you don't see him the way I do."

"He looks a little scary." Sara thought the Pope looked far from able to comfort anyone. "But maybe he's not."

"Well, I wouldn't be scared if he set his big hand on my head to bless me." Mary let the buckets down with a thump, several coals rolling out and along the floor.

"Mary O'Dowd! Don't be lifting such heavy weights. I could have done that for you!"

Mary tutted. "Don't fuss. I'm grand." She grabbed a brush and shovel and started to sweep up the mess, humming tunelessly.

Sara thought to change the conversation. She drained her cup and said, "I saw Dearbhla Finnegan the other day and she looked bate out. All shrivelled into herself. We always suspected she was up to something, what with all those strange men coming and going."

"Ah, dear old Dirty Dearbhla."

"Mary!" Sara clicked her tongue. "If your mother was here, you'd get a right telling off!" She laughed. "I hear the daughters have taken over the business."

"Ah, Dearbhla will be glad of a rest."

"That's true."

Both women chuckled.

The grandfather clock struck twelve.

"I must be going." Sara set her teacup on the worktop and reached for her coat.

Outside, the chickens clucked loudly. A few specks of rain pattered against the window, tracking downwards in random patterns.

Mary lifted the newspaper that lay folded on the chair. She stood reading the front page before flinging it down. "Dear Lord!"

"What's wrong?" Sara asked.

Mary picked it up and showed it to her. "Seventeen years old. One of those RIC men was only seventeen years old."

"Dreadful, I know," Sara buttoned her coat, her lips set tight, "but we can't afford to be pulled down by it." She would keep her emotions in check. She'd had enough crying to last a lifetime. "But I'm afraid there's little decent people like us can do to stop it."

Mary sank back into the rocking chair. "It's not good. Not good for anybody."

"Well, don't you be thinking about things like that. This baby will need you in the best of form. Let's both try our best to keep our spirits up."

With that, Sara gave her friend a warm hug and let herself out.

Chapter Eleven

It was that time of evening when the gloom floats like a mist and trees can be mistaken for people. The day had been warm but now the heat had gone from the sun with the promise of a cold cloudless sky.

Dan had been watching them from the shadows of the trees as they embraced; disgusted and excited in equal measure. One of his 'comrades,' who was related to the girl's family, had told him they'd be here. It had made Dan wonder whether the bitch should be taught a lesson. And why he'd hawked that bloody heavy bucket and sack all the way from the forge in expectation.

Waiting a while, in case they'd settle themselves on the ground and he could witness something more intimate, he leaned against the trunk of a sycamore tree, feeling the sharp nobbles digging into his back. Disappointingly, the pair seemed content to nuzzle one another like young affectionate ponies. He hadn't even been able to see a bare titty or a white thigh, let alone them riding.

After they parted, the youth headed off towards Beggarstown and the girl stood fixing her mane of hair, shaking it from side to side, humming to herself. Her long tresses fell well below her waist and, in the failing light, it looked like bleached flax. She was slight, clad in a thin, ill-fitting dress that could have been a hand-me-down.

Dan grabbed her from behind.

It was so easy, like bringing down a wounded deer. She struggled in vain, crying out shrilly, her head thrown backwards. Pinning one arm round her throat, he clamped his other hand over her mouth. "Shut your trap, missy or I'll shove a rag in your mouth. Keep deadly quiet if you don't want harmed."

The girl went limp in his grasp. He could smell scullery and washboard from her. It reminded him of his Grainne, and he felt momentarily shamed. Stamping on that thought, he set his mind to the task in hand. Forcing her arms behind her back, he bound them with twine. He pulled her towards a tree and wound more twine around her body, securing her to the trunk of a sycamore. She shook uncontrollably, her gaze downward as he worked to fix the final knot in place.

She whimpered, "Don't hurt me, Mister. I haven't done anything wrong."

"Oh, indeed you have, you slut. And now you're going to pay for it." The balaclava muffled his words, a good thing he thought, as she might recognise him from his voice.

"Where does that young bastard live? Now tell me the truth or I'll be forced to do things I don't want to."

The girl cried, "I don't know, Mister. I don't. He's just a boy I know." She shivered, her thin shoulders moving up and down in time to her sobs.

"I'll repeat. Where does this bastard boy of yours come from?"

"I told you, I don't know. Not exactly. Somewhere near Beggarstown." She struggled against the tree. "He wouldn't ever tell me. Said that the least I know, the safer for me."

"So how the blazes did you meet?"

"He came to our house once." Tears rolled down her face.

"And why would he come to your house?"

She shook her head. "He asked me if I'd like to see him. Just for walks, mind."

"So, you think it's all right to be cavorting about with a feckin' British soldier!" Dan snorted.

Snot trickled down from her nose. "Mister, please. It wasn't anything wrong we were doing."

Dan pulled the knife from the back of his trousers. How easy it would have been to have killed them both when they were petting. He should have stuck his knife right through that soldier's heart. But he might have been armed and now he'd missed his opportunity. However, he was going to enjoy giving the little hussy a haircut.

He grasped her hair and wound it in his hand like a skein of rope.

The girl yelled, struggling after seeing the glint of the knife. He pulled a rag out from his pocket and shoved it in her mouth, making her gag. She spat it out on the ground.

He bent down to retrieve it and forced her mouth open before shoving it inside again. As she wrestled her head from side to side, her teeth clamped about the rag, he whispered in her ear. "Make one more noise and I'll slit your throat." He drew the tip lightly across her neck, a small bubble of blood forming on her white skin.

He pulled her face up to meet his. He could see the terror in her eyes, the pleading of her pathetic face. "This is what collaborators get." He took the knife to her scalp.

Tears continued tracking down her face as she clenched her eyes shut.

When most of her hair lay on the forest floor, he looked for the bucket he'd brought with him.

Damn, the blasted tar was beginning to set. Raising the bucket above her head, he tried to tip the contents onto her scalp. Nothing. He took a stick from the ground and attempted to stir it.

It had the consistency of congealed porridge.

Exasperated, he took his knife and plunged it into the gloopy mess. He slathered her face and scalp with the black substance, some of it getting on his hands. Loading his knife again, he attempted to spread it over her breasts and down her thin legs.

Then, holding the sack upside-down, he tipped the contents over his victim.

Feathers fluttered down. Some stuck to her head. For good measure, he pressed a handful of feathers over each of her breasts, their firmness stirring him. He patted some up her thighs and, momentarily, thought of releasing his belt buckle before realising he could be left covered in tar.

The girl spat out the rag and called for help.

Reaching for the knife again, Dan held the blade close to her throat. "Another word from you and, so help me God, I'll sink this blade into your dirty, slutty throat. Do you hear me?" He slapped her hard across the face.

She nodded, then turned away from him, her shoulders hunched. A few feathers floated from her scalp onto her bare arms.

***

Pat and Liam were returning from fishing when they heard the screams. Pat stood still, pulled on Liam's arm and squeezed it. "Did you hear that?"

"Someone's calling." Liam put a cupped hand to his ear. "Someone's calling for help!"

Pat dropped the fishing equipment he was carrying onto the ground. "Wait here." As he started to run, he shouted, his head turned back. "Liam, stay there!"

Liam set down the basket cradling the floundering trout and hobbled after his father, who was running in the direction of the setting sun. "I'm coming too!"

In the velvet-green light, Liam could just make out his father, his arms waving, yelling into the night air. "I'm coming! Help is on its way!"

***

Dan heard voices as he finished sticking the last of the feathers on the girl's body. Fuck! Shoving the sticky knife into his belt, he turned on his heels and sped in the opposite direction to the voices. As he ran, he could hear the girl shouting for help.

Within a few minutes, he was wheezing and sweating profusely. Stopping to catch his breath, he pulled off the balaclava and stuffed it in his pocket, then wiped his tarred hands on the legs of his trousers. A couple of loose feathers dislodged from his clothes. He sneezed, the sound disturbing the crows who squawked and wheeled above him. He drew in large gulps of air, hoisted his trousers up and refastened his belt a notch. Then, in spite of the stitch in his side, he ran on.

When he felt he was far enough away from the girl, he slowed to a walk. From the edge of the forest, he took the low road; infrequently used by travellers due to its potholes. Eventually, he reached the closed doors of the forge. A loud creak issued as he swung open the main door. A wall-mounted gas lamp glowed dimly from inside. Declan lay asleep on a hay bale, his mouth open. Beside him, the end of a cigarette glowed red on the floor.

Dan stamped on the smouldering butt. He kicked at Declan's feet and the lad awoke with a start.

"Get up, you lazy bugger." Dan growled. He pointed at the cigarette butt. "You could have started a fire with your carelessness."

Declan sprang to his feet. "Why are your hands and clothes all black?"

"Army business." Dan tapped his nose, leaving a dot of tar on it. "Now get me some turps so I can clean myself up."

***

Pat followed the yells of help, eventually reaching the tree where the girl was tied.

"Good God!" He could just make out the slight form in front of him, the twine around her waist and chest.

She moaned as he approached her. "Don't hurt me Mister." She seemed to shrink back from him.

"You're safe now, girl. I'm here to help you." He used his penknife to saw through the twine that bound her. He felt revolted. How in God's name could someone leave somebody in this state?

"Who the divil did this to you?"

"I don't know," the girl sobbed, running her tarry hands over her matted hair. "I thought he was going to kill me!"

Pat pulled a handkerchief from his pocket and tried to rub some tar off her face.

She winced. "And he shore me like a sheep!" She pulled at her stubbled hair.

"The bastard! Excuse my language, young lady, but it was a cruel, despicable act. I'm sorry for you, Miss, I truly am." Pat looked at the mess in front of him, the girl's clothes, torn, her small head crowned with tufts of matted black hair. "We'll need turpentine to get that stuff off."

The girl sank to the ground, where she sat, her knees pulled up towards her. "Mam won't have turpentine, just soap."

Pat hunkered down to face her. "I've turpentine at home. My wife will help you get cleaned up."

At that moment, Liam arrived and stood, frozen with shock.

"This poor girl needs our help, not someone to gawk at her." Pat offered his hand out to the girl who took it and allowed herself to be pulled to standing. He nodded to Liam. "Now, go get the fishing tackle and make your way home. I'll be right behind you."

As Liam limped ahead, Pat hoisted the shivering girl into his arms, and began the long walk back to his house.

Chapter Twelve

From inside the parlour, Mary heard Liam's lopsided footsteps approaching the door. She pulled back the curtain. Liam was on his own. Where was Pat? The two of them had gone fishing hours ago. As Liam unlatched the door, she stood waiting for him, her outstretched hands ready to take the fishing-rods and basket.

"I was getting worried about you, out gallivanting." She wagged a playful finger at him. "And your da had better be here soon if he wants his stew hot."

Then she saw the state of him, gasping for breath, the words coming in fits and starts.

"Da's not far behind..." He put a hand to his side. "He's carrying a girl." He hobbled past her and sank unto a chair. "She'd been tied to a tree and messed up with tar!"

"Dear Jesus! Why would anyone do that?" Tarring someone was a brutal punishment, a humiliation for fraternising with the enemy. It was hard for Mary to understand how anyone could justify such an act. "I'll go get turps."

Taking an oil lamp, she scurried to the shed, where she peered at the different bottles lined up along the shelf. Selecting a ribbed bottle, she opened it and sniffed. The pungent smell of turpentine hit her nose.

Back in the parlour, she studied the label in the lamp light to make sure. Turpentine: for superior cleaning. Pulling several rags from under the work top, she opened an old newspaper and spread it out in front of the fire. Placing her milking stool on top of the paper, she turned to Liam as he stood near the hearth, warming himself.

"Take some stew from the pot, get it into you and then off to bed," she told him.

"I could help?"

She shook her head. "I'm sure the poor cratur won't want an audience."

He nodded in acknowledgement.

Hearing footsteps approaching the house, Mary opened the door, standing aside as Pat came in and deposited the girl carefully onto the stool. Both stood looking at the trembling waif; her body blackened and scalp matted, with eyes staring into the distance.

"Where did you find her?"

Wiping his hands on a rag, Pat fought to catch his breath. "Near the banks of the Bawn, on the Beggarstown side."

On bended knees, Mary placed her hands lightly on each of the girl's dirty arms. "You poor child."

The girl whimpered, plucking a few feathers away from her skin. From under her breath, she said something about her mam.

Mary felt Pat's calloused hand pull her gently to her feet. His rough cheek brushed ever so briefly past hers. Then, he set a wooden chair in front of the stool and pulled it back slightly so that Mary could sit on it, facing the girl.

"Now child, you're safe here. I'm going to clean you up." Mary leaned forward taking the girl's limp hands in her own. "What's your name?"

Sobbing, the girl replied, "Sorca Miskelly."

"Oonagh Miskelly's daughter? From Carnspindle?"

The girl nodded, tears streaming down her face.

"Who was the brute who did this?"

Shaking her head, the girl pulled her hands away and tugged nervously at her filthy dress.

Mary put her hand tenderly under the girl's chin and lifted it so that their eyes met. "Now, no more crying, Sorca." With her other hand, she beckoned Pat to her side. "I need a clean nightdress and socks from my dresser." She twisted round to where Liam was sitting, spooning food into his mouth, while gazing in the girl's direction. "Now, what did I say about getting off to bed?"

Liam nodded and gulped down the remainder of the stew before wiping his mouth on his sleeve. "I'm going now." He slid out of his seat, leaving the empty dish on the work counter.

As he struggled upstairs, Pat squeezed past with the fresh clothing. "We'll talk about this in the morning, son."

Pat set the clothes on the rocker beside Mary. "I'm thinking I should cycle to the local barracks and tell the RIC. Get them to catch the blaggard!"

"No!" Sorca stood up suddenly and started to shake. "Please, no. My uncle's in the police, and I don't think he would want to help me." She stood with clasped hands, her blue eyes darting between Pat and Mary. "Mam and he don't speak."

"There, there, child. "Mary took hold of the girl's shoulders and directed her back to the stool. She looked up at Pat. "After I get her cleaned up, she can spend the night here and go home tomorrow." She went to the basin and filled the kettle. "Best let Mrs Miskelly know Sorca's with us."

Pat took the kettle from her hand and hung it over the fire. "You're right." He stroked his chin. "I'll cycle out to Carnspindle." He went to Mary, slid his arm round her waist and kissed her lightly on the cheek. "Then tomorrow, I'll have a think about what the right thing to do is."

He pulled on his coat. As he opened the door, a shard of moonlight fell across the parlour floor. He stepped outside, and the smell of the hedgerows seeped into the house, freshening the fug of sweat and tar in the parlour.

Mary heard the familiar sound of Pat pulling the bicycle out of the shed and giving it a shake as if bringing it to life. After a screech or two from the pedals, she heard him ride off into the night. She could picture the dynamo of the bike throwing a searchlight out in front of him, and Pat hunched, bat-like, over the handlebars.

Meanwhile, Sorca sat silently on the wooden stool, her hands on her lap. Mary's heart bled for her. This young woman, most undeserving of such a mean and callous attack.

With turpentine-soaked rags, Mary rubbed at the tar on the girl's skin. Then, using scissors, she cut the black-matted remains of hair from the girl's scalp. Finally, a pumice stone and soap scrubbed away the remaining tar.

After what seemed like hours, the girl's head resembled that of a new-born chick. The skin on her face was red and blotchy, and her eyes puffy. However, dressed in a laundered nightdress and socks, at least she smelled fresh.

Collecting the feathery, tar-stained clothing, Mary scrunched it up in newspaper and threw it on the fire. It blazed a fiery red in front of them. "Thank God, you're not scarred. If the tar had been hot, you would have been left with burns." She threw slack on the fire, causing it to spit and hiss. "And your hair will grow again. Now, let's get you ready for a good night's sleep."

"Thanks, Missus," the girl replied, her voice somewhat tinny and hesitant. "Can I go outside...?"

"Of course. I'll show you where it is and wait for you." Mary placed the girl's feet into an old pair of boots and drew a shawl around her shoulders before leading her, by lamplight, to the outside lavatory. Standing waiting, Mary rubbed her arms to warm them. She looked upwards. The stars sparkled above her, unfazed by events beneath them. A light breeze ruffled the leaves of the birch tree overhanging the chicken coop. As she brought Sorca back down the path, a waft of lavender met them.

Once back inside the parlour, Mary settled the girl in Pat's rocking chair. There, she sat swaying, as though keeping time with the ticking of the clock.

"Will you have a taste of stew? A cup of tea?"

Sorca shook her head. "No thanks, Missus. But water, please."

Mary filled a glass from the pitcher and handed it to Sorca, who sipped at it with shaking hands.

"I'll be back in two ticks." Mary said to her.

Upstairs, she removed two starched sheets, two blankets and a counterpane from her dresser and took them downstairs. She made a makeshift mattress in front of the fire and helped Sorca to get settled.

"Thank you, Missus." The girl's eyes flickered as Mary pulled the covers over her shoulders. Within minutes Sorca was asleep.

Later that evening, finding herself unable to sleep, Mary heard Pat tiptoeing across the parlour and up the stairs.

As he got into bed, he told her of Mrs Miskelly's reaction to the attack on her daughter. "She nearly fainted in front of me, cursed the British Army and the IRA at one and the same time. Pleaded with me to tell no-one about what happened tonight!"

Mary put her arms around her husband, the scent of hair-oil and sweat strong on his skin. "Oh Pat. That's dreadful. She must be really scared, poor woman."

"I know. I'd love to help her, but I don't know how."

She kissed his neck. "Let's try and get some sleep."

He reached for her hand and squeezed it, letting her warm her cold feet on his.

Chapter Thirteen

Early in the morning, after Sorca had picked at a bowl of porridge, Pat took her home on the back of his bicycle. Before leaving, she hugged Mary, promising to visit in the future.

"When my hair has grown a little and your baby's here." She ran her hand over the stubble on her scalp, her eyes misting over.

Mary tied an old scarf around Sorca's head. "In case there's prying eyes."

She watched from the door as Pat pushed hard at the peddles, the girl riding side-saddle, clinging tightly to his waist.

Although Liam was exhausted from the evening before, Mary insisted he go to school. "It'll do you good. You need fresh air and something to occupy your mind other than poor Sorca."

She tidied away the remains of the boiled egg she'd made him as a treat. Before he left, she reminded him not to be telling his friends about the night before. "Talk of what happened last night and what we did could bring unwanted attention."

Liam seemed confused but agreed to keep quiet. Watching him limp down the lane, his canvas schoolbag slung across one shoulder, Mary felt a deep ache within her chest.

He'd have to know some day about his past. Meantime, there was a baby on the way and the trouble in Ireland was getting worse. It seemed that the time was never right. Would he really be able to keep last night's events to himself? She wasn't sure. He couldn't be expected to understand the danger it might land them all in, if others knew they'd helped the girlfriend of a British soldier. Pat would need to have a good talk with him. To explain the way things were.

On Pat's return, the table was set with mugs and a loaf of freshly made soda bread. Mary stirred the tea in the teapot before setting it on the table.

"We need to think how we'll best explain things to Liam. He'll be hearing all sorts of nonsense at school."

"I've been thinking about it too." Pat buttered a slice of bread and took a bite, holding it over his cupped hand. "This evening…"

There were two light knocks at the door, as though someone had used the knuckle of one finger. Sara. Mary would know that sound anywhere. The door creaked open.

"Hello! Anyone at home?" Sara walked into the kitchen shaking her hair out from under her felt hat. "Mary... Oh Pat! How are you?" She stood, a basket in hand, her eyebrows furrowed together. "I'm sorry, have I got the wrong day?"

Pat put his bread down and swallowed. "Good morning, Sara."

Mary got up from her seat. "No, we said Monday, and Monday it is." She helped her friend out of her coat. "Pat's just having a bite to eat before work." She hung the coat on a hook at the door and set the hat on top. "He'd an early morning message to attend to before breakfast, and he's half starved." She looked over at her husband.

He smiled thinly and took a drink from his cup. "I am that. But next door's plough needs a new axle, so if you'll excuse me, I'll just take my food with me and leave you two ladies alone." Pat stood up and offered his chair to Sara. "Mary here will be glad to talk to you."

Pat reached for his jacket from the hook by the door but swung round suddenly. "I know you, Mary. You'll be going over the whole blessed business with Sara." A small pulse throbbed at his temple, and he ran his fingers round the back of his shirt as though it was too tight. "Mary, just bear in mind that the poor girl won't want more trouble at her door. We all need to be careful about what we say." He looked towards Sara. "And Sara; I'd be glad if, perhaps, you wouldn't mention this to William."

Sara, her face suddenly pale and frowning, nodded. "Of course."

Pat wrapped some buttered bread in a sheet of newspaper and took a few gulps of tea. "Thank you, Sara. I know you're a woman of principle." He pulled on his jacket, shoved the parcel in his pocket and opened the door. "Goodbye, ladies."

Then, without looking round, he drew the door shut after him.

It closed with a thud.

The clock ticked loudly.

Sara eyed two feathers on the floor, black and sticky. She held one up, studying it in puzzlement. She took the feather and set it in the coal bucket, searching for a handkerchief from her sleeve. "Euch!" Gingerly, she opened out the cotton square and wiped her hands. Several, other blackened feathers lay on top of the slack. She stared at them. "What happened last night?"

The kettle whistled. Mary lifted it off with both hands and wet the tea. "You mind the the Miskellys from out Carnspindle way?"

Sara knew the family; for wasn't Mr. Miskelly away to the asylum after going berserk one day in the Main Street? And didn't the rector call for the RIC, and didn't it take two policemen just to calm him down? It was just the saddest thing. But people said he was made feeble-minded by the Great War and wouldn't the asylum be the best place for him?

Setting clean mugs and tea on the table, Mary added a jug of milk and two fresh slices of bread. Sara looked at her, her eyebrows slightly raised. "So, what about the Miskellys?"

Mary swallowed hard before slowly recounting what had happened to Sorca, and how herself and Pat had helped her.

Sara sat still for a while before speaking. "How dreadful. Why pick on a young girl like Sorca Miskelly?" She patted her hair, smoothing it back from her face. "Poor mite." She lifted her cup of tea in her hands, studying the small flecks of cream floating on the top. "William says the IRA are getting more daring, day by day. He says this new war's going to get worse before it gets better."

"Well, I hope he's wrong."

"And I don't like William going up north to the Unionist rallies." Sara looked at the floor. "I'm afraid of the wrong people getting to know."

A blast of wind rattled the chimney of the cottage. The rooks, who had been nesting there, took to the air, their harsh cries cutting through the quiet of the countryside. A few stray leaves danced outside the window.

Mary looked at her friend's face. Not for the first time did she see fine lines and greying hair, but this time she saw something new: fear.

"We're safe here in Lisowen," Mary said weakly. "Nothing's going to happen to you or William." She patted her friend's arm.

"William's not so sure." Sara buttered some more bread and took a bite.

"And why do you think that?

"Hasn't he taken to sleeping with the shotgun loaded and ready at his side."

"No!"

"I shouldn't be saying." Sara ate the rest of her bread and drank up her tea before taking the crockery to the basin and lowering the plate and mug into cold water. "Now, best I be going." Drying her hands on a work cloth, she lifted her coat off the hook by the door. "You must be exhausted after the night's shenanigans, and you're going to need your strength for the baby." She reached for her bag. "You'd do well to get some rest." She wagged her finger playfully at her friend.

"I'm glad you called." Mary got up and rubbed her back with a little groan. "Sure, who else would I have to tell the likes of what happened last night? She rearranged her skirt and smoothed out the creases.

"And who else do I have to tell about my own fears?

"Well, thank God, then, we have each other." Mary smiled. "Please stay a little while longer. I'll only sit and brood about what went on last night."

Sara set her coat and bag on one of the chairs. "Well, if that's how you feel, I'd be glad to stay a little longer."

"I do."

They talked some more and then, after a while, Sara declared that she really should be going. William had taken Richard up to the school, and she'd promised to collect him around eleven o'clock. Before leaving, she set a small jar of castor oil on the worktop. "It helped ... you know... bring the baby on..." She clicked open the latch at the door.

"Sounds drastic," quipped Mary. "But thank you." She chuckled, standing at the door watching her friend stride out, her head held high, until she turned the corner out of sight.

***

When Pat returned, Mary recounted Sara's worries for the safety of her family.

"I can't say I'm surprised. William would do well to keep his views to himself." He picked up the newspaper and scanned the headlines. "I know he travels to Belfast to attend those Unionist meetings." He lifted his eyes to meet hers. "Not a word to Liam about it in case the wrong people get to know. Caution and common sense are what's needed to see us all through."

He reached across the table and took her hand in his. He squeezed it tight. "Let's speak to Liam tonight about his education. With his leg the way it is, it's best he puts his energies into his schooling." He sighed. "As for what happened last night, he needs to know that there can be no excuse for that sort of thing. Perhaps by studying, he can stay out of trouble and have some sort of future."

Chapter Fourteen

It had been six months since Old John had been to Lisowen. Down the wide street he plodded, one hand clutching a sack, the other grasping the handle of a small brown suitcase.

It was the first hot day of spring, and his shirt stuck to his skin, sweat trickling down his back from the heat of the midday sun. On the path in front of him, chaffinches pecked at a piece of bread that had fallen out of a workbag. As he approached, the birds scattered, their brown and white wings fanning out before him.

Old John glanced sideways to the yawning interior of the forge and saw the bullish blacksmith cuffing the ear of a youth. He averted his gaze. It didn't do to get involved in matters that weren't his concern. And Dan O'Toole was not his concern.

Across the road, the local priest was clipping at his laurel hedge.

"Grand day, Father," Old John shouted to him, swinging the sack onto the other shoulder.

The priest looked up, both hands holding the clippers as though about to cut the air. "Good to see you back again, Old John. Hope you'll come to Mass sometime soon."

"I'll be there tomorrow, Father!" Old John held up the case as a substitute for waving.

Today was his birthday. April 1st. April Fool's Day. He was forty years old. The last time he looked in a mirror, he had been shocked and saddened at the man looking back. How could he have turned into this hunchbacked old codger? The few strands of slate grey hair and the ridges etched deep in his face added to the illusion of a man who might pass for twenty years older. It was as though his name expected him to act out the lie, to trick his customers into thinking that they were dealing with a man of advanced years. He smiled wryly. No bad thing in his line of work.

Leaving the forge and parish house far behind, he made his way to the cottages and farms on the outskirts of the village.

Life could be so much worse, he thought, recognising Liam O'Dowd, the boy with the limp, a tattered schoolbag clutched under his arm. He overtook the boy with ease, calling out a cheery Hello. Even he, with all his wares to carry, was faster than that poor cripple.

He had his freedom, fresh air in his nostrils, no-one relying on him and him relying on no-one. The tannery and factory chimneys of Dublin were things of the far distant past.

Trudging uphill, he came to the bend in the road not far from his next customer's house. When his breathing became hard and laboured, he sat down on the roadside to rest. He inhaled deeply, the smell of grass and hedgerow delighting his senses. Across from him, a field full of sheep and their newly-born lambs nibbled the grass. Tufts of wool, caught on barbed wire, fluttered in the breeze. He rose and plucked clumps of wool off the barbs. It felt soft and prickly, and warm in his hand. After gathering a good few handfuls, he stuffed them deep into his trouser pocket.

He sat down again, with his back supported by a stone wall, eating an apple he'd kept for his birthday. The sourness of the flesh made his mouth water and when it came to the pips and core, he munched his way through, only spitting out a tiny piece of stalk that had lodged in his teeth. He wiped his mouth on his tattered sleeve and allowed himself to think of his favourite customer, the blacksmith's wife, who was next on his list.

Such a hauntingly beautiful creature, Mrs O'Toole. Never had he set eyes on a finer woman. He pictured her jet-black hair, her pale skin, her slim figure. His mind strayed briefly into some improper thoughts from which he quickly withdrew, mumbling a few Hail Marys in recompense.

He would admire her from a distance. Life in the company of a female such as Mrs O'Toole would be limited to sharing nothing more than a cup of tea. Any other arrangement was unthinkable. She was a married woman and, even if she wasn't, he wouldn't stand a chance. Fate had decided that he should make his way through life alone, and he'd come to accept that as his lot.

Picking himself up from the lane, he brushed the gravel off the backside of his threadbare trousers, before gathering his sack and suitcase together. As he neared the house, he reflected that it was good to know that Dan O'Toole was occupied in the forge and not at home. O'Toole was someone to be avoided. From what he'd seen, that man was a bully with no manners and it was a mystery that a woman as beautiful as Grainne O'Toole was his wife.

He announced his arrival at the cottage with the tinkling and clanking of pots and pans from his burlap sack. Wrestling his way up the snaggy bramble path, his face lit up as he saw the lady of the house cleaning the front doorstep with a scrubbing brush, a pail of water at her side.

She looked round, dark hair framing her porcelain face.

"Oh, hello, Old John. What have you today?" She eased herself up and held her dainty hands out towards him, her face shining from carbolic and curiosity. "You know I've enough mothballs to sell to my neighbours?"

"Mrs O'Toole, I've much better than mothballs." Old John raised his battered cardboard case to eye level. "Pray, if you have time, let me show you the contents." He paused, then added, as though revealing a long-kept secret, "Inside – please witness – the most beautiful ribbon this side of Dublin or Paris or Lisowen" He set the case on the ground and dropped the sack with a clunk. "Now, only if you have time, Mrs O'Toole. You being such a busy lady." He took off his flat cap and bowed in front of her. "I don't want to take you away from your domestic affiliations."

Leaning over the bulging case, he snapped the clips, causing it to spring open. A flurry of velvet ribbons, peacock feathers, organza headscarves and gingham squares flounced up from the receptacle.

Standing back reverently, arms outspread, he presented his chest full of treasure.

***

It was unusual for Dan O'Toole to return home during the day. His habit was to take bread and dripping with him to work and wash it down with a pint of porter at McGinn's on the Main Street. There, he could meet with the others and keep up to date with what the British were up to and what business needed attention.

McGinn himself was a supporter of the cause and could turn a blind eye when Dan or the other army members needed it. At times, when they needed total privacy, they were given the back-room snug. Today, McGinn's green door was closed. Several barrels of porter had burst and flooded the bar. The young lad who'd crashed the barrels on delivery, had been sacked and sent away with a flea in his ear. Black liquid seeped out onto the road, wetting the shoes of those gathered, expecting their lunchtime pints. The new delivery of beer wouldn't arrive 'til the next day and disgruntled customers murmured their disapproval. Sweat trickled down McGinn's face as he tacked a notice about the closure to a piece of board.

"Get your finger out of your arse, McGinn, and get this place back to normal," one youth complained. "I'm parched for the want of porter."

The assembled crowd laughed.

McGinn approached the boy and gave him a playful slap on the back. "Of course, young man." Then catching Dan's disapproving eye, he pulled at the youth's ear, who yelped in discomfort. "Just watch your fecking mouth," he threatened. "Talk to me like that again and you could end up regretting it." He let the boy go but fixed him with a stare. "I know people. People who know how to get short-arses, like you, to show respect.!"

The crowd grew silent, except for Dan. "You tell the little fecker, McGinn!"

"Sorry, Mr McGinn." The lad shook his head, his face pale. "I don't know why I said that." He slunk off, head down, to join his friends who stood chatting with the pretence of normality.

McGinn finished putting the final tack in the poster. The crowd had dissipated but Dan held back.

McGinn scratched his backside, his face red and puffy. "I saw that bastard Leavy at the train station in Kilkenny last week, and I could hear him asking for a ticket to Belfast."

Dan hoisted his trousers up and retied the baler twine securing them. "Did he, indeed."

"And when I looked in the paper, didn't I see that a fecking Unionist rally was taking place the very next day?"

Dan tapped his temple. "That sort of information is very useful." He pulled a cigarette from a packet in his jacket pocket and held it, unlit, between finger and thumb. "Some people shouldn't be allowed to live quietly in these parts." Lighting the cigarette, he inhaled deeply. "I would prefer our own sort to prevail. Some of that other side like to lord it over us." He tapped McGinn's shoulder. "Know what I mean?"

McGinn nodded.

Dan slapped his back, letting McGinn know that they were of the same mind.

Chapter Fifteen

The wind whipped a pair of embroidered ladies bloomers from Old John's case and blew them to rest at Grainne O'Toole's feet.

She laughed. Setting the scrubbing brush down, she put a hand to her stomach and then to her sides. The giggles had taken a hold of her and try as she might, she couldn't stop. She wiped the tears from her eyes with the backs of her hand. And the expression on the old man's face, well it just made everything worse. He stood there, cap in hand, his eyebrows raised, a faint lop-sided smile on his crumpled face.

"Forgive me, dear lady." The old man lifted the offending garment between finger and thumb and, holding it over the open case, released it.

Grainne looked away to gather her composure.

Cows in the adjoining field poked their heads over the brambles, as though to get a better view of the scene in front of them. A few loud 'moos' rang out. In front of them, high up on the washing line, Grainne's underclothes swung to and fro.

The tinker caught sight of the laundry too. He stood, mesmerised by lily white garments writhing in the wind. He could imagine them on the woman in front of him. An image of her lounging on her bed, her dark hair falling about her delicate shoulders, flashed before him. He closed his eyes, then blinked them open. A gust of wind caught several further items from his case. He rushed to retrieve them, muttering a few mild curses under his breath.

Strewn on the path were several peacock feathers, a few strands of ribbon and two delicately embroidered handkerchiefs.

Grainne gathered together the peacock feathers that lay next to her feet. She stood, holding them, their vibrant purple and green a sharp contrast to her pale skin.

Tentatively, Old John reached out his hand to take the feathers from her. "I'm so sorry, dear lady, for that unwanted exhibition of my wares." As he leaned towards her, he thought he could smell rose petals. His fingers grazed her forearm, the touch of her skin as soft as silk.

She looked at him directly and smiled. "Don't mind me. I found it funny."

He placed the feathers back in the case. "I'm so glad. It was stupid of me to embarrass your good self."

"No, no. I'm perfectly recovered." She bent down, picked up the scrubbing brush and threw it into the pail, splashing water on the step. "Please come inside and show me what's new. It's a while since I've last seen you." She helped him push the oddments back into the case and click the buckles shut. "You'll take a cup of tea?" She cocked her head to one side.

"If you insist, dear lady." The old man's face seemed to glow.

For the first time, Grainne noticed his yellowed teeth, a few missing on the bottom row.

***

Dan sat down on the wooden bench opposite McGinn's and lit a cigarette. The crowd had dispersed, leaving him alone with his thoughts and his grumbling stomach. He patted his belly. Those hunger pangs were annoying him, but there'd be no pickled eggs with a pint today. He'd go home, have bread and tea with his wife. He hitched his trousers up and tightened his belt under his paunch and ambled off in the direction of his house.

As he walked, he thought about Grainne. Often, she'd go to the monastery to buy eggs or pick wildflowers. She was in the habit of lining the flowers up in jam jars in front of the kitchen windows. He snorted. Just let her be home so she could put the kettle on for him, and butter him some bread. Pity that she said so little. Then, the thought of the smell of her hair and skin began to arouse him. With luck, the babies would be sleeping.

He put a spring in his step.

***

Grainne directed Old John to the outside lavatory after he'd enquired about the facilities.

"And where's all the family today?" he asked, washing his hands on return with water from the pail.

She told him that the boys were now working, the girls at school and the babies napping. Stepping into the house, she filled the kettle from the water jug and hung it over the fire.

She heard a slight cough behind her and looked round. The pedlar stood at the door, his suitcase in one hand, his large sack in the other.

"Please, come in." Grainne pulled a chair out from the table. "Sit yourself down." She set about making the tea and laying the table.

Old John balanced his case on his lap and snapped the buckles open. This time, he opened the top with care. Extracting a few items, he laid them out on the table. Coloured ribbons, lace shawls and a hand mirror brightened up the drab surface.

Grainne smiled. Thank goodness Dan was at work. If he could see all this, he wouldn't be best pleased. And as for making tea for a travelling salesman? Well, he'd no need to know. And he'd no need to know of her fondness for Old John. Her precious feelings were her own. The only thing she could lay claim to. Keeping quiet meant he'd no reason to hurt her. Later, she'd tell him that she'd spent a ha'penny on some essentials at the door.

"Where have you been today, Old John? Who did you visit before coming here?" Selecting two ribbons, one blood red, the other pale violet, she laid them across one hand, stroking the velvet with her fingers.

"I went a little out of town, to a place I've never been, an orphanage on the Beggarstown Road."

Grainne felt her heart begin to thump. "Oh. Did they buy from you?" She hoped her voice sounded normal.

"Far from it. God forgive me, the nun who came to the door had a face like thunder and a voice like a dog's bark." Old John produced more ribbons from his suitcase and laid them on the table. "Eyebrows more suited to a man and, I'm sorry to say, she gave me short shrift."

Grainne dug her fingers into her palms. Sister Columbanus. The woman who'd shaped the course of her life. "I'm not surprised."

"You know her?"

"I do." Grainne stopped herself from going further. She blinked a few times and thought back to her wedding day.

Old John blew on his tea before taking a mouthful. "I did see some children looking out from an upstairs window. I admit to feeling sorry for them; abandoned like that."

She shook her head. Many's a time she had been the child watching visitors coming and going from that upstairs window, knowing there was no hope of leaving.

Old John looked at her, his hand stroking the whiskers on his jaw. "This jam is indeed delicious." He took a bite of bread, a few crumbs catching on the front of his collarless shirt.

Grainne bowed her head, not wishing him to see the moisture in her eyes. "That's good."

He tapped the table lightly with his knarley fingers. "Mrs O'Toole, it's very Christian of you to share your provisions with me but I sense a discomfort in you this day."

"I'm not…" she shook her head. "I'm afraid, I'm no Christian!" The words jumped out before she could catch them back. "I can't believe…" At this, she felt a lump in her throat and her eyes begin to swim.

"Tell me, Mrs O'Toole," he gently pressed her. "I think, if I'm right, that you carry a worrisome burden."

She began to sob. "I'm sorry."

"Would it help to tell me what ails you so?"

"No, no, I'm just being silly." Then the tears started to roll. When she tried to fight them back, she felt herself choking.

Old John leaned forward and handed her a large clean linen handkerchief. She dabbed her eyes, then blew her nose.

"It might help to tell me. I assure you, it'll go no further." He raised his eyebrows, creating deep wrinkles in his forehead.

She shook her head and screwed the wet handkerchief into a ball in her hands. "It was the word, Christian. I heard it every day from the nuns."

"You were at a convent school?"

"No…," she hesitated, before saying, "I was brought up in an orphanage. The orphanage that you visited this morning."

Old John nodded. "I too, had a difficult childhood. But I'm lucky now to be where I am. In fact, my life today holds much joy."

He leaned towards Grainne. She could smell apple pips on his breath.

"And why would a lovely lady like you be so troubled?" he continued.

She swallowed hard. Old John was not a gossip. She was sure of that. He lived a solitary life and could be trusted, surely? Then something released inside her, as though a door had swung open, the latch undone. She took a deep breath in, and her story poured out like a river that had burst its banks.

Her parents had died when she was a baby and the church had taken her in. Beaten, if she got a word of a prayer wrong, she made enemies of the nuns for questioning everything. Why didn't priests and nuns marry one another? For that, she had to stand all day beside the cold statue of the Virgin Mary.

The old tinker sat, his hands cupping his chin, staring into her eyes.

"I even questioned what the Immaculate Conception meant." She felt heat rise from her neck to her face.

Old John pursed his lips.

"Instead of an answer, I got twelve whacks across the knuckles; one for each apostle, from Sister Columbanus." Grainne rubbed her hands together as though she could still feel the pain.

"Well, it's good that when you left, you met Mr O'Toole."

She nodded, looking suddenly embarrassed. "Indeed," she said, rising from her chair. "I'll just go out to the press, to top up the milk jug." She lifted the jug and left Old John with his tea.

How could she tell him everything? It was so shameful; the bank notes that changed hands between Sister Columbanus and her husband-to-be. That woman had worn her down with her argument as to why she should marry. Why throw away the chance to lead a respectable life? Where would she find herself if she didn't? In the workhouse or out on the streets? Did she want a life of sin?

Grainne remembered, vividly, the day he had arrived, how she had to stand in front of him. Him, looking her up and down. The cut of him, his belly hanging over his trousers, and the smell of horses and manure.

She remembered the wedding ceremony of fifteen minutes. The old priest rattling through the proceedings, with Sister Columbanus as witness. Then leaving the orphanage, with a small bag of belongings and a large measure of dread. Dan waiting for her outside, his eyes black and piercing, a sheen of sweat on his forehead.

She patted her chest and wiped her eyes with her fingertips. Old John would be waiting for her. She poured milk from the pail into the jug and swung the door open to the parlour.

"I shouldn't have burdened you like that," she apologised.

"Ah, Mrs O'Toole. Some people think they are Christian but are very un-Christian. Then others are Christian but don't even know it." He reached across the table, lightly covering her small, pinched fingers with his large, rough hand. He cleared his throat, bowing his head. "Would you allow me to say a prayer?"

***

As Dan approached the front door of his house, he could make out two heads at the parlour table. He scratched his chin. Who could be visiting? Grainne didn't have any friends. He sneaked along the wall and peeked his head round the side of the window to get a better look.

Two heads almost touching.

Gasping, he screwed up his eyes to get a better look. Sitting at the table was his wife, her coal black hair wound high on her head, her eyes downcast. The other person with his back to him was male, almost bald save a few strands of hair, his face within inches of Grainne. They were holding hands.

Dan felt rage grow within him. His heart racing, a sudden sickening pain gripped his stomach. What the fuck was going on?

A spade, half hidden in the hedgerow, caught his eye. Seizing the implement, Dan padded silently to the door of the cottage, pressing his ear to it.

He could hear the man mumbling.

He carefully undid the latch and slid through the doorway. The couple were engrossed in some incantation.

"Forgive us our trespasses and those who trespass against us…"

Dan raised the spade above his shoulder and brought it crashing down upon the sparsely-haired skull of Old John.

Chapter Sixteen

Dan laughed as he shook his fist at the motionless body. There was blood oozing onto the floor. "That'll teach you, you bastard!" He dropped his spade; the clank echoing off the walls of the room.

Grainne wailed, a banshee wail, her head clasped between her hands. Upstairs, the babies started to cry.

Stepping over the man, Dan grabbed his wife by the shoulders and shook her. "And what were you up to with this fecker?" He locked eyes with her. "Tell me!"

"He was praying for me!" She stared back at him. "You despicable man."

He felt her struggle against him, her eyes fixed on the man on the floor.

"Praying for you?" he snorted. "What the fecking hell? He doesn't look like a priest to me."

"It's Old John you attacked...and he wouldn't hurt a fly."

"The pedlar?" Releasing his grip, Dan watched her crouch beside the man, placing the end of her apron against the wound, a red bloom forming along its edge.

Grainne leaned over the shabby form and placed her face close to his. Dan heard a low whimper from the floor, like the sound a wounded rabbit would make, its paw caught in one of his traps. Tugging at a cloth hanging from the back of a chair, she replaced it for the bloodied apron.

Dan paced the room. "What got into you, Grainne? Letting him sit with you like that?"

She looked up at him, her mouth set in a tight line. "I invited him in."

"You invited him into my house?" He felt the urge to strike her welling up inside him.

He resisted.

He needed Grainne. If he beat her, she might run away. He thought of how Brian Lavery's wife was found hanging in the forest, having endured years of force at his hand. Stupid cow.

Grainne must stay.

Old John groaned and moved his head side to side.

Dan rapped the table with his knuckles. "There you are. It was only a graze."

"Only a graze?" Grainne sat on the floor, taking Old John's head and laying it gently on her lap as she held the cloth against his head. "Thank God, you haven't killed him!"

He watched her stroking the tinker's forehead, as though soothing a fevered infant.

She looked up at him, her eyes blazing like coals. "If you'd killed him, you could be spending the rest of your life locked up!"

He sprang back. This was too much to take. He raised a hand towards her. Then an image of his mother cowering from his father and himself crying in the corner came to mind. No. He held his hand for a minute, caught the defiance in her eyes and let it drop. Grainne would calm down. Maybe he'd been too rash in attacking the intruder. She would get the old man sorted and on his way. And that would be the end of it.

He stood shifting from foot to foot, watching her as she cradled the pedlar's head, the cloth congealed to his skin.

The door rattled open and three of his daughters tumbled into the kitchen from their walk home from school.

He waved his hands at them as though shooing geese down the lane. "Get out, the lot of you!" He didn't need a gaggle of girls adding to the events that had just unfolded, bursting into tears on seeing their mother, her bloodied hands nursing the skull of some elderly man. He snatched the daisy chains from their hands and stamped on them as though stubbing out a cigarette. The girls began to howl as yellow blotches stained the floor.

"Can't you see that we're dealing with someone?" he demanded.

The howls grew louder. The girls covered their eyes, weeping and tugging at one another's skirts.

Grainne glared up at him. "The girls will stay and help with Old John." She instructed Bernie to bring her a basin of water, and Rosy to fetch a clean cloth.

"Aagh" A gurgle came from Old John. He moaned, thrashing about. "I'm not so bad now, Mrs O'Toole." He tried to raise himself onto one elbow but slid back down onto the floor. "Give me a minute or two...and I'll be on my way."

"You're going nowhere, Old John. You're staying in this house until that wound's healed."

Dan banged his fist on the table. "He won't be staying here! Did you not hear him say he was fine and ready to go?" He reached for the cigarette packet inside his jacket and then remembered that he'd smoked his last fag some time ago. Dear God, he needed out of this house. Away from young girls whining, an old man groaning and the anger of his wife.

"I'm off out!" He would go get himself some tobacco. Hoiking his trousers up, he opened the door, then turned his head. "When I get back, I expect that scoundrel to be gone!" He slammed the door shut.

The air seemed thick that day. It was pressing down on his head, the taste of hot tinder sharp on his tongue. There would probably be a thunderstorm later. That was what was needed. He set off in the direction of McGinn's. Then, remembering that the pub was probably still closed, he cursed McGinn and his public house.

A small dog ran out from behind a tree, bounding towards him. Lifting his foot, Dan kicked out, catching the animal in the soft under belly. The dog yelped and limped off to lick its wounds within the safety of the hedge.

Dan started to feel better.

***

Old John wheezed as he struggled to sit upright. "I'm grand now. Really I am," he panted.

Grainne eased herself up from the floor. "I don't think so. That's an awful bad gash you have." She returned with a mug of water. "It'll take a day or two to heal." She held the water to his lips and encouraged him to drink. "Don't worry, Old John. I'm going to make sure that you're nursed back to strength. There's a decent woman lives up Carnspindle way, who'll take you in for a night or two. I'm sure of that."

Taking a coin from a tin that she kept in her sewing box, she dropped it into her apron pocket.

***

Having bandaged Old John's head, Grainne and Bernie supported the stumbling man on the long walk to Oonagh Miskelly's house.

Finally, they arrived, panting and out of breath. Old John muttered something incomprehensible as he lurched unsteadily beside Grainne. Having knocked, Grainne waited until she heard footsteps and the door creaked opened a fraction.

A young woman, with uncommonly short hair, peaked round the corner. "Yes?"

"Is your mother there?" Grainne felt Old John's knees buckle. She clasped him tightly as an older woman appeared behind the girl.

"Mrs O'Toole? Is that Old John beside you? For the love of God, would you bring him in?"

Mrs Miskelly and the girl helped Grainne drag Old John to a bed in the corner of the room.

Old John was rambling. "Thank the Lord, for he is great, for those that are kind shall inherit kindness, and those that are bad shall be smote, and those that are smote shall lie down and die…" And so he continued until he was laid on the bed, his head cushioned by a pillow.

Grainne unlaced his boots and pulled them off. Mrs Miskelly placed an old blanket on top of him, tucking it in around his shoulders. Old John's eyes flickered closed.

Grainne offered Mrs Miskelly a sixpence to look after him. The woman took it and threw her arms around her. She smelled of starch and soap. The sound of infants crying came from an adjoining room and the girl was sent to tend them.

As she prepared to leave the house with her own daughter, Grainne looked around. Washing lines were strung from every corner of the parlour. She thought it strange that on a good day such as this, the washing wasn't outside on the line. It was then that she noticed something strange. All the undergarments drooping from the lines, belonged to men.

Chapter Seventeen

Liam loitered at the stone school wall, listening to his friends talking while the singing rhymes of the girls, with their skipping ropes, drifted along on the warm air.

The conversation about the current situation ricocheted between the boys.

"Sean Corvin's joined the RIC."

"Silly fecker. Why be a policeman? Does he want to get himself shot?"

"I've heard they get ten shillings a day," one boy said, "and have the best of guns." He raised his arms and, with his clasped hands, swung them round making a ratatatat sound.

"Sean had better watch himself, for the IRA are out to get them," another boy piped up. "My da says they want to teach a lesson to anyone siding with the British."

"Well, my da says that the Black and Tans have tanks that can roll right over anyone who gets in their way."

"The Black and Tans are feckin' British bastards. The IRA'll fix them too. Boot them out of Ireland." A boy kicked at an imaginary football, his leg flung high.

One of the boys nudged Liam. "Who are you for, Liam?"

Liam wasn't sure how to answer. His da hated the Black and Tans but had supported the police in the past. Things were all muddled. He wasn't sure who was right or wrong.

He rolled a stone back and forth under the boot of his good foot. "I'm for keeping me head down and letting them all get on with it!"

The boys guffawed.

Father Flaherty, who was taking the religion class that day, strode over, his cassock flapping. "What's all the talk about here?"

The oldest lad answered, his hands in his pockets, a cockiness about him. "We're just having a political discussion, Father."

The priest jutted his head forward from his body. Liam thought of an eagle perched high on a rock, ready to swoop down on its prey.

"Well, I suggest you keep your political discussions to yourselves. These are dangerous times for young lads like you to be getting all het up." Father Flaherty clapped his hands. "Now, time to get back into class."

The boys trudged up the steps to the school door and slunk inside, followed by the girls, jostling and elbowing one another, their chatter echoing along the school walls.

***

That evening, when Liam had finished his homework, he thought over the schoolyard conversation. His father sat with his new spectacles on, his newspaper held up, his elbows on the table. His mother, her head bowed, stitched her needlework, brushing stray curls away every so often.

"Lads at school were talking about...you know... the police and that."

Da lowered his newspaper to the table. "And?"

"Why are you so dead against the Black and Tans, if they're here to help the police?"

Da folded his newspaper and set it in front of him. "They're a ragbag of British soldiers who've no respect for anyone." He unwound his spectacles from around his ears and set them to the side. "I'm afraid they're an ill-disciplined rabble. Not fit to uphold the rule of law."

"So, the IRA are right to fight them?"

Da pushed his chair back, got up from his seat and paced the floor. "No-one should be fighting. It's all wrong."

Mam left her needlework to the side. She rubbed her hands over her bulging belly with circular strokes. "Most people want nothing to do with this trouble."

"Your mam's right. We're peaceable people. We don't want a fight with anyone." Da unrolled the cuffs of his shirt down and buttoned them at his wrists. "Education, Liam. "Education is the way forward. Stay in school. Maybe go to college?"

Liam poked the fire with a stick, before throwing it on the flames where it crackled and burned. "Like those involved in the uprising. Weren't they a lot of college boys?"

Da shook his head. "What a waste of a good education. They should have used their efforts to concentrate on speeches, not violence." He inhaled deeply. "They were fools, those lads, and more beside."

Mam groaned as she wriggled herself back into the spine of her chair. "Well, we'd like you to think again about school. We've been saving."

Liam shifted in his seat, then scraped the legs of his chair back from the table. He placed his injured foot on the floor with a thud. "Just because I've a bad foot doesn't mean that my hands don't work." He limped to the bottom of the stairs. "You won't need to worry about me mixing with bookish Irish patriots, for I won't be staying on at school."

"Liam!" Mam struggled out of her chair and tried to hug him.

He pushed her gently away. "I'm not staying a minute longer than I have to and that's that." He called over his shoulder as he hobbled up the stairs. "You think I can't do much but I'm telling you... this foot's not going to hold me back!"

***

Mary heard Liam's bedroom door shut and slumped back into her chair. Pat kneeled in front of her and took her hands in his. He leaned forward and kissed her gently. She felt his rough stubble on her cheek and smelled the faint damp of his woollen sweater. She sat upright. "To be honest, Pat, I'm in two minds. You left school at fourteen and you turned out all right."

"But I'm not handicapped." Pat raked his fingers through his thick hair. "And Liam's clever too. If he'd more school years behind him, he'd be able to get a decent job."

"That's true." Mary nodded. "Please God, he won't get mixed up in any trouble. Surely, he's more sense." Then the thought of him staying at school, travelling to Kilkenny, or beyond, for college made her feel anxious. If he went away, he might never return.

"Liam knows right from wrong, Mary. He's a good lad. Just too young to know what's best."

"I hope that's true." Mary resumed her needlework and lowered her voice. "I was thinking that we should be telling him about his parents." She held up the christening robe she'd been embroidering for the baby. "After the baby arrives."

"That wouldn't be the best time, my love. Think about it." Pat picked a stray nugget of coal from the hearth and threw it on the fire before brushing his hands. "But I agree it needs to be soon."

Chapter Eighteen

Sara peered over William's shoulders as he read the Lisowen Gazette. He smelled of blackboard chalk and turf fires. "What's in the news today?" She noticed that his hair was thinning, with a bald patch the size of a florin, visible, the skin red and shiny. They were both getting older.

He turned round and grinned. "There's to be a variety show in Donnybrook Hall," he chuckled, reading from the newspaper. "Suitable for children and women of sensitive natures, apparently. A kaleidoscope of singing, dancing and storytelling." He shook the paper in front of him, as though shaking water off an umbrella, and laid it to one side.

Patting his shoulders, Sara took the newspaper and scanned the advertisement before setting it down. "It'd be nice to go as a family." For a second, she thought about the twins and imagined the boys sitting either side of her in the hall, their faces gleaming. Then, just as quickly, she let the image fade. "I mean it'd be nice to take Richard." Stretching over the large wooden table, she wiped side to side with a wet cloth fashioned from an old cotton vest.

William stood up from the rocking chair and took the cloth from her hand. He threw it onto the work counter. "Why not? We could do with a night out. Some fun. Some laughter."

She dried her hands on the front of her apron. "There are refreshments too, after the show. There's tea for the adults and lemonade for the young ones."

William took her hand and, holding her close, rocked her gently to and fro. "What about taking those schoolchildren whose parents aren't taking them already? What do you say?"

"I'd be thinking that's a grand idea."

"That's settled then. It'll be us and the schoolchildren."

Sara smiled. It had been some time since she'd seen her husband in such good form, and it was a welcome change to have him talking about something other than politics.

***

Permission from the parents was sought and William was delighted with the overwhelming response. He'd sent a note home with all the children informing parents that if they couldn't afford the two pence admission, a payment wouldn't be necessary.

"Most of these children will never have seen a show," he said to Sara. "I'm sure you don't begrudge a little of our savings to give them that opportunity."

"Of course not," she responded enthusiastically, knowing that they themselves could ill afford it. Her mind flitted to Mary and her worries about bills. Thank the Lord, money wasn't an immediate concern for them. William's teaching provided a small, regular income, but for many in Lisowen, money was scarce. How families managed to feed twelve or thirteen young mouths, let alone clothe them, was beyond her.

***

Arriving at Donnybrook Hall early, Sara stood with William, the other teachers and their pupils by the large wooden doors. In one hand, she held Richard's arm, the other clutched twenty-two concert tickets. The children held hands, skipped on the spot and chattered excitedly one to another.

As Sara looked back and around the long queue of people, she caught sight of Mary, Pat and Liam. She stood on tiptoes waving, as did Mary. Pat grinned and touched his flat cap. Liam, who was now almost the height of Pat, waved too.

At five minutes past seven, the crowd began to grow restless and, when the doors opened, an excited wave of villagers flooded into the hall. The pupils took the first two rows, with the two teachers sitting directly in front of William and his family.

"Look, Mummy." Richard pointed to the pastel bunting strung across the ceiling. "Look at all the little flags."

Sara smiled and patted his head.

At the front of the hall, to one side, a small band of musicians sat tuning their instruments. A large black curtain was drawn across the stage. The children whispered one to another, guessing what might be behind it: a snake charmer, a magician, performing dogs? Their expectations grew to fever pitch. The hall was bulging to bursting point. People who couldn't get seats stood at the back and to the sides. The air was thick with the smell of hair pomade, lavender cologne and sweat. Women fanned themselves with flimsy programs. Using long poles, some of the organisers opened a few top windows to let in much-needed air.

The conductor, Sidney Simmons from Beggarstown, raised his baton and tapped it on the wooden lectern. The audience shushed. A medley of show tunes followed with the audience invited to clap along.

At last, the curtains to the stage opened.

The backdrop was of the Irish countryside; hills and valleys splattered with sheep having disproportionately long legs and oddly human expressions.

A tall man and a short woman, dressed extravagantly in furs and feathers, walked onto the stage. Mr and Mrs Funnybones. A thin ripple of laughter spread through the audience.

"I say, I say, I say. What did the doctor say to the patient who thought he was a pair of curtains?"

Mrs Funnybones held her hands out and rolled her eyes upwards. "I don't know, Mr Funnybones. What did the doctor say to the patient who thought he was a pair of curtains?"

"Pull yourself together, man!" Mr Funnybones doubled over, shaking with laughter.

William elbowed Sara's arm. "I hope there's something better to come," he whispered.

She elbowed him back.

After several more jokes, the Funnybones flounced off the stage.

"Unfunnybones, I'd call them," one wag proclaimed, causing the biggest ripple of laughter in the hall so far.

Two swarthy men in dress suits and sporting huge, waxed moustaches followed. A single fiddle sounded a few screechy notes. The band took hold of the melody, increasing in volume after a couple of faltering bars. The men stood side-by-side, hands clasped, eyes glazed, shuffling their feet. Inhaling deeply, they began to sing.

William leaned close to Sara and whispered in her ear. "What a horrible dirge! Have you a sock handy that we could throw on the stage?"

Sara knit her brows and put a finger to her closed lips. The younger children were shifting on their seats. After several ballads, a palpable sigh of relief could be heard when the final song was announced.

From somewhere back in the audience someone shouted: "Enough of the caterwauling. Get the dancers on!"

A few snorts of laughter followed before the audience clapped both in sympathy for the singers and anticipation of the grand finale: Irish dancing.

As the singers left the stage, a team of dancers took their place. Ramrod straight, toes pointing, arms pinned to their sides. The conductor raised both hands and, as he dropped them, the band played a jig. Two young men clattered across the stage, the noise of their hard shoes echoing from wall to wall. Four girls in black velvet dresses, green Celtic designs flowing from their capes, imitated the steps of the men. The audience clapped and whooped, adding their approval at the end of the routine by stamping their feet. The jig was followed by two reels and The Waves of Kerry.

Sara tapped her feet as the children clapped their hands in time to the music. Catching a sideways glance at William's face, she could tell he was enjoying himself too, a broad smile on his lips. She beamed at the children around her, their little faces lit up with delight.

An encore followed and the dancers received a standing ovation. Then the compere announced that refreshments would be served at the back of the hall.

Sara reached for her handbag. Just as the band were about to put their instruments away, she saw a man, his belly hanging over his trousers, run to the front of the hall and whisper something to the conductor.

It was Dan O'Toole, the blacksmith!

He turned round and clapped his hands as he faced the audience, shouting, "Before…before …we have supper, the band will play a song to mark the birth of our new nation!"

The band-members looked expectantly at their conductor. He leaned forward and spoke to them in hushed tones.

Sara wondered what song they would play.

The blacksmith puffed his chest out and wiped sweat from his brow. "Please stand for Amhrán na bhFiann: The Soldier's Song. He gestured again to the conductor, who shuffled side-to-side, mopping his brow with a handkerchief. It appeared that he was unfamiliar with the tune. A couple of the violin players played a few introductory chords.

Dan flung his hands out, encouraging the audience to stand.

People shuffled to their feet.

William turned to Sara, his hand pinning her arm firmly to the armrest of her seat. "How dare they think of playing that song! We're certainly not standing."

She could see his cheeks were flushed, his eyes narrowed.

"Sit down, children." William released her hand and stretched his arms out, preventing some of the children from moving. "Don't get up!" He put his hand on the teacher's shoulder in front of him as she was leaning forward, about to rise from her seat. "It's not the official anthem. Tell the children in front to stay put!"

The teacher nodded. She tapped on her colleague's shoulder and whispered something in her ear.

Sara's stomach churned. She felt eyes boring into the back of her neck and heard voices, low and questioning. Time seemed to slow. The heat rose from her toes to her scalp. She could feel the beat of her heart, thumping against the thin fabric of her Sunday blouse. Her hands, clasped tightly in her lap, were damp and clammy.

"Why aren't we standing, Mummy?" She felt Richard's breath from the funnel he'd made with his hand against her ear.

She hissed back softly, "Daddy doesn't want us to stand." She patted his knee. "Be a good boy and sit still." She heard similar questions from the pupils, now fidgeting in their seats.

Everyone was on their feet excepting William, his family, the teachers and the schoolchildren. Sara could see to her left, that her friends from the church were standing. The rector was also out of his seat. Mary, standing to her right, looked round with eyebrows raised and a sympathetic expression on her face. Sara gave a tiny shrug.

The room grew silent.

The conductor of the band looked round. Sara saw him stare at her. There were red patches on his face and his lips were pursed tight. He shook his head. Whether he was in sympathy with her or not, she couldn't tell. She thought he was a Protestant, a member of the church in Beggarstown. Where would his allegiance lie?

Then, with arms held high, he turned to the band and indicated for them to play.

The audience sang with gusto. She had no doubt that the volume had been turned up to fever pitch to demonstrate the patriotism that William's actions had stirred. William sat statue-like, looking straight ahead.

When the band stopped, a roar of clapping and stamping of feet broke out. Some young lads attempted to reprise the anthem with raucous bellowing. The crowd, however, began to move out of their seats, heading to the back of the hall where refreshments were being laid out on trestle tables.

Sara saw Dan O'Toole fighting his way past the crowd, beads of sweat on his forehead.

Panting, he stood in front of her, his eyes dark and menacing. "Why didn't you stand, Madam?" he demanded.

William pushed himself in front of her, guiding her gently to the side. He cleared his throat. "Because that song is not an anthem, and it shouldn't have been played. It's nothing more than a republican rebel rouser."

"So, that's your opinion, is it?

"It is indeed. There's only one anthem here."

"Your British King has no place in Ireland now."

Sara could see the blacksmith's eyes bulging, spittle on his bulbous lips. She pulled at her husband's sleeve. "Please William. We should go."

"I've nothing more to say to you, sir." William turned his back on the blacksmith, pulling Sara beside him.

As she struggled to the back of the hall, Sara caught smatterings of comments from the audience: Disgraceful. Stupid. Spectacle. She felt William reach for her hand. She let him take it. It lay limply in his palm.

She heard the teachers talking to one to another, sharing their discomfort at what had just happened. As she drew near to them, they changed the subject.

"It was a fine show now, especially the dancing. What lucky children."

As soon as she moved past, however, she could hear them returning to their concerns. Could their school be targetted, and would they all be safe?

She jolted William's arm. "We can't stay for supper." She gave his hand a shake. "Please, William."

William looked at her and nodded. He addressed the children and teachers nearby. "Ah. It's late now, children. Too late to stay." He patted some of them on the head. "We'd better get you back to your mammies and daddies. As a special treat, however, we'll have lemonade and cake tomorrow in school."

Sara sighed: a huge dose of humiliation plus the prospect of making cake and lemonade for twenty mouths! Suddenly, there was a rush of cool air on her face. Thank the Lord! Someone had unlocked a side door.

She helped corral the children together and they tumbled outside into the calm of the night air.

Once outside, she prayed that she'd only imagined the word 'Traitors!' following them. Why couldn't her husband have just stood up like the others? She'd seen some of them, standing silently; the words of the song foreign and unfamiliar. Surely, that was enough of a protest? But she knew her William only too well. It was so like him to stick to his beliefs and principles.

It had been a horrible experience for herself, but despite it all, in some strange way, she found herself admiring him.

Chapter Nineteen

As the audience made their way out of Donnybrook Hall, the band finished the last dregs of tea and tidied the music into their satchels. Apart from the unpleasantness at the end, all agreed that the evening had gone particularly well. Now it was time for home.

Dan stood at the main doors, a cigarette balancing between his lips. "Did you enjoy yourselves, now?" he asked one family, tousling the children's hair and shaking the hands of the parents. Behind them, he could see the clerical collar of the local priest. "Ah, Father Flaherty. How are you? Good man, yourself." He thought the priest owed him at least a handshake instead of a grimace. Feckin' dour-faced aul cleric!

He puffed on the last fragment of his cigarette, before throwing the butt on the floor and stamping on it. As he did so, he considered what had just happened and Leavy's outrageous slur against the new state. He'd stamp on that feckin' Protestant neck if he got the chance. The bloody cheek of the man! There'd be no forgetting that incident in a hurry.

"We'd best be going." The band members pushed past him, their battered violin cases banging against their legs. Sidney Simmons, the conductor, brought up the rear.

Dan put his hand out to shake the conductor's hand. "Grand do, it was now, lads," but the man turned away from him as though he hadn't heard him. Dan shook his head. Ignorant fecker. But he could do with a lift home and knew that the conductor owned a motor car.

As they stepped outside, Sidney locked and bolted the hall doors before offering his fellow band members a cigarette. The accordion player and the pianist declined, saying they had to be off up home, but two of the violinists hung back.

Dan jostled forward holding his hand out and the cigarette pack was stiffly offered to him.

"Ah, thanks now." He extracted a cigarette and clamped his lips around it before pulling his matches from his pocket. He struck the match, then cupped his hands around the flame while sucking deeply.

The conductor struck his own match, lit his cigarette, then offered it to the remaining men so that they could light theirs. They stood together, chatting, the glow of their burning cigarettes partially lighting up their faces. Dan listened in on the conversation, but it was all about tone and pace and vibrato. Words that meant nothing to him.

"Good work now, with your instruments and so-on." Dan, his cigarette between two fingers, waved it in circles. He leaned in towards the huddle. "A grand aul racket you made."

The three men broke off from their conversation. Now, he had their attention.

"That man, Leavy, is a bloody fool." Dan sucked hard on his cigarette, the rawness of it hitting the back of his throat. He waited for a response. With none forthcoming, he took a deep breath in. "I'm sure you'll agree that there's no place in Ireland for disrespectful fuckers like him."

The men turned their backs on him and started to talk among themselves. Dan felt a sudden rush of anger.

"Ah. You're of a different mind?" His voice raised, he could feel the heat of blood rushing to his face.

One of the violinists stubbed his cigarette out with a few taps of his shoe. "None of us here want to see trouble," he muttered under his breath, his voice thin and reedy.

Dan grumbled, struggling with one hand to pull his trousers up as far as his overhanging belly. "No-one gets into trouble if they mind themselves properly. If they know what's good for them."

From over the hill, the roar of the truck could be heard long before it screeched to a halt beside them. Several men jumped out, the heavy stamp of their boots on the ground betraying who they were. Army. When Dan heard the accents, he knew they were British soldiers. He braced himself. Fuck! They've come for me.

One of the men pointed at the violin cases and called out in a clipped English accent. "I take it that you're part of a band."

Sidney cleared his throat. "Indeed, we are."

The soldier snorted. "Do any of you here know this lad?" He shone his torch on a boy, his face bruised and his nose bloodied. He sat, pathetic, on the floor of the truck, his hands bound together with baler twine.

Dan recognised him as Conal Shaunessy, the son of one of his comrades. "No." he said, averting his eyes from the boy's.

The bandsmen shook their heads.

"That's a pity." The soldier approached Dan and tapped him lightly on the shoulder with his baton. "He said that someone in Lisowen would vouch for him," he laughed, "as a law-abiding citizen."

He leaned close enough to Dan so that Dan could smell the brilliantine in the man's hair. "And something else. A while ago we stopped and listened as your concert was winding up."

The soldier pointed to the boy. "This little runt was outside with his friends singing at the top of his voice. His friends ran off, but we managed to catch him." The soldier sneered. "The Soldier's Song? A bloody IRA baiting call!"

The realisation of what was to come hit Dan a millisecond before the soldier's fist connected with his stomach.

"You should have finished your concert with God Save The King!

Knocked off his feet, Dan curled himself into a ball as the punches rained down on him. Beside him, he could hear the yells and curses of the musicians as they, too, were subjected to the same treatment. Within a couple of minutes, it was all over. The truck had disappeared into the night and the men, bloodied and beaten, lay gasping on the road, wondering what had just happened.

One by one, they struggled to their feet, gulping in air, spitting out blood. Brushing themselves down, they swore at the soldiers who had dared to attack them.

Sidney, panting to get the words out, spoke first: "Bastards, the lot of them." He wiped his mouth with a linen handkerchief.

Dan groaned. How dare those feckers disrespect The Soldiers Song! He felt gut-wrenching rage, raw and visceral. It wouldn't be long till he'd put a bullet through that feckin' army captain's head.

***

Back at home, Mary and her family sat together in front of the dying embers of the fire. Mary was finding it hard to get comfortable with the baby almost due. She got up and walked around the parlour, watching Pat stoke the coals, encouraging them to light.

"I feel so sorry for the Leavys, especially Sara," she said. "I could see the frightened look on her face when Dan O'Toole confronted her."

"He's an ignorant brute, that blacksmith." Pat set the poker down with a clank. "I'm sorry for the family, too. But William's just inviting trouble. I'm afraid there's plenty out there who share Dan O'Toole's views." Sliding himself into the rocking chair, he nodded at Liam. "Well, son. Did you have a good time.?"

Liam smiled. "Yes. I liked the Funnybones best." He poured himself a mug of water from the jug on the sideboard. "I think William Leavy is a stupid man." He gulped down the liquid, wiped his mouth with his hand, then banged the cup on the table. "Why wouldn't he stand and sing like everyone else? Out in the playground at school we all love singing the Soldier's Song. Where's the harm in it?"

"I won't hear a word like that against Mr Leavy." Mary stood glaring at her son, her eyes blazing. She took the mug from the table and cupped it in her hands; the cool of the tin against her palms. "William Leavy is a decent man and far from stupid. He just happens to have different views about things.

"What sort of views?"

"Well, we feel that we are Irish citizens, but Mr Leavy considers himself to be British."

"But he lives in Ireland!" Liam shook his head.

Mary brushed a stray curl back from her face. "And his sons lost their lives fighting for Britain."

"As did the sons of some of our Catholic friends." Pat stood up and held his hands out towards the fire. "Liam, don't think that there isn't more than one way of seeing things! People's views should be respected, not threatened!"

Later that evening, when Liam had gone to bed and Pat had slacked the fire, Mary pottered about the worktop, tidying away the crockery. "I don't like to see Liam so single-minded. He's like a sheep with blinkers. If there is such a thing."

"Don't worry, my dear. He's still young. Give him time." Pat lit a candle, setting it in a brass holder before blowing out the gas lamp. Ghostly shadows danced across the walls.

As they made their way upstairs, with Pat in front, he said, "After all, would we have had the same views as our parents at Liam's age?"

Mary stood on the stairs, chuckling. "Of course not, Pat. Sure, didn't we think they knew nothing, and we knew everything!"

Chapter Twenty

It was one of the few Sundays that Liam and his parents didn't go to Mass. Instead, early that morning, as Liam stood barefoot in the kitchen, his father set a pot of creosote and a paintbrush on the table and told him to paint the fence out the back.

"Now? At seven o'clock? Where's Mam?"

"Upstairs."

"Why isn't she down here, making breakfast?"

"She'll be staying upstairs today."

"Why?"

His father had just handed him a glass of milk and hacked a piece of bread from a loaf when a yell rang out.

"Is that Mam?"

"The baby's on the way."

"The baby? Is everything alright?"

"She's managing... but it's maybe time to get Nurse Armstrong." His father pulled on his coat and opened the door. I'll not be long." He left the door swinging half open, with Liam staring after him.

Liam heard the rattle of the shed door as his father pulled the bike out. He watched in amazement at the speed of his father's legs propelling the wheels down the lane. A screech from upstairs made him jump. He'd never heard his mother make that sort of noise before.

He struggled over to the stairs, a wadge of soda bread in one hand "Da'll be back very soon. Hold on, Mam!"

His mind in a quandary, he tried to think what best to do for his mother. He knew how the baby had to come out and that the nurse would do the final pulling. What was about to happen filled him with dread for his mother.

And what if his mother was in trouble? What if she was in real danger? After all, the grocer's wife had died as her baby was being born. He decided to wait ten minutes and then, if his father wasn't back, he'd go in and see if he could help.

They were the longest minutes of his life. The second hand of the clock crawled by as loud groans came frequently from upstairs. At last, the door flew open and his father, a dumpy woman and a large tapestry bag filled the space.

The woman dusted herself down and mumbled something about the uncomfortable ride on the saddle of the bike. "What a pity my bicycle tyre chose to be flat. Sure, I thought I was never going to get here alive!"

She wagged her finger at his father who held up his hands in apology. The midwife unpinned her hat and laid it on the table, replacing it with a starched white headscarf, which she pulled from her bag. "Hot water! Clean towels! Get rid of the boy!" she instructed.

Thank God! Some minutes ago, Liam had imagined himself looking away from his Ma while tugging on a baby working its way out from between her legs. It had been a very disturbing thought. Leaving his father scrambling for the kettle, he took his pot and brush and went outside, closing his ears to Ma's screams.

At the back fence, he prised the lid from the rusted pot with his penknife. Then, with a brush dripping dark brown liquid, he set to work.

Paint. Dip. Paint. Dip. Paint. Dip. Paint.

A baby sister or a baby brother? His mind flew off far into the future. In it, he could see himself pushing a little one on a swing fashioned from an old crate. He could hear the gurgles of delight. There would be yells: "Don't stop!" Fat little legs would kick and urge: "Higher, Liam!"

He saw himself take a tiny hand and parade his brother or sister round the yard. He, or she, would gently stroke Bobby's mane.

There would be fun the whole year long. Springs and summers for tadpole catching, butterfly chasing, bluebell gathering; autumns and winters for bonfires, toffee apples and sled rides on icy paths. He could picture a red-button nose, lips puffing out clouds of steam, a tiny head in a warm white bonnet.

It could have been fifteen, or fifty, minutes before he saw his father again, clambering down the stairs, waving frantically, running towards him, his eyes like saucers.

His father's strong hands reached out and clasped him to his belly, shaking him gently side-to-side. He felt alternately embarrassed and pleased.

"Liam," his father's breath was on his ear. "You've a sister! Come and see for yourself!"

*****

She owned the softest skin he had ever touched. He stroked her tiny fingers and toes. They had the feel of his mother's red silk ribbons that she wore on special occasions.

"Can I please hold her?"

"Put your arm under her little head. Be careful."

With trembling hands, he sat on the bed beside his mother and cuddled his little sister. "She's so small."

A new chapter had opened up for Liam, like one in the story book that the pedlar sold. You would turn a page and a whole town, with spires and rooftops would magically shoot up in three dimensions. Now Fionuala was here, and he was a big brother. He could see his mother watching him, her eyes flickering, her gaze dreamy.

"She's beautiful, isn't she, Mammy?"

"She is that."

He tenderly handed Fionuala back to his mother and struggled off the bed. "She's going to love all the things I'll show her."

As he stood at the open door of the bedroom, Liam could hear his father downstairs talking to the nurse.

"Would a dozen fresh eggs be enough?"

"I'd rather have money, Mr O'Dowd."

"Of course."

He heard the rattle of the coins in the tea tin, then a few words of thanks from both parties. Liam peered over the bannister. The nurse was taking off her headscarf and apron, stowing them into the bottom of her large bag.

"Now, I've got to get back to my brother," she said. "He's a bark like a fog-horn since he came back from America."

Liam thought that funny. Why would anyone bark? There was a clank of what looked like metal tools being stowed away into the midwife's bag. Then he heard the nurse instructing his da on how to make broth. She launched into a lecture on the need for men to know how to do the jobs women do all the time.

"Thank you, Nurse. Very useful." Da was shifting about from foot to foot.

"She needs lots of time to rest." Nurse Armstrong donned her felt hat, stuck a large hat pin through it and clutched her bag to her chest. "I'll walk back, if you don't mind, Mr O'Dowd."

"Of course." Da had the door open, ready. "And thank you again."

At last, the nurse was gone, and peace returned once more to the kitchen. Liam went back to his mother to tell her that Da would be making lunch.

"Oh, your father will be pleased to be rid of the earwigging." His mother chuckled, her face a blotchy red colour. Her hair was no longer curly. Instead, it lay in damp strands on the bolster. "Now, go and give him a hand to sort out the kitchen."

As he heaved himself downstairs, clutching the bannister, Liam thought of something he could make for Fionuala. He'd make her a little cart and if his da could find him some wheels and some rope, he'd be able to trail her round in it. Da was in the kitchen cutting the string between the sausages with his penknife. He'd the frying pan ready, with a knob of dripping in it. Liam felt his stomach skip at the thought of the fried sausages.

This is what it feels like to be happy, he thought.

***

Liam was sent to tell Sara the news.

She opened the door to him. Richard was beside her, a teddy trailing from one hand.

"A baby sister!" Sara exclaimed. "How wonderful! Come in till I get something for you to take back to your Mammy."

"She's called Fionuala."

"Fionuala. What a lovely name." Sara recalled Mary talking with fondness about her Grandmother Fionuala.

Standing in the scullery, looking as to what best to give Mary as a food parcel, she could hear Liam in the parlour asking Richard about his teddy.

"That's a very nice teddy. Does he have a name?"

Richard, in his baby voice, answered, "Carson. Edward Carson."

Sara winced. Richard had heard that name mentioned several times by his father and had latched on to it.

Liam laughed. "Very pleased to meet you, Mr Carson."

She took from the scullery shelf a pot of her newly-made gooseberry jam and a small, boiled cake, oozing black molasses. The smell of the cake still lingered and made her hungry. For an instant, she thought about sending the jam on its own, before wrapping the cake in some old newspaper that was stored in a tin bucket on the floor. She packaged the two items together in a piece of muslin. Muslin would come in handy with the baby, too. Back in the parlour, she handed the bundle to Liam.

"Thank you for the gifts." He smiled broadly at Sara, and she realised that he wasn't quite sure of how best to address her, his mother's best friend. Auntie wasn't right, Sara too familiar and Mrs Leavy much too formal.

"Bye-bye, Richard. Bye-bye, Mr Carson." Liam shook Richard's hand first, then the teddy's.

Sara watched him hobbling down her lane, the cloth parcel tucked under one arm. Having told Liam that she'd call the next day, she reminded herself that the knitted bonnet still required a few hours of work.

Sara felt joy for her friend and her new baby. Mary truly deserved this happiness. She felt a sudden twinge deep within her chest. Her boys. They were never too far away from her thoughts. So many years had passed since their birth but the memories were still strong. Such a difficult time she'd had, delivering the twins. The midwife hadn't been able to manage on her own and the doctor had been called for the final hour. A whole day and night she'd laboured, William pacing the floor, unable to rest.

The sound of giggling brought her back into the moment.

Richard was gabbling. "Mr Carson wants to go with me to meet the new baby. Mr Carson will be very gentle with the new baby."

Sara thought of how Mary would be tickled to know of teddy's name. But, she wondered, what would Pat think? Would he find it funny too?

***

A few days later, Pat trailed into the kitchen, his mouth downturned, his arms hanging heavy.

The baby was making tiny gurgling noises from the cot. Mary waved a cloth doll above her head. She looked up. "What's wrong, Pat?"

"It's Nurse Armstrong."

"What about her?"

He cleared his throat. "She died this morning."

"What?" Mary put the doll on the table. "How?" She shook her head, her brow furrowed.

Pat looked away. "Diphtheria. Her brother was ill when he came back from America. Apparently, he's on the mend but...she couldn't be saved."

Liam shivered. The fire was roaring, but the atmosphere in the cottage had suddenly chilled. An uneasy silence ensued. Whatever his parents were thinking about, it wasn't good.

Chapter Twenty-One

"Tomorrow we'll clean this house from top to bottom." Mary ran her fingertip along the mantlepiece and then the dresser, looking for traces of dirt. "And I mean every nook and cranny."

Pat took a deep breath in and sighed. "Are you sure it's necessary?"

"Well, look at the way Nurse Armstrong disinfected everything when she tended me. And she never stopped rattling on about infection. Even after the baby arrived, she was still telling me how to keep the germs at bay."

"God rest her soul." Pat crossed himself. "Unfortunately, all her disinfecting didn't help save her."

"But Fionuala's only a few days old. Little ones are very delicate." Mary's mouth drooped at the corners.

Liam stared at her. "But you clean the house every day. Isn't that enough?" What exactly did his mam mean by delicate?

Mam shook her head. "Best we give the house a thorough going over, just in case."

Mam and Da started talking about what should be done first and who would do what and did they have enough soap for the linens, and bleach for the work top.

Liam shook his head. What was all the fuss about? Their house was always spotless. Mam was forever wiping the table with a cloth and running the broom over the floor if so much as a crumb dropped onto it. It was sad about the old nurse, but hardly surprising. She must have been well past forty, if truth be told.

Mam lifted Fionuala, who was whimpering, out of her cot, then turned to Liam. "Why don't you take Fionuala outside and round the house. The fresh air will do her good, and your da and I can make a start in here."

Liam was pleased. Mam trusted him to mind the baby. Carefully placing Fionuala over his shoulder and securing a shawl around her, he unclicked the latch on the door and stepped outside.

Steadying himself and his heavy boot, he placed his palm on the baby's back and let her curl her warm little head into his shoulder. She smelled of lemons and baby sick.

He looked down at the tiny bundle. At only a few days old, she didn't do much. He rocked her gently.

Some day, he thought, *she'll wake up from her bed and call out for me.* But for now, he'd just have to bide his time. Even if she wasn't interested, a tour of the yard to see Bobby, the stray kittens and the hens would help her get to know her home.

As he limped around the farm, his mind turned to the old nurse who'd died. His parents seemed very worried. He tucked the shawl more securely around the baby's shoulders and whispered in her ear. "But don't you worry, Fionuala. Your big brother will keep you safe."

***

The next day was taken up with the continual boiling of kettles, scrubbing of floors and hanging wet sheets and counterpanes on the line. Pat insisted on doing the heavy work. He beat the bolsters and eiderdowns, and Mary boiled the sheets and pillowcases with bleach. Liam hated the smell. It made him feel like retching. It reminded him of his hospital visits when his leg was bad, and it made his foot ache again.

His mother fed the last sheet through the mangle while his father held the baby close to his chest, speaking softly to her in a voice that was new to Liam. "Sure, that's ninety-nine percent of the germs gone and the one per cent left will die of loneliness." He took Fionuala's tiny hand in his and grazed it with a kiss.

Mam folded the damp sheet and laid it on the pile in the basket. She patted Da's back and Liam felt re-assured. His parents had worked hard to make sure that the house was clean as a whistle. Things could return to normal. He'd go back to school tomorrow, see his friends and all would be well.

***

A couple of days had passed when, late one afternoon, his father came in from the butchers and placed a brown paper parcel on the table. "Some rashers and sausages." He nudged Liam who was sitting at the table doing homework. "Our favourite."

Mam said something to Da in a low voice that Liam couldn't quite make out. She was feeding the baby, its little head nuzzled into her blouse.

His father cocked his head to one side. "Old Ikey has diphtheria?" His face seemed to drain of colour. "Who told you?" He struggled out of his jacket and hung it on the hook behind the door.

Mam shifted slightly, tucked Fionuala into the crook of her arm, then buttoned up her blouse. "Teresa, who does his messages. It was herself who told me." She held up the woollen crocheted blanket that was draped across her lap. "She made this for Fionuala."

"That's nice." Da didn't look at the blanket. His eyes were staring ahead, as though he could see through walls and out to the hills faraway.

Mam shifted the baby up against her chest and began patting her back. "Young Ikey's not doing well either, according to Teresa. Apparently, the doctor had to cut his throat open to give him ease."

Da closed his eyes. "Aah now, Mary."

"Would that not kill him?" Liam felt a cold chill run from his head to his feet.

"It's a medical thing, Liam. Helps the person to breathe." His mam shrugged, clutching Fionuala to her with one hand. "It's not like this." She drew a finger from her free hand across her neck. "But this." She poked her finger at her Adam's apple. "The doctor makes a hole into the throat."

Da shuddered. "Enough now. Please Mary, you'll put poor Liam and me off our supper."

Liam waited for his mam to laugh or say something witty. She was always jesting with Da, but she didn't even smile, just rocked the baby. He looked from one parent to the other. What were they thinking? Then, something that had been niggling him, came to mind. A year ago, his uncle had died suddenly, giving them all a terrible shock. "Was it diphtheria that killed Uncle Eamonn?"

Mam laid Fionuala gently back into her cot. "No, that was Spanish flu. Far worse. So many Irish people died. People actually dropped dead in the streets of Dublin." She leaned over the cot, tucking the blanket around the baby's shoulders. "Dreadful time, it was. Thank God we weren't much affected here in Lisowen."

"Thank God, indeed." Da rubbed his chin. "Poor Eamonn, may he rest in peace."

Mam crossed herself, then took the meat parcel to the worktop and unwrapped it. From underneath the worktop, she took a handful of potatoes from a sack, and a knife from the dresser drawer. She started peeling and chopping the potatoes into quarters, both palms of her hands pushing down on the knife.

The noise of the knife on wood grated on Liam's nerves. His mam was vexed; probably about what she and Da had been talking about: diphtheria, Spanish flu, germs. He hated the very sound of the words. He felt scared, again, for himself and his family. People talked about fighting infection. But how could a baby fight?

***

A few days on, his father came in after unblocking a drain at Donnybrook Hall. It had been raining steadily and he kicked off his muck-clad boots before flopping into the rocking chair. "Sure, I just can't get heat into me today." He rubbed his hands alternately along the length of his arms.

Ma looked up from her darning, her face pinched with concern. Putting the kettle on the range, she went out to the scullery and returned with the tin bath. "We'll get you warm." She turned to Liam. "Nurse the baby for me, son, while I get your da bathed."

Liam took the gurgling baby from her cot and paraded her around the kitchen. Saturday night was always bath night, but this was only Friday. He hoped he'd get to take his regular bath the next day, along with the warm soda farls and hot milk that always came after. He whispered gently into Fionuala's ear as he walked around. "This is the clock, this is the table, this is the fire, and this is the dresser."

Unbuttoning the top three buttons of his shirt, his father struggled to pull it off over his head. "I heard today that the old spinster from Carnspindle is dead."

"Mattie Hay? But she wasn't old." His mother helped to free his father from his clothes, folding them in a neat pile on a chair nearby.

Water slopped over his father's knees as he lowered himself into the steaming tub.

His mother placed the clothes on the chair. "Mattie wouldn't have been more than forty-five." She plucked at a loose thread on Pat's shirt and raised her eyebrows. "Was it …?"

"I believe so."

Liam watched his mam sponge his da's back.

As he ran a yellow block of soap over his arms, his father muttered, "I'm afraid that Mattie's brother is ill from it too."

"The brother that helps on the farm?"

"The very one." Da placed the soap on the floor, where it skittered about, coming to a halt at the foot of the rocker. "It'll be hard for them, with the cows and milking, there's no doubt. Maybe I can help them in some way?"

Liam saw a look flash from his mother to his father. A look of pleading. Nothing was said. He laid Fionuala gently into her crib. A hard ball formed at the back of his throat and caught his voice so that it shook when he spoke. "Are we going to get diphtheria?'

"No, of course not." His mother avoided his gaze as she poured another kettle of water into the tub.

His Da quickly pulled his knees away from the scolding water.

"But it can kill you?" Liam said.

"Old, frail people, Liam. Don't you worry."

"But you just said that Mattie Hay wasn't old."

He looked at his mam for an answer, but she just fussed about, wiping splashes on the floor with an old cloth.

After a while, Da broke the silence. "I'll end up like a walnut if I stay in here any longer."

Liam offered to fetch towels and his da's nightshirt. When he came back with the old linen cloths, Da stood up gingerly and stepped out of the water. Mam threw one towel over his shoulders and wrapped another round his waist. With a third, she mopped splashes off his chest and flicked water off his feet.

Da stood in front of the fire, warming his hands, his chest bare, a few drops of water glistening on his back. "Now, that did me the world of good." He turned round and blew a kiss in Mam's direction. "I'm right as rain now."

Mam held the nightshirt towards him. "Get your nightclothes on and wrap a blanket round you! I'm not having a half-naked man cavorting about my kitchen." She folded one of the threadbare linens and laid it on the table, her gaze on the flames.

Liam could see through his Mam. She was pretending that everything was normal, but he could tell from her face that it wasn't. The steam had caused her curls to lose some of their spring, and her lips were set in a straight line, a few fine lines visible around them.

He tapped his fingers lightly on the table. "I'll fill you a hot water jar, Da. It'll keep your feet warm."

Da smiled. Mam smiled. Then they said something to one another that he could only catch part of. Did he hear them whisper that he was brave or good?

***

That night, rain lashed against the bedroom window. The baby wouldn't settle. Despite Mary getting up a couple of times to offer the breast, the baby refused and cried sorely.

She laid her hand across the baby's cheek and tapped Pat on the shoulder. "Are you awake?"

"No," he mumbled.

"She's hot, Pat."

He gave a little cough. "She's fine, my love. Go back to sleep."

Chapter Twenty-Two

Mary set her bare feet on the wooden floor and felt the cold air seeping through the cracks. Pat appeared to be sleeping, having been restless for most of the night. Mary lifted the whining baby from the cot and, with the back of her hand, rested it lightly across Fionuala's forehead. Dear God, she was burning up!

The clock struck five. Outside the birds were starting their dawn chorus, their constant twittering a background annoyance.

She held the little one against her, feeling the struggles of the tiny fists and legs. "Ssh. Ssh." There was a deep sickening feeling in the pit of her stomach. Then she realised that Pat was standing beside her, his hand clammy as he placed it over her own. As he bent towards her, she could smell the sourness of his breath.

"I've listened to Fionuala crying all night, my love. Pat struck a match and lit the candle on the bedside table. The room took on a ghostly glow. He cleared his throat. "I should go get the doctor. I think it best to go now."

She felt the heat from his hand on her shoulder, then a squeeze. Resting her head against his chest, she heard the thump of his heart. "Maybe it's quinsy? That would make a baby sick."

He coughed. "Ay. Maybe so. But best that Dr O'Neill sees her."

She looked at him, her eyebrows knitted together. "Are you ailing too?"

"Not a bit of it. Just a niggle in my throat."

"But it's barely morning, Pat, and he's the other side of Lisowen."

"Don't you worry. I'll pedal that yoke of a bike like a demon. The good doctor can drive me back in his motor car." He kissed her on the cheek, then stroked the baby's forehead. "He'll know how to cure our Fionuala."

Struggling into his clothes, he searched on the floor for his work-boots. "Don't be fretting now," he told her.

Mary watched as he hurried away from her, the thud of his boots like those of a soldier on a mission.

As the front door slammed behind him, Liam's door creaked open. "Where's Da off to?"

"He's gone to get the doctor." Mary rocked the baby to and fro in the cradle of her arms, but the infant struggled and cried. "Fionuala's not well."

"What's wrong with her?"

Mary lowered the crying infant back into the cot. She put her arms around Liam. She felt the warmth of his bed on him, and smelled the staleness of his night clothes.

"She's got a bad dose of something."

"Diphtheria?"

"No, no. I'm sure not." She turned her back on him. "It'll be croup or German measles, or some other baby ailment. Little ones pick up all sorts of things."

She patted the baby's head, but Fionuala twisted and turned. Lifting her back out of the cot once more, she let the baby nuzzle into her neck. The crying stopped. Mary stroked the tiny head with its covering of fine, dark hair. It felt like the down of a new-born chick. "Now, Liam, your sister's settling. Go back to bed and get some sleep."

Liam reached out his hand to touch Fionuala and finding a bare foot, patted it gently. "Don't worry, Fionuala. The doctor will have medicine to make you better."

After Liam closed his bedroom door behind him, Mary rolled herself onto her bed, opened her nightgown, and attempted to ease a milk-swollen nipple into the baby's mouth. The baby latched on but spat the nipple out almost immediately, moving her head side to side, refusing to feed, a strange rasp coming from her chest.

Every now and then, Fionuala seemed to stop breathing and Mary would hold her own breath until she saw the little chest moving again. Closing her eyes, she prayed to God, the Virgin Mary and all the saints. Please God, help her.

***

A little later, Mary heard the roar of a car, then Liam hobbling down the stairs. Clutching her precious child to her, she followed him, calling to Liam to light the gas lamps. Even though dawn was breaking, the sky had a darkness to it and rain still pattered against the windowpanes.

The car pulled up outside the door.

She turned to Liam. "Sit yourself in the corner and don't be disturbing the doctor. He'll need space and quiet to cast his eye over your sister."

As she laid Fionuala in the blanket-lined drawer near the smouldering fire, the child cried out, then whimpered.

She heard Pat, his voice heavy with concern, before the door opened and the cool morning air raced in to envelop her. She pulled her shawl around her shoulders.

Dr O'Neill tipped his hat to her as he entered. He was wearing a cloth mask over his nose and mouth. The sight of him put a fright in her.

"I'll wash my hands and then I'll examine her." His words were flat and expressionless.

Pat muttered something to the doctor, who discarded his hat and coat on the table. In the gaslight, his forehead had a pale sheen about it, the lines round his eyes deeply etched.

Dr O'Neill addressed Mary. "Can you pour me a basin of water, Mrs O'Dowd?"

She nodded and tipped water from the pitcher into the enamel bowl on the worktop.

Having washed and dried his hands, the doctor pulled back the covers from the crying child and placed the back of his hand on her forehead. "She has a high temperature." He sighed, then pressed around her neck with his long fingers. "And her glands are swollen."

"She'll be all right, won't she?" Mary gripped a drying cloth tightly in her hands and wound it into a tight coil.

The doctor opened his bag and rooted around in vain for something. He ran the back of his hand across his forehead. "I'll need a teaspoon, Mrs O'Dowd."

Mary rattled the drawer of the dresser and searched among the cutlery. The doctor stood as a surgeon would, his hand ready to receive an instrument.

"I need you to hold her completely still so that I can look into the back of her mouth."

Mary gathered Fionuala into her arms. Pat stood next to her, his fingers stroking the little feet. Dr O'Neill pushed him gently to the side. Holding the spoon end, the doctor forced the crying infant's mouth open and inserted the handle deep into the baby's mouth.

Mary fought back tears as her child struggled and gagged.

The doctor peered inside, moving his head this way and that. Liam, now out of his seat, watched closely.

"Stay back, boy!" the doctor snapped.

Mary saw the fierceness on the face of the doctor. "Liam, son, do as you're told."

The doctor turned to the fire and threw the spoon into the flames. "I'm sorry. I've no better way to sterilise your spoon." He stood staring at the flames. "I'm afraid the infant has diphtheria."

Mary howled, her face buried into the baby's chest. Pat put his arm round her. Liam said nothing.

"The infection has formed a sticky plug over the back of her throat. That's why she's finding it hard to breathe."

Mary's whole body convulsed. She could feel Pat's arms hugging her tightly. Then she felt Liam hugging her, too, and his wet tears on her nightdress. She wanted Pat to get rid of the doctor and let her have her time with her baby.

The doctor went to the basin again and scrubbed at his forearms and hands. "Don't give up hope. I saw ten cases yesterday and only three are unlikely to survive. For the next forty-eight hours, you'll need to boil kettles and create steam."

"Of course, Doctor, we'll start right away," Pat replied, his voice faltering. "We'll do that, won't we, Mary?"

She nodded.

Paid from coins in the tea tin, the doctor dropped them into his pocket, where they rattled against other coins. "I'm leaving an embrocation to rub on her chest and some aspirin powder to bring down her temperature." He fished two little brown paper packages from out of his leather bag and set them on the table. "The RIC are putting up quarantine notices. No-one is to leave Lisowen. There's to be no school or church for now. It's hard on us all, I know."

And then he left, muttering, "More homes to visit, diagnoses to make."

***

The rosary beads slid silently through her fingers, a low repetitive murmur from Mary's lips accompanying the high-pitched crying of the sick child.

Pat slouched on the rocking chair beside her, his eyes closed. Every so often, he coughed.

Once more, Mary lifted the wheezing Fionuala from her blankets and cradled her.

Liam put water in the kettle and set it beside the steaming pot. Rivulets of water ran down the walls.

Pat sat up and called to Liam, his breathing laboured. "A little drink of water to slake my thirst, please."

"Yes, Da."

Mary watched as Liam poured water into a mug and handed it to his father. As he gulped from the glass, she saw damp patches under Pat's arms. She laid the baby back into the makeshift cot and went to him. The heat of her husband's head against her palm made her pulse race. "Goodness, Pat, you're running a fever."

"I'm fine, Mary." Pat went to rise from the chair but slumped back. "Just a bad cold."

Blood drained from her face; the realisation dawning on her.

Chapter Twenty-Three

Sara slid two fine sheets of paper into an envelope and licked the seal. Writing letters to a fellow bereaved mother took it out of her. In some ways, she wished she could rid her head of all things to do with the war. But that would do her boys a disservice. To recall the memories of her sons to a woman whose only child shared the same fate in the trenches was both bitter and sweet.

Richard sat on the floor, banging a saucepan with a wooden spoon, the noise echoing off the walls.

"Please stop, Richard!"

"Why can't I go and see the ducks?" He threw the spoon down on the floor.

"You know Daddy doesn't want you leaving the house." She retrieved the wooden spoon from the floor and replaced it with a pencil. "You could get sick." Setting an old newspaper out on the floor, she wrote his name in big letters at the top and encouraged him to copy it.

"I don't want to write my name now and I won't get sick!" He set the pencil down, crossed his arms and pouted.

Sara felt sorry for her son. What did he know of quarantine? In one way, she was glad that it was only boredom that three-year-old Richard felt. He couldn't sense or understand the current danger. Besides this diphtheria epidemic, the country was in turmoil, senseless killings happening on a daily basis. The fight for Irish unity was never far away.

"Please, Mummy. Please let's go and see the ducks. They'll be very, very hungry." He pulled at her skirt, his eyes wide and pleading.

She felt herself waver. What harm would it do? A short walk. William had gone to the school to attach a poster about the epidemic to the front door. He said that he'd wait a while in case any child turned up, then he'd shoo them back home. After that, he'd sort some papers out that could be worked on at home and be back by lunchtime. Sara shook her head. For him, going out didn't seem to be such a problem.

"A necessity," he'd told her, "I won't be gone long."

Sara's mind flitted to Mary. How would she be coping? A newborn baby and everyone up to high doh. She'd be worried, like Sara, but, knowing Mary, she'd be keeping herself and the family safe. The visit to see baby Fionuala, the day after her birth had been difficult for Sara. She'd been too upset to stay any longer than a few minutes, caught up as she was in her own silent grief. Over two years now, but the pain was still raw.

She'd cuddled the new-born infant, left a gift of a knitted bonnet and hastened away with the excuse of the chimney sweep calling. It was the smell of the baby's neck that had done it. As she'd nursed Fionuala, she'd been transported to the day she'd cradled her own twins. Arthur, the first to be born, a slippery coil of limbs and a mop of thick black hair. Samuel, the smaller, had less hair and was more compact. She recalled the wide grin on William's face when he saw his sons for the first time, and she'd had a fleeting glimpse of that wonderful feeling of unbounding joy and fulfilment.

Now, Mary had a boy and a girl, while she had only Richard and those fading memories of her sons. She shook her head and chastised herself for envying her friend's good fortune.

She heard paper being ripped. "Richard? No, please! You'll break the pencil!"

Richard was scribbling on the newspapers, digging so hard with the pencil tip that he was tearing the paper.

Fresh air. That's what they both needed. What if they went out but didn't go near the Main Street? A walk up the back road to the part of the river where the ducks gathered would allow Richard to throw some crumbs. Then a quick walk to the O'Dowds, just to check on how the baby was doing. She wouldn't go in, of course, just leave some barmbrack wrapped up at the door. They'd be back well before twelve.

Sara opened the bread bin and sliced a heel off a loaf. Then, thinking ahead about what would be a suitable bribe for her child, she washed a carrot and sliced it into sticks. "Maybe we can go out to post a letter, then go to the river."

Richard looked at her, his eyes wide. "And feed the ducks?"

She nodded and he jumped up and down, then ran around the room with his short arms flapping in the air shouting, "Yeah!"

When he had calmed, she kneeled down to take his hands in hers, locking his eyes with hers. "We can't be away long. We'll feed the ducks and, afterwards, we'll stop by to check on little Fionuala."

"Can I hold the baby? I'll be very careful?"

She shook her head. "Not this time. We're only calling to see how they're doing."

***

With a sense of freedom tinged with guilt, Sara pulled the door behind her and, holding Richard's small hand in hers, stepped out. The night before had been stormy and, every so often, they had to step over the branches that had fallen from the trees.

The wind blew against them as they walked, thin ribbons of sunlight glinting out from behind dark clouds. Making their way up the narrow road leading to the river, she looked about her. No-one to be seen. How were the farmers minding their animals?

The only sounds to be heard were of a rickety barn door rattling and the distant mooing of cows. As she approached the post box, she lifted Richard under his arms to let him slide the letter into the metal slot. The sun had retreated, leaving a steel-coloured sky.

"Come on, Richard, the ducks are waiting to be fed." She gave his arm a gentle tug.

She felt agitated at the river but let Richard throw crumbs to the ducks as promised. They swam towards him, creating symmetrical ripples in the water, their bright plumage a contrast to the way she felt.

"We're in a real hurry today, so I think we need to get going again," she told her son.

He frowned at her and she patted his head, feeling the dampness of it. Putting the back of her hand to his forehead, she reassured herself that he didn't have a temperature.

"What about something nice to chew, while we walk up to Auntie Mary's?" She bent down to his level and held out a carrot stick.

He smiled and took the offering.

They walked on.

***

The lane to Mary's house was strewn with branches and leaves blown down by the wind. Jackdaws screeched overhead, and an old newspaper lay beside the hedge, its pages whipping violently side to side. It felt more like winter than spring and, looking ahead, she saw the distant pattern of rain heading towards them. She buttoned up her coat.

Richard ran ahead, his grey knee socks falling round his ankles, his shorts held high by braces. He hid by the side of the house as she rattled the knocker.

No answer.

She knocked once more, wondering where they all could be. Surely, Mary and the baby would be inside. They'd know about the quarantine. Could they be out for a walk round the farm? She held her hand to her forehead, as though trying to spy a ship on the horizon. The stone walls of the monastery stared back, as did the sheep in the neighbouring field.

At least, Pat and Liam must be around somewhere, she thought. She set her basket down and cupped her hands round the corners of her mouth. "Hello! Is there anyone at home?"

She heard the scrape of an upstairs sash window being pushed upwards.

"Mary?" Sara looked up at the long, unkempt hair hanging from the face above her. "What's wrong?"

"Just stay where you are, Sara!"

"Why?" She felt a spit of rain on her face. "What is it, Mary?"

"Diphtheria."

Her hand flew to her mouth. She felt her heart race wildly. "Who's ill, Mary?"

"Pat and the baby. They're sick these last two days."

She heard the tremble in Mary's voice. "And yourself? And Liam?"

"Well enough."

"Where's Liam?"

"Gone to draw water from the well."

"I'll get help, Mary!" She heard the crying of a baby. "I'll get the doctor." She tried to keep her voice calm, but her words seemed to tumble carelessly from her mouth. "The doctor will make them better."

"The doctor has been and gone."

"Did you get medicine?"

She heard a faint, "Yes."

Richard came running back to her side, dragging a large branch behind him that he swished around.

She kneeled in front of him. "Be a good boy and wait there."

He threw the branch down. "I want to go in and see the baby!" He pursed his lips and clenched his fists.

"Richard, please!" She set her bag on the step and shouted up to Mary. "What can I do? Shall I come in to help you?"

"No, you mustn't! Keep yourself and your family safe."

"I can't leave you like this."

"Yes, you can." Mary's voice grew louder. "And you will. Stop the germs getting to you and Richard."

"Can I get you food at least?"

There was a pause. Looking upwards, she saw Mary wiping her eyes with the back of her hand. "That would help, for I need Liam here to help me. Stay there a moment."

Sara waited. A little while later, she heard the clank of something falling beside her feet. She reached down and looked inside the small cloth bag to see three pennies. A faint smell of lavender hit her nose. She looked up.

"For milk and butter. Just leave them on the doorstep."

Sara heard groaning. A man groaning.

"I have to go." The window was shoved shut.

With moisture in her eyes, Sara put the cloth bag in her pocket and left the house, holding her son's hand. He toddled along beside her, his reluctant feet tripping every other step or so. Halfway down the lane, she turned and looked back. The washing line was empty. The windows were closed. No smoke rose from the chimney. It was as though the very heart of the house had stopped beating.

Chapter Twenty-Four

Dan took a drag from his cigarette as he balanced on the back legs of his chair. He blew smoke-rings into the air. Quarantine was a fecking bugger!

His younger son, Declan, went to pass him, a hammer in one hand and two pieces of wood in the other. "I heard Brendan Mooney's very sick. They say his neck's the size of a bull's. Can't speak now the doctor's made a hole in his throat."

"Is that so?" Dan stubbed the cigarette butt on the floor with the toe of his boot. "I'll be looking for another apprentice, then." He put his arm out to bar Declan's way. "Pity your useless friends had to be given the heave-ho."

"Sure, Daddy, you've me and Phelim to rely on." Declan cocked his head to where banging could be heard coming from the outhouse. "No better men than your sons!"

"Well, the two of you lazy bastards had better show me some commitment! What are you making anyway, with all this commotion and carry-on?"

One of the girls piped up from the table. "They're making a motor car, Daddy."

Her sisters, seated beside her, hooted with laughter.

Declan set the wood on the table and shook his fist at them. "Well, none of you lot will be getting a ride in the go-cart." He glared at them, before stomping out the back door.

From the yard, Dan could hear arguing and yelling. Phelim, with his whiney voice, was demanding that he should have the bigger hammer.

Jesus Christ! This house and family were getting on his nerves! Never before had he been cooped up like this. The fecking animals in Dublin Zoo had more space to pace around!

Thank God, his Grainne was well. He'd forbidden her to go further than the bottom of the lane. He stared at her, sitting there opposite him, on the rocking chair. She cradled the baby, her jet-black hair trailing from a purple ribbon, two faint blotches of colour on her porcelain cheeks. The simple dress she wore sat low on her shoulders and he watched the gentle rise and fall of her small breasts.

He sidled over to her and planted a soft kiss on her neck. "You're a fine woman," he whispered.

She put a finger to her lips, turning her head towards the fire. "Don't wake the little one."

He kept his ground, inhaling her freshness, her fragrance. Her skin smelled of apples. He whispered back, his lips brushing the fine hairs on her neck. "Put the baby in the cradle. Come upstairs with me."

The three girls, who were sitting at the table peeling potatoes over newspaper, giggled.

He glared at them, his eyebrows narrowing. "Get back to your work, you silly girls."

They covered their mouths with their hands, stifling their chortles, elbowing one another in the ribs as they jostled together on the bench seat.

Suddenly, there was a loud crash from the outhouse.

"For Christ's sake, what is it now?" Dan slapped the table so hard that some potato peel bounced up and ended on the floor. The child who had been sleeping in the corner on a blanket, lifted his tousled head and started to cry.

Blast those children. No school to go to, no work to keep them occupied. Just a half hour's peace with his Grainne – not too much to bloody ask for? Was it?

The crunch of a bicycle on the gravel path approaching the house drew him to the window. A young man, wearing the uniform of the RIC, set the bicycle to one side. He reached into his trouser pocket and withdrew a cloth mask, the strings of which he tied behind his head. Rummaging in his other pocket, he extracted a crumpled piece of paper.

Dan flung open the door before the policeman had time to knock. "What business have you calling here?"

Startled, the policeman took a large step backwards and struggled to pull the mask over his mouth. "We're under orders to call with everyone in Lisowen." He held out the dog-eared piece of paper at arm's length, as though about to make a speech. "It's to make sure you know about the quarantine."

"I can't fecking hear you with that muzzle round your mouth." Dan reached forward, snatched the paper from him and started to read it.

The policeman pulled his mask down so that it hung around his chin. "I was going to read it out to you! Now, I don't have any more copies."

"Too bad." Dan looked at the typewriter print slanting across the page. "If I were you," he leaned forward pointing a grubby finger at the man, "I'd get away back to the barracks. We're all coming down with throats and chests in this house." He coughed loudly and spat phlegm from his mouth, a glob landing not far from the man's feet.

The policeman, wide eyed, jerked his head back and pulled his mask back up over his mouth. "I'm only doing my job, Mister!"

Grabbing his bicycle, he slung one leg over it and hurtled away, a violent squeak issuing from the wheels as he pedalled.

Chuckling, Dan read out loud:

DIPHTHERIA OUTBREAK IN LISOWEN!
Diphtheria causes fever and a sore throat, and is highly contagious.
Schools, churches and public houses closed until further notice.
Diphtheria is a notifiable disease.
Magistrates will prosecute those with infection in public places.
Residents should restrict all journeys to those of necessity.
By order of the Kilkenny Health Department.

"Sure, we knew all that, didn't we? Haven't we heard the feckers out with their loud hailers? The bloody dogs on the street have been covering their ears." Holding the page, Dan slapped it with the back of his hand. "Do the feckers think I'm deaf?"

Once inside, he tore the paper in half and threw it on the fire. He watched the flames lick over the print as the paper crinkled and curled against the hot coals. Shifting in his trousers, he hoisted them up to where his belt strained tightly under his belly.

The girls were bickering as to who had peeled the most potatoes and who deserved a rest.

Dan gripped the table, his knuckles white, his eyes narrowed. "Shut up, the lot of you!"

The baby howled.

"There, there, my darling." Grainne sat stroking the little one's head, who cried pumping her tiny fists in the air.

"I'm going out!" Dan grabbed his jacket, hauled it over his shoulders, pulled his flat cap onto his head and slammed the door behind him.

The air was cool, the sky colourless. The stormy weather had abated. Dan walked out onto the Carnspindle Road, his arms swinging freely, glad to be out in the open. He thought he could smell decay in the air, and the silence unnerved him. It was as though the wildlife was in quarantine too. Only a rat lying dead at the side of the road; bloodied, its entrails swarming with bluebottles, caught his attention. As he looked down at it, the smell made him gag. A couple of magpies circled close-by, awaiting their opportunity to feed.

He strolled on towards Beggarstown, no person or vehicle passed his way. He would stop short of the crossroads as he'd heard that the police were blocking the routes in and out of Lisowen. Then, he'd circle back by the river.

After walking for a half hour, he could hear the unmistakable hum of an army van puttering over the hill. He threw himself into a ditch, peering out at the road through blades of grass. The ground was cold and hard beneath his belly, the earth damp and musty.

"The fucking Black and Tans," he muttered, spotting the dishevelled and unmatched uniforms of the soldiers sitting in the back of the vehicle. Pity his comrades weren't there with him. Armed. A Thompson sub-machine gun to boot. Then they'd have greeted the bastards with a hail of bullets. Filled them full of holes from here to fucking Timbuktu. He pointed his finger at the disappearing van and bent his middle finger, as though cocking the trigger of a pistol.

"I'll get you next time, you British scum!"

Why he had felt the need to hide, now seemed ridiculous. As far as he could tell, no-one knew of his past, nor suspected him of any wrongdoing. Those fires, started so far away from Lisowen, were months back now. Besides, he kept no weapons in his home, just in case the auxies or the Tans called. They wouldn't find anything more in his house other than a bunch of screaming brats and his beautiful wife.

Clambering out of the ditch, he brushed off the grass and twigs with a couple of swipes of his flat cap. A pint or two of porter would have been the thing today, but McGinn's would surely be closed, being in fear of the magistrate's wrath.

Recalling a bottle of potin he'd secreted in the forge, he decided to head there. Better sleeping at the smithy for a night than returning to that madhouse of a home.

Chapter Twenty-Five

Sara hurried along, dazed, encouraging Richard to keep up with her. She'd have to get home, and quickly. William would be really alarmed if she wasn't in the house. He'd be furious, too, to think she'd disobeyed him, but thank God that she had. Once she'd told him, she could see about helping the O'Dowds.

As they sped past the hedgerows, Richard pointed out cows in the fields and a small black kitten that darted out in front of them. "Look, Mummy! Look, look!"

"Yes, yes. I see," she answered, her mind elsewhere.

Only an army van puffing fumes high into the air, full of fresh-faced boys in uniform, caught her attention. For an instant, she thought of Arthur and Samuel.

Richard tugged on her hand. "What's dipeerer?"

She took a deep breath. "It's where people have sore throats and coughs, and aren't very well."

He seemed content with this answer, kicking stones as he hopped and skipped beside her.

***

Finally, they were home to the familiar creaks and smells of the parlour. The clock struck twelve as she hung up their coats and, taking a poker, she searched for life through the slack heaped high on the fire.

Soon, she heard the familiar crunch of William's boots on the gravel outside. She stood at the door, her heart thumping, ready to meet him, preparing what she would say.

Kissing her cheek, he straightened up and took a step back. "My dear!" He took his hat off and held it with both hands. "You look as though you've just seen a ghost. What's wrong?"

Richard ran to his father's side and tugged at his sleeve. "We went to see Auntie Mary and the baby's sick, and Auntie Mary's husband's sick."

"What?" William threw his hat on a chair.

Richard threw his arms round his father's leg. "They've got dipeerer."

"After everything I said!" William thumped the table, his face like granite. "Why would you put yourself and Richard at risk?" He paced the floor, his footsteps loud, his voice angry.

"Daddy's cross," Richard sobbed. "Why are you cross, Daddy?'

Sara felt hot tears stinging her eyelashes. "It's not as you think. We didn't go into the house." She twisted her wedding ring round her finger, digging the band deep into her flesh. "I just needed fresh air and we went to post a letter. I stayed away from the Main Street. I never thought for one minute…"

A feeling of dizziness enveloped her. She sank to the floor, crying, choking the words out through great gulps of air. "Oh, William, just think if it was us. What would we do? What can poor Mary do? A sick new-born and a sick husband. Dear Lord above, I can't bear to think of it."

She felt William's arms around her, helping her up from the floor and into a chair. "Now settle yourself, my love." His face softened. "Give me time to think. It's just the shock of what you did that vexed me so."

He took Richard, pulled him up into his arms and rubbed the tears from his son's eyes with his thumbs before setting him down. "Your Daddy's not cross. He's just worried." He dug deep into his pocket and held up a wrapped sweet. "Now, off upstairs to play until you're called down."

"Thank you, Daddy." Richard, the sweet clenched tightly in his fist, hurtled off upstairs.

Sara took Williams's jacket from him and hung it on the coat stand. "Did any of the children turn up at school?"

"Yes, a handful showed, in spite of the warnings. I only kept them long enough to hear their news." He took her hand in his and held it tight. "I now know of seven who've died: Nurse Armstrong, the two old craturs up the hill, Sarah and Arthur Bolt, and Molly Doherty's two little ones. Apparently, there's not a house in Main Street where someone isn't ailing."

Sara swept the stray hairs back from her forehead and put her fingers to her temples. "Dear God! That's awful!"

"I'm truly sorry for the O'Dowds. I really am." William rose from his chair and stood in front of the fire.

Sara could see the veins on his neck throbbing the way they always did when he was worried.

"We can't be anywhere near them, but we can leave food and medicine outside their house," he decided.

She laid her head against his neck and hugged him. "Thank God, we're of a mind." Feeling a twinge of guilt at having been so ready to enter Mary's house, she slid the lavender coin bag from her dress pocket and held it out so that he could see it. "Mary threw coins down to me, in this bag. For food."

He pushed her away and pointed to the fire. "Burn it! Drop the coins in boiling water. Then wash your hands." His face was drained of colour.

He shook his head, and she felt both stupid and chastised.

"We mustn't touch anything from their house," he explained.

Sara emptied the coins into a small enamel bowl, then flung the little bag into the fire, where it fizzled; the smell of lavender bursting forth. After boiling a kettle, she scalded the coins before adding cold water and washing her hands.

Richard was called down, and they ate their broth in relative silence, most of the talking coming from Richard, who chattered on about the ducks and the kitten he'd seen earlier.

When they'd finished their food, William pulled another sweet from his pocket and passed it to Richard. "You're to keep that until after I'm gone. Then, you're to play quietly and be a good boy for your Mummy." He pushed his dish to the side and wiped his mouth with a handkerchief.

Sara cleared the dishes to the sideboard. "I'm sure Richard will be very good."

"I'll be very, very good." Richard stuffed the sweet into the pocket of his shorts and started playing with his wooden train on the floor.

William touched her elbow and beckoned her to the corner of the room near the door. He lowered his voice. "Let's make a start. You prepare what you can, and I'll go to the dairy. Hopefully, I'll get there and back without any problem." He reached for his hat and jacket. "Though, Lord knows there only seems to be the army willing to be out on our streets. The poor ruffians they're after are home and hiding under their beds. I'll wager there'll be no homes turned upside down until the diphtheria germs have disappeared."

"And when will that be?" she whispered, afraid of what he might say.

He shrugged.

"Will you take the horse and trap?"

He slid his long arms into his jacket and placed his hat on his head. "The horse needs reshoeing but I'm damned if I'm going anywhere near O'Toole's forge."

"It's a long way to walk." She frowned, aware that it would take him most of the afternoon to get to the dairy and back.

"I'll wait till after quarantine to get things fixed. Shanks's pony will have to do for now," he replied. "After quarantine, I'll take the horse to the forge in Beggarstown."

Richard looked up from the floor as his father opened the front door. "Can I eat my sweetie now, Daddy? Now that you're really going?"

William grinned. "Yes, son, eat your sweet now."

Richard unwrapped the aniseed ball and shoved it in his mouth "Thank you, Daddy," he blurted, his mouth full of drool. He reached for his teddy and waved his paw at his father as he left the house. "Edward says thank you, too."

Sara smiled weakly at her son's delight, then solemnly turned to the task in hand. Taking a block of cheese and several rashers of bacon from the press, she wrapped them in old newspaper. She looked for other food she had to spare and found some cabbage, carrots and a few pieces of mutton. She would make stew and colcannon and bake bread. Wearily, she started to peel potatoes. Could her life be measured in boiled potatoes? Perhaps if you laid them end to end, they might stretch from Dublin to Kilkenny. Silly thoughts. The clay caught under her fingernails, stinging the skin that she'd scrubbed earlier.

***

Some hours later, William returned. He came in the door, set a small sack on the table and, with his coat and hat still on, held his head in his hands.

Sara looked at him in alarm. "What happened?" She poured him a glass of water.

He took it from her and sipped slowly.

Over an hour it had taken him to get to the dairy, what with going along the back roads. And then, when he'd arrived, he found the doors padlocked. The men were closing early. They'd been nervous, looking all about them; jumpy and anxious, and not just about diphtheria. A dairy out beyond Beggarstown had been burned to the ground, apparently in retaliation for a barracks being attacked. Worse still, a workman had been shot. Word had it, that their dairy might be next. Only by pleading, did he persuade the foreman to open the door and fetch him some butter and milk. Next time, the man had said, we might not be here, for we're worried for ourselves and our families.

Sara couldn't believe it. As if people hadn't enough trouble without looking over their shoulder. And the murderers and bullies were supposedly acting on her behalf, upheld by the Crown? William had been shocked too, said that he'd speak with the local RIC who were good men, not the sort of people out to destroy lives and livelihoods. Those soldiers drafted to help the police were getting totally out of hand.

Sara turned her attention back to the work in hand, stopping to put supper on the table, then working on till the early evening. Before bedtime, there was enough food to fill her wicker basket, as well as a small flour sack to take to the O'Dowds' the next day.

***

She watched William leaving the cottage early the next day, her wicker basket hung awkwardly over his arm and a full sack of flour thrown over his shoulder.

He strode out with purpose; his tall, erect frame a dark figure against the murky morning light.

Chapter Twenty-Six

Mary opened the door quietly to Liam's bedroom.

He stirred and moved himself up onto his elbows. "How's Fionuala today?"

She crossed herself and inhaled slowly. "Your sister passed away last night."

His face crumpled, his eyes blinking back tears.

"Liam, I wish I was telling you something different."

He threw back the covers and turned to sit on the edge of the bed, staring at the floorboards. "Now she'll need the priest. And how will we have a wake and a funeral? And Da? Da doesn't seem to be able to do anything yet."

Mary took him in her arms and held him tightly. She could feel his heart beating, thumping against her chest. He smelled of his father's sickness and she stifled the bile from rising into her mouth.

"I know." She caressed his head. "Liam, we have to be brave." She slid a hand under his chin, stroked the sides of it, felt the sharpness of its contours.

He lifted his blue eyes, fringed by long eyelashes. "Is Da going to die too?"

She shook her head. "I pray to God, he won't."

She left him to dress and, sometime later, took him gently by the hand and led him downstairs, the familiar scrape of his boots on the steps a strange comfort to her.

"You need to say a proper goodbye to your sister."

***

The infant lay as still as a doll would, perfect and beautiful, an ivory crocheted blanket pulled up to her shoulders, her pale eyelids closed.

"Are you sure she's gone?" Liam looked at his mam.

She nodded and he could see her closed lips tremble.

"Could you not be mistaken?"

She shook her head and looked away from him. "I'm sorry, Liam. I'm so sorry."

He put his hand against Fionuala's cheek. He felt the chill from her skin. She wasn't warm and snuffly anymore. He felt a heaviness in his throat. Leaning over, he planted a tiny kiss on her forehead. "Rest in peace, Fionuala."

He straightened up, caught sight of his mam, a handkerchief held to her eyes and stuffed his feelings deep down inside himself. "I'm going upstairs." He turned and hobbled to the staircase.

He went into his room and beat his fists against the bolster, beating so hard that feathers floated out. He beat on and on, until his shoulders ached and he had no more fight left in him.

Then, settling his breath, he stood up, went to the basin and ran a cold cloth over his face. He opened the door of his bedroom, closed it softly behind him and went in to his da.

***

Mary steadied herself with two hands on the sideboard. Was Pat to die too? She offered a silent prayer into the morning light. Then, brushing her hair back from her face, she returned to the laundry, hauling sheets from the basin, laying them on the drainer, cold water trickling onto her foot.

There was a knock at the door. Sara? It was yesterday that Mary had spoken with her, dropped the money to her from the upstairs window. She crossed the room to the door, opened it and stood back.

William Leavy stood in front of her. "Mrs O'Dowd."

The formality of the greeting cut into her. In all the time Mary had known Sara, she had but exchanged a few pleasantries with her husband. She took him as serious, somewhat stern, missing Pat's rambling ability to chat about little or nothing, or crack a joke.

"How are you managing?"

She swallowed hard and composed herself. "Fionuala breathed her last some time ago." She looked away. "I've laid her out as best I can. I know there can't be a wake." She hung her head, glad that her hair obscured her face. "Pat's still with us. Just."

William took his hat off and shook his head. "I'm so very sorry. I truly am. I know Sara will be heartbroken for you." He shifted from foot to foot. "And yourself?"

She shrugged. "I'm surviving. As is Liam. God's honest truth, I don't know how I'd have coped alone." A gust of wind whipped about her face. "But Pat's a dreadful worry. He scares me with his coughing and his voice is not one I recognise. It's as though he's choking." She put a hand to her throat. "He can't seem to get breath in or out of him."

"Ah now, Mrs O'Dowd – Mary."

She saw him physically struggle to ditch formality, the discomfort in his body.

William wrung his hands together. "Thank the Lord that Liam and yourself are well."

He stood before her, a couple of yards away, awkward, hat in one hand, the basket and sack in front of him on the path. The sun shone into her eyes, making it difficult for her to see his face. Although, for most of the time, he kept his gaze downward.

"God has a plan for all of us. He's taken your little daughter to be with him, but God willing, he'll spare your husband." William looked up at her briefly. "Sara and I will pray for you all."

He spoke the words so softly and with such sincerity that, for the first time, she sensed the shyness of the man; his true nature.

There was a hand on her sleeve.

Liam stood beside her. "Da's calling for you."

Mary glanced down at Liam, and then back at William. "I'm sorry. I've got to go."

William pointed to the basket and the sack that lay in front of him. "I'm leaving food for you here, on the path. And I'll be back tomorrow to check on you." With that, he turned away, put his hat on and walked down the lane.

***

To Sara it seemed like an eternity until she heard William stamping his feet to shake the muck from them, at the door. She set the sock she was darning to the side.

He came into the parlour, unlaced his boots and sat silent in the large wooden chair at the fire. Richard gave his father a hug before turning his attention to a set of dominoes.

Sara waited for William to speak.

He lifted Richard from his seat and set him on the ground. "Upstairs, young man, and get your book out. I'll be up to read to you very soon. Mummy and I have things to be doing."

Richard tugged at his father's sleeve. "What sort of things, Daddy?"

"Things that you don't need to worry about." William patted him lightly on the head.

Richard scrambled up the stairs, shouting as he went, "Don't be long, Daddy!"

Sara filled the kettle from the jug of water and hung it over the fire. "Did you speak to Mary?"

He nodded.

"And you left the food?"

"I did." His voice was weak and reedy. He took one of her hands in his and stroked the back of it. "The baby's dead."

Sara gasped. "Oh, how awful!"

He cleared his throat. "Pat's hanging on but isn't doing so good. Liam's well enough, though."

"Oh, William!" Her mind flew back to that terrible day when she got the news about her sons. She felt her stomach turn, a sick feeling rising through her. But now was the time to be strong for her friend.

William went into the scullery. Sara took a few deep breaths and followed him inside. He was raking through nuts and screws in an old tobacco tin, a hammer and nails in front of him on the small table.

"What are you doing?"

"I'm going to make a coffin for the baby, and then dig a grave for her." William kept his back turned away. "I had time to think as I walked back. There's a small wooden crate in the shed. Maybe you could make it suitable with linen and whatnot."

Sara nodded and whispered, "I'll do that."

Later, with Richard asleep, she rummaged in her trousseau drawer for satin and lace. William set the crate on the table and sanded the edges, removing splinters and protruding nails. They worked together by gaslight.

Sara, her head bent over the linen, kept the stitches as small and even as possible, weaving cream ribbons of lace around the exterior, and lining the inside with a small feather pillow.

By nightfall, the coffin was ready.

***

She awakened as William got up from bed and dressed. The day had hardly yet broken but there was enough light to make out the contours of the room. She slipped her bare feet into her boots. "You'll need breakfast before you leave."

"No need, my dear. I'll drink some milk, then be on my way."

"But you must have more than that to line your stomach." With her unlaced boots on her feet, still nightgown clad, she went downstairs and made milky porridge. When finished, she added a thin drizzle of honey.

He ate hungrily, scraping the remains of the bowl with his spoon.

From the downstairs window, a thin blanket around her shoulders, Sara watched him leave; this time carrying a sack containing the tiny coffin with one hand and a spade in the other.

***

Mary laid another cold flannel on Pat's head. He called out, then coughed. She put her cheek to his. Still hot.

There was a noise outside. Someone was working, shovelling, moving stones about. She drew back the curtains. A watery sun glowed down from a pale sky. A man was digging, his hat and jacket thrown to one side, his sleeves rolled up.

A mound of soil was stacked up neatly to one side. When the man straightened to put a hand to his back and stretch, she saw that it was William Leavy. The hole he had dug was under the tall weeping willow, its branches swaying gently in the breeze. Mary clamped her hand over her mouth. Fionuala's grave.

Behind her, Pat called out for water. She went to him, helping him sup tiny sips from an enamel cup, her hand supporting the back of his head, his hair wet and pasted to his head, his breath the smell of vinegar.

She looked at her husband; beads of sweat on his brow, wheezing, gasping, his eyes flickering. It should have been him digging the grave for their baby. He would have wished to do this, this most personal of acts. God forbid that he, too, should lie cold and dead beside Fionuala.

She drew a shawl about herself and went back to the window. William had a small sack with straps around it, which he was measuring against the sides of the space that he had dug.

He turned round, looked up and, on catching her gaze, bowed his head.

In bare feet, in case Liam should wake, she tiptoed downstairs and opened the door. She called out softly. "I won't come closer." She adjusted the shawl to cover as much of her nightdress as possible. "I'm grateful to you for doing this. I truly am."

He looked up at her face and gave the slightest of nods. She clutched the door frame, fearing her legs might buckle.

He brushed the dirt off his hands and trousers, and held up the tiny coffin with its satin padded lid. "Sara worked hard to get it right. I'll leave it here for you to bring inside."

Mary wiped a stray tear away with the back of her hand. "Thank you." She couldn't think of what else to say. She felt like a husk; hollow, devoid of thought, empty of purpose.

"I thought to return tomorrow at noon, if that suits?" He looked at her. "I'll see if one of the priests is willing to come with me."

She pulled her shawl close to her, suddenly aware that it had slipped. She couldn't bring herself to worry about it. "Thank you," she repeated.

She watched him clean the dirt from the spade by smoothing it on the grass. Securing his shirt buttons at the wrists, he perched his hat on his head, threw his jacket over his shoulder and took the spade in his hand.

He looked round at her.

She raised a hand, held it motionless in the air, and then he was gone.

***

Dan was out for a walk again. No feckin' magistrates orders would keep him at home. Quarantine had been going on too long, in his opinion, and it was time to get back to matters of importance: ridding Ireland of the British. Word had it that the dairy workers had been threatened by the Tans. Well, something would have to be done about that.

As he turned onto the road towards the Main Street and forge, he glimpsed a figure coming down the road, something over one shoulder. Screwing up his eyes, he saw that the man was tall and wore a hat with a brim. As he approached, he realised who it was. Well, I'll be damned, it's that blasted Protestant, Leavy. What in the name of Jaysus would he be doing with a shovel?

On passing, William Leavy tipped his hat at him, spoke no word and walked straight on. Dan, in return, scowled back, angry again for the man's outrageous protest against the Soldier's Song.

In an instant, he realised that he'd missed his opportunity. Far better would have been to have asked outright why William Leavy was breaking quarantine rules.

Too late.

Further on, he came upon an old, deserted hovel. He'd passed it many times and now he wanted to take a better look. It could make a suitable place for an interrogation, for no-one for miles around would hear the cries or protestations.

He pushed the door open. One rusted hinge still held. Two birds that had been nesting flew out the door and something small and furry disturbed the leaves on the floor. Filthy but perfect! Even the roof was mostly intact. If he had to force information from someone, this would be where they'd go. He went outside.

With his back to the stone wall, he fished for his cigarette packet from his jacket pocket. Selecting a cigarette, he tapped it several times on the box before running it under his nose and inhaling the aroma. He struck a match, and inhaled deeply, drawing hard on his cigarette. The brief sting of the inhalation was a pleasure to him, and he blew the smoke out in short puffs.

Where the feck could that bugger Leavy have been going? Then, it came to him. He tapped ash on the ground. No-one feckin' takes their spade from their farm unless they're going to dig a hole and hide something. Arms or money. One or other.

Of course! It would be money. If Leavy had guns, he would keep them at home. Well, he might be needing them soon for his own protection.

Money! A schoolteacher like him would have gathered a bob or too together over the years.

The rich bastard!

Dan's mind turned to ways of parting William Leavy from his fortune.

Chapter Twenty-Seven

Mary was hanging washing on the line, two pegs held between her lips, glad of the warm sun on her face. Pat was slowly on the mend and that was a relief, but Fionuala's passing had taken its toll on all of them. Time was needed for the pain to soften. She pegged a nightdress to the line. But there'd be no forgetting Fionuala. She looked up, squinting, hoping her little girl was somewhere up there, high above, safe in the arms of angels.

As she heaved a thick counterpane over the line, she heard the leaves rustle behind her, and someone clear their throat.

"Beg your pardon, Missus."

She let go of the washing and turned to see a uniformed man standing behind her. He wore the distinctive dark green serge of the Royal Irish Constabulary, his legs sticking out from the bottom of his trousers, as though he'd suddenly sprouted a couple of inches overnight. He looked vaguely familiar. Had he been at Liam's school? But she didn't want to stare, and his face was mostly hidden by an overly large, peaked cap.

She looked from his cap to his socks, and the policeman self-consciously tugged at his trousers in what seemed to be a vain attempt to stretch them. "I walked up over the grass. That's why you didn't hear me." He pointed to a bicycle abandoned on its side at the bottom of the lane. "That blasted contraption has a puncture."

Mary pegged the counterpane to the line. "Ah, that's a pity."

"Missus – you'll be glad to know that quarantine is over."

She crossed herself. "Thank the Lord."

The policeman produced a small, well-thumbed notebook from his bag. "Could I trouble you to answer some questions regarding the recent epidemic?"

"Of course. What would you like to know?"

"Did anyone in this household die from diphtheria? Any burial take place? Authorised or otherwise?" He took a small pencil from behind his ear and held it poised; ready to write.

Mary swallowed hard. "My baby died … on the second of last month. She's buried under the tree there." She pointed towards the small plot under the weeping willow, the dark brown soil mounded and fresh, a small wooden cross at one end. "We plan to move her to the churchyard… when the time is right."

The policeman hung his head, avoiding her gaze. "I'm sorry for your loss." He wrote something in his notebook, then hesitated, the pencil poised. "The baby's name and the mother's name?"

Mary inhaled deeply. "I'm Mary O'Dowd and my baby is Fionuala O'Dowd."

He continued writing. "Anyone else affected by diphtheria?"

"My husband." She picked up a sheet from the basket and slung it over the line. "He's getting better, but he's still not right." She straightened the linen and secured it with the pegs she was holding. After drying her hands on her apron, she scooped the empty basket into her arms and turned to face the policeman.

"Why do you ask?"

"These details will go to the Town Hall in Kilkenny. As well as that, the local doctor wants to know." The policeman lifted the flap of his leather bag, stowed the notebook inside and reset the pencil behind his ear.

"Dr O'Neill?"

"Yes, he's making records about the epidemic."

Mary swallowed. She wasn't sure if you could ask a favour of a policeman. "Would you mind, if you're talking to him, to tell him that Patrick O'Dowd is still not well recovered."

"Would you like him to call?"

"I would, and I'd be most grateful."

"Of course, Missus. I'll let the doctor know."

As he walked away, Mary thought to herself that the RIC man could be no more than sixteen or seventeen. Then she realised who he was. Ruari Corvin's brother. Both had joined the police.

When she came into the house, Liam was seated at the table. In front of him, on newspaper, lay the springs and cogs of an old clock. His tongue protruding from between his teeth, he held a screwdriver and a dirty cloth in the palm of one hand. "Who were you talking with outside?"

"It was an RIC man, a young slip of a lad. Not much older than you. I think it might have been Ruari Corvin's younger brother."

"Sean Corvin? He was a good lad and looked out for me at school." Liam set the screwdriver down and glanced upwards as though searching for an answer.

Mary looked at him quizzically. "Is that so?" She couldn't remember Liam telling her of anyone looking out for him. He'd obviously kept that from her so as not to be worrying her.

Something stirred in the back of her mind. "His brother, Ruari, is stationed down in Kilkenny, or so I heard. Your da thought so much of him, the way he helped the day of your accident, and how nothing was too much trouble for him." She shook her head, a few stray curls swaying about her face. "Ah, I remember his lovely, freckled face and that broad smile of his as though it was yesterday."

Liam poured a drop of oil onto a cogwheel in front of him and rubbed at it with the cloth. "I haven't seen either of them since Sean left school...and I thought he was stupid joining the RIC."

"Well, he probably wanted to follow in his brother's footsteps." Mary wondered what their mother thought. Would she have tried to change their minds?

"Did he have a gun?"

"What a thing to ask!" Mary placed a metal tray on the table. "If he did, I didn't notice. He came to say there's no more diphtheria to worry about. Thank the Lord." With both hands she carefully lifted the clock face onto the tray. "Now, set all your other bits and bobs on this please." Taking the oil from him, she placed it on the drainer; the stickiness and smell of it lingered on her hands. She rubbed them on her apron. "So, it'll be back to school next week."

Liam sighed.

After making tea, she poured a cup for Pat and buttered a slice of soda bread. Placing both on an enamel plate, she climbed the stairs to where Pat was propped up in bed, his back supported by two bolsters.

Standing in the doorway, she caught sight of him staring sorrowfully through the open window at the weeping willow. She blinked back a tear. It wouldn't do any good for the two of them to flounder in a sea of despair.

She forced a smile. "I brought you tea."

He looked round, his face breaking into a smile, his chest heaving wildly.

She could hear rattling as he breathed. "I've been thinking, Pat." She set the plate on the bedside table. "What you need is a really good tonic. One that'll get you back on your feet."

Pat reached for the mug and took a slurp. "Is that so?"

"What about some slippery elm or sulphur and treacle electuary?" She chuckled. "Something to put hairs on your chest!"

"Have I not enough of those already?" He laughed, then cleared his throat. "Did I hear you talking to someone outside?"

"A policeman. He came to say that quarantine is over."

Then she told him about asking for the doctor to call. Pat protested but she fussed about him, shaking out the eiderdown and puffing up the bolster. The doctor was calling and that was that. She kissed the top of his head and walked out of the room, clicking the door softly shut behind her.

She'd decided not to say that the policeman had been Sean Corvin. Pat had been concerned when Ruari had joined the police a few years ago. She offered up a prayer to God to keep Ruari and his brother safe.

Politics and policing tended to get Pat all het up. Pat had written to his cousin in Cork advising him to leave the RIC. Life was becoming too dangerous for Irish police officers, Pat had said.

Best keep him free of such vexing matters, she thought.

Back downstairs, she took the tea tin down from the shelf and shook the contents onto the table. A few forlorn coins rolled out. Two shillings and sixpence! It would last them a couple of weeks. Hopefully, it wouldn't be too long before the doctor would see Pat. Put him to rights so that he could get back to work.

***

Later, after Liam had left to get messages, Mary heard a car draw up outside. She opened the door for the doctor.

He tipped his hat to her and brushed past, his flustered face looking around the parlour. "Baby?"

Mary shook her head.

He put a hand on her shoulder, and she caught a strong whiff of disinfectant from his clothes.

"I'm so very sorry. Unfortunately, it's often the little ones..." He set his hat on a stool and his bag on the floor. "And your good man?"

"Still in bed. I'll take you up to him."

The doctor insisted on seeing Pat on his own. "Less fuss," he said.

When, eventually, he came back downstairs, his stethoscope still round his neck, he went to the basin, rolled back his shirt cuffs and washed his hands.

Mary held a small towel out to him.

He dried his hands, concentrating on his fingers as though trying to unscrew them from their joints. He took the stethoscope from his neck and laid it on the table. "I've counted over seventy in Lisowen that succumbed to diphtheria. And eighteen deaths." Hanging the towel back on the hook by the basin, he deftly re-fastened the buttons of his
shirt sleeves.

Mary took a deep breath in. "But why isn't Pat getting better now that the fever has gone and he's eating again?"

Dr O'Neill stood by the fire, his hands clasped behind his back, staring at the flames. "Your husband's heart has been damaged by the infection."

What does that mean, Doctor? Won't he recover?" She wondered if it was him or his housekeeper who polished his shoes, the leather gleaming in the firelight.

The doctor opened his bag and put the stethoscope inside. "I'll leave a prescription for digitalis powders." He closed the bag with a thunk and took hold of it in one hand. "The medicine will help, but from now on, Pat needs to take things easy. And I mean very easy. He mustn't put strain on his heart."

Mary took the tea tin down from the shelf, placing it on the table, ready to pay the bill. "What about work? When can he get back to work?"

Dr O'Neill put his bag down. "I'm afraid that things have to change. He can't be lifting heavy weights or exerting himself. I've suggested to him that he finds something light to be doing." The doctor tapped the table with his long fingers. "I have to go. Now that the epidemic is over, the militias are out and about. No doubt, I'll have more bullets to extract from young men before the week is over."

Mary searched for coins in the tin, rattling the pennies against one another, looking for the sixpence she knew was there. A thought came to her. "Rather than money, maybe you'd like some freshly laid eggs?"

Dr O'Neill pursed his lips. "Eggs?" He picked up his bag. "Ah yes. I'll take your eggs."

When the doctor was ready to leave, he clutched his medical case in one hand and a small, worn pillowslip filled with eggs in the other. "One last thing, Mrs O'Dowd. Marital relations. Pat must be very careful." He opened his eyes so wide that Mary could see the fine blood vessels radiating out to the eyelids. "I'm sure I don't need to spell out the dangers of," he sniffed, drawing his nostrils together, "the physical side of marital relations."

Mary felt the heat rising in her face. "I understand."

"Good. Good." Doctor O'Neill used the pillowslip to wave a goodbye. "That's good then... that you understand."

She closed the door on the doctor, her heart thumping.

Back upstairs, Pat demanded to know everything that the doctor had said.

"He says that you're to be taking things easy when you're up and around again."

Pat looked at her sadly. "He told me that too." He beckoned her to him with the crook of a finger. "Come here, my love. I need a hug or two to warm my bones."

Mary put her arms around him.

He rubbed his nose against the nape of her neck. "You smell of fresh daisies."

"Do I indeed? And you, Pat O'Dowd, smell of too many days spent in this room." She stroked his hair. It was losing its colour, losing its thickness.

He wasn't the strong, able man she'd married all those years ago.

But he was still Pat. She kissed his forehead, the tip of his nose, both cheeks, then held his face with both hands.

Pat wheezed. "Steady on, woman."

Mary straightened up and placed both her hands on her hips. "Now, let me tell you, you big eejit, how we're going to manage our marital antics when the time is right." She untied her boot laces, kicked away her boots, lifted the counterpane and climbed in beside him. The bed creaked. "I've already got a few ideas."

Chapter Twenty-Eight

Mary was outside feeding the chickens when she heard the car. A far-away phut phut. Probably the old judge off to the courthouse in Kilkenny. Liam had left for school and Pat was still in bed.

The rumble of the car was getting nearer. Scanning the hillside to see where the noise was coming from, she saw the vehicle cresting the stone bridge near the monastery.

After an early morning shower, a rainbow had appeared arching over the countryside. She smiled. Pat used to joke about what they'd do with the pot of gold, if they found it. She was to buy a silk dress; he would be fitted for a tweed suit. Together, they'd take a first-class train carriage to Greystones and parade along the seafront with the best of them.

"Blessed Mother of God!" Mary exclaimed, realising that the car was coming up the lane. She left the bucket to one side and wiped her hands on her apron.

The car was getting nearer. A uniformed man had his gloved hands on the wheel and a woman, with a large, brimmed hat, sat behind him. Who were these people?

The car stopped in front of the cottage and the tall chauffeur, wearing a navy-blue peaked cap, stepped out. "Mrs O'Dowd?"

Mary nodded and, hesitantly, held out her hand out, which he ignored. Instead, he went to the passenger side and opened the door. The young woman, dressed in a modern cream chemise with a string of pearls about her neck, one hand securing her hat, the other holding a small, beaded bag, stepped daintily onto the muck-smeared path.

She held out a lace-clad hand. "Mrs O'Dowd? Cecelia Farstairs."

Mary stepped forward and shook her hand. It felt so weak and small in her own. "Pleased to meet you, Miss Farstairs."

"Lady Farstairs," the chauffeur interrupted, flicking a piece of fluff off his shoulder and avoiding eye contact with Mary.

Mary gulped. A Lady visiting their own wee cottage. "Lady Farstairs, you are most welcome."

"Oh, please don't stand on ceremony. Your husband called me Miss Cecelia, and you must too."

"My husband?"

"Yes. Your husband is Patrick O'Dowd, formerly from Killogen, County Cork?"

"Yes, yes. That's where he grew up."

The chauffeur coughed, coming round to the woman's side and audibly whispering, "Are you sure you want to be left here?"

Lady Farstairs pursed her lips. "Yes, I do. I owe a great debt to this good woman's husband."

Mary's eyes widened like saucers. What in Heaven's name could Pat have done to warrant this visit?

The chauffeur doffed his cap to his passenger. "Very well, ma'am. I'll go and get petrol."

As the car drove away, Lady Farstairs shook her head. "Forgive my weasel of a driver. He's only been with us a month and I'm afraid he's a dour old stick."

Mary smiled, thinking it best not to pass comment.

The young woman rattled on, "Daddy thought I shouldn't be making this trip at all, and if he knew I'd broken my journey, he'd be cross. But then, I'm afraid Daddy's suspicious of just about everyone and everything now."

She smiled broadly, two dimples forming, and Mary decided, then and there, that she liked this woman.

"It's your husband I called to see. And now I realise that I was foolish. I should have written." Lady Farstairs shook her head. She touched her ear as if to check that her pearl earring was still attached. "He's not here?" She looked about as though she hoped he'd pop up and surprise her from behind one of the bushes. "Silly me. Of course, he'll be at work." The woman's shoulders drooped, and she stared into the distance.

Mary took a step to the side, kicking over the bucket of grain. She tutted and hurried to lift it but the spilt grain had already attracted attention. Chickens clucked and pecked around the two women's feet. Mary flapped her hands at them. "I'm sorry, Lady Farstairs. Those greedy chickens don't know how to stop."

Lady Farstairs smiled in acknowledgement.

Wind rustled the leaves of the sycamore tree beside them. Mary shivered. "Please. It's chilly out here. You must come inside. You're in luck, Lady Farstairs, Pat is at home." She hesitated. "But I'm afraid he's not very well."

Lady Farstairs frowned. "Oh, that must be concerning."

"He didn't fully recover from diphtheria. In fact, the doctor tells me he's unlikely to get much better."

"I'm so very sorry to hear that!" Lady Farstairs rubbed her arms. "Well, if it wouldn't be too taxing, could I possibly see him? Even for a few minutes. I should really like to speak to him."

"Of course. Please come into the house." Mary ushered Lady Farstairs through the front door and into the parlour. The smell of cabbage, from the previous night's meal, enveloped them as they walked in. A full basket of washing hung over the fire.

Mary winced. "It's all in a bit of a state, I'm afraid."

A gloved hand was waved dismissively. "Your house is charming."

"Before I tell Pat you're here, you'll take some refreshment? A cup of tea?

"Very kind, Mrs O'Dowd. Thank you. I feel that I've chosen a bad time to call. I was just hoping for nothing more than a quick word with your husband."

"And where are you headed?" As soon as she'd said the words, Mary regretted her candour.

Happily, Lady Farstairs displayed no signs of annoyance. "I'm on my way to visit my cousin and her new baby in Kilkenny. She's married to the Reverend Russell."

Mary nodded. "Your cousin is married to the Dean of the Cathedral?" She'd often heard Sara speak with fondness about the Reverend Russell.

"The same lady." Lady Farstairs smoothed the pleats of her dress with her hands. "I'm afraid to say the match was not so popular with my aunt and uncle." Then, as if realising she was saying too much, she took the newspaper from the table and looked at the headlines. "Poor Ireland. When's all this violence going to stop?"

Mary looked at the woman in front of her, not much more than a child. She tried not to stare. There was something beguilingly innocent about this young woman, her rouged cheeks giving Mary the impression of a painted doll.

The fire spat a few sparks onto the floor. Mary stamped on them and brushed them to the side. "Oh, where are my manners? You shouldn't be standing! Please, sit down."

Setting the newspaper down, Lady Farstairs sat in a high-backed chair opposite the rocker. Opening the clasp on her handbag she rummaged inside it. "When we had the trouble at the start of the year, your husband was so courageous. I never got to thank him properly." She pulled a lace handkerchief from the depths of her bag and twisted it in her fingers. "You see, I was taken off to hospital and remained there for several months."

Mary, her brow furrowed, tapped her chin absentmindedly. "Lady Farstairs, I'm quite confused. Are you talking about the fire at Killogen?"

"Yes. My house." Lady Farstairs looked at the floor. "At least it was."

"I'm so very sorry. I hadn't realised." Mary filled the kettle and hung it over the fire, pondering over what she'd just heard. So, this was to do with the last time Pat worked for Lord and Lady Killogen. This young woman had to be their daughter. "Pat came straight home after the arson attack." Mary put a hand on the table, as though to steady her thoughts. "He told me he'd helped in getting people out of the house, but he didn't want to talk of it." She brushed a few crumbs off the table into her cupped hand and dropped them in the hearth. "I knew he'd been upset by the whole affair, so I never asked more."

"It was indeed upsetting. It wasn't just me who was injured. Our pet Labrador and her two puppies didn't survive.

"He didn't say anything about the dogs." Mary shook her head. "How sad. No wonder he didn't want to speak of it!"

Lady Farstairs blinked, a trace of moisture on her eyelashes.

The ticking of the clock filled the room. Mary busied herself making tea, sighing with relief on opening the biscuit tin and finding two pieces of shortbread. Pat had talked to her about the Lord and Lady Killogen, or jokingly Lord and Lady Muck. The name Farstairs, was unfamiliar.

When Mary handed Lady Farstairs a cup and saucer, she took it and set it down on the floor. She beckoned Mary with a gentle wave of her fingers. "I should show you this." She delicately rolled her silk sleeve up to her elbow and held it out towards Mary. "This could have been my whole body, if it hadn't been for your husband."

Mary had to stop herself from visibly recoiling. Underneath the clothing was an arm that looked as if it had been skinned. An unpleasant sensation shot fleetingly through her body.

"Your husband was helping my father in getting everyone outside. You see, the fire had started so suddenly and there was pandemonium. I was looking for the dogs, going through every room." She dabbed her eyes. "I was frantic to get to them and I thought I heard barking from the downstairs library. When I opened the door, the oak timbers were burning and the room was filling with smoke. Then one of the tapestries hanging on the wall caught light." She gripped each elbow tight to her stomach. "It fell on my shoulder and my dress caught fire."

"Please, Lady Farstairs, don't go on. This must be distressing for you." Mary closed her eyes and tried to think of something else.

"No. I must tell you what happened next. Someone broke a window and climbed in. The next I knew I was being rolled tightly in a rug." She looked directly at Mary. "It was your husband!"

Mary put a hand to her chest. "Thank God he did." She crossed herself. Then she recalled the bandage that Pat had worn on one hand for a while. To cover a little cut, he'd said, dismissing it as nothing much.

"Your husband is a true hero, and you should be very proud of him!"

A door creaked open upstairs. "Mary?"

Mary could hear Pat, wheezing, trudging down the stairs.

"Mary?" he called. "I've thought of some new things we could try out tonight."

"You have a visitor, Pat!" Mary called out.

Pat reached the bottom of the stairs and stopped.

Mary caught his eye, her face crimson red.

He looked at Lady Farstairs. "Miss Cecelia."

Lady Farstairs, her cheeks flushed, looked up at him. "Yes, it's me. I came to thank you for saving my life."

***

Mary helped Pat to the rocking chair. He grinned at her, his eyebrows slightly raised, a gesture that meant please forgive my indiscretion. She plumped up the cushion behind his back as he eased himself down.

Lady Farstairs, who had stood to welcome Pat, sat down, taking her teacup in hand. She took dainty sips from it, her little finger raised. Mary wondered what she was thinking.

Mary caught Pat's eye. "Pat...you are one dark horse." She smiled at him, shaking her head.

Pat clasped his hands and leaned forward in his seat, clearing his throat. "I just did what anyone else would have done. And then I wanted to forget about it."

"As we all did," Lady Farstairs added.

"And Mary, the last thing I wanted to do was upset you. What with your fondness for animals."

Mary shuddered.

The ticking of the clock grew louder.

"Lady Farstairs has made a detour from her journey specially to see you, Pat." Mary unhooked a cup and reached for a saucer from the dresser. She set them on the table. "Will I pour you a cup?"

He nodded.

Mary tilted her head to one side, a smile on her face. "Would you like a warmer, Lady Farstairs?"

The young woman smiled in return. "Yes, thank you."

Pat shuffled in his seat and gave a little cough. "Now tell me, Miss Cecelia, what's happened to your family since I saw you last."

Mary listened as Lady Farstairs explained to Pat that they were now staying with relatives and that they would be moving soon, but weren't sure where. Many families living in houses like theirs were afraid. So many of the big houses had been burned down, left in ruins, their owners forced out. Some people had even left for England.

"I'm sorry to hear that, Miss Cecelia." Pat rubbed his cheeks, then rested his hands on his lap.

He looked up at Mary and she could tell that he wasn't sure what to say next. Mary thought about making some comment about the weather.

Lady Farstairs set her cup and saucer on the table. She looked from one to the other, her face beaming with childlike delight. "I'm engaged now." She held out her hand towards Mary and waggled her ring finger. "To Lord Gilroy."

Mary studied the ring. Five red rubies, set in a thick gold band. The dark red stones twinkled back at her. But most evident was the scarring on the woman's hand and the patchy discoloured skin. "Congratulations, Miss Cecelia."

"Thank you. We're to be married before the month is out."

"Well, that's just grand." What else could she add? Whether Lord Gilroy was a good and kind man was none of her business.

She refilled Lady Farstairs' cup halfway. The young woman lifted it and the saucer with both hands, resting them on her lap.

Pat wheezed a little, his hand over his mouth. "Wonderful news, Miss Cecelia."

"Terence, I mean Lord Gilroy, has a house up north." The childlike delight disappeared, replaced with a more sombre mood. "That's where we'll live."

Mary saw the tremble in Lady Farstair's hand, her cup rattling against the saucer. *Poor soul*, thought Mary, *she can't be much more than eighteen, and to have to leave her family and move up north? How awful.*

"Oh, but where are my manners?" The young woman looked in Pat's direction. "I came here expressly to thank you, not to talk about me."

A rap came at the door.

Relieved by the interruption, Mary got up and opened it.

The uniformed man was back. "Lady Farstairs?" He poked his head through the door and looked around, his nose twitching as though he'd just smelled something bad.

"Yes, Hempenstall?" Lady Farstairs waved her hand at the man without looking up. "Wait for me in the car."

She stayed another five minutes, enquiring after Pat's health before asking, "And your son, the boy who got hurt in the ploughing accident?"

"Good of you to remember Liam, Miss Cecelia. He's doing fine." Pat replied. "Sadly, the epidemic took our little baby."

Lady Farstairs shook her head and whispered that she would pray for them.

After some silence, she snapped open her beaded bag, undid a coin purse and handed half a crown to Mary. "Please give this to your son."

Mary inhaled sharply. "That is too kind, Miss Cecelia. Liam will be thrilled." *I'll put it away for a while*, she thought, *for when the time is right.*

Lady Farstairs promised that if there was anything she could do to help, she'd be honoured to do so. She would write to them. She said it was a pity that Lisowen was so far away from her new home. Pat could have been such a help at the new house.

Pat cleared his throat. "Thank you for thinking of me, Miss Cecelia. Just give me a little while yet and maybe, someday, I'll travel up north and give a hand."

Mary kept a sigh from escaping her lips. There would be no way she'd let Pat travel all that way, let alone work again in someone else's house.

Outside, the chauffeur opened the passenger door for Lady Farstairs. With her hand on her hat, she dipped her head and stepped into the car. The chauffeur used the starting handle to bring the engine to life. With his eyes averted from Mary, he clicked open the driver's door, slid in and, with a puff of exhaust fumes filling the air, drove off.

Chapter Twenty-Nine

Dan had been assigned a task. Some blasted woman was running a laundry for the British Army. He was to put a stop to it. Deal out some suitable punishment. He looked at the grubby piece of paper his superior had given him. He was to go to Carnspindle and find a cottage set back from the road, opposite the deserted mill. The house was owned by a Malachy Miskelly. The same man had fought for the British Empire in their fecking war. Dan cleared his throat and spat the contents out on the pavement. Bastard!

Apparently, since Miskelly's return, he'd gone doo-lally and was only fit for the asylum. He'd been locked away there, and now the man's wife had an arrangement with the local army barracks. They left clothes with her on a weekly basis. She'd launder them and have them ready for collection, when the next lot of dirty washing would arrive.

"The fecking bitch!" Bad enough, her husband fighting for the British, but his wife cleaning their bloody britches? Inexcusable!

***

The cottage wasn't hard to find. The broken walls of the mill – overgrown with ivy – loomed large on the road in front of him. Opposite, a grey plume of smoke rose from a chimney partially hidden by a large oak tree. *Good*, he thought, *nice and isolated*. He walked up to the cottage, looking this way and that, in case anyone should see him.

When satisfied there was no-one about, he pulled his balaclava over his head and yanked the iron jemmy from the bag he was carrying. He strode to the door and banged hard with his fist.

A young woman with untidy, short hair answered. She looked familiar but before he could think who she was, the girl backed away and ran screeching to the back of the house. Screaming for her mam.

Dan stepped through the doorway and took in the spectacle before him. Washing hung haphazardly around the parlour. Steam rose from wet garments hanging over the fire. A pile of men's underwear was stacked neatly on the table. Beside them lay the army uniforms.

A large, ungainly woman, with a small apron tied round her waist, peered out from the scullery, two small grubby children clinging to her clothes.

"Who are you?" The woman called out, her face distorted in fear, her voice shaking. When she saw the iron bar in his hand, she cowered. "What do you want?"

"What blasted business are you carrying on here?" Dan smacked the iron bar onto his hand.

The woman started to cry and the children buried their faces in her skirts, howling. "Don't hurt us… please. We'll starve if we can't earn money. My husband's in the asylum; bad with his nerves."

Dan hooked an army jacket, that had been drying, onto the end of his iron bar. "You should have found yourself some other job," he snorted. Swinging the garment in front of the fire, he slid the jacket off into the flames.

The fire roared up and the smell of damp fabric burning filled the room.

Dan rapped the jemmy on the table, beside the clothes. "Burn them."

The woman stared at Dan. "Burn them?"

"Burn all these fucking clothes. Heap them on the fire."

The woman howled but stood motionless.

The girl who had been hiding in the scullery, piped up, her voice trembling. "Do as he says."

"But they'll be here soon to collect what's dry." Her mother shouted back.

Then it came to Dan. The girl he'd tarred! The bitch had a soldier for a boyfriend.

His mind began to whirl. The woman had said they. How many? Two? Three? Maybe a fucking battalion of them. Why hadn't he brought Martin and Ger with him? As he thought this, he grabbed a bunch of the clothes that had been lying on the table and flung them on the fire.

Then, turning on his heel, he ran out through the door.

Chapter Thirty

Mary was worried. What were they going to do for money? The question churned over and over in her mind, with no satisfactory answer. They were having to use the savings they'd put away for Liam's education, and that money was dwindling, unlikely to last more than a few months. It hurt Mary, like an open sore, that they'd no alternative.

The hens, the sow, the piglets and their two acres of land were now her responsibility. Liam helped but she hated seeing him toiling in the fields after school, the sweat of hard work on his brow. The only sliver of a silver lining was that Liam's deformity had been almost forgotten now that other issues had come to the fore.

Thank God, she'd been able to persuade Pat to forgo heavy lifting. "I want you around when Liam's married and there's grandchildren to entertain. Don't you go and die on me!"

"Yes, my dear," Pat had replied with a cough and an impish grin. Recently, he'd been able to come downstairs, shuffle out to the shed and potter about. His back, once ramrod straight, was now bowed. With his stooped walk, Pat reminded her of her father. No bad thing, for her daddy had been a kindly, pleasant invalid. Wheezing continually, Pat often looked for his rocking chair, sinking into it with a sigh. There, he would rock gently for hours, his eyelids half closed.

***

Sara had called several times since the epidemic, and always with food. She brought brown bread and barmbrack, warm from the oven, gooseberry jam and a listening ear. Pat would greet her warmly, then say that he was in need of a nap. Would Sara excuse him? And off upstairs he'd take himself. Mary loved the fact that he knew when not to be around.

It was on such a day that Sara came to visit, Richard having been left at the house of a church friend who had a boy of a similar age.

"Won't he love that?" Mary recalled Liam at that age, chasing after a hoop with a stick. "I'm sure they'll be getting into all sorts of divilment, as young boys should."

She jiggled the dresser drawer open and took out two knives. From a plate rack, she lifted down two white side plates. Sitting on either side of the table, they each nursed a cup of tea, freshly baked bread in front of them, butter and jam to hand. As Sara topped up the teacups from the teapot, the conversation turned to Pat.

"How are you managing, with him not working?" Sara leaned forward a little and caught her friend's eye."

Mary shrugged. "I keep hoping the doctor's wrong and he'll get better."

Sara turned her gaze downwards as she buttered a slice of bread. "Are you going to be all right?"

"We're getting by." Mary thought about the pound notes rolled up in newspaper at the bottom of the potato sack. For Liam's future. "Now sup that tea, and tell me if its stewed and I need to make a fresh pot."

"You know if you need anything, you just have to ask." Sara took a tiny sip. "The tea's fine." She pursed her lips. "Promise me you'll do that."

"I will." Mary took a bite of bread, a small dollop of green jam falling onto the table. "Thank you... Liam's been a great help."

"But he's still only a young lad" Sara cocked her head to one side. "And I know you want him to be doing well at school."

Mary picked up the tongs and placed several coals on the fire. "To tell the truth, I'm worried about him falling behind." She turned to face Sara, a strained look on her face. "He's often too tired to do homework, and Pat and I are long past being able to help him."

"You worry too much. I'm sure he's doing enough."

"Perhaps."

Sara reached for the newspaper that lay folded on the rocking chair. "Did you hear the latest? Another barracks out Carlow direction attacked. A policeman murdered." She shook her head. "Then the Rossakiltey creamery? Burned to the ground."

"Pat says he can't understand these reprisals on innocent people. The creameries out of action means the farmers are affected too." Mary pulled a curl back behind her ear. "How does getting rid of creameries help the Crown?"

"We can't make it out at all." Sara wiped crumbs off her dress. "William says the troops from England are supposed to be defeating the IRA, not wrecking businesses."

Mary shook her head.

Both women sat for a while, neither speaking, before Mary turned the conversation to the new clothes shop that was to open on Main Street. The fabrics, the differing lengths of skirt, the embellishments and the prices were discussed at length.

Eventually, Sara set her cup on top of her plate and brushed her hands together. "Time to be getting home. William and Richard will be wanting their dinner." Digging her hand into her coat pocket, she placed two toffees on the table. "William sent these for Liam." She kissed Mary lightly on the cheek and threw her coat over the crook of one arm. "I'll call back next week."

Soon after she left, Mary heard the creaking of Pat's footsteps on the floorboards upstairs. *I'll go up and sit with him*, she thought. Often, she just wanted to talk about Fionuala. All they had to remember her by was a tiny lock of wispy, blonde hair. She and Pat would often touch it as it lay in its little velvet lined box. She'd go now and take the box out from the top of the dresser drawer.

Blinking a couple of times, she rolled her shoulders, secured her hair back from her face with a clip and climbed the stairs.

Chapter Thirty-One

Later that evening, as dusk descended, Mary lit the two parlour oil lamps. Arcs of amber-coloured light flickered around her. The fire hissed, spitting specks of coal out. She took her needlework bag, eased into the spine of a wooden chair and pulled out the green embroidery thread. Sitting opposite Pat, she heard the familiar rasp from his lungs, his head hidden behind a newspaper.

Liam pushed the jotter he had been writing on to the side and struggled out of his seat. "I forgot to check on Bobby." He hobbled to the door. "I'll go make sure there's hay and water in the stable." The door closed behind him with a gentle thud.

Wetting the tip of a thread with her lips, Mary pinched a few frayed ends of thread together and held it up to her needle. "He's a grand lad, our Liam." She delicately eased a strand through the eye of the needle, pulling a length of it out.

Pat rocked slowly in his chair. "He is that."

Liam came back into to the house, his hair flopping over his eyes, his cheeks blotched red. "I gave Bobby extra rations."

"Thanks, big son." Mary watched him sit down to remove his boots, his head bowed over them, his frame young and supple. She wished there was some way that his foot could heal. She looked over at Pat, his eyes half closed, rocking in his chair. She wished that he would heal, too. Pushing these thoughts to the back of her mind, she returned to the shamrock design she was embroidering on a linen napkin.

Liam washed his hands at the basin, shook them dry and ran them over his trouser legs. He yawned. "I'll just finish off my sums before bed."

"Good lad," Mary said. "I'll heat you some milk."

"Thanks, Mam." Liam opened his jotter and flicked through the pages, a pen and bottle of ink at the ready.

Mary poured milk into a pan and hung it over the fire. When bubbles started to form, she filled two mugs, setting one in front of Liam and the other beside Pat, who whispered a Thank you and clasped his hands around the steaming cup. He stared ahead, his eyes fixed on the fire.

"I wish I could take my bike and go fix the pump at Whelan's, like I promised to do months ago." He took the milk and blew on it before sipping; the milky skin formed white marks on his lips. "Ah, those jobs will have to wait till I'm better."

"There's lots of other things you could do." Mary tapped her fingers on the table. "Right here. Like fixing watches and clocks, while I go to work somewhere nearby."

Pat pursed his lips and raised his eyebrows. "Doing what?" He tilted his head to the side, his breathing loud and noisy.

She stretched across him, her blouse buttons straining, and opened the newspaper out, flapping the pages, searching for the one she had marked. Laying the folded newspaper on his lap, she pointed at an advertisement she had ringed in pencil earlier that day.

Pat cleared his throat. "Cleaning lady wanted. Must have good credentials. Apply to Colonel Wishart, Killentulley Barracks." He looked up at her, his brows knit firmly together, shaking his head. "You clean up at the barracks? Work for the British Army? Help keep everything shipshape for the Empire?"

She thought about saying something: that they couldn't afford to be choosy but, instead, she took a deep breath in and blew the air out as though letting the pressure out of a tyre. Snatching a duster from beside the basin, she walked around the room, flapping at some stray cobwebs hanging from the rafters, trying to calm her beating heart.

"It would pay well."

"I've no doubt, for they'd need to be paying danger money!" Pat took a handkerchief from his pocket, holding it briefly at his chest as he gathered his breath. "That's a job for the Protestants. Not us! At one time, when the Home Rule Bill looked certain, I might have sided more with the British. But I'm afraid we were misled."

Mary shook the duster out over the fireplace. She would hold her tongue. "It was just a thought. Maybe, I could ask at the monastery if they need help with cleaning?"

Pat chuckled. "The monastery could certainly do with a good clean, but I don't think the monks would part with their money for that reason."

Mary folded the duster and set it on the worktop. "But if the place is dirty?"

"And would you think the monks worry about that?" Pat looked at her, his eyes twinkling.

Liam blotted his work carefully with a scrap of newspaper. "The blacksmith is looking for help. I saw a notice pinned outside the forge." He pushed his chair back, the legs scraping along the floor. "Brendan Mooney used to work there before he died of diphtheria. Now there's only the blacksmith and his son."

Mary crossed herself. "God rest the poor man's soul." She looked up at the Sacred Heart hanging over the mantlepiece. "And that of our little Fionuala." She turned to Liam. "Dan O'Toole isn't what I'd call a decent man. I'd be none too happy about you working for him. Besides, what about school?"

"We're off soon for the holidays. It'd just be for a few weeks."

Pat stirred in his seat. "It would be hard, physical work, son. You're already doing enough here at home."

Mary looped a stray curl back behind her ear. "I'm not sure you'd be what he's looking for."

Liam stared at her, his eyebrows furrowed. "You mean because I'm crippled."

"Now, Liam." Pat beckoned him to his side. "I don't think the blacksmith would want a young lad, not yet broad-shouldered, working at the forge."

"But I've been outside these last few weeks doing heavy work on our farm."

"And besides the work, Dan O'Toole has a bad reputation."

"Why, what's he done?"

Mary and Pat exchanged a look. There was nothing they could say, only rumours to go on and didn't they think it was wrong to go by rumours?

The clock struck eleven o'clock. Pat cleared his throat, coughing into a cupped hand. "That man doesn't have a civil bone in his body. Don't be surprised if he gives you short shrift."

Liam's mouth broadened into a smile. "That means yes?"

Mary's mouth tightened. "I suppose so."

***

The next day after school, Liam stopped by the forge on the way home. He was thankful that Padraig and Finn, who used to bully him, were long since gone, leaving only Declan. But Declan on his own, he could cope with.

174

Approaching the forge, he saw the unmistakable bulky figure of the blacksmith, standing outside the open doors smoking, his belly overhanging his trousers. From inside, he could hear the loud clank of an anvil on metal. Liam guessed that it was Declan hammering on a horseshoe.

Liam took a deep breath. "Mr O'Toole?"

Dan threw his cigarette butt on the ground. "That's me."

"I'm here about the job."

Dan raised his eyebrows, the stray dark hairs sprouting out at all angles. "You?"

"Yes." Liam puffed out his chest, attempting to conceal his bad foot behind the other, causing himself to wobble. "I don't mind hard work."

Dan put his hands on his hips, threw back his head and guffawed.

Declan came to the door, his pasty face moist with sweat. On seeing Liam, he moved closer to his father. "What does the cripple want?"

Dan clipped Declan's ear. "Back to work, you lazy fecker. It's none of your business."

Declan, holding his ear, turned to scowl at Liam before slouching back into the forge.

Dan took a step towards Liam, coming so close that Liam thought the blacksmith might cuff his ear too.

"So, you think you're strong enough to work here." Dan reached out and felt along Liam's arms as though inspecting an animal. "Maybe there's a bit of muscle there. Enough to feed the horses, shovel the shit into a pile, scrub out the outhouse." He pointed to a small shed with a nicotine-stained finger. "Full of rats and rubbish. Maybe you could spruce it up. Take the rubbish to the dump at the river." He chuckled. "It should be interesting work for a boy like you." He peered at Liam's foot, shaking his head. "Now, I can't pay you a full wage, as you've got your handicap."

Liam felt a rush of heat to his face.

"But if you manage to do a good job, there'll be money for you at the end of the week."

Liam held his hand out to Dan, who looked at it, spat in his own hand, then squeezed Liam's hand tightly.

"Any slacking and there won't be any pay."

Liam stretched his fingers to ease the pain. "Thank you, Mr O'Toole. I'd be pleased to work for you. If it's all right with you, I'll start next week."

Chapter Thirty-Two

Old John looked out of the window as the rain fell on the streets of Dublin, his mind casting back to the horrors of Spanish flu. It was little more than a year since it had all been declared over. People had dropped dead on days like this; on the wet pavements of Dublin, with masked police having to carry the bodies away. Back then, the newspapers had been full of dreadful stories. Poor families, who shared a single room, wiped out, and no medicine nor cure to be had for love nor money.

Living with Aunt Rose in her dreary house had not been easy. It had been a petrifying time, every cough or sniffle convincing him that he had succumbed to the dreaded flu. Potatoes, stale bread and dripping had kept them both alive, and when Old John finally emerged from captivity, he was determined that he'd never stay put in one place again.

With the escalating violence around Cork and Kilkenny, he'd returned to the city of his birth and the streets he knew. Somehow, he felt safer in Dublin, as though familiar surroundings could shelter him from the growing turbulence in Ireland. He had left Lisowen not knowing that he had left in good time, well before the first case of diphtheria was discovered.

So, here he was, back with Aunt Rose and her increasingly erratic temper and waywardness. She was getting forgetful too. Unsure, at times, of who he was, then suddenly recalling that it was she who'd called him Old John first.

"You were always an old head on young shoulders," she'd say. "Wise beyond your years."

When he had first knocked at the door, however, she had looked at him as though he was a stranger.

"It's me, Aunt Rose," he'd said. "Old John."

She'd shaken her head before a sudden flash of recognition caused her face to brighten. "Old John. Old John." Then, just as quickly, a look of suspicion took over. "Oh, I expect you want to stay again."

"If I could have a bed for a few nights, I'd be most grateful, "he said.

She looked him up and down before suddenly smiling. "Old John. Old John. Come in."

And he'd walked in to peeling wallpaper, musty smelling rooms and a leaking roof.

Every day, he had hawked his wares around the sooty tenements, earning enough to feed himself and pay for his keep. When he read, Small Town in Ireland Quarantined Due to Diphtheria Outbreak, he'd been shocked. Lisowen had been shut down, with the police preventing residents from leaving or entering. How were those poor people going to endure the ravages of yet another deadly disease? As he read the news unfolding, he became increasingly alarmed at the rising death toll.

Aside from the diphtheria outbreak, Lisowen was suffering in other ways. From having been a peaceful little backwater, there seemed to be growing tensions within the communities. While going door-to-door selling his wares, he'd avoided entering into any political discussions. He knew that feathers had been ruffled, dander raised. There was a call to arms and he'd no time for that. As long as he had a bed for the night and a warm meal, he was happy. And as for which side he was on? Well, he couldn't quite work that out, for what would it mean to a man like him?

After a few weeks at Aunt Rose's, he knew he had to get back on the road. He felt that he was slowly dying inside, the greys and blacks of Dublin felt like a shroud to him. He needed to see countryside. The green of the fields and the blue of the sky. When he heard that the quarantine had been lifted in Lisowen, he had himself a bath, clipped his whiskers and got himself ready for the long trip ahead.

"Goodbye, Aunt Rose." He kissed her sunken cheek and pressed a florin into her palm as they stood together at the open door. *Surely to goodness, this would be the last time,* he thought. Then, he felt uncharitable. She might not last another winter. He clicked open his suitcase and took out his most expensive shawl. Woven from alabaster-coloured linen and fringed with hand-made lace, he'd had another recipient in mind for this delicate garment.

As he draped the shawl over Aunt Rose's shoulders, her tired eyes suddenly came alive. "Thank you. Thank you."

She ran off to get something and returned with an old cardboard shoe box. "For you."

He took the parcel from her, seeing in her the look of the young woman she'd once been. "Take care, Aunt Rose. I'll call back before Christmas."

***

Old John got off the bus in Lisowen's Main Street and looked about him. People were going about their business, just as they had when he'd last been there. The bus stop was only a few yards from the pawn shop and that would be his first port of call. One of the Dubliners, close to destitution, had paid for a much-needed kettle in foreign coins. Now, he'd see if the pawnbroker would take those coins off his hands. He walked in to the tinkle of a small bell.

A thin man, with an angular face, stood at the counter and greeting him with a smile. "Old John. Long time it is since I've seen you. Good day to you, sir."

"Good day to you too, Mr Bartholomew." Old John set the coins on the bench. "Now tell me if these yokes are of any use to you."

The pawnbroker held a coin between his thumb and finger, and peered at it through a magnifying glass. "From France or Belgium, I'd be sure. If I were to guess their history, I'd say one of the soldiers brought them back." He tilted his head to the side. "But talk of that war isn't popular now among certain quarters."

"Any use to you?" Old John asked, already guessing the answer that would follow.

The pawnbroker shook his head. "Sorry."

Old John laid his suitcase and burlap sack on the ground. From the top of his sack, he pulled out the cardboard shoe box that Aunt Rose had given him and lifted the lid.

"Now, that's more like the thing." Mr Bartholomew took the candlestick from the box and looked underneath it. "Solid brass. That's good. A shilling I'd give you, if it pleases."

Old John held his hand out to shake that of the pawnbroker's. What luck. He felt a warm glow in his chest. "Now tell me, please – for it's some time since I was last here – what happened during the epidemic?"

"Shocking time, we had." The pawnbroker reached for a cloth and a small tin of liquid and began polishing the candlestick. "Nurse Armstrong, the midwife, was the first to go."

Old John took his cap off and held it in one hand. "Sad, sad. A generous woman. Always bought from me, even if only a dish cloth."

"Ay, a good woman, for sure." Mr Bartholomew breathed on the brass and rubbed it fervently with his cloth. "Tragic that her brother brought the diphtheria from America."

Old John shook his head. "Is that a fact?"

"And didn't he survive while his sister died."

"I read they had to quarantine the whole town. Stop the disease spreading."

"You heard right. A dreadful time we had those days, corralled in our own homes like animals."

"Ah, now, I suppose it had to be done."

The pawnbroker screwed the top back on the tin. "That's what the magistrate said."

"And who else succumbed?"

"The Ferris children, one-eyed Ikey, Mr and Mrs Mulvenna, and little Finbar Dooley. A few from Main Street, that I know of. Then, there's the poor O'Dowd family."

"What happened there?" Old John laid his threadbare cap on the mahogany counter.

The pawnbroker set the candlestick holder to the side. "Mary O'Dowd's baby died but a few days old."

"Ah, no!"

"And that fine husband of hers is now an invalid. All the life bate out of him."

"I'm sorry to hear that." Old John filled his lungs with air. The inside of the shop smelled damp and fusty. He rubbed his nose. The question that had been foremost in his mind had to be asked. "What about the blacksmith? How did his family fare during it all?"

The pawnbroker leaned forward across the counter, his hands supporting him. "It would take a dose of something shocking to fell that brute of a man." He sucked on his gums, his cheeks hollowing. "I believe his family was one of the few not to have been affected."

Leaving the pawn shop, Old John offered up a prayer of thanks that the beautiful Grainne O'Toole had been spared. However, against his better nature, he couldn't stop feeling sorry that the blacksmith still lived.

***

"What are you doing there, Old John?" the farmer asked. "Don't you know you're awful close to a fairy ring? No good'll come of treading too near those wee people."

Old John was alarmed. He'd heard many a story of misfortune for those that dared to desecrate such places. An old teacher of his, who declared it all nonsense, had died, struck by lightning while attempting to fell a tree on the edge of a fairy ring. For an eleven-year-old boy, that incident had left a deep impression. To this day, he'd decided that he'd stay well away from fairies and their territory.

"God bless you for telling me." Old John tugged his suitcase out from under the shelter of a fuchsia bush and pulled out the stakes from the oilcloth he'd stretched out on the ground. "I'll find somewhere else to sleep."

The wind whipped up the groundsheet as Old John struggled to tame it. He glanced up at the slate grey clouds hanging heavy and threatening.

The farmer took off his flat cap and scratched his head. "I don't like to think of you lying out this night with the possibility of rain." He rummaged in his trouser pocket and produced a long key, which he held out to Old John. "It's for the barn over there." He pointed to a wooden building, situated on higher ground.

Old John looked at the barn. Why anyone would build their barn on such an exposed piece of land was beyond him. Far better would have been to build in the lee of the land, sheltered from the elements and close to the farmhouse.

The farmer saw him looking and shrugged. "My father built it before he died. Loved peace and quiet and a good view, he did. Liked to sit with his pipe at the door and watch all the comings and goings at the barracks."

Old John could see the merit in that. From the barn, you would be able to see for miles around. The monastery and the spires of the churches would be visible too. He looked forward to sitting with a mug of tea and taking in the beauty of the landscape.

The farmer straightened the flat cap on his head. "I keep it locked for fear of fugitives, but you can come and go as you wish. As long as you lock it after you. And I'll not take a penny from you."

Old John beamed back at the man. "For a couple of days, till I get myself around the village. I thank you. Then I'm off to Tipperary."

"For as many days as you need."

Old John felt his heart do a little jig. Maybe he would stay a week or two. A roof over his head, and not having to pay for it, would be just grand.

***

Old John lengthened himself out on the straw in the barn, resting his head on the pillow of his rolled-up jacket. With the small side door open, he looked out at the fields ringed in stone walls, a few sheep dotted here and there. Most notable was the RIC barracks no more than a hundred yards away. He was amazed at the changes that had taken place, the fortifications, the sandbags stacked high around the walls, the perimeter of barbed wire. Just below the barracks and beyond, the Bawn river meandered lazily through the countryside.

He got up and walked outside. Dipping his enamel mug into the barrel, he supped cool water from it, enjoying its refreshment. From the corner of his eye, he could see a stout woman approaching, carrying a bucket in one hand and a basket in the other.

The farmer's wife, her face ruddy, held out the bucket towards him. Inside, was a cloth and a large bar of yellow soap. "For your ablutions," she said.

"Thank you, good lady. Too kind." Old John doffed his cap.

From her basket, the farmer's wife lifted out a muslin-wrapped parcel and handed it to him. "There's some cheese for you and bread off the griddle." She put the basket down and put her hands on her hips, catching her breath.

"I thank you again, good lady."

"Sure, you're only as good as the bowl you're baked in," she replied. She took the empty basket and ambled away, leaving Old John pondering over the meaning of what she'd just said.

He opened the food parcel. The bread was still warm. A small, wrapped twist of butter that lay beside it, was melting; yellow drops falling onto his hand, which he licked off. The cheese smelled rich and earthy. His mouth watered. He would dine well that night.

Later, as he eased down into the hay, he heard the scrabble of field mice moving around him. Every so often, the blades of straw would move, shake gently, then settle. He smiled at the thought that, underneath him, a whole family of little creatures were getting on with their lives.

Running his hands over his head, he touched the gouge of a scar that was still there. The injury, acquired at the hands of the blacksmith, was now well healed and he said a little prayer for Mrs Miskelly for nursing him back to health. He recalled the lines of washing strung from rafter to rafter, the smell of bleach and the constant haze of steam. For her to have to run such a laundry and take such a dreadful risk, vexed him sorely.

With that troubling thought, he fell into a deep sleep.

***

Business was good over the next couple of days. The epidemic had left women craving new ribbons and frippery. Old John counted his money out onto the straw of the barn floor. One shilling and sixpence. He whistled under his breath.

Then his thoughts turned to Mrs O'Toole. She, too, would want new things and she, too, loved ribbons and lace. He'd stocked up with both in Dublin, keeping her especially in mind. Old John felt his hands dampen and his pulse start to race. He'd a sudden image of Mrs O'Toole wearing a finely embroidered chemise and knickerbockers, brushing her jet-black hair in slow even strokes. He mopped his brow. Oh, how good it would be to see her again.

But first there was the matter of her husband. The last thing Old John wanted was another encounter with that beast of a man.

Chapter Thirty-Three

The following day, Old John didn't feel well. After thrashing about most of the night, he'd woken to beads of sweat on his brow. What the divil was wrong with him? Surely, not diphtheria! But the infection was long gone from Lisowen. Perhaps a day staying put would suffice. The weather was warm and having the heat on his bones would do him good. Just the thought of taking it easy made him feel a little better.

Old John dozed in the barn, waking from time to time to sip some water before drifting off again. He'd visit Mrs O'Toole on another occasion, when he was more like himself. Later that afternoon, he felt well enough to make some small repairs to his clothes. He got out his needle and thread, and set about mending the seams of his well-worn coat. As a young boy, Aunt Rose had taught him how to sew. She'd been a dressmaker and declared that Old John had a steady, sensitive hand. A willing learner, Old John had learned how to tack, hem and even follow a pattern.

In the main, his skills were used in repairing his own shabby clothes, giving them new life when seams started to fray and hems unravel. Now, he turned his attention to the sheep's wool he'd collected. He pondered on how to construct something warm and cosy for winter nights when forced to sleep outside.

Taking his old cap in hand, he stuffed as much wool as he could between the tweed fabric and its torn lining. Repairing the tears with fine stitches, he sewed a square of rabbit fur to the exterior. He pulled the newly padded cap down over his head. *Good*, he thought, *it still fits even if it feels quite strange*. He set the cap on the ground in front of him.

He pulled a threadbare scarf out of his coat pocket and another from the depths of his sack, and stitched the sides of both together. Then, he stuffed wool between them and attached one end of the padded scarf to the side of his cap. He placed the cap on his head and wound the padded scarf around his face and behind his neck. A large safety pin secured the scarf to the other side of his cap.

Withdrawing a pocket mirror from his suitcase of wares, he held it up in front of him. With the cap pulled well down on his head, only his eyes were visible. What a sight! His head and neck seemed grossly inflated. But no matter. Who would see him and what if they did? The stuffed woollen garment would serve him well when the nights drew in and there was no prospect of a bed for the night. And, because business had been good, he still had money to buy himself a new cap and scarf when next down Main Street.

Feeling much better, Old John decided that his feeling ill-at-ease had been caused by nothing more than a head cold.

Throwing the side door of the barn open, he let fresh air and the scent of the countryside flood in. From where he sat, his back supported by a bale of straw, he'd full view of the barracks where three policemen were loading a truck with crates.

***

Sean Corvin was worried.

He'd only been a policeman for a few months and wasn't the whole of Ireland up in arms? He'd joined to help enforce the law and now it seemed that enforcing the law was just about impossible.

And hadn't he signed a contract that would keep him in the RIC for at least five years?

Had his father been right all along? Had his brother been wrong? The rows that Ruari had had with their father. But Ruari had his mind made up. He'd be a policeman like he'd always wanted to be, and the family would be proud of him some day. Then it was Sean's turn. No, they couldn't talk him out of it either, even when his father claimed that the force was in disarray. Sure, hadn't it been infiltrated by the IRA?

And if you aren't informed on, you'll be a target for the flying columns out on the dusty side road. With men in ditches waiting to ambush you, his father had said.

I'll be fine, Sean had reassured him. Stop all this worrying. Sure, won't I be able to bring some money home to you?

It was only when his mother had pressed a St Christopher into his hand, her eyes brimming with tears, that it had started to hit home. However, Sean had reminded himself, Ruari was two years joined and he seemed to be doing fine. Sent down to Kilkenny, to the big barracks where all was well.

When he first came home to visit, he'd talk about going after illicit stills and unlicensed dogs. But times had changed since then and Ruari didn't say much now when he came back to see his parents.

Sean tugged at his trousers. Why the blazes hadn't they given him the right size? He'd ask his mother to try and let them down next time he saw her.

And now he was being left on his own at the barracks while his two superiors swanned off to Kilkenny. They were under instructions to remove most of the newer weapons to the city. But someone had to stay and mind the remaining arsenal, or so they'd told him. He was aware that the barracks might have to close. There were too many vague threats, that much Sean knew. And what with all the present trouble, the force could end up retreating to the garrison in Kilkenny. Anyway, it was for those further up the chain-of-command to decide.

As they were preparing to leave, his superiors had told Sean that he wasn't to worry. Lisowen was a sleepy law-abiding place. And didn't he have weapons at his disposal? The older policeman had put his hand on Sean's shoulder. "I don't need to warn you, young Corvin, to be vigilant."

Sean tapped the Webley revolver by his side with the palm of his hand. "I'm well trained, sir," he'd said, feeling anything but.

"And there's a strong possibility we'll be getting reinforcements before the week is out." The older man tugged at his jacket sleeves.

Sean wasn't sure what he should say. He'd heard a senior policeman declare the Black and Tans both a plague and a Godsend. He kept quiet.

"We need more local police to help." The younger RIC man pulled his peaked hat down over his head. "Last thing we want are the fucking Black and Tans on our backs!" He smacked a fist against his other hand. "I'll not be staying around if we're to be lackeys for the British cause."

"Now Mick, don't get yourself upset. As long as the pay packet gets to us every month, that's the main thing." The older man threw a wooden crate into the back of the van. "Put your ideals away in your breast pocket, for they won't put food on the table."

Sean Corvin watched in resignation as his colleagues left in their noisy vehicle, a trail of black cloud issuing from the exhaust.

***

Old John saw the policemen drive away. He wondered what it would be like to drive, sit at the steering wheel, move the gear stick and race along country roads? Ah, he'd probably never know.

Grey clouds scuttled overhead as the young policeman walked around the barracks, pulling at the shutters and rattling them. He'd a gawkiness about him, his dark green tunic too wide in the shoulders, his legs too long for his trousers. He looked this way and that as he checked the padlocks.

Old John turned his gaze to the surrounding countryside. What a view. He looked out at the Bawn River glinting in the sunlight, and the forest, its trees in full foliage. Further afield he could even make out the sandstone tower of the monastery.

Then something, not too far away, caught his attention. He sat forward and rubbed his eyes. A darkly-clad figure was creeping along the stone wall in front of the barracks. What the blazes! The figure stopped, crouching well down behind the wall. Old John got up from where he was sitting and stood peering through the open door. A man, his head covered in black material raised his arm out over the wall. There was a loud bang. The policeman put one hand to his chest, struggled to pull his gun out with the other and returned fire.

A series of shots rang out. Old John stood statue-still, his heart thumping so loudly that he could hear it in his ears. The policeman was now on his knees, one hand clutching his side, the other hand still firing his gun.

The gunman began running backwards, his weapon raised. He stumbled over the root of a small tree stump and landed on his back, the gun flying out of his hand and up into the air. Scrambling to his feet, he rubbed his leg and hobbled at speed towards the trees. Within a few seconds he was gone.

Old John ran as fast as he could towards the barracks. In front of the stone wall, he saw the gun lying on the ground. He reached down to lift it, its handle still warm from the gunman's hand. He thrust it deep into his jacket pocket.

As he neared the fallen man, he saw that the farmer's wife had arrived before him. She was cradling the boy's head in her hands. The farmer followed shortly after, panting, his flat cap in hand. Old John walked slowly up to them, watching the young man's blood bloom out from his body.

The woman closed the policeman's eyes with her fingers and laid his head gently on the ground. The farmer shook his head, his mouth pursed tight. "Poor Sean Corvin. His first real job, and a good lad too. Slaughtered!" He crossed himself. "And all for what?"

Old John hung his head. He felt his stomach heave, sour water rising into his gullet. He swallowed hard.

"Did you see anything, Old John?" the farmer asked.

Old John slid a hand over the bulge in his jacket. "No. Nothing."

Chapter Thirty-Four

Father Flaherty arrived, summoned by one of the farm hands. Old John stood back, his head bowed. The farmer's wife clasped a folded bedsheet. After the priest had said the last rites, he took the sheet from her and drew it gently over the victim.

A few people had arrived at the barracks, having heard the shots. The priest addressed them; his long face sombre. "Please let this be an end to the bloodshed! Getting involved in a senseless spiral of violence will do nobody any good."

One villager, who Old John recognised as the rag and bone man, shouted at the priest. "He should have known better than to have joined up on that side."

Another man chipped in. "Awe, you're right there, Brian. That boy's father should have steered him away from the British.'

A few others echoed these sentiments.

Father Flaherty used his large hands to press down the growing discontent. "Please be minded that a young lad has lost his life." He swept his hooded eyes around them all. "Show some respect!"

The farmer's wife wagged her finger at the dissenters. "You should be ashamed of yourselves! Let the poor boy rest in peace."

A general murmur of agreement followed, with some people voicing their annoyance at those who had just spoken.

Father Flaherty raised his hands again. "Enough! Let us pray."

The crowd silenced. Most of the men removed their caps. The rag and bone man and two others beside him hung back, their flat caps defiantly still covering their heads.

***

Mary and Sara were returning from shopping when they saw the crowd outside the barracks. As they approached, they could see Father Flaherty surrounded by people.

Mary strained to see what the commotion was about. She touched Sara's sleeve. "Something's happened or all those people wouldn't be out on the street."

A woman, who Mary recognised, came towards her. "Don't go any further, Mary."

"Why not?"

"Sean Corvin's been shot. The priest is just after saying some prayers."

"No!" Mary gasped.

Sara's hands flew to her face. "Dear God!"

A horse and trap arrived, people standing back to allow it through. Mary clutched Sara's arm as the body of the policeman was gently carried up onto the back of the trap. The driver looked round to check that the body was secure, shook the reins and the horse trotted slowly off, its hooves echoing heavily along the road.

"Ah, they're taking him home to his poor Mammy and Daddy," one woman said to another.

"Good Christian people too, the Corvins. I know them well," her friend replied. "Always sending what little money they have spare to the missions."

The rag and bone man spat close to where the policeman had fallen. "Well, he isn't the first, and he won't be the last."

Grabbing him by the collar, the farmer locked eyes with him. "How dare you!"

"Surely to God, they're not going to fight!" Mary exclaimed, feeling a trickle of sweat run down her back.

Father Flaherty strode over and pulled the two men apart. "Go home both of you, before you regret it." He turned to all the onlookers. "Go home, the lot of you and ask forgiveness for your sins."

Old John sat on the side of the road, his head in his hands. He must be in shock, thought Sara. Poor old man. She hoped he hadn't witnessed the actual shooting. That poor boy would have been about the age of her sons. She put a hand to her chest to calm her breathing and thanked God that Richard was at a neighbour's house.

Then she thought about William. He'd be outraged, demanding that the police find the killer. Leave no stone unturned in doing so. It made her feel uneasy, to think of him and what he might do.

"I want to stop by the church on the way home, before I get Richard," she said.

Mary nodded. "Say a prayer for us all while you're there."

***

The crowd had gone. All that was left was the dark red stain of Sean Corvin's blood on the gravel.

Old John staggered back inside the barn. Standing against the closed door, his body shook violently. He clenched his fists, then unclenched them. What was it with these people? Did they not know right from wrong?

Feeling a deep sense of sadness, he sank into the hay, covered his eyes with his hands and wept.

Chapter Thirty-Five

They came that night when the household had retired to bed. Mary heard the roar of the truck at the door, the scream of the brakes. She clambered out of bed, went to the window and looked out. The harsh lights of the lorry shone straight at her door. Several uniformed men bounded out. She gripped the windowsill, the sweat gathering on her palms. What did they want, these men?

Pat called out, "Who is it?"

"I don't know. Just stay put while I go down and see."

Then came the battering on the door. "Open up! Open up!"

Mary ran down to open the door and they stormed in past her, their torches piercing the darkness. throwing the chairs upside down, opening the drawers, scattering their contents over the floor.

She saw a man with a black raincoat and a tin hat, and another in khaki trousers and a dark green jacket. The Black and Tans! Sent from England to help the RIC. She recalled the stories she'd heard, how the Tans could turn people out of their houses, people like herself and Pat, who'd done nothing wrong. Some innocent people had even been murdered.

She felt the blood drain from her face, her breath coming in short pants. Would they kill them too? "What do you...want from us?" she asked.

They shone their flashlights at her face. "Any weapons kept in this house, Madam?"

The accent was unfamiliar to her, the voice heavy with menace. Mary shook her head.

"Any weapons upstairs?"

"No!" she cried, her voice strangled.

In the glow of the flashlights, a uniformed man, with a high forehead and his hair slicked back, tapped his baton on the table. "An RIC officer was shot the other day. We're following leads on the culprit."

Pat, holding a lit candle, hung his head over the bannister.

"What's going on, Mary?" he coughed.

Liam came out of his room and called down, "Are you all right, Mam?"

She looked up. "Stay there, the two of you." She indicated to Liam, who was standing beside his father. "Don't move."

Two of the men clattered up the stairs, their boots echoing harshly.

She ran after them, her bare feet catching on the hem of her nightdress.

"Out of the way. Let us do our job," one yelled as he brushed past Pat and Liam.

"Nothing to fear if you're innocent," the other guffawed.

Pat clung to the handle of the candleholder as it flickered in front of him. Mary came to his side and steadied him. Liam took the candle from Pat and set it on the floor. The flame dipped then flared again, casting ghostly shadows on the walls.

They watched as the bedrooms were searched. A chamber pot was pulled out so roughly that it slopped its contents on the floor.

"Whoops-a-daisy!" one man exclaimed.

"Someone here knows how to piss themselves silly," the other hooted.

After they'd upended the mattress and pulled the bolsters out of their covers, they rooted around, pulling clothing out of the dresser drawer. Pat swore under his breath as one man held a pair of Mary's bloomers out in front of him, laughing raucously.

Pat gasped for breath, then coughed violently. "So, you think… we're all corner boys… out murdering?" His voice broke.

"Shinners." The man spat on the floor. "You've an answer for everything."

"Please!" Mary pleaded. "My husband's not well!"

In the glow of the candlelight, she could see Pat's face; his cheeks sunken, his lips pinched tightly together.

Liam's room was next to be searched. She saw the mattress being tossed to the side, drawers pulled out and heard: "Nothing here."

From downstairs, she heard the men being called by a superior. The filthy language they used and them all laughing.

"Gave them a right old fright, that lot."

"Well, fuck them all, the dirty scum."

"Come on, there's more houses to do before we're done."

And then, it was all over.

Mary released her hold on Pat and Liam. "Thank God," she whispered.

She felt weak, sick to her core, but what would this do to Pat? She guided him downstairs, his breathing coming in fits and starts, unable to utter a sentence without distress. She eased him into the rocking chair. Liam took a chair that had been upended and turned it over, seating himself next to Pat.

Mary returned upstairs and surveyed the mess. Then she said a prayer of thanks. Thank God they were all still alive.

***

Sometime later, with the gas lamps in the cottage burning, Mary set about putting the parlour to rights. Liam jostled the final drawer back into place in the dresser. He gathered up the mess from the floor: the dominoes, the draughts, her embroidery, and set them on the table. She lifted her needlework, now stained with muddy footprints.

"I'm sure this can be washed," she said, and he nodded.

Liam reached down to the floor and held up two pieces of the ornament of St Francis that had sat for years on the mantlepiece. "I'll see about mending this tomorrow."

With Pat huddled into the rocker, a cushion at his back and a large rug about his shoulders, Mary took a mop and bucket upstairs. She lifted the Bible that had been flung on the floor and ran her hands over the leather cover, thankful that it was still intact. She righted the upturned chair and lifted the clothes, strewn across the floor, piling them onto the bed.

She hadn't heard him approach, but suddenly Liam was beside her. He hoisted the mattress from the ground and threw it back on the bed with a thud, before heaping the bed linen on top.

"Bastards," he murmured under his breath.

She put a hand on his shoulder and squeezed it. Taking a wet mop, she sloshed it over the urine-stained floorboards, deciding to scrub them properly the next day.

***

When, eventually, the room had been put to rights and the beds remade with fresh linen, she went down to Pat.

He was coughing continually. She laid a hand across his forehead. "Goodness, Pat. Not again!

Liam looked up. "I'll help you to bed, Da."

194

He came over to his father and, with Mary's help, tried to lift Pat from his seat.

Pat fell straight back down. "Leave me be, you two," he wheezed. "Leave me a blanket and a pillow, and I'll sleep here".

Reluctantly they left him, tucked up as comfortable as they could make him.

***

Liam tossed and turned. Sleep would not come, no matter how hard he tried. Sean Corvin had been murdered, and now this. The Black and Tans. Their house searched for weapons. How could those so-called policemen force their way into his house and think that his family had anything to do with Sean's death?

Why would they do that?

His thoughts turned to his da and the strain of the whole thing on him. Those bastards deserved to be punished. His head felt as though it might burst from all the anger that seethed within him.

Early the next morning, Liam crept out of bed and down the stairs. Momentarily, he held his breath, so still was the rocking chair. He gritted his teeth. Surely not. He touched his da's hand, relieved to feel its warmth.

Pat stirred. He opened his eyes and looked at Liam. "Son?"

Liam inhaled deeply. Thank God.

Chapter Thirty-Six

Mary strode out towards Sara's house. She'd left without a basket or handbag, her coat flapping out from her sides, her curls untamed. Fury raged inside her chest, anger pulsed through her veins. Why would those men have targeted her family? How could they possibly imagine that herself or Pat or Liam had played any part in Sean Corvin's murder? Hadn't they all been horrified at his killing?

Her family home had been violated. Violated by thugs. Thugs who would have mothers like herself. Mothers, who, if they knew what their sons had done, would tell those boys to be ashamed of themselves.

These garbled thoughts, and more, whirled round and round in her head. She'd needed to do something other than sit at home and seethe. With the school term over, Liam would stay with Pat today. It was a blessing that Pat seemed no worse. He'd even tried to calm her down. Why not go to see Sara, he'd suggested. She'd agreed. A walk up to Sara's house would be good. The last thing he'd said was for her to mind what she'd say, on account of where William's loyalties lay. She knew where he was coming from, she'd told him, but Sara would know what to say, or not say, to her husband. Mary was sure of it.

Arriving at the Leavy's door, she rapped twice with the brass knocker and stood back.

The door creaked open.

"Hello," she called out, about to go in, but then stepping back.

William stood in front of her smiling. "Hello, Mary."

She tried to smile but her lips trembled.

"Sara and Richard went off early to the Sunday School outing."

Mary could feel tingling behind her eyes. She blinked. "Of course. She told me they were going, and I forgot." She looked down at her boots.

"Is anything wrong?"

She felt suddenly as though her chest would crumple under the weight of her feelings. She let out an involuntary sob.

William cleared his throat. "I've time yet before I need to go out." He caught her eyes as she looked up. "I think you should come in."

***

From a small tin, which Mary knew to contain Sara's assortment of tinctures and liniments, William held out a small dark bottle. "The paleness of your face tells me you've had some horrible shock. Is it Pat or Liam?"

"Neither." She looked away.

"A thimbleful of brandy?" He pulled the cork off the top of a tiny bottle and sniffed it. "For medicinal purposes." He poured a measure into a glass and handed it to her.

Holding it to her lips, the smell of it made her shiver.

"Drink it back. It'll settle your nerves."

She tipped her head back obediently, and swallowed the liquid. It warmed the back of her throat and made her hold a hand to her chest.

"Can I be of help in some way?" William recorked the bottle and set it back in the tin.

"No," she patted her chest once more, "but thank you."

"But something bad has happened." He took the tin and set it back on the sideboard. "Something to do with that poor policeman being shot?"

She drew a deep breath in. "We had a visit, last night...On account of it."

She grasped her hands together and squeezed them tight.

"The police?" His face had a look of concern, the eyebrows slightly raised, a softness about the mouth. "And they searched your house?"

She nodded.

"And they frightened you?"

She nodded again.

He leaned forward in his seat, facing her. "Tell me what they did. I'll see to making a complaint."

"No!" She looked at him in horror. "That could make things worse. Please no."

***

Making him promise that he wouldn't go near the police, Mary told William what had happened. It made her heart race to talk about it, so she skipped over the cruelness of the jeering and the language used, and the way those men had leered at her clothes.

William sat, his hands clasped in his lap, his face betraying his true feelings. He looked angry.

When she finished, William got up and walked to the mantlepiece. He picked up the picture of his sons. "Those men that called with you, those newly assigned members of the RIC, should be rightly ashamed." He stared at the faces of his boys. "And I've heard that many of them, had fought in the Great War." He shook his head. "I'm ashamed. Those men are not fit to wear their uniforms. Not fit to serve!" He set the photograph carefully back in its place. "If I'd thought for a minute that Samuel and Arthur …" his voice trailed off.

"It's not your fault." Mary could see the hurt in his eyes. A different type of hurt from what she was feeling. "And this has nothing to do with your sons. You're a good man, and Samuel and Arthur were fine, young lads."

He turned to face her, his arms hanging by his sides, the hands balled in fists. "I'm so very sorry."

"Thank you." She met his gaze for an instant.

"I promise you I won't take this matter further, but won't you reconsider? There's local men in the Kilkenny RIC." He cleared his throat. "Are you absolutely sure?

"Pat's been wary of the RIC for some time. Says the rules have changed."

"I see." William nodded slowly, then sat down opposite her. "And how are Pat and Liam?"

"I left Pat sleeping. He took a bit of a turn last night but there was colour in his face when I left him. And he ate a little porridge. Liam's angry, of course, but he'll calm down, I'm sure."

"Please tell them how horrified I am to hear of what you went through. I want no part of those policemen's vicious campaign. They don't speak for me or my views."

***

198

She said goodbye, and set off down the lane. The air had a coolness about it and there was a faint smell of something burning. It wasn't just her family that had been hit by grief. The Leavys had had their fair share too. No-one in this life was immune.

Chapter Thirty-Seven

Liam left his house early for his first day at work. It would take him at least a half hour to reach the forge, but he was glad of the fresh air. The events of the last few days had left him in shock.

Sean Corvin dead and buried? The boy who helped him when he was being bullied. Sean, who was a lad just like himself. He thought of the older brother, Ruari, now stationed in Kilkenny. Ruari, who Da had liked so much when he worked with him before joining up. Now, Ruari would be wanting to get his hands on his brother's killer. No doubt about that.

Then, the Tans arriving at his house. Those bastards storming in, turning everything upside down. Scaring the wits out of his parents. His poor da, so weak and unable to do anything. And now his mam seemed to shake and tremble at any loud noise or bang.

It would be good to start working. Earn some money and take his mind off the whole horrible goings-on. Although it had been raining, the clouds had parted, allowing shards of sunlight to shine through. Feeling the warmth on his shoulders, he drew strength from it as he approached the closed doors of the forge.

He knocked several times with his knuckle.

Dan poked his dishevelled head out of the window. "Ah, Hop-along." He dusted his hands together. "Wait here." He disappeared back inside.

Liam felt heat rising up his neck. He hadn't heard that cruel nickname, other than from Declan some years ago. But he wouldn't let it upset him. He was here to work. He heard metal tools clanking, the crash of something falling to the floor, then Dan cursing, followed by more jangling noises. Liam thought of his father's shed; neat and tidy, nuts and bolts stored on shelves in tobacco tins, spanners and pliers hanging from hooks on the wall.

After a couple of minutes, Dan appeared at the door, and handed him an old shovel and a tin bucket with a lopsided handle. "Now let's see how good you are with the feckin' rats." He jutted his head out from his neck, his nostrils flared. "I want the shed free of those buggers!" He sauntered back into the forge, whistling.

Liam hobbled to the shed, unsure of what to do. At home, if a rat had been seen, his father would lay a trap. With a shovel, he didn't think he could get near enough a rat to hit it, let alone kill it. Pulling back the bar of the lock, he screwed up his eyes and peered inside. He gagged. The smell of something festering caught his nose. He could see the half-eaten carcass of a small animal, and the tail of a large rat vanishing through a hole in the wall.

Creaking the door fully open, he surveyed the mess in front of him. An entanglement of old, rusted pieces of machinery took up most of the space. Newspapers were stacked haphazardly against the walls, pieces of chewed up paper strewn across the floor. Shattered panes of glass perched precariously on top of broken wooden crates.

Liam cursed inwardly.

Looking up, he could see light coming through two large, gaping holes in the corrugated iron roof. The only window in the shed was so dirty that the glass appeared opaque. A pot of tar lay on one side, the spilled contents black and congealed. With the door fully open, he saw black rat droppings, the size of peas, everywhere. The stench made him retch.

Stepping back outside, he filled his lungs with fresh air.

Declan cycled up, screeching to an abrupt halt. He stood astride the bicycle, his feet firmly planted on the ground, elbows on the handlebars. "I was wondering how a useless cripple like you," he nodded toward the shed, "could catch any rats."

Liam turned his head away, sucking his teeth, fighting back the urge to reply.

On hearing Dan guldering his name, Declan abandoned his bicycle at the side of the water trough and scurried into the forge.

Liam breathed a sigh of relief. *Thank goodness Declan's scared of his da*, he thought. *That'll keep him off my back for a bit.*

Examining the shed, Liam decided that everything inside it would have to come out. That way, there would be nothing left for the rats to feed on.

He started by carrying out the broken bricks and stacking them neatly outside, then turned his attention to the large plates of shattered glass. Using a matted piece of material, he cautiously carried the glass to where he could lay it up against the outside wall. A rusty bit of engine cut welts into his hand, with parts of the metal breaking off as he hauled it along the ground, gouging deep tracks into the gravel.

Returning to the shed, he saw what lay partially uncovered under some dirty sackcloth.

A plough.

An old plough like the one his father used to own before he replaced it. It took him back to the day that had changed his life. His heart raced furiously. He took the shovel and beat at the plough. The noise reverberated around the walls. Then, fearing that the commotion would cause Dan to investigate, he gripped the plough handles and, groaning, dragged it from the shed.

His own strength both amazed and appalled him. Something of the man inside him had reared up. Suddenly, he thought of his father, barely able to carry a bucket of coal.

Shaking the cramp from his injured leg, he looked around. Dotted at the base of the trees were masses of purple foxgloves. He could hear the low drone of bees clamouring around them. He breathed in the smell of grass and the freshness of summer. Sparrows chirped high up in the trees and putty-coloured butterflies fluttered by, the edges of their wings black, as though dipped in ink. He took a handkerchief from his pocket and wiped sweat off his brow. *Back to the work in hand*, he thought.

After a few hours, he'd lugged most of the shed's contents outside. Attempting to gather the rat droppings from the shed floor with the shovel, Liam considered asking Dan for a yard brush. Reluctantly, he limped up to the forge doors, which had been pulled partially closed.

Two bicycles lay beside Declan's. Liam realised he'd been so occupied, he hadn't noticed anyone else arriving.

He cocked his head around the entrance. Dan and Declan were arguing about something, so engrossed in their discussion that they didn't see him as he peered inside. In addition to the blacksmith and his son, two men slouched by the wall. Liam recognised them as Martin Blaney, the butcher, and Ger McKenna from the knacker's yard. Liam hung back a little, shuffling his feet to announce his arrival.

Startled, they looked up in surprise.

Dan walked up to him, so close that Liam could smell lard on the blacksmith's breath. "I hope you're not snooping, boy."

"Sorry, Mr O'Toole. I just need a brush to sweep the floor of the shed."

Dan pointed a finger at him. "I don't like snoopers! Now heed that well!" He pulled his cigarette packet from his pocket, extracted a cigarette from it and put it in his mouth. Striking a match, he cupped one hand round the end of the cigarette as he lit it. "I don't have a brush." He inhaled deeply. "What's wrong with your hands. Not big and manly enough?"

Declan, Ger and Martin sniggered.

"And there's no need to take all the rubbish to the dump. Most of that stuff can be burned." He handed Liam his packet of matches. "When the shed's spotless, let's see you make a bonfire. Now scram!" he roared. "There's a tin of petrol by the forge door. That should start it nicely."

***

Dan gazed out from the open doors of the forge. The tip-off about the Tans coming down to Lisowen had caused him and the boys to take a little trip into the woods the night before. Just in case. Cold and damp, it had been, but now the Tans were away, empty-handed, terrorising some other hapless buggers. Well, there was more than one way to skin a cat, and Dan would take them out one by one if he had to. *One by fucking one*, he thought. *Let them all rot in Hell.*

Dan looked out at Liam struggling to pull corrugated iron out of the shed. The boy was bent over the metal, heaving and pulling for all that was worth. Dan smiled. He'd made a good decision in taking that cripple on to work for him.

He was on his own now. Declan had been sent off to get him more cigarettes and Martin had gone back to work. Ger had stayed longer, somewhat agitated about recent events, but he was also now away. Ger had done what he'd been tasked to do, Dan reassured him. But still, Ger was worried. After all, he'd lost his weapon.

"Ah, feck it. You did well. Worth the loss of a gun." Dan had taken a piece of chalk and added a mark to the inside of the forge wall. "The gun can be replaced."

Eventually, Ger had left with a new Smith and Wesson revolver wrapped in oilcloth, which Dan had pulled from the depths of the coal bunker.

The fire in the forge was smouldering and he'd let it go out. He'd done enough work for the day, even though it was still early. He took his cigarette packet from his pocket and pulled out the last cigarette. Striking a match, he sucked hard and inhaled. All in all, this was turning into the most satisfactory of days.

The cripple had heaped a great pile of wood and rubbish together. The tin of petrol stood at the ready. Beside the bonfire stood a heap of scrap metal, and Dan wondered why he hadn't considered the value of it before. If he was lucky, the rag and bone man might give him a shilling for it.

Every so often, he had watched the cripple doing his back-breaking work. The boy was a determined fecker; he'd give him that. He'd worked harder than Declan, who snuck off frequently, to smoke, or piss, or God knew what, in between shovelling coal and hammering on horseshoes.

Dan blew several smoke rings, watching them distort and disappear. It was time for Declan to get involved in the armed struggle. Discipline was what was needed to make a man of him.

He turned his mind to the plans for the following day, a snoop around a troublemaker's house. Smiling, he drew hard on the end of the cigarette butt before throwing it on the floor and stamping on it. A certain someone deserved to be shaken up a bit.

Looking out from the forge door, he watched as Liam threw petrol on the bonfire. "Steady on, Hop-along."

The boy had obviously no experience of lighting fires. Mesmerised, he watched Liam strike a match and throw it on the pile.

The wind caught the flames and soon the fire became an inferno. It brought Dan back to Cork and Kildare. Burning those houses had helped him avenge his poor, starving grandmother all those years ago at the height of the famine. Fuck them all. The lord of the manor ignoring her plea for food! And Grandma at the door, a dead baby cradled in her arms and children hanging on her skirts.

Declan broke into his thoughts as he came running towards the bonfire with a bucket of water. He swore fiercely as he hurled water at the fire, soaking Liam at the same time. "That little fecker of a cripple will have the forge burned down," he screamed, his head turned towards Dan.

Dan sauntered over and caught his son by the shoulder. "Some fires need left to burn. Do you know nothing?" He clipped Declan on the ear. "Leave it. It'll go out eventually."

Declan handed him the cigarettes he'd bought and, without comment, slunk off into the forge.

Liam shook his head, his sodden shirt plastered to his skin.

Dan slapped him hard on the back. "Good work, Hop-along! You can come back tomorrow and sort the metal out for selling. Then, I'll get you up on the roof of the forge. The gutters need clearing. When that's done, there's whitewashing and creosoting." He turned, hoisting his trousers up, working his lumpy body down into them. "And I don't want to even smell as much as a rat again! Do you hear me, Hop-along?"

"I'll be back at eight tomorrow, Mr O'Toole," the boy said and, with a tired limp, hobbled off towards home.

Chapter Thirty-Eight

As Sara and Mary strolled towards Beggarstown, woodpigeons cooed from the thick of the forest and the scent of wild roses and honeysuckle drifted by in the air. A blazing sun shone down, with only a few puffs of clouds dotted across a deep blue sky. Sparrows cheeped incessantly, tending to their fledglings before darting into the hedgerows through white elder blossom.

The friends had the day to themselves. Mary was still reeling from the shock of the Tans searching her home and Sara knew it was not the time to burden her friend with new worries. So, she walked, tight-lipped, holding her thoughts and anxieties to herself. She was glad that William had offered to look after Richard.

"I'll get him to help me whitewash the privy," he'd said.

And she could picture the two of them, paintbrushes in hand, Richard's old clothes stained with paint. *Ah, nothing a bath and carbolic wouldn't remove*, she thought. She took off her hat and fanned her face with the brim.

"Liam has a job." Mary put a hand up to shield her eyes from the bright sunlight. "For the summer holidays."

Sara wondered what it could be. Jobs were in short supply in Lisowen for men of working age.

"He's helping out at the forge."

"With Dan O'Toole?" Sara tried to disguise her shock. That horrible man. So, this was what Mary's family had to do, in order to pay bills. "And how is he getting on?"

Mary blinked a few times. "He's only been there a couple of days and yesterday he came home filthy and exhausted with a deep cut on his arm. Could hardly eat his dinner before going to bed."

Sara thought back to the concert in Donnybrook Hall, the way that O'Toole had frightened her. Why Mary and Pat would agree to letting Liam work for that brute was beyond her. She thought of saying something but swallowed hard instead.

Mary sighed. "Pat and I don't like him being there, but Liam still seems keen." She picked a dandelion from the roadside and blew white, fluffy seeds into the air.

Sara felt a trickle of sweat on her back. It seemed to her that the sun was terribly warm. "And how's Pat?"

Mary let the stem of the dandelion slip from her fingers. "Ah, you know...just the same."

"Well, it's good that he's no worse." Sara pulled the brim of her hat tightly down on her head, tipping it forward to shade her face. Then, noticing that her forearms were tinged red, she adjusted her thin shawl to cover them.

They passed the priest ambling beside an old man stooped over a stick. Father Flaherty touched his hat. "Quare day for a dander, ladies."

"Good day to you, Father," Mary called out.

"Good day," Sara added, briefly wondering how a church minister could earn the title 'Father.'

Then, they heard the clanking of Old John and his wares; his saucepans and kettles banging together as he trundled down the path. He stopped when he got to them and, giving a little bow, caused his pots and pans to sway precariously. "Good day to you both, dear ladies."

They said their Hellos and asked after his health.

"I'm well enough, with thanks to you both for enquiring." He looked upwards at the sky and then turned his gaze back towards them. "But my heart is sore for that young man just killed at the barracks."

"Us too." Sara said. "Such an awful thing for anyone to do." Her mind flashed briefly to her sons, long gone.

Mary crossed herself. "God rest that poor boy's soul."

Old John repositioned his bag onto his back. "Ah, God will need to be answered to on Judgement Day." He almost lost his balance, from the sudden adjustment of his burden, but soon steadied himself. "I hope...to call...with you...both sometime...soon." He puffed the words out, two at a time.

"Of course, Old John." Sara smiled at him. "We'll look forward to your visit. Won't we, Mary?"

Mary grasped the handle of her basket with both hands. "Indeed."

Old John smiled, showing his uneven, stained teeth. "I am indebted, ladies."

They exchanged their goodbyes.

Once out of earshot, Mary brushed a few curls back from her face and secured them with a clasp. "Dear old man."

Talking about the dead policeman had unsettled Sara. She pulled her shawl up over her shoulders. "Let's go up to the Bawn River."

Mary looked at her quizzically. "Whatever you say. But it's a bit off the beaten track."

After ten minutes or so, they reached the hump-backed bridge and took some time to look down at the water flowing lazily over the pastel-coloured rocks. From there, they followed a well-trodden path off the road.

Arriving in a clearing, Mary flopped down on the ground. After checking first with her hand that the ground beneath was dry, Sara joined her. Mary took two small green apples from her basket and set one gently on top of Sara's lap before biting into her own. She screwed her face up at the sharpness of it. Dappled sunlight shifted through the leaves, sparkling off the granite rocks dotted along the riverside.

Mary took another bite from her apple. "Now, tell me what's vexing you. I know you well enough to know that there's something on your mind."

Sara brushed a fly away from her face. "You've enough to be thinking about, without my worries too."

Mary looked at her, eyebrows raised. "Enough of that. Well, tell me?"

With her apple clenched tightly in her fist, Sara launched into her story. How, two days ago, she'd come home from the butchers to find the front door swinging open. How she'd berated herself for forgetting to lock it, William having asked her to use the key on account of the current trouble. How, when she'd walked into the parlour, there were shards of glass all over the floor and, worst of all, face down among it, her picture of Samuel and Arthur. She'd been so upset, thinking that she'd been careless, that the wind had knocked it off the mantelpiece. But then, as she was about to clear up, she saw a cigarette butt on the floor. It appeared as though someone had deliberately destroyed her photograph of her boys.

Mary put a hand to her mouth. "Holy Mother of God!"

"I got the brush and pan out, and swept everything up."

"And William?" Mary threw her apple core into the bottom of a large fern.

"He doesn't know. He'd left early that day for Kilkenny with Richard. They were going to the book shop." Sara sat bolt upright, staring straight ahead. "Thank goodness there was another framed picture, the very same, that sat in Grandmother's house till she died. It's on our mantelpiece now."

Mary touched her arm lightly. "Of course, you'll tell him."

Sara shook her head vigorously. "I'm worried how he'll react and what he'll do? He can be so hot-headed. He might well go to the police. Can you imagine the trouble that would bring the village? "She pulled a daisy from the grass and plucked the petals off methodically, one by one. "If I just hold tight, it might all come to nothing."

"You'll keep this from your husband?"

"If it keeps us all safe."

"You're sure?"

"I am."

A cool wind blew through the beech trees.

Sara shivered and reached for her shawl. A few stray rays of sunlight escaped from behind a pewter-coloured cloud. "You need to be home for Pat and Liam."

The two friends retraced their steps. At the top of Mary's lane, they embraced.

"Take care." Mary gave Sara's arm a gentle squeeze.

Sara smiled weakly and walked away.

Approaching her house, she saw William and Richard outside, kicking a ball. William's clothes were unblemished, while Richard's shirt had splodges of whitewash all over. They waved. When she eventually caught up with them, William opened his arms towards her.

She ran towards him and gave him a hug, burying her face deep into his neck.

Chapter Thirty-Nine

A few days had passed since Liam had taken the job at the forge. At the end of each day, he'd drag himself into the house, haul his boots off at the door and flop into a chair.

In addition to lacerating his arm an on an old piece of corrugated iron, he'd twisted his injured ankle. "Climbing down off the roof," he'd told his mother.

Mary wondered what Dan O'Toole would ask Liam to do next, but tried not to fuss. Knowing Liam was in pain, she mixed an aspirin powder into his glass of milk. But she felt uneasy. That brute of a blacksmith didn't care for her son's safety. Any amount of money wasn't enough if Liam had another awful accident, or a wound went gangrenous.

At the end of the first week, after Liam had gone to bed, she sat with Pat; both of them nursing tea in enamel mugs. She sipped from her cup, tendrils of steam rising up in front of her.

"I don't think it's right that Dan O'Toole is making our son work like this," she said. "He's using him as a slave. Look at what's happened so far. He's cut his arm and injured his bad foot."

Pat took a deep breath and nodded. He held his hand firm against his chest as he spoke. "It vexes me too, truth be told. We don't need money so badly that he has to put himself in danger."

Mary set the cup down and got up from her seat, taking a poker to rake the fire. But they did need money.

Pat wheezed. "Liam has enough here to occupy him on our bit of land, and that's being neglected. Maybe, it's time for him to stop school."

Mary sighed. "Maybe so. Perhaps after Hallowe'en?" She hoped not but she knew how much money remained. They could maybe make it last another couple of months.

***

Liam came home the next day to the smell of freshly-made pancakes. He sank into the rocking chair and undid the laces on his boots. With a grunt he pulled them off, taking more time with his damaged foot. "Where's Da?"

Mary set the butter dish and two plates on the table. "He's gone to bed. Said he'd be down later." She scooped a pancake onto a plate. "Told me under no circumstances are you to eat the whole lot, and that he's looking forward to his share." She chuckled, pointing the wooden spoon at him. "You know your da and pancakes."

The kitchen smelled hot and sugary. Mary leaned over the griddle, spooning globules of batter from a large white bowl, which she cradled in one arm. "Your da and I think you should stop working at the forge and concentrate on the farm."

Liam sat at the table, a knife and fork clenched in each fist. "Because you think I'm not up to doing both?

Mary deftly flipped a pancake. "Of course not."

"But the money?"

"We still have some of our savings left." She hoped the expression on her face didn't give her away.

"Really?"

She scooped several pancakes onto Liam's plate, setting some aside for Pat. "The money your da made when working at the big house in Cork." She hated lying.

Liam munched his way through the sticky pile of pancakes, licking his lips and wiping them on his handkerchief. "To be honest, I'd be glad to have an excuse to leave the forge." Slathering another pancake with butter, he sprinkled sugar on it and, folding it in two, raised it to his mouth. "That man's a slave-driver." He gave a half chuckle. Sometimes, I even feel sorry for Declan."

Fat spat from the griddle onto the fire. Traces of batter began to burn, wafting smoke into the kitchen. A fine haze spread out from the fireplace.

"Dear Jesus!" Mary ran to the front door, opened it and, grabbing a cloth, set the smoking griddle on the front porch step. Waving her hands, she tried to disperse the smoke as if guiding sheep into a pen. She closed the door on the griddle and turned to Liam. "Good. Just tell him that your parents need you for ploughing." She winced as she thought back to Liam's accident. "Sorry."

Liam shook his head. "I'm over that long ago."

She came to him at the table, hunkered down and hugged him tightly. She could smell the butter and sugar from his breath. "I'm glad." She eased herself up with a little groan, and squeezed his shoulders, aware of their increasing breadth. "I know your da will be glad too. We can't have our big son wasting away!"

Later that evening, she opened the door to retrieve the griddle. The fields were illuminated by thousands of stars and a crescent moon shone down. She inhaled the fragrant night air, a cooling breeze on her arms.

Pat had been pleased at Liam's decision. She should be pleased too, but the niggle of other things was on her mind, not far away. She was worried for Sara and the break-in. And it wasn't that long since the Tans had thrown her own house upside down. Things were bad in Ireland. But she didn't want to tell Pat about her worries, for the slightest annoyance seemed to set him back. She grabbed the griddle, shrugged her shoulders and stepped back inside.

Chapter Forty

The next afternoon, Sara, with young Richard in hand, called on Mary.

"I dug these carrots up yesterday. Too many for our needs." She deposited the vegetables, neatly wrapped in newspaper, down, their green stalks vibrant on the dark wood of the sideboard.

Mary set them in a basket underneath the worktop. "Thank you. I'll make stew tomorrow. Pat and Liam will love that."

The sound of hammering could be heard coming from outside.

Sara raised her eyebrows. "Pat?"

"He's repairing our old bird table." Mary poured milk into a tin mug and offered it to Richard.

He rapidly glugged the contents down.

"Richard, why don't you go upstairs and play in Liam's room?" Mary took a box of dominoes out of the dresser drawer and handed it to him.

The little boy said thank you and scrambled up the stairs.

Sara sat at the table, nibbling the nail on her ring finger. "I still worry about someone having been in our house." She lowered her voice. "It's a threat. I'm sure of it."

Mary spooned tea leaves into the teapot before adding boiling water and swirling the pot. "Would you not tell William now?"

Sara shook her head. "He went off to another of those Unionist meetings up north yesterday. This time in Armagh. He gets a lift from the man who owns the bookshop in Kilkenny." She twisted her wedding ring round her finger. "They're away from early morning to very late at night. I worry about him until he's back and in the door."

Mary crossed herself. "I can understand that." She poured two mugs of tea and handed one to Sara.

Sara took the cup and, feeling the heat from it, set it on the table. "How's Liam getting on at the forge?"

"He's finishing with that job, thank God." Mary took a sip from her mug. "I've decided to go round the doors, ask if anyone needs cleaning or mending done."

Sara raised her eyebrows but said nothing. She opened her handbag and reached inside, pulling out a half crown which she set on the table. "This is a present for your birthday. I was going to buy you a new shawl, but you could maybe put this to better use."

"But it's not till next month."

"It's a bit early, that's all."

Mary took the coin and wagged a finger at her friend. "It's too much." She held the coin between finger and thumb. "But thank you."

***

Returning home with Richard, Sara screwed the mincer onto the table. From the cold safe outside, she brought the shin bone into the parlour. Having sliced the fat and flesh from the bone, she pressed the meat into the mincer and turned the handle. Swirls of freshly minced beef tumbled out onto an enamel plate. Richard knelt on a chair, his chin in his hands, watching wide-eyed.

The door creaked open. "Hello! Anyone at home?"

Richard scrambled off the chair and ran to his father, who scooped him up and threw him high above him. The boy giggled before wriggling to be put down.

"Now, be a good boy and fetch me down the book I left beside my bed." William patted his son's back.

The boy dashed upstairs.

Sara wiped her hands on her apron and gave her husband a peck on the cheek. He looked drained.

"What's wrong?" she asked.

"The IRA are at their murderous work again. Two more policemen dead on the road to Kilcreen. They used dynamite, this time." William clenched his fist. "Then another village turned upside down and two young lads shot." He shook his head. "I don't want young Richard to hear any of it."

"Of course not." Sara certainly didn't want Richard frightened.

Later, after a dinner of minced beef and cabbage, and Richard having been read his bedtime story, Sara told William of the conversation she'd had with Mary. She was on the point of telling him how scared she was when he went off up north but thought better of it. Maybe she'd bring the topic up at the weekend. "You know, poor Liam's not strong enough for the job at the forge. Mary says he's coming home each day with all sorts of injuries."

"He should stop then." William wet his thumb and leafed through the newspaper.

"It's not so easy for the family, with Pat unable to work."

William raised his head and looked at her, his eyebrows knit together. "Liam should be able to concentrate on his schoolwork, not working for that hallion, O'Toole."

"Mary knows that. But they're a proud family..."

William sat in his chair, his large feet planted wide on the floor, his spectacles swinging from his thumb and forefinger. "I might be able to help."

"They'll never accept charity."

"I know, my dear, but it would be easy for me to give Liam a little help with his schoolwork. Then, if he was coming up to the house, I'm sure there are many jobs I could find for him to do. Jobs, I'd pay to have done."

"What sort of jobs?"

"For a start, I need to get the horse to the forge in Beggarstown and the cart needs fixing too." William linked his fingers together and stretched out his arms. "Then, there's all those chores around the house you're always going on about. The hinges on the back door, the shelf that you want up in the scullery, the leak in the roof of the stable –" his mouth sagged. "All those tasks that Samuel and Arthur could have helped me with."

Sara nodded. "I'll talk it over with Mary tomorrow. She can speak to Pat." She shovelled slack on the fire, dampening down the flames. With luck, the fire would still be going in the morning. "At the end of the day, it will be up to Liam," she said.

Chapter Forty-One

Mary had been delighted, when Sara told her of William's offer. If Liam had extra help with his schoolwork, he might, one day, be able to get a good job.

Sara smiled at her from over the rim of her mug. "It's what William loves doing best; helping young minds develop." She took a sip of tea, then set the mug down. "And there's lots of little jobs that Liam could help William with."

"Then we won't feel indebted." Mary clasped her hands lightly on her lap. This arrangement could suit both families.

"We'll work something out."

"Now, no feeling sorry for us!" Mary, a wide smile on her face, wagged her finger at her friend. But the whole idea sounded perfect. William wouldn't expect Liam to do anything he wasn't capable of and, if there was a lot of work, then a little payment would be justified.

"Hopefully, Liam will like the idea." Sara pursed her lips together, thoughtfully. "At the end of the day, he might not be as keen as you are."

***

"Well, what do you think?" Mary lifted the dinner plate from the basin of water and wiped it dry with a cloth. "Mr. Leavy needs help with some jobs," she said as she dried her hands on the cloth and hung it over the hook beneath the worktop. "And he's willing to go over your schoolwork in return."

Liam listened to her, his face expressionless. "I don't think it's such a good idea," he answered, his head down.

Pat cleared his throat. "And why not, when Mr Leavy is kind enough to offer to help you catch up at school?

Liam set down the piece of wood he'd been sanding on the parlour table. Specks of sawdust floated into the air. "You know if my friends found out about it, I'd never hear the end of it?"

Mary lifted up the piece of sanded wood that Liam was using to repair her trinket box. "Why would your friends be bothered?" She ran her fingers over the wood, feeling the smooth, warm surface beneath her touch.

"A Catholic boy being helped by a Protestant teacher?" Liam looked at her.

Pat stood up. "Then your school friends are not good friends." He shifted from foot to foot, running his hands over his legs as though to get the blood flowing. "And I hope that when you've thought about this, you'll realise that it shouldn't matter."

"I'll think about it." Liam replied, his voice flat.

Mary lifted a bracelet from the broken jewellery box. She draped the brightly-coloured baubles across her hand, recalling her delight when Pat had presented it to her one Christmas. She fastened the bracelet over her wrist and shook it down her arm, catching the light on the cheap stones. "You were so looking forward to helping your little sister learn to read and write. You would be doing good in her memory by improving on your schoolwork."

A burst of sunlight brightened the parlour, casting a small rainbow on the white wall opposite the window.

Liam felt a hard lump in the back of his throat. He hadn't forgotten Fionuala, just tried not to think about her too much. He looked at his da, whose gaze was elsewhere. His mam turned her head from him, but he could see tears glistening on her eyelashes.

Would it be so bad to get extra help with spellings and sums? Being good at school wasn't something he thought about much but passing exams could help him find work. He thought about his older friend, Aidan, who was now the station master. He'd done some extra exams. And it would be easy to help Mr Leavy with some jobs, a lot easier than working at the forge. William Leavy had helped them, after all, at the time of the epidemic.

Anyway, Liam thought, *my schoolfriends won't need to know, for I'm not planning on telling anyone.*

Liam ran a finger over the dimple in his chin. "Maybe, I could go for a couple of days."

"That's the spirit." His father caught his gaze.

"But," Liam leaned back on the chair, balancing on two legs, "if things don't work out, I'll go up to the knackers yard and see if they need someone to work there."

Mary hoped not. The thought of Liam coming into the house with the smell of dead animals lingering on him, made her feel sick. She looked up at the Sacred Heart hanging above the worktop and silently appealed for help.

They sat round the table for the rest of the evening, Liam finishing the repairs on the trinket box and his father advising him on how to do it. His mother polished their boots. With a hand inside a boot, she shone the leather with a small brush before setting it neatly on the table on an old piece of newspaper. Liam inhaled the smell of polish, listening to the noise of the bristles whooshing gently as his mother brushed to and fro.

After the boots were tidied away, his mam said she'd go to bed, leaving Liam and his father sitting on opposite sides of the table, finishing off the last repairs to the wooden trinket box.

"Did you hear what happened in Cork?" Liam gave the box a rub with a cloth before setting it to the side. "What the British have done?"

Pat eased himself back into his rocking chair with a sigh. "It would be so easy to get angry. And anger can get out of control. And that can lead to rash decisions." He pounded his chest with his fist, wheezing. "I don't want you to be swayed by those who are prepared to fight." His father struggled out of his seat and began pacing the room. "Cannon fodder – that's what those young lads are, who sign up."

"Don't worry, Da." Liam shook some slack on the fire. The flames flickered out. "Some of my pals are wanting to fight the British, but I don't want to be fighting with anyone." He gave a wry chuckle and added, "I'd hardly be fit to be a foot soldier anyway."

"You're more capable than you think, Liam. Look at the work you did at the forge. A man with all his limbs in working order would find that tough."

Liam felt something inside him stir. A deep, comforting feeling. "You've nothing to worry about, Da. I won't get involved in anything. Anyway, what happened to Sean was despicable."

"Indeed, it was." His father took a deep breath in. "Thank God to hear we're of a mind. Let Ireland sort itself out, for there'll always be people who aren't happy." He rapped the arm of his chair with his knuckle. "It's a problem with no easy solution."

Liam lay awake that night. For a long time after his accident, he'd viewed himself as nothing much more than helpless. He mulled over the conversation he'd had with his father.

Tonight, for the first time, he saw himself differently. He was of value.

***

Liam dreaded handing in his notice at the forge, but it had to be done. He had shrugged off his mam's offer to accompany him. To have his mother speak up for him would have made the whole business even worse. He'd do this on his own.

He knocked at the forge door, sweat slick on his palms. The door creaked open and Dan's unshaven face peered out.

"Ah, Hop-along. You're early." Dan O'Toole lumbered out, his collarless shirt smudged with oil. "The horses need fed, then I want you back up on the forge roof. There's slates that need fixing."

"I'm sorry, Mr O'Toole, but I'll not be staying. I'm handing in my notice."

Dan's eyes narrowed to slits. "Who the feck do you think you are? Think you're above this work, do you?"

Liam looked at his boots. "No, it's not that."

Dan gathered phlegm in his mouth and turned his head to spit it out. "Couldn't stand the pace of a decent day's work, Hop-along?" He glared at him. "Ach, limp away back to your mammy and daddy! There are others that'll only be too glad of a decent job."

Liam kept his eyes focused on the ground in front of him. "Sorry." He noticed that Dan's boots had splatters of muck all over them. "I'll be going now. Thank you."

Dan fistled in his trouser pocket for something, produced a coin and threw it down where it rattled off a stone. "For the week just past." He turned on his heel and tramped into the forge, grumbling.

Liam leaned down, picked the coin up and looked at it. Thrupence for a week's work? Surely to goodness what he'd done had been worth a florin at least? He thrust the coin in his pocket and waggled it around.

Where was his penknife? He searched on the other side, shaking the material furiously. He was sure that he'd had his penknife with him. It had been given to him by his father on his last birthday. Just before diphtheria hit.

Liam shuddered. Why had he brought such a precious thing to the forge? Not more than two inches in length, it had an intricately carved ivory handle made from an elephant's tusk. He remembered thinking it could help him cut away at the base of the weeds sprouting from the shed floor. But he could have as easily hacked at the weeds with a spade.

Why hadn't he left the knife at home? He felt sweat on his palms and his heart pound wildly.

The knife must have dropped out of his pocket when he was leaning over, clearing out the shed or while working around the forge. He searched his pockets again, then pushed his finger down deeply. The stitches had separated to reveal a tiny hole. That was it. The penknife must have slid out through the gap in the lining.

He hunted around his feet, and was about to look further when Declan sidled out of the forge, chewing on a piece of straw.

"Hey cripple!" Declan strolled over and stood in front of Liam, grinning. "I knew you wouldn't be any good." He took the straw from his mouth, crumpled it in his hand and flung it at Liam's face. "Feck away off, why don't you?"

Liam ignored Declan, resolving to leave and come back in the early morning. As he walked home, he recalled his mother telling him about the penknife. His father was given it for work he'd done in Cork. Apparently, it could fetch a lot of money at auction.

"How much?" he'd asked, but his mother had refused to say.

Later she'd given him an old, tin pastille box that she'd lined with a scrap of velvet. "That will keep your penknife safe," she'd said.

He'd loved the gift, using it to whittle away at birch sticks, making a bow and arrow which was the envy of all his schoolfriends.

He had to get that penknife back.

Tomorrow, he'd be up early and go to the forge. He'd seen where Dan kept the spare key to the forge. It was hanging in a corner of the shed, which was never locked. He'd use the key to have a quick hunt around inside, and if the penknife wasn't there, he'd scour the area outside.

What a dunce he was to have put himself in this situation. He hit his head with the palm of his hand. Fingers crossed, he'd find the penknife before anyone else.

Chapter Forty-Two

Liam couldn't sleep. Fitful dreams of himself at the forge, up on the roof, hauling rusty corrugated iron away and Dan shouting at him, kept him tossing and turning all night.

At last, hearing the dawn chorus, then the clock strike six, he leaped out of bed. Once dressed, he crept barefoot down the stairs, before pulling on his socks and boots.

He unlatched the door with a gentle click and stood outside for a while to calm his breathing. Cool air blew the hair back from his forehead. He looked around. The sky was brightening but the fields still had a silver-grey sheen about them. Far in the distance, a cock crowed.

Half an hour to the forge, a quick scout around and, hopefully, he'd find the penknife. With luck, he'd be home before anyone noticed.

If his mother asked what had him up so early, he'd tell her that he was out feeding the chickens and pigs, so that he could meet friends later to go fishing. That would please her. Besides that, he'd say that he intended calling with Mr Leavy, see about making an arrangement with him. That would please her even more. He could easily throw some food out for the animals later in the day when his mother was occupied elsewhere.

As he hobbled along, he passed a robin trying to catch a worm and resisted the urge to stop and watch it, or to blow some of the dandelion clocks that littered the roadsides. There was only one thing on his mind and that was to find his penknife.

On nearing the forge, four coats swung from the tethering post, their arms gently waving. Recognising Dan's scruffy tweed jacket as one of them, and another as Declan's, Liam clenched his fists in dismay. Damn! What had them here at this time? Dan wasn't in the habit of opening up till eight. Quieting his footsteps, Liam tiptoed the remaining distance. The only option was to sneak around the perimeter as quickly as possible, hoping that the penknife had fallen outside.

Treading carefully through the weeds at the side of the forge, his eyes scanned the ground for any sign of his precious knife. Voices carried out to where he was crouching, and he strained to hear snippets of the conversation. He heard mention of a raid and, stopping in his tracks, held his breath. So, it was true after all. Dan was involved in the armed struggle. Had he also been involved in Sean's killing?

Liam looked up at the window, open overhead above the trough. If he could just haul himself up, he'd have a better chance of hearing what was going on. Placing his hands on the wall, he inwardly groaned as he climbed onto the water trough. His hands slid over the rough plaster, scraping a thin layer of skin off one palm. He winced, small flecks of blood appearing on the white of the wall. He stood with his good leg on the edge, wobbling precariously. Keeping his head bowed, he could just about make out the conversation.

The first voice he recognised belonged to Dan. "Feckin' barracks burned like there was no feckin' tomorrow!"

Liam heard other men laughing, then Declan's unmistakably whiney voice. "But didn't it take three goes with the paraffin to get it to catch?"

There was a moment's silence, then Dan guffawing. "Pity that feckin' cripple isn't around anymore to help. He'd make a great arsonist. Built the finest bonfire I've ever seen!"

Howls of laughter broke out from within the forge.

Liam felt his cheeks redden. He wanted to punch Dan hard on the nose. He felt a ball of anger gather deep in the pit of his stomach. Wobbling, he steadied his foot on the trough. The conversation turned to something different.

"Now, we're going after a Protestant fecker. A bloody know-it-all." It was Dan speaking again.

"What's he done to annoy anyone?"

Liam heard something about Unionist rallies, then smatterings of the conversation that followed.

"Feckin' Brit!"

"And the bastard has money buried for didn't I see him carrying a spade? I'll be interrogating the fecker…!"

"You might have a job getting the truth from him."

"Not if I'm holding a gun."

"When?"

"Saturday evening."

Liam gasped. Saturday was only five days away. Suddenly, he felt his body quiver and his balance give way. He put his hands to the wall and dug his nails into the whitewashed stone. He was going to fall. He braced himself. His shirt sleeve caught on a small nail. He heard a rip, felt the ground slap his back and the wind leave his body.

He writhed silently among the nettles.

Waiting.

***

"What the feck was that?" Dan withdrew his pistol from the back of his trousers, his knuckles white around it.

Declan shrugged. "That crippled fecker didn't do his job properly. I saw a rat darting out from under the trough this morning. That's probably it."

"More like a sack of spuds hitting the ground." Dan swivelled his neck.

"I didn't hear anything." Martin ran his hand over his bald head. "If it wasn't rats, it might have been a cat or a dog."

"Check all round. I'll put a feckin' bullet in the guts of anyone we catch snooping." Dan pulled his trousers up with his spare hand. "And I'll kill any animal with my bare hands that sniffs around here looking for scraps." He cracked his knuckles.

Ger undid the latch and swung the forge doors open. He darted out, running around the side, circumnavigating the building. Then, with Dan watching him, he ran round again, looking out towards the hedgerows and trees. Martin skited off in the opposite direction.

Declan looked back and forth, then trailed after Ger.

With narrowed eyes and thin lips, Dan stood at the front entrance, still clutching the pistol, scanning the road in front of him.

***

Liam lay winded and stinging from head to toe. He could hear the men hunting for him. It wouldn't take long for them to find him lying there and, at the very least, beat the living daylights out of him. Or maybe they'd just shoot him?

He shook with fear.

He spied the water trough. It was longer than the height of him and surrounded by nettles and fern. Frantically, he rolled underneath and slid his body out of view, pulling nettles and bracken around him. Easing closely into the wall of the forge, he pulled the foliage up around himself, creating a dank, mossy cave.

Just in time.

Someone ran past the trough.

A large, uncomfortable stone lay under his back, and he put his hand underneath him to remove the sharp object. His hand felt something smooth and polished. His penknife! He slid it into his pocket. Now, he'd just have to wait it out, keep deathly quiet and pray that no-one would think to look under the trough.

He heard footsteps at the side of the forge, then talking, snippets of sentences, Dan berating Declan. The runner came past the trough again and feet stomped about through the wet grass before stopping.

He held his breath.

Someone must surely sense his heart pounding, his hands sweating, he thought. Unable to remember who the saint in charge of fugitives was, Liam sent a prayer to all the saints in Heaven to protect him. With his hands latched around his head in as tight a ball as possible, he waited to be dragged from his hideout.

Instead, he heard someone stop nearby, the rustle of clothing being adjusted, then a man relieving himself. A rivulet of warm urine wet his shoulder. Then, after what seemed like an eternity, the man left.

***

Dan scoured the countryside. Nothing. Just the sight of a woman pushing a pram, two children at her side.

Panting, Ger arrived back at the forge door, his chest heaving. "If someone was out there, then they got away pretty quick."

Declan sauntered round. "No-one to be seen. False alarm." He held his hands out. "I'll get the fire going inside. Get the work started." He disappeared into the forge.

From round the other corner, Martin arrived back, his chest heaving, his hands on his knees, struggling to catch his breath. "I didn't see anyone either."

Dan swayed from side to side, the rumble of a growl in his belly. He'd heard something. No doubt about it. Surely to God, some bugger wasn't on to him?

His pistol still in hand, he cursed as the woman with the creaking pram approached, two young children struggling to keep up in her wake. Ger and Martin stood outside, lighting up cigarettes. Dan wanted them gone. It might seem suspicious, the three of them together.

But it was too late; the woman had seen them.

***

Liam heard more footsteps followed by the scraping of wheels of some sort of cart approaching the forge. There was the sound of children whining and chattering and, from inside the forge, he could hear the banging of the anvil. He exhaled a sigh of relief. Surely, if they were getting on with their work, they'd decided not to look any further.

Then he heard Dan speaking gruffly to a woman, and she, with an equally gruff voice, spoke back at him.

***

"Mr O'Toole!"

Scowling, Dan secreted his pistol down the back of his trousers. "Mrs Hanna. What brings you out so early at the scrake of dawn?"

The woman sniffed, ignoring the question. "Could you weld the handle of me pram back into place?" She jiggled the offending part with one hand. A piercing cry issued from inside the carriage. "Be quiet now, Seamy and Siobhan." She pulled the hood back to reveal two podgy babies lying face to face, one's little hand on the other's nose. Beside her, two young girls were poking at each other.

Dan could feel the precarious positioning of the gun as it slid to the crease of his buttocks. He was about to tell the infernally annoying Mrs Hanna that he'd too much work to do to be working on her pram, but the bitch rattled on.

"My Seamus says you could fix this yoke in less than five minutes." The woman leaned over and, with a flat hand, swiped each of the children hard across their legs. The girls cried and pulled their mother's skirts for attention.

"Bridie says I'm a slather, Mammy!"

"I did not, Mammy!"

"I'll slather the both of you, if you don't shut up!" Straightening herself up, Mrs Hanna pointed a finger at Dan and waggled it. "My Seamus says this is the very type of job that a workman like you could do. Weld something back into place."

"Now, Mrs O'Toole –"

"So, you'll do it for me, won't you?"

The girls howled louder. The woman shook a fist at them. "Make any more noise and when I get you home your daddy will really give you something to cry about."

The girls sobbed quietly, their chests and shoulders heaving, the sniffles slowly subsiding.

Dan put his hand to his buttocks to stop the pistol from sliding further. "Jesus Christ," he muttered, barely able to contain his irritation.

"Jesus Christ what?" The woman scrunched up her face and leaned towards him.

Dan caught a whiff of stale onion on her breath.

"And why are you standing like that?" demanded the woman. "Is there something wrong with you?

"I'm grand, now." Dan scowled, easing the pistol up with the palm of his hand until it caught in his waistband. The insolence of the woman! Speaking to him like that! Only the fact that her father had been a senior member of the IRB subdued him somewhat.

"Well, can you mend the thing or not?"

"Not now, Mrs Hanna. I've too much work on."

The woman looked at the empty paddock and back to Dan. "Well, when do you think you might be able to fix it?"

Dan dug the nails of his hands into his fist. "Leave the contraption with me, and I'll have it ready tomorrow."

The woman perched a knuckle on each of her ample hips. "And what am I to do with the babies? Throw one over each shoulder and clatter on up the road with these two bawling beside me?" She glared in the direction of the girls, who were both still rubbing their legs.

Dan backed away. "If you just give me a minute…now… to tend to the fire, I'll see what I can do." He disappeared into the forge.

Smirking, Ger and Martin followed the blacksmith, closing the doors behind them. Inside, Declan stood banging a farthing on the stonework surface, flattening it with a mallet. Dan extracted the pistol from his trousers, stuffing it into a sack of coal propped in the corner. He squeezed his hands together, took a step towards his son and cuffed his ear.

Declan rubbed the side of his face. "What did I do?"

"What about the bloody fire?" Dan pointed at the ashes, grey and cold. "And furthermore, did you actually bother to look?" he snorted. "Think I didn't see you taking a piss out by the trough? Any fecker spying on us had ample opportunity to escape."

"That monster of a cat that belongs to the priest shot off when I ran round the corner," whined Declan. "But I checked all round just in case."

Ger scratched his backside. "That bloody cat. The 'oul priest dotes on it. Can't understand what anyone sees in a bloody cat," he grunted.

"Could be good target practice, though." Martin cocked his finger and made the sound of a gun firing.

Chapter Forty-Four

Mrs Hanna banged loudly on the forge door. "Dan O'Toole, will you come out and tell me if you're going to fix this yoke or not?"

Dan clenched his fists. "I'm just instructing the lads on the day's work, now, Mrs Hanna," he yelled back.

"Well, do you think I've all day to stand here?"

The forge door swung open. "I'll fix it for you, if you just give me a moment." Dan cursed inwardly, wiping a trickle of sweat from his forehead with the back of his hand. He wanted this blasted woman gone.

The babies in the pram started crying. Mrs Hanna leaned forward and jiggled the side of the pram, the two young girls hiding behind her skirts.

Dan caught a whiff of something acrid and unpleasant.

"Well, get a move on, won't you," muttered Mrs Hanna. "These babies need changing."

***

Liam heard banging on the door of the forge. The gruff-voiced woman had shouted for Dan O'Toole to come out and, now, some sort of argument was underway.

He clenched his teeth. He would go now. Rolling out from the confines of the trough, he used his elbows to shuffle to the back wall of the forge.

Once there, he pulled himself to standing, flattening himself against the cold stone. The smell of urine rising from the shoulder of his shirt sleeve forced him to turn his head the other way. Shaking, he took a deep breath and limped, as fast as he could, away from the forge, towards the trees.

After reaching the relative safety of the thicket, he looked behind to satisfy himself that he wasn't being followed. Thank God! His legs felt like jelly, and his heart as though it might burst out through his chest.

For the next ten minutes or so, he slunk through the forest before finally stopping to rest in a little clearing. He smelled awful. Arriving at the river's edge, he took off his shirt and washed it, glad for the coolness of the wet fabric against his skin when he redressed. Splashing water on his face did little to calm the intensity of the itching, however, for the nettles had been vicious.

The gravity of what he'd just heard was beginning to sink in. Dan's gang were planning to attack someone. A local Protestant, who was rich, and had buried money.

Dan was no more than a criminal. He'd happily attack and rob a rich man that he had a grudge against. Of one thing Liam was certain: he couldn't tell his parents. His father wasn't strong enough and it wasn't fair on his mother. She'd enough to worry about.

He lay back on the ground for a moment, allowing the rising sun to warm his body. It was up to him to stop Dan. And there was no way he'd go to the local RIC. For all he knew, they would call for those bastard Tans to help.

Besides, Sean Corvin was dead, and Liam didn't know the other men in the local barracks. There was only one other person he could trust, Sean's brother, Ruari. Even though Ruari had joined the RIC, he was a decent fellow. And he was big and strong.

Liam struggled to his feet and carried on walking along the water's edge, still thinking about Ruari. It was such a pity that he hadn't seen him in a very long time, for unlike his brother, he'd never been stationed in Lisowen. Ruari had gone to the big barracks in Kilkenny.

He had to find him. Ruari would know what to do and how to stop Dan with his cowardly plan.

Chapter Forty-Five

Dr Peter O'Neill ate the cold remains of his dinner for an early breakfast. Seated at his mahogany table, which had been handed down through generations of O'Neill's, he faced a picture of King George hanging beside the wall clock. He recalled, nine years ago, standing with his elderly father among the throngs of people, trying to get a glimpse of the Royals in their carriage as they paraded down Grafton Street. It had been a wonderful day. Now, the portrait of King George bore stains of mildew. Peter considered replacing it with something more current. Where would he go in Dublin to get a replacement? Surely, he wouldn't need to go to Belfast. Belfast was a horrid place; dark and dismal, with the shipyard looming over the city like a malevolent giant.

The dying embers from the previous night sparkled red from under the grey ash. The housekeeper wouldn't be in till midday. A wife would have made his breakfast. In some ways, he was sad that he'd never married. Now fifty-two, he'd lost the heart to go looking. At least, he reflected, he had no-one to nag him, annoy him, expect attention from him, or worse, look for money for frivolous things. *Ah well*, he thought, *I've more than enough to occupy me with my patients.*

These musings were cast aside when he considered the prospect of the next couple of hours. In his spare time, he loved to fish. Whether the day was cold or hot, it didn't matter. It was the lack of wind and the stillness of the water that he liked most, and often that time came just around dawn.

He stuffed a hard-boiled egg into one of his jacket pockets and a wadge of soda bread into the other. Pouring a glass of water, he gulped it down in one go, a slow trickle making its way down his unshaven chin. Gathering his fishing tackle, he left the house with his canvas bag slung over his shoulder and a spring in his step.

This was the time of year he most enjoyed. He strode out towards the river, the countryside shrouded in a semi-darkness, with only the hint of daylight to come. Tiny droplets of water from overhanging trees dripped onto his head, and the road squidged muddily beneath his feet.

Approaching the riverbank, he made out the ghost-like form of tall Father Flaherty, his fishing rod outstretched. He noted the priest's collarless shirt and tweed trousers. Divested of his clerical clothes, Eamonn Flaherty was like any other man out early to enjoy a morning's fishing. It struck Peter that he, too, without the uniform of his stethoscope and doctor's bag, was also such a man. The anonymity pleased him, for the reliance that patients placed on their doctor to heal them could sometimes feel overwhelming.

Peter held up his bag and tipped his flat cap. "Good day to you, Eamonn!"

"Fine day it's going to be, Peter," Eamonn replied.

This had become a common meeting place, not by design, but not against design either. A loose arrangement, a 'perhaps I'll see you here another time' sort of arrangement and the only time they shed formality to use each other's Christian names.

On the riverbank, beside the priest, a pathetic trout lay flapping, its iridescent scales glistening in the gathering light.

Peter pointed at the fish. "Dinner taken care of?"

"I'm looking forward to it already." Eamonn chuckled as he patted his belly.

The men took up different positions on the riverbank. There they stayed fishing in companionable silence, as the morning light chased away the last vestiges of darkness.

After a while, and without further success, Eamonn Flaherty suddenly cleared his throat and turned to the doctor. "I don't mind telling you, I'm worried about the current state of things."

Peter set down his fishing rod on the bank. "Me too. That young policeman shot going about his day's work. Dreadful business altogether."

"Dreadful indeed. A good young man from a good family." The priest set the trout he'd caught in the bottom of his cloth bag, then wiped his hands on his trousers. "But other people see things differently. I hear all sorts of disquiet when people leave after Mass."

"In particular?"

"The distress caused by the Black and Tans."

"I did hear something about that from some of my patients." Peter sank down to sit on the ground and rubbed his hands together.

"They've turned half of Lisowen upside down. Frightened innocent people." Father Flaherty withdrew his fishing line from the water and set it down on the grass. "They don't bother people in the bigger houses. Or those of their own religion."

Peter shook his head. "They're not supposed to be here to threaten those that have no part in the fighting."

Eamonn sat down beside him, his eyes fixed on the eddies in the centre of the river. "But I'm worried about where this all will end." He plucked at a few blades of grass, sifting them through his fingers.

They sat silently, the only noise that of the water burbling as it cascaded over roots and rocks. Peter O'Neill shifted uncomfortably from where he was sitting. He could feel the damp grass on the backside of his trousers. He thought of several words of placation, but discounted them all and remained quiet, until he said that he really should go.

"The first patient will be sitting outside my door in less than an hour," he explained.

As they were about to leave, Father Flaherty picked up a small stone and threw it out into the fast-flowing river. The ripples widened out, their circular pattern merging softly with the calmer water at the sides.

"No-one can rightly lay claim to this land. We're here together, enjoying the river. We can both see it and hear it, but we can't own it. Within minutes, the river will have changed and there'll be new water and different fish."

Peter slapped his hand on Eamonn's shoulder. "Now, there speaks the philosopher!" .

***

Liam, his heart still pounding from his escape, was picking his way along the muddy path by the riverbank when he saw the men.

His skin itched around his shirt collar and his face was on fire. Already, he was thinking of the explanation he'd need to give his mother. She would wonder how the nettles could have stung him all over and his clothes got so dirty. A partial truth would have to be told. He'd admit to losing the penknife while working at the forge. While trying to retrieve it, he'd fallen into a clump of nettles.

With the sun glinting through the trees, he could make out the silhouettes of two men, one taller than the other, standing together by the river. Then he heard the unmistakable bass tones of Father Flaherty, and both men came into view. The other man was Dr O'Neill, his hair unkempt, in need of a comb.

Damn, thought Liam, *I'm going to have to explain myself.*

"Liam!"

"Hello Doctor." Liam fixed his gaze on the ground.

"What brings you here, Liam, so early in the day?" Father Flaherty looked at him, moving his head side to side. "What happened to your face? It's the colour of a boiled ham."

"I took a tumble into nettles, Father."

"That's a nasty looking rash." The doctor took a few steps forward so that he was standing next to the priest. "Why don't you come by my surgery later on and I'll give you some calamine."

Liam looked up briefly. He could feel the doctor's eyes boring into him. "I can't, thank you, Doctor. I told my da I'd work in the fields today. But don't worry, me mam is good with remedies for rashes."

The priest leaned towards him, his piercing eyes fixing him with their intensity. "Were you fishing, Liam?" He looked this way and that as though expecting to see a rod or a fishing net.

"No," Liam answered. "I was out looking for my penknife, Father. I dropped it yesterday and had to retrace my steps." He pulled the penknife from out of his pocket and laid it on the flat of his hand. "But luckily I came upon it."

Father Flaherty moved closer, dropping his rod and bag to one side. Liam smelled the fish off him.

The priest looked down at the knife. "It's a fine knife, indeed. With an ivory handle, no less!"

Dr O'Neill agreed.

Liam felt hot and clammy. "I need to be getting home now." He slid the penknife back into his pocket.

"Of course." Father Flaherty smiled. "Tell your mammy I'll see you all at Mass on Sunday."

"Thank you, Father. Good-bye, Doctor O'Neill."

The doctor nodded. "Good-bye."

With a sigh of relief, Liam hobbled away.

Chapter Forty-Six

Declan had been looking for a suitably secluded spot to carry out some target practice.

He wondered what had come over his da, asking him to take the gun that day rather than work in the forge? Maybe it was that nonsense of him thinking someone had been snooping around.

"I want you to be able to hit bullseyes with this," his da had said, before handing him the pistol. "Don't come back until you're as good a shot as this man here," and he'd winked at Ger, slapping him on the back.

Well, his da would soon see how gruelling the day's work at the forge was when he'd have to do it alone.

Declan had never been entrusted with a weapon before. It was good to feel the coolness of the metal in his hand. His mind flickered over the conversation he'd heard that morning with Martin and Ger present. There'd be more reinforcements coming from Britain, and the IRA would be attacking the bastards with more than just guns. Dynamite. Feckin' hell! Then, there was that other man they'd be going after.

With an old tin can in one hand and his father's pistol in the other, he cast his gaze for somewhere to perch his target. He'd already tried, unsuccessfully, to shoot a blackbird out of the trees. This should be easier.

He took aim.

***

The priest and the doctor were heading home; the priest, the fitter of the two, leading the way. Suddenly a shot, followed by two more in quick succession, rang out from among the trees.

The men stopped, their eyes darting to look around them.

"That was close." Eamonn, his shoulders hunched, put his hands on his thighs.

"Someone shooting rabbits?"

"I hope you're right," replied Eamonn, with less certainty.

The leaves rustled and there was the snap of a twig underfoot. Tentatively, Peter pulled back the branches and peered through the gap. "There's nothing there." He laid his back on a large tree trunk, his breath coming in short pants. "I think we're just nervous, what with everything we've been talking about."

"Perhaps." Eamonn nodded. "And we all know how much everyone round here likes rabbit stew."

Peter bent down to lift an empty cigarette packet from the leaves at his feet. "Someone passed this way not long ago."

"Young Liam?"

"He wouldn't be a smoker, I don't think."

Eamonn shook his head. "I worry about that lad. I really do."

Peter scrunched up the packet and put it in his cloth bag. "But the boy has made a remarkable recovery, in spite of his injury."

Father Flaherty waved his hand. "It's nothing to do with his injury."

"What then?"

***

Declan had dropped to the ground when he saw the men approaching, shuffling his body between two thick clumps of fern. With his body flat on the forest floor, he made out two voices. Surely the Tans wouldn't be patrolling in the forest? Feck it. They were coming his way.

The words became louder. The men had stopped. One pulled back a branch not far from him. He held his breath. They were talking about rabbits. Rabbits, for God's sake! Then he recognised one of the voices. It was that of the priest, Father Flaherty. The other man had a more highfalutin tone. Was it the doctor? He could see their shoes, the smaller feet of the doctor and the long, black-laced shoes of the priest. He heard them talking about Liam. Liam, the cripple? Why would they be interested in anything to do with that cretin?

***

Eamonn Flaherty stared into the distance. "Liam has still to learn the real truth about his parents."

"About his adoption?"

"The boy doesn't know. Yet."

Peter unslung the bag of fishing tackle from his shoulder and set it down on the ground beside the priest's. "I thought the O'Dowds would have told him by now."

"No, not yet. I asked Mary recently." Eamonn looked up at the leaves of the overhanging trees. "I remember the whole affair as though it was yesterday. Mary asking me to baptise the baby and telling me about his parents, who'd both passed. Asking me to keep it to myself, protect the child from prejudice."

Peter cocked his head to one side. "Why would she ask that?"

"Liam's mother was Protestant."

Peter let out a sigh. "Ah now. For a Catholic family, that could be difficult, no doubt."

Eamonn straightened his collar and unrolled the sleeves of his shirt, fastening his cuffs. "Ah now, I really must be going." He hoisted his bag up unto his shoulder. "Please God, I'll be back in time to take Mass!"

The men hurried off, half walking, half running.

***

'Liam, the cripple!' Declan's scrunched his eyes together, hardly able to believe what he was hearing. That no-good cripple was an orphan. And not just an orphan. A feckin' Protestant too!

He waited a few minutes after the two men had left before rolling out from under his canopy of ferns. Elated, he set the tin can up on a branch. He cocked the weapon as his father had shown him, spat phlegm to one side and stepping ten paces back, held the pistol in front of him. Taking aim, he pulled the trigger. "Take that you feckin' bastard!"

But the gun was out of bullets. Searching in his pockets for more bullets, he realised that he'd used all he'd been given. *Feck that*, he thought, *I suppose it's time to be going.*

Whistling, he made his way back to the forge. *Tomorrow*, he thought, *I'll have a grand time telling that scrawny cripple who he really is!*

Chapter Forty-Seven

Liam returned from his ordeal to find his mam in the parlour scrubbing clothes. Kneeling over the tin bath, a washboard in hand, she rubbed at the collars of his father's shirts. The smell of carbolic soap caught the back of his throat. His mam looked up and drew her wrist across her forehead, her hands red and raw. "Where were you this morning?"

"At the forge."

She scowled. "And why would you be back at the forge?"

"I lost my penknife."

She dropped the soap in the water, splashing water on herself. "Your father's precious gift to you?"

"Don't worry, I found it."

"Thank God! Your da treasured that knife." His mam dried her hands on her apron, struggled up from her knees and hugged him.

Liam felt the damp heat of her chest. She released her grip and surveyed him, her eyes flickering up and down his body.

"What in God's name is that rash round your face and neck? And your hands too?" She sniffed. "And you smell dreadful."

Liam swallowed. "I had to get under the trough at the forge to look for the penknife. It was full of nettles."

"Did you rub it with docken?"

"I didn't see any docken leaves."

"Hmm. It'll have to be porridge then. I'll make it now and you can slap it on when it's cooled."

Liam knew that arguing would get him nowhere. His mother had a bee in her bonnet for certain remedies and he was just thankful that he wouldn't need to wrap a sock around his throat or rub his chest with bacon fat.

His father's heavy footsteps could be heard on the stairs. "What's all the talk about?" he called out.

Once down, Pat shuffled towards his seat, his chest heaving. He stopped to put his hand on Mary's shoulder and kiss her curls. Turning to Liam, he beckoned him to his side and slung his arm around his shoulder.

Liam stiffened. His da might look for more in-depth information than his mother had been happy with.

"What, I'm not allowed to hug my big son?" Pat frowned, a hurt look on his face.

Liam felt his father's hand on his back, pulling him close. Suddenly, he felt off-balance. Should he tell his parents about Dan and his gang? Was he right to keep this from them?

"What happened to your face?" Pat coughed several times into his hand. "Ah, gone are the days… when a father… could hug his son like a child." He continued to cough, alternately thumping his chest and rubbing it.

"Liam's been stung by nettles. But it's nothing that cold porridge won't soothe." His mam put her hand on his da's back, steering him into his rocking chair. "I think you should rest. Close your eyes and take a little nap. I don't like the sound of all that coughing."

His da sighed. "You worry too much, my dear."

Liam, thankful that he'd kept to his resolve, left his mam fussing over his da and said he needed a rest. He'd come down later for the porridge treatment.

Once upstairs and sitting on his bed, Liam thought again about getting to Ruari. He'd have to take the bus to Kilkenny. Then, he remembered he'd given his mam his three thrupenny bits towards his new boots. He'd no money now.

Maybe, tomorrow, he could go and see William Leavy. Surely, if he worked hard, Mr Leavy might give him enough to pay for a bus ticket.

He pulled his boots off and stared briefly at his misshapen foot. How would things have been if he'd never been injured? He couldn't hope to know. But of one thing he was sure; he was alive while Sean Corvin was dead. His mind turned to what he'd heard at the forge. Could Dan have shot Sean? Or was it Ger or Martin who had done it?

Liam lay back on the bed and closed his eyes. And who was Dan after now? Who was the Protestant, who was rich and had money to bury? He didn't know many rich people, only those who owned motor cars: the judge, the doctor, the pawnbroker, and the man who owned the quarry. It could be any, or none, of them.

Liam felt exhausted. Sleep came quickly, taking him away from his turmoil to a faraway land of peace and tranquillity.

Chapter Forty-Eight

The following day, Declan woke with a start. Had he been dreaming? Then, he began to remember where he'd been and what he'd heard the day before. That cripple isn't who he thinks he is. Leaving his little brother sleeping, his thumb still trailing from his mouth, Declan dressed himself hurriedly. He was glad that Phelim was away to Dublin, for the size and smell of him had been hard to take. Two to a small bed was much easier. The girls were already up and away, leaving their bed a mess of sheets and pillows and blankets.

Downstairs, his mother was in the kitchen cleaning out the fire, setting the rolled-up paper in the hearth for the new day. She looked at him briefly, her face set in its usual wearied expression, her long dark hair loose about her face.

"You're up early."

"I've something to do before work." He smelled the baby's sour milk off of her. "Somebody I need to see."

The baby lay asleep in the cot, arms outstretched, palms upwards. From outside, Declan could hear the chatter of his sisters on their way out to fetch water from the well. Ignoring his mother, as she did him, he went to the press and brought in a bottle of milk with a loaf of brown bread.

He held the bottle to his mouth and gulped the milk down noisily. Tearing a chunk of bread off with his teeth, he chewed it; his mouth wide open.

"Your father will be wanting bread and milk," his mother said, without looking round. "Don't make him cross."

"I've left him some." Declan put the half-drunk bottle of milk and the tooth-marked loaf he'd been eating on the table.

Dan lumbered down the stairs half-dressed. A faint guttural growl heralded from his throat. "Were you eating my breakfast, boy?" He pointed to the remainder of the loaf. "Is that all you've left for me?" Dan took Declan by the ear, fixing him with a stare. "Don't you know that your father comes first in this household!" Then letting go of him, he went to his wife, taking her waist in one arm and kissing her neck.

She stood motionless.

"You smell so good," he mumbled.

Declan lifted his boots from where he'd kicked them off at the hearth and thrust his feet into them. "I'll be up at the forge, shortly!"

His father didn't look up, as he stroked his mother's arms. "You'd better be, lad."

As Declan laced his boots, he saw his father whisper something in his mother's ear.

Unlatching the door, with his jacket in hand, Declan looked round. His parents were climbing the stairs, his father at the rear.

***

It was a clammy day, with the gathering clouds promising a downpour later on. Declan whistled as he cycled towards the O'Dowds'. With luck, the cripple would be outside feeding the chickens. He'd often seen him at this time, from afar, as he rode past on his way to the forge.

Rounding the tall, brick walls of the monastery, the O'Dowds' small farmhouse came into sight. He got off his bike, pushed it to the side and peered into the distance. Suddenly, he spied Liam. With a bucket in one hand, limping down the lane, Liam came into view. That lollop, that cretinous roll. Declan shook his head. What a useless fit-for-nothing piece of shite. He cleared his mouth of phlegm.

Leaving the bicycle supported by the hedge, he sauntered towards Liam calling out, "Hey, cripple! I've something to tell you."

"There's nothing you could tell me that I want to hear." Liam made to walk round him.

"Oh, but there's something I think you really should hear." Declan caught hold of Liam's sleeve.

Liam struggled to free himself. "Get off me, you fecker."

Declan held tight. "Now, that's not a nice thing to call me when I'm just trying to pass on some helpful information."

Several boys came round the corner, laughing as they made their way down the road. A stout lad carried a football. Declan let his grasp weaken.

"Liam!" the stout lad called out. "Is that ejit annoying you?"

Liam waved. "He's just going." He scowled at Declan, then turned to his friends. "He has to be up at the forge to start work or his da'll give him a hiding."

The boys laughed, then carried on up the road, calling out to Liam to join them later in the top field.

"We need you for goals!" the stout lad shouted.

Once again, Liam attempted to pass Declan, but Declan barred his way.

Liam set the bucket on the ground. "Tell me whatever it is and then push off."

Declan put his hands in his pockets and jutted his head forward. "It's a pity your mammy and daddy didn't have the guts to tell you," he sneered.

Liam felt anger rising up from his stomach. "Leave my parents out of this!"

Declan was so close that Liam could smell the sourness of his breath.

"The problem is that they aren't your parents." Declan straightened up and shook his head. "Your so-called parents should have told you long ago; that you never belonged to them!" He looked at Liam, a cruel twist to his mouth. "You're an orphan!"

A few drops of rain began wetting the ground in front of them. From far away there was a faint roll of thunder.

"Shut up." Liam clenched his fists so tightly that he could feel his nails piercing his flesh. "That's just rubbish!"

"Ask your mammy!" Declan pointed his finger at him. "Who isn't your real mammy at all," he chuckled. "I'm telling you, cripple, when you go up home, you'll find out that I'm right." He threw his head back and laughed. "I heard the priest talking about you. And do you know what's even worse?" He shook his head. "You're a feckin' Protestant!" Then, whistling tunelessly, Declan sauntered slowly towards his bicycle.

"Fuck away off!" Liam shouted after him, rage coursing through his body. He thought the bullying days were long gone. But why would Declan take the time to come over and tell him such a story?

His mam would soon put him right.

***

Gathering up the bucket containing grain, Liam stumbled to the chicken coup and tipped the grain out in one go. The hungry chickens trampled over one another to get to the food. The rain was beginning to take hold and he limped hurriedly towards the front door. Trembling, he opened it to find his mother stirring a pot hanging over the fire. As the smell leaped out to greet him, his stomach turned.

"Where's Da?"

"He's having a lie-in this morning." His mother grinned, waving a spoon at him. "I'm making your favourite stew for tonight." She lowered the spoon into the pot, extracting a small amount of liquid that she blew on. With one hand cupped under the spoon, she offered it to him. "Try it."

He shook his head. "No thanks."

"What's wrong?" She sipped from the spoon and laid it on the table. "You love stew." She went to put her hand on his forehead. "Are you coming down with something?"

He brushed her off. "I'm fine, but I'm not hungry."

The fire shot a burning splinter of coal onto the floor. She jumped and hurried to get a brush and shovel. She brushed up the smoking nugget, tossing it back on the fire.

"What's bothering you?" She hung the shovel on the hook of the companion set. "You're always hungry."

"Not today."

"And why would that be?"

"I just need," he swallowed hard, "to know that I'm your son."

Mary took his shoulders in her hands. "Has someone been saying something to you?"

He looked her straight in the eyes. "Am I? Am I your son?"

***

"Oh, Liam." Mary felt as though someone had punched her in the stomach. The pain so strong. She put her hands to her belly. "You are very much my son."

He shook his head. "Am I? I think you're lying." He turned to her, his lips closed tight, his face ashen.

She took a deep breath. "Oh, Liam!" She tried to hug him, but he turned his back on her.

"You're not my real mother, are you?" He stood peering out of the window, staring at the stone-ringed fields, the sheep huddles, the green canopies of the sycamores.

"It's not as you think," she whispered.

He banged his fist against the wall. "And Da isn't my real da either," he sobbed. "I so hoped it wasn't true. I so hoped that Declan O'Toole was lying!"

Mary tried once again to put her arms around him, but he flung them off. She fell backwards, managing to steady herself with the arm of the rocking chair.

"Liam, please!" She went to touch his back, but he shifted away.

"Don't come near me!" He turned towards her, his eyes red-rimmed, his arm outstretched, the palm of his hand keeping her at arm's length.

Oh, why hadn't she told him long ago? She felt afraid. What was he going to do? Tears rolled down her face, dripping onto the front of her apron. She put the back of her hand up to wipe them away. "I'm sorry. I'm so sorry, Liam."

He stood looking out the window, facing away from her. "You'd better tell me how you came by me and... and I want the truth!"

He spat the words out so slowly and with such venom that Mary felt as though he were striking her with a stick.

"I am your mammy, Liam." She wiped drips from her nose with her fingers. "I'll always be your mammy." She walked to him, her arms outstretched, tears cascading down her cheeks. "Your father and I have always loved you, as though you were our own." Her whole body shook. "Sit down and, and I'll make tea."

"Tea?" he laughed harshly. "Tea?" He turned round to face her. "Tell me now!"

She pressed her palms together as though in prayer. "Please." She pointed to Pat's room. "Don't wake him. Yet."

Outside, the rain poured down. It thumped hard on the roof and battered the windows of the house.

Liam sat down at the table, his arms crossed, his face like stone. She sat facing him. She rubbed the sides of her face and, with a quiver in her voice, she began.

"Long before your da and I got married, your da was coming up from Cork to visit his uncle, Father Oisin, at the monastery. I had an old aunt, Aunt Brid, who helped with the cooking there, and that's how we met; when I was visiting her. We got on so well, Pat and I." She put her hand to her wedding band and twisted it round.

"Da came up to Lisowen every few weeks, even when his uncle passed, making an excuse that he was helping the monks with little jobs." She clasped her hands together. "And then, he proposed."

Liam tapped the table with his fingers. "And?"

"Well, even after we married, your da still had to work in Cork, for times were hard. I stayed here with my mother, who wasn't well."

"That year, your da was working with his cousin, Canus, at the big house in Cork. Canus had a sweetheart, Ann. A beautiful little thing, Pat told me, blonde with blue eyes. She was a kitchen maid." Mary took her handkerchief from her sleeve and rubbed her nose.

"They loved each other and wanted to marry. But there was a problem. They were of different religions and both their families were dead set against it."

Liam glared at her. "And what has this got to do with me?"

"Everything Liam. Everything."

"They couldn't bear to be apart." Mary lowered her voice. "They ran away to Dublin and then Ann got pregnant, and they had you."

Liam held his head in his hands. "Uncle Canus was my father?"

"Yes, Liam." She looked at him as he slowly raised his head, a look of horror and disbelief written all over his face. "I'm afraid Canus got ill with consumption and Ann couldn't cope. Your da went to see them and came back to tell me the state they were living in. The house was stone-cold, and there was barely enough food to feed them. Pat wanted to bring you all back to live with us here in Lisowen. That was the plan, but a few days later Canus took a turn for the worse and died."

"And my mother?"

"When Canus died, the neighbours said they'd never heard such wailing and grieving. One of them offered to mind you while Ann went out for fresh air. She went down to the docks and when she came to the side of the Liffey…" Mary got up from the table and reached for her rosary beads from the mantlepiece. "…she slipped."

"She drowned?"

"Her mind wasn't right. She wasn't herself."

Liam hunched his shoulders and stared at the floor.

"Oh, Liam. You were only a tiny baby." Mary sucked hard on her cheeks. "And I'd had so many babies die before they were born." The words spluttered out like water from a boiling kettle. "Your da and I went to Dublin and brought you back with us. When we saw you, our hearts melted." She ran her fingers over her rosary beads, the familiar soothing feel on her fingers. "We decided to bring you up as our son." She started to sob; her head bowed.

"And how much longer were you going to keep this from me?"

"The time was never right!" Mary got up from her chair and walked to the sideboard, running a cloth along the surface. "When you had your accident, we thought it better not to upset you. Then, when your daddy got ill and Fionuala died…it wasn't right either."

"So instead I had to hear it from Declan OToole?" Liam balled his fingers into his hands. "Was that better?" He reached for his coat. "I need to go out."

"But it's lashing with rain!"

The door swung shut, leaving Mary alone, wishing she could turn the clock back, fearing things would never be the same again.

Chapter Forty-Nine

Mary felt an ache in her chest, like the pain when she lost little Fionuala. How was she to tell Pat? He'd be distraught too. Had they lost Liam? Was he so badly hurt that he'd never trust them again? It was the look in his eyes that had frightened her. His expression so cold and hating.

She hurried upstairs to their bedroom and blurted everything out to Pat, sobbing every now and then into her embroidered handkerchief.

When she finished, Pat collapsed back unto the pillow. He stared up at the ceiling. "Well, he had to find out at some stage. We both knew that." He lifted the counterpane and swung his bare feet to the ground.

Mary dabbed her eyes and rubbed her nose. "But will he forgive us?"

Pat took her hands in his and held them tight. "He'll need time to settle his mind."

"But he's so dreadfully hurt."

I know." Pat got up and paced about the bedroom floor, his breathing laboured. "But he needs time to take this all in. He needs time to think."

Mary left Pat to get dressed. She wasn't so sure. Time might set Liam's mind even more against them. She futtered about the parlour, setting a bowl of stew out for Pat. Then she set one out for herself but, after taking a sup, couldn't stomach more. She got up and dusted the Sacred Heart and other ornaments on the mantlepiece.

Eventually, Pat came downstairs and ate his stew, gazing every so often into the flames of the fire. "We need to bide our time and leave well alone."

She gave him an anguished look. "How do I do that?" She poured herself a glass of water and slowly sipped at it. "What I need now is a walk."

"In the pouring rain?"

"I'll go up to Sara's. Do you mind?"

"If it helps you, then go."

Mary hugged him in his seat and felt the frailty of his body; the bones of his ribs against her.

Pat looked out towards the window, the pitter patter of rain on the glass. "The rain's going over a little. By the time you get back, chances are Liam'll be home and in a better frame of mind."

***

When she got to the Leavy house, Mary's stockinged feet and boots were soaking.

Sara opened the door and let out a small exclamation. "What brings you here?"

Richard ran towards her calling: "Auntie Mary," and throwing his little arms around her wet skirt. She patted his head then squeezed her eyes tight before blurting out, "Liam's found out, Sara. He knows."

Sara dropped the scrunched-up newspaper she'd been using to clean the inside of the windows. "And it wasn't you or Pat that told him?"

Mary shook her head.

Sara took Richard up in her arms. "I'll get this young man occupied, then put the kettle on. William's away to the post office, for I'm expecting a parcel from relatives in England."

***

Mary lifted the scalding tea to her lips and took a tiny sip. "Declan O'Toole overheard the priest talking about Liam and his real parents. And then Declan told Liam."

Sara poured herself a cup and held it between her hands. She shook her head. "The dirty little scoundrel."

"He is that." Mary leaned forward. "And then I had to tell Liam everything. It broke my heart to tell him how his mother died, God rest her soul." She crossed herself.

"But you knew it would have to come out eventually."

"We should have told him long ago." Mary poured a little more milk into her tea. "I know that now."

The women supped their tea in silence. Upstairs, they could hear Richard talking, making conversation with imaginary friends.

Sara drained her cup and brought it over to the worktop. "You need to give Liam time to come to terms with things."

"Pat said that."

"Well, he's right."

The sound of footsteps at the door made both women turn around.

The door swung open. William walked in, shaking the rain off his coat and hat. He smiled when he saw Mary. "Good morning, Mary. How are you?"

Mary nodded, "Well, thank you, William," her manners overriding her true feelings. "I just stopped by for a short while, but it's time for me to be going." She reached for her handbag.

"And Liam? I thought he was coming over to see me. Arrange some lessons. Why don't you tell him I'd be free to see him tomorrow morning.?" William set the canvas bag he was holding on the floor.

Mary feigned a smile. "I will, of course."

Sara lifted the bag. "Did you pick up the parcel for me at the post office?"

"I did, it's in the bag."

Sara opened the flap of the bag and took out a brown paper parcel, which she set on the table. "What else have you in here, my love? Bricks?" She put her hand in and took out a large hardbacked book.

William coughed. "I borrowed it from the rector."

Sara scanned the title: "Unionism in Ireland."

Chapter Fifty

Liam stumbled aimlessly down the road. How could his so-called parents have hidden the truth from him all this time? He rubbed his pounding forehead between his thumb and forefinger. Now everything about him was nothing more than a lie.

The rain came down in sheets and soon his clothes were soaked. He made his way off the road and into a deserted hovel, where he sheltered under its leaky roof. From the ground, he picked up a discarded cigarette pack. Opening the box, he pulled out a half-broken cigarette and ran it under his nose. It smelled of the forge.

It made him think of Declan and the cruelness of his most recent taunt. How could this be happening to him? Was his injury and his sister dying not enough pain? He opened his mouth and screamed, beating the wall of the hovel with his fists until he could feel blood trickling across his knuckles. Until he'd no more breath or strength. Sinking to the ground, he held his head in his hands.

Eventually, when the rain eased, he struggled up and headed out onto the main road. From there, he took the road past the recently abandoned police barracks. Without stopping, he put his head down and dragged himself on up the hill. Where he was going, he didn't know. He'd walk on and maybe rest a while behind the farmer's barn that loomed large on the horizon.

As Liam approached the barn, one side of the main door swung open. An old scarecrow-type man – his clothes patched and faded – was dipping his tin mug into the water barrel and supping from its edge.

The man called out to him. "Is it Mary O'Dowd's son?"

"Old John?"

"Ay, tis me." Old John set his mug down and held his hands out from his sides. "Did you not recognise me from my deportment?"

Liam exhaled. "I wasn't sure."

He'd only seen Old John a couple of times. From what his mother had said, Old John was odd but good natured. She'd sympathy for his hard way of life and the fact that he was always on his own.

"For the love of all the saints, what are you doing out in the elements?" Old John held his hands out to the rain.

"I needed a walk."

"And why would a lad like you need a walk?"

"I just did."

Old John beckoned him inside. "Well, come inside the barn and take shelter."

Liam stood his ground. "No thanks. I'll be on my way."

"Well, wait a while till the precipitation is over. "Old John brushed the hay from his clothes and raked away the few strands that had got caught in his hair. "You'll catch your death in elements like these."

"I'll be getting along, thanks."

"Well, I'm not a man to do a dacent cratur harm, now." Old John moved inside the barn door and took a couple of steps back. "Please... come in from the rain. It would be good to share a word or two, for a person like me can be lonesome at times."

Liam thought about home. So what if he stayed away for a while? Besides, home didn't seem like home anymore. He hesitated, then said, "Thank you," and walked into the barn, leaving a couple of yards of space between himself and Old John.

Old John gestured for him to sit.

Liam hunkered down against the half-closed barn door, resting his back against it. The wood felt scratchy but warm. Despite the distance between them, Liam could smell tobacco and sweat from the old man.

"Well, tell me and the sheep out there," Old John spread his arms wide, his ragged and battered coat stretching at the seams, "what's ailing you, young man."

"It's nothing."

"Nothing is it? To be out in the rain and drenched through in order for a walk, is it?" Old John scratched his head. "Ah, you must think I'm away with the fairies."

"It's my own concern."

"Well, I'll bid you good day then, if you won't talk to me. I'm rightly put out, for who would I tell if you were to say anything? I haven't a soul in the world to call my own."

Liam felt a lump form in the back of his throat. "I don't have either."

"Well, that's a nonsensical answer, if ever I heard it. What about your good parents?"

"They're not my parents," Liam whispered. He jabbed his fingers into the ground beside him, feeling fragments of hay catching in his fingernails. "I'm an orphan."

"Is that so?" Taking a pipe from his pocket, Old John pushed tobacco into it with his thumb.

"I'm angry because I didn't hear the truth in the right way."

Old John took matches from his pocket and lit the pipe, puffing several times to make sure that the tobacco had caught. "Oh, you are, are you? Well, if it's the truth you've heard, what's right or wrong about it?"

Liam could hear Old John's breathing, deep and regular, and see the old man's wrinkled face in the glow of the pipe embers. He thought to himself that Old John might be of an age when death could be a strong possibility.

Old John leaned forward, his pipe clutched in one hand. "Would you like to hear of my upbringing, for it might help you see things in a different way."

"I don't see how," Liam shrugged. "But if you wish."

Old John gave a little cough, then breathed out several puffs from his pipe. "My life..." he looked upwards as though composing his thoughts. "I was born in the workhouse. My dear mother, bless her soul, I recall her face but little. Her skin was smooth and her breath was sweet, that I do remember. The pleasure of knowing my father, that I never had. He was a jobber, I believe, moving from town to town to find work."

Old John sucked on his pipe. Liam rubbed his legs and shifted from side to side. The floor of the barn was unwelcomely hard and Old John seemed in no rush to tell his story.

"My dear mother died young; the flame of life snuffed out by the machinations of a Dublin laundry." Old John took another puff. "Aunt Rose was my saviour, and I was no more than a whippet when she offered me solace. But she was prone to the melancholia." He scratched himself, first under one armpit then the other. The pipe jiggled from between his lips. "On her good days, though, she taught me how to sew."

Liam had never heard of a man who could sew before. He briefly wondered about the garments Old John might have made.

"But Aunt Rose's husband was cruel. He enjoyed the exercising of his jaw most every day, along with the twack of a strap." Old John scratched the back of his head, brushing away some strands of straw. "Ah now, but the Lord took him with a dose of the typhus."

He took several more puffs. The rhythm of this and the calm way in which he talked was a salve to Liam's troubled mind. Old John was most certainly a strange man, but gentle with it.

"When I was twelve or so, I obtained employment at the tanner's yard. That smell, I swear, will inhabit and obstruct my nostrils to my dying day."

"But you sell things now?"

Old John chuckled. "Indeed, I do, for when the tanner's yard closed, Aunt Rose suggested I try my hand at peddling wares. Twas she called me Old John, professing me to be old before my time. Declaring my vocabulary to be most well developed for my young years." Old John tapped the remains of his pipe on the stone floor. "I'm awaiting now to hear the vagaries of your childhood."

Liam rubbed his eyes. "Another time perhaps, thank you." He shifted from where he was sitting, pins and needles shooting through his legs. He shook them, stood up and hobbled towards the door.

Old John got up too. "Very well, then." He groaned as he straightened his back. "But I tell you, young man, that no-one else knows my story and the telling of it to you has been of benefit to me." He called after Liam, "I advise you to go converse with someone. For I believe it will help."

Chapter Fifty-One

The cool air and soft haze of incense hit Liam as soon he walked into the chapel. At the back of the church, he glimpsed Father O'Flaherty hovering around the altar. Greatly relieved to see the priest, he hobbled up the aisle, stopping briefly to genuflect and make the sign of the cross.

Two women were dusting the pews. He recognised one as the postmistress and the other as Mrs Hanna, the butcher's wife. They turned at the sound of his boots scraping along the wooden floor.

"Liam," Mrs Hanna called out, beckoning him to come to her. "What brings you here in this awful weather." She looked him over from head to toe "Why you're sodden. Is it just to be out of the rain?"

"Hello, Mrs Hanna." He could see his wet footprints on the floor when he looked down. "I'm here to see Father Flaherty."

When he continued walking up the aisle, she scurried after him. "Something urgent you're needing to speak to the priest about. Your poor father, is it?"

Liam turned round. "No...no. He's well enough, thank you."

The woman stood facing him, peering at him from under hooded lids. She smelled of polish. "It must be awful for you and your mother now." She looked down at his bad foot. "What with your..." She flicked her duster at the seat of the wooden pew, "and your daddy not well and your little baby sister passing." A small, sly smile played across her lips, eerie in the flickering light of the candle-lit chapel. "It can't be easy for your family."

The postmistress joined them, nodding in agreement.

Liam felt heat rising from the base of his neck. Busybodies, the pair of them.

Liam!" Father Flaherty swept down the aisle, his cassock swishing on the ground, throwing up specks of dust. "Why don't you come through to my office?" The priest took him by the arm and led him swiftly away from the women. He leaned towards him whispering, "I'm presuming you didn't risk a soaking just to come here and pray?"

"No, Father, I came to see you." Liam could hear the two women talking about him in hushed tones. He desperately tried to close his ears. "Long ago, you told me that your door was always open."

"Of course, Liam. I'm glad you feel able to talk to me." Father Flaherty opened the door to the church office and ushered him inside. "Please, sit down." He gestured to a mahogany chair with a brown, studded-leather seat.

Liam slid onto the chair, grateful for the heat off the fire, stacked high with turf.

Father Flaherty sat down facing him. "So, what's troubling you?" A large black cat leapt up from the floor and onto the priest's lap. He stroked it with his long fingers.

"I know that I'm adopted," said Liam.

The priest set the cat down and rubbed cat fur off his hands. A small plume of black fluff rose into the air. "Your parents told you?

"No." Liam ran his hand over the wooden arm of his chair. "Declan O'Toole heard you talking about me to the doctor." He dug a fingernail into the wood, gouging out a tiny indentation.

The priest put his fingers to his lips. "Oh Liam, I'm so very sorry."

The cat meowed, rubbing its body on Liam's legs, then scratching its paws on the rosewood floor.

"Doesn't matter now." Liam hung his head, his gaze fixed downwards. "I had to find out some day..." he hesitated, "but I came to ask you something else."

There was a knock at the door. "Father!" a woman's voice called. "Would yourself and Liam like some refreshments?"

"No thanks, Mrs Hanna. Not now," Father Flaherty replied. When the footsteps had retreated, he turned his attention back to Liam. "What did you want to ask?"

Liam shifted on his seat. "I know that my real mother was a Protestant, so what does that make me? What am I?"

Father Flaherty eased a finger around the inside of his dog collar. "First of all, Mary and Pat have raised you as their son, and have been the most attentive of parents to you. Secondly, you are a Catholic. I can assure you of that."

"But is that true, Father?" Liam shrugged his shoulders. "Considering that I was deceived for all these years."

Father Flaherty got up and opened a drawer in the mahogany writing desk. "I want to show you something." With both hands, he removed a large leather-bound book and laid it on the desktop. As he turned the pages some newspaper cuttings and photographs became dislodged.

"This is what I'm looking for." The priest held both sides of the book apart, his fingers splayed. "Christenings: July 1906." Slipping a photograph out of its attachment corners, he handed it to Liam.

The photograph showed several couples holding babies, while a young Father Flaherty, with a full head of hair, stood to the side. Liam recognised Mary, wearing a white dress embroidered with flowers, her hair plaited and swirled around her head. Beside her stood Pat, neat in a three-piece suit and felt hat, his arm around his wife's waist.

Liam stared at the photo. He couldn't quite make out his parents' expressions, but he thought that they had smiles on their faces. The other parents stared straight at the photographer; their faces contrastingly serious.

The priest sat back down, one hand stroking the cat that weaved around his legs. It purred loudly. "I recall thinking, all those years ago, that yourself, Pat and Mary would make such a happy family."

Liam hung his head, unsure of what to say. He knew that Father Flaherty was a good person and would tell him the truth. His head swam with competing thoughts. He'd been lied to all these years, but by the very people who seemed to really care for him.

The room was warm, sunlight blazing through the windows. Liam could feel sweat trickling between his shirt and his skin.

Father Flaherty leaned towards Liam, his long hands on his knees. "I will never forget the conversation I had with your mother at your baptism. How glad she was to have you. But I recall that she was sad too, for the circumstances around your real parents' passing." He closed the book and held it tightly in both hands. "I know we can find it hard to sort through these different feelings. But your parents did what they felt was right, and I respect them for that."

"But they didn't tell me the truth, Father."

"I know you're angry, Liam, but remember they took you in at a time when the only other option was to go to an orphanage. Life there would have been very different for you."

Liam swallowed hard, his voice breaking. "But they could have told me long ago."

"I'm sure they were intending to. Often adults find these situations difficult. What they did do, was with the best of intentions. They brought you up as their son and they brought you diligently here to this church, of which you are a full member."

From outside the door, Liam could hear a metal bucket clanging, then whispering.

He shifted in his seat. "I'll go now." He set the photograph on the desk and limped to the door.

"Wait." Father Flaherty opened a drawer, withdrew an old envelope and slid the photograph into it. He held it out. "I'd like you to have this."

Liam took the envelope. "Thank you, Father." He left the room, brushing past the postmistress with her mop and Mrs Hanna with her duster. The cat shot out after him. "Goodbye Mrs Hanna. Goodbye Mrs..." he muttered.

They looked at him strangely as he walked away from them, the sound of his boots clacking unevenly echoing through the church.

Pushing open the solid door at the front of the chapel, he walked outside into the glare of the sun. Holding the envelope firmly in one hand, he headed off in the direction of his home.

***

Mary opened the door. "Liam... Thank God, you're back! I was worried sick about you." Instinctively, she reached forward to hug him, then held back. She scanned his face. "Please forgive us."

He looked at her, this strange person. She suddenly appeared smaller, a shadow of her former self.

"Can I heat you some milk?" she asked.

"If you wish," he mumbled.

"I'll do that then," she said and went outside to the press.

He was glad she hadn't hugged him or asked about the envelope which he had set on the stool. He opened a couple of buttons of his shirt and slid the envelope inside. He'd secrete the picture away in his room when he got the chance.

He sank into Pat's rocking chair, his mind working slowly over what the priest had said. These people had been good to him.

He watched as Mary hung the pan of milk over the fire, her red curly hair falling round her face. Earlier that day, she'd been crying and he hadn't cared. She'd deceived him all these years and she deserved to be punished. But the anger had left him now, replaced with something sad and empty.

He drank his hot milk and ate warm, buttered soda bread. "Where's Da?" The last word caught in the back of his throat.

Mary set the milk pan back on the fire "He's resting upstairs. I'll go up and let him know you're back." Mary flapped around him, cleaning crumbs off the table. "I think he's got a bit of a chill."

Liam felt suddenly alarmed. The thought that his da might take a turn for the worse was too much to bear. He saw his mother catch the look on his face.

"Don't worry, we've all had a lot to deal with today." She moved close to him and he could smell mutton stew on her. "Liam…"

"Yes?"

"Nothing." She blinked.

He could see teardrops glistening on her eyelashes. He placed his empty glass and plate beside the enamel basin and went upstairs. Creaking the door open to his father's room, he called out, his voice low and taut. "Are you not well, Da?"

"I've been better, it's true to say." Da gave a little cough. "We are so sorry, so very sorry you had to hear the way you did."

Liam walked over to the bed. "Why didn't you tell me?"

"We wanted to, but… we just couldn't." Da looked away from him, his eyes fixed on the window. "We should have, I know."

"I wish you had."

"I wish so too."

"You're not sick again, are you?"

"No. I'm not sick. I'm annoyed with myself, that's all." Da propped himself up on his elbows, then gestured for Liam to sit beside him. "Even if you think we're not your parents, we have always felt that you belong to us. Do you understand?"

Liam nodded. "I sort of do."

Da shifted, struggling to make himself more comfortable.

Liam took his father's arm, leaned him forward and beat the bolster into shape. "Just rest, Da. Mam and I need you fit and well."

Da pulled Liam to him and patted his back. "Thank you, son," he whispered.

When he came down to the parlour, Liam looked at his mam: her plump body, her curly red hair. It was going to take some time before he could put his trust in her again. Somehow, it was easier with his da.

She smiled at him. "How was he?"

"I think he's just tired."

She nodded, then taking hold of a pair of bellows, attempted to bring life back to the fire. The black coals glowed red, tiny licks of flames bursting forth.

As Liam watched the fire take hold, other thoughts flooded into his mind. "I'll go see Mr Leavy tomorrow about the schoolwork and the jobs he has lined up."

His mam looked round, smiling. "He's expecting you to call, so that will be just grand."

The flames subsided and his mam started to pump the bellows once more, the gentle whoosh sound filling the space of the room.

The events at the forge swam in front of his mind's eye. Those horrible men laughing about him. Then Dan O'Toole telling his cronies that they would target a Protestant. Somehow, O'Toole had to be stopped.

Mary smoothed the curls back from her face. "I'll try not to be bothering you. Give you time to settle yourself." She rested the bellows against the hearth. "I know you've a lot on your mind."

Liam gave her the hint of a smile. If only she only knew.

Chapter Fifty-Two

Liam stood fidgeting in Mr Leavy's parlour. He'd been in this room many times, but always with his mother. Now, he was here on his own and he felt nervous. Mr Leavy was a headmaster and he might get cross if Liam couldn't answer his questions. And there were other thoughts whirling round in his mind: Declan, Old John, Father Flaherty, Dan. Not to mention everything about who he really was. He'd woken up that morning resolving to forgive his parents. It would be hard, he knew that, but he'd try.

Mr Leavy came back into the parlour from the dining room, the wire of his spectacles dangling from one hand. "Come through, Liam, and we can make a start on some lessons. We'll have peace this morning, for the family's away doing messages."

'Thank you, Mr Leavy."

"Just schoolwork today, for there'll be other days when you can help me."

"Of course." Liam took his hands from his pockets and straightened up. That was a pity, for he'd been hoping to help with some proper jobs today. "Whatever you think best."

"So, what subjects need brushing up?"

"Probably everything."

Mr Leavy looked bemused. "Well, maybe we could make a start with some maths." He went to the bookshelves behind the table and extracted a jotter and a pencil, setting them on the table.

Liam looked around the room. Above the fireplace hung a picture of a youthful, bearded man in a military uniform." As he glanced at the portrait, he was aware of Mr Leavy looking at it too.

"A great man, King George." Mr Leavy placed both hands on the table as he gazed at the man's face. "I remember the welcome he got in 1911 when he came with the Queen to visit Ireland. I'm glad to say, I was there to see him." He tucked his thumbs into his jacket lapels. "He's overseen the expanse of a wonderful Empire. Brought medical care, education and the railways to backward places like India. Helped this country too."

Liam pursed his lips. "I didn't know that."

Mr Leavy gestured for Liam to take a chair, a soft tone to his voice. "I wouldn't be expecting you to know much about the Empire."

Liam sat down. He couldn't imagine the King visiting Lisowen now. He'd be a sitting duck for the snipers. How could he be loved in 1911 and hated in 1920?

Mr Leavy slid jotter paper in front of him and handed him a pencil. "We'll start with some multiplication, shall we?"

For the next hour or two, Liam recited his multiplication tables and worked at sums. As he struggled with long division, he glanced up to see Mr Leavy reading from a large hard back book. The gold embossed title on the green cover was clear: Unionism in Ireland.

A bespectacled face appeared over the top of the large tome and caught his eye. "Just concentrate on what you're doing, please."

As Liam returned to his work, a pamphlet fell from the book and dropped beneath the table.

Mr Leavy stood up and excused himself. "I'll be back in a minute."

As the door closed, Liam bent down and picked up the pamphlet. He stared at it. The cover was adorned with the colours of the British Flag. Rally in Guild Hall, Armagh, August 1st

He dropped the pamphlet back on the floor and went back to his seat. His mind was racing. Dan had been furious about someone going to a rally. Then, Liam remembered the row at Donnybrook Hall.

Mr Leavy came back into the room with a glass of milk, which he set in front of Liam. "Shall we move on now to comprehension?"

"Excuse me?" Liam's thoughts were elsewhere. "I'm sorry, Mr Leavy, but I don't feel the best and I think, if you don't mind, that I should go home." He rubbed his stomach. "I should have said earlier, but I've a bit of a sore belly. My food feels as though it's not settled. I'm worried that I might …you know…sick it up."

"Eh, of course, Liam." The headmaster looked concerned. "We'll carry on with English tomorrow afternoon, if you're feeling better."

"I'm sure I will." Liam struggled up, his high-backed chair creaking. "Thank you for helping me with my sums. I'm grateful. I really am."

He grabbed his jacket and hurriedly left the house. Hobbling away, he started piecing everything together. Mr Leavy was a unionist. A unionist who might be going to a rally. And that whole business of Dan going after a Protestant he thought had buried money during the epidemic – well, Mr Leavy had come to the house to help with little Fionuala's burial.

How could he voice his fears to Mr Leavy? The headmaster was a sensible man and might not take a boy like him seriously. And then again, if he did, he might head straight for the police, and the bastard Black and Tans. Telling his parents was out of the question. Liam's mind flitted over those people that he might turn to. His own schoolteacher? But Mr McNamee was not a pleasant man. Father Flaherty? What would he do if he knew? A man of the cloth might not wish to be involved. Then Ruari came to mind again. With all the events of the last days he'd forgotten about trying to contact him. Ruari in his RIC uniform would be the man to call at the Leavy house. Mr Leavy would take Ruari seriously and get the family to leave. Once the Leavys were safe, Ruari could decide what was to be done about Dan.

And the bus fare to Kilkenny to summon Ruari? Liam was skint. Once again, he racked his brains. Who could he turn to for money? His parents would be suspicious as to why he needed it, and he couldn't possibly steal from them. He thought of his schoolfriends but knew that they never had much to spare.

Then he thought of Old John. Would he lend him the money for the fare to Kilkenny?

***

Old John was outside the barn, washing his face in a small metal basin, when he saw Liam approaching. "Ah, I trust I find you in finer fettle today."

"Yes, thanks." Liam shuffled about uneasily.

Old John dried his face with a cloth and poured the water from the basin on the ground. It sloshed over the stones creating small rivulets. "What brings you this way again?"

"I came to ask a favour." Liam steeled himself for a possible refusal. Old John might have spent all his money.

"It's a favour you're seeking, is it? And do you think an oul soul like me might be able to grant such a favour?" Old John looked at him, the deep lines about his eyes crinkling.

"I need the bus fare to Kilkenny. I need to speak to someone there. Urgently"

"Well, I was thinking of doing some commerce in the environs of Kilkenny. Could I deliver a message?" Old John raised his eyebrows.

Liam could see thick dirt under his discoloured fingernails. He hesitated. It had been troubling him that his mam and da would worry if he stayed away from home all day. Indeed, they might think that he'd run away. But to entrust Old John with his news?

"Ah, you're not sure if a man of my deportment might be trustworthy or not. There's many a shifty unsavoury type about these days, I'm sad to say." Old John looked at him, his eyes wide, a softness about his mouth. "I can only but vouch for my own behaviour."

"I'm sorry, I'm not sure..."

"Would a prayer help?' Old John scratched his head.

In that moment, and before the prayer was said, Liam knew that Old John going to Kilkenny was a much better idea. He bowed his head as Old John intoned.

"Dear Lord, bring clarity, and correct and noble thinking to this young man's mind. Amen."

As soon as Old John had raised his head, Liam had the words out of his mouth. "Could you go to the Kilkenny barracks and find an RIC friend of mine?"

"Well, that should present no problem."

"He has to be told, and in private, that there's a threat to someone's life."

Old John raised his eyebrows, his eyes wide. He stared at Liam. "Pardon me?"

"I know of a plot to kill someone."

"And how, young man, did you hear this?"

"By chance. I was outside the forge, looking for something I'd lost when I heard Dan O'Toole talking to some men about who he planned to shoot."

"And you didn't perchance, pick this up incorrectly?

"I swear to God above! The blacksmith plans to shoot a Protestant this Saturday night. Someone who's dug the ground up." Liam started to sniffle. "I'm sure it's Mr Leavy, for didn't he bury our Fionuala?"

Liam saw the look of horror on the old man's face.

Old John put his hands to his scalp. "Dear God above." He closed his eyes and mumbled something.

"Only my friend, Ruari Corvin, who's an RIC man, can be trusted. My da's been suspicious of most of the police for some time now, and if the Black and Tans got to know, there'd be more problems for us all in Lisowen."

"And have you told your father?"

"He's too ill." Liam cleared his throat. "I want him kept out of this."

Old John nodded, the lines on his forehead knit deeply together. "We should warn the Leavys now."

Liam shook his head. "They need warned, but at the right time, for I'm worried that Mr Leavy will go to the police himself. Ruari's the only policeman that can be trusted. He's a good man." Liam drew breath. "He'll know what to do and he'll not have the Tans involved.'

"And it's planned for Saturday?" Old John brought his hands to his neck. "The day after tomorrow?"

"Saturday night."

"Then, yes, Liam. I'll catch the bus for Kilkenny tomorrow morning. I'll be sure to find your friend. Then he can do what's best."

Chapter Fifty-Three

The next day, as Liam fed the chickens and cleaned out Bobby's stall, his mind kept pulling him away to Old John and how he'd get on that day.

Having visited Kilkenny two years ago, Liam could picture the barracks. A little bigger than Lisowen's, Kilkenny Barracks might house five or six policemen. He recalled they'd been constructing a new building next door, something to do with the army.

He imagined Old John reaching the barracks' door and asking to speak to Police Officer Corvin. He'd wait a few minutes and then Ruari would come out. Ruari would tower over Old John. He could picture Ruari with his thick brown hair visible under his cap, his boots shining, immaculate in his uniform. In his mind's eye, he could see Old John take Ruari to the side of the barracks. A long conversation would follow. Things would be said and plans made. Ruari would place his broad hand on Old John's shoulder. "You can count on me," he'd say.

Then Old John would catch the late afternoon bus back to Lisowen.

Bobby whinnied and Liam patted the warm flank. Ruari Corvin could always be counted on to do the right thing.

***

Old John stepped down off the bus at Kilkenny Bus Station. It had been a year or two since he'd last been there and he couldn't remember having ever seen the barracks. He'd abandoned the idea of trying to sell door to door. This task was much too important.

He stopped a young man on the street. "Excuse me young sir, and I'd be looking for the RIC establishment, if you'd be so kind."

The man looked him up and down before answering. "You'll not get near it, for aren't the army moved in and settled there. Feckin' sandbags stacked as high as the Cliffs of Moher!"

The man wore a plaid suit and smart shoes. *That man has money,* Old John thought. *A lawyer or doctor, or someone who bets cannily on the horses.* "I beg your pardon, young man, but could you elaborate?"

"It's only the police and army that goes in or out. The whole place is barbed wire all round and Tommys sitting about with rifles and the like. A feckin' fortress!"

Old John thought the man's uncouth tone and voice to be at odds with his clothes. Must be a gambler, he decided.

The man pointed down the road. "Sure, you're not more than a hundred yards from the building. A stone's throw will take you there."

Old John thanked him and headed off in the direction he'd been shown. Rounding the corner, he groaned. It was exactly as he'd been told. Two army trucks were parked outside the fortified building, and soldiers strode in and out of the entrance. The mix of colours: dark green police tunics and the khaki-coloured trousers told him immediately that the Black and Tans were billeted there.

He clenched his fists. It was as he'd feared. The police were no longer run by the police. He approached one of the guards. "I'd be looking for an RIC officer by the name of Ruari Corvin."

The guard scratched his head and turned to his colleague. "You know a Ruari Corvin?"

The other lad sniffed and answered in an English accent. "And who wants to know, for most of the local police have been relocated." He leaned forward and sneered at Old John. "Get lost now, will you?"

Old John felt dizzy. "Eh, I'll be on my way, thank you."

The two men turned their backs on him, their chat peppered with curses.

Old John's stomach churned. This wasn't good, and what was he to do now for young Liam? He looked up to the grey sky for divine intervention, but none seemed forthcoming.

When he got back to the bus station, he saw two bus drivers with the side panels of the bus open, working at the engine, and a queue of anxious onlookers. He made his way to the front and cleared his throat. "Will I be able to get back to Lisowen this evening?"

One man looked round, his face smudged with grease. "Sorry Mister, but this bus isn't going anywhere soon. I think you'll have to wait till tomorrow."

Old John felt his pulse race. The clock on the red brick wall of the bus station showed half past four. If he started walking now, he'd be back well after midnight. And those hills were going to kill him. But, with nothing else for it, he put one foot in front of the other.

***

At half past four, Liam was sitting with Mr Leavy learning about commas.

"Commas are important," said Mr Leavy, "but they can be tricky."

The work was dull and repetitive. Every so often, Liam found himself almost blurting out his fears, but he managed to hold them back. As he battled to keep his concentration, he thought about Old John. He'd be leaving Kilkenny now. Then, doubt crept into his mind. What if he couldn't find Ruari, or Ruari couldn't get away?

William Leavy reached for the page that Liam had just written and looked at it, checking for commas, adding a few. "Not bad, but room for improvement." He sighed. "We'll go back to grammar another time." Unwinding his glasses from around his ears, he set them to the side and rubbed his temples. "Maybe tomorrow you'd help me get the trap fixed, for the springs need replacing and it'll take the two of us to do that."

Liam, grateful to have the excuse to go, got up from his seat. "I'd do that willingly, Mr Leavy."

"Excellent." Mr Leavy smiled broadly and opened the door from the dining room.

Liam took his leave. "Thank you, Mr Leavy. I'll be back tomorrow early." Please God, with Ruari.

***

Liam bolted down his supper and, sliding his plate to the side, pushed back his chair. "I'm going round to Aidan's to return a football card that he loaned me."

His mam looked at him, her eyebrows raised. Then her face lit up. "Aidan who has the sister with red hair and dimples?"

Liam cringed. "You mean Kathleen?"

Da wheezed, then laughed "Don't be long."

267

"I won't," said Liam, as he eased his arms into his jacket.

Once outside, he headed off in the direction of the barn where Old John was staying.

When he finally got there, the place was deserted. Damn! Old John should have been back long ago. Surely, he was as good as his word! Tomorrow night was looming large and what was he to do if Ruari couldn't come?

He returned home, weary and worried. Telling his parents that he was tired and needed his bed, he climbed the stairs to his bedroom.

Tomorrow, Liam thought, *it might be up to me to save the Leavys!*

Chapter Fifty-Four

Old John staggered into the barn just as streaks of morning light
were breaking through the dark sky. The final effort of climbing
up the hill had left him breathless and totally exhausted. Pulling
his boots off, he realised that the blisters on his feet were bleeding.
The smell of sweat and blood made him gag. As he tugged off his
socks, one of his toenails got caught in the wool and pulled away.
Dipping his mug into the bucket of drinking water, he poured it
over his burning feet to cool them. After drying them with a rag,
he laid his head on the straw and fell fast asleep.

***

That morning, Liam came down to the parlour in a state of
agitation. He'd hoped to be the first person up, but his mam was
already stirring a pot of porridge hanging over the fire.

She glanced up at him. "Morning, son..."

Liam saw the pinched look on her face and sensed her unease.
"Morning."

"Did you sleep well?"

"Well enough, thank you." He wasn't going to tell the truth
about his dreadful night of tossing and turning, wondering how
he was to tell Mr Leavy that his life was in danger.

His mam placed a spoon and a bowl of steaming porridge on
the table. He sat down, blew on it and spooned it hurriedly into
his mouth.

She looked at him with a sideways glance. "You'll burn your
throat forcing hot food down you like that." She set a glass of
water on the table. "What's the hurry?"

"I want to be up early with Mr Leavy this morning. He needs
help in fixing the trap."

"But it's only gone seven o'clock."

He gulped his water down, then pushed back the chair with a
loud scrape. "The job might take most of the day."

"And when will you be back?"

"Don't know, Mam. When the work's done." He tried to smile at her but grimaced instead. He reached for his jacket and opened the door. Without looking behind, he closed it tightly and hurried off down the lane.

**

Old John was awoken from a dream by loud banging on the door. In the dream he'd been waltzing with Grainne O'Toole; himself in a top hat and tails and Grainne in a long, flowing pink dress, her hair tied back in red ribbons. He sat bolt upright from his bed of hay, his pulse racing, taking a moment to realise where he was. "Who's there?"

"It's Liam."

Old John struggled up, flinching from the pain in his feet, and shuffled to the barn door. He put the key in the lock, turned it and swung the door open, screwing up his eyes as daylight flooded in.

"Well? Is Ruari coming?" the boy asked, his young face open and earnest.

Old John felt his toes throb. "He'll be here this evening with some trusted pals, but we're to warn the family first. Ruari is on duty all day and can't get away till later. He said to me – most categorically, and with plain-speaking language – tell the Leavys to leave their house, for the police are on their way."

"I'm so glad you got to him," Liam shivered from the cool morning air, "I was afraid he'd be out on patrol somewhere."

Old John moved slightly, shifting his weight from one foot to the other. "We should both go to see the family, for I think that the serious nature of this threat requires a delegation." He groaned from the pain in his feet. "Just give me time for my ablutions and to take some sustenance."

Beckoning Liam inside, Old John set about preparing himself for yet another walk.

Liam chewed his fingernails as Old John ran a wet cloth over his face, then washed some bread and cheese down with a mug of water.

Then the pair set off, both hobbling; Old John moaned gently while mumbling Bible verses under his breath. They kept their heads down, straining against the prevailing wind. Liam thought about his home as he walked, replaying in his mind how Declan had goaded him. He could see now that Pat and Mary were just human like himself. Human beings that made mistakes. He'd seen their anguish, and it was up to him to accept what they'd done and forgive them. The priest had been right, his parents could not have done more for him.

Liam looked up as the Leavy house come into view. Mrs Leavy was outside polishing the brass knocker. She looked round as the two of them approached.

Old John set his cloth bag on the ground with a groan and bowed awkwardly. "Ma'am."

"Liam? Old John? What brings you both here?"

"You've got to leave the house!" Liam blurted out. "The police have sent us to warn your family." He took a deep breath in. "You're not safe here."

Sara's hands flew to her cheeks. "No! This can't be true!"

"The boy is telling no lie." Old John took off his cap and held it in his hand. "I'm afraid to say that his message is totally accurate and with no hint of trickery." He tilted his head to one side. "May I speak to your good husband, please. There's things that should be said, man-to-man."

Sara nodded slowly, holding her polishing cloth in one hand. She opened the door, calling for her husband to join them. She turned to Liam, kneading her duster with her fingers. "How did you find out about this?"

Liam felt his face flush red. "By chance. I heard some men plotting against you."

"Yes, what is it?" William came out, his spectacles on, holding a folded newspaper in one hand. "Liam? Old John?" He took off his glasses. "By the look on your faces I can tell that something's not right."

"Indeed," Old John mumbled. "I'm afraid it's all wrong."

William stood back a little. "Please, come in. Both of you." He set the newspaper on the table. "Old John, come through to the dining room. Liam, if you'd kindly take a seat in the parlour."

Liam followed Mrs Leavy into the parlour where Richard was playing with his toy train. The child's little face brightened into a wide grin. "Liam, come and play trains with me." He held his toy up to show him.

Liam hunkered down beside the child. "I've a good idea. Why don't you come to my house and bring your train?"

"Yah!" Richard tugged at his mother's skirt. "Can I go? Please, Mummy?"

"And I think my mam and da would like your Mummy and Daddy to come too."

Liam looked up to see Mrs Leavy wringing her hands together, her face pale. She brushed a stray strand of hair back from her face. "Yes, we'll all go, Richard. But first I need to do some things. Be a good boy and put your train and teddy and your books in here." She handed Richard her wicker basket.

Liam kneeled down and took Richard's teddy from the chair beside the fire. "Mr Carson thinks we'll all have a grand time at my mam and da's house. Isn't that right, Mr Carson?" Liam made the teddy's head nod in agreement.

Richard jumped up and down. "Hurrah, Edward says he wants to go!"

Through the half open dining room door, Liam could hear snippets of Old John's conversation with Mr Leavy. Old John was talking about the RIC, who would be coming. But the family should leave soon, well before the evening. Then he heard Old John groaning, asking if he might sit a while as his back was troubling him. Would that be an inconvenience or discommode? Liam heard him ask Mr Leavy.

No. Please stay as long as you need, he heard Mr Leavy say. But you'll appreciate, that I'll need time to help my wife with the packing.

Liam glanced at his mother's friend before averting his gaze. Her face was such a poor colour; she looked as if she might collapse at any time.

"Don't worry, Mrs Leavy. You'll be fine when you get to our house" Then Liam remembered that he'd have to prepare his own mam. He felt his pulse race. "But first I need to go home and tell Mam and Da that you'll be coming."

***

Liam made his way home as fast as he could. Thank God, Old John had found Ruari. He'd never even considered how difficult if might be for Ruari to leave Kilkenny Barracks and get to Lisowen. Now, as he limped up the path towards his front door, Liam felt a huge surge of relief.

He hoped that his da would still be in bed. The less upset for him the better. But it was important now, to tell his mam.

When he opened the door, he could see her shaping soda farls on the work top.

She looked round as he came into the parlour, her hands white with flour. "What has you back so soon? Did you get the trap fixed?"

"No, Mam. I need you to listen and you're not to interrupt me." As he fixed her with his eyes, he could see the look of confusion, almost hurt, on her face.

His mam's face crumpled. "Is this to do with your da and me? Are you going away?" She wiped her floury hands on her apron and turned to him, her mouth trembling.

Liam shook his head. "No Mam, this isn't to do with Da or you. It's the Leavys."

"The Leavys?" His mam sank into the rocking chair in front of him. "What about them?"

Liam thought carefully about how much he should tell her. "Well, there's a threat to their lives."

His mam clutched her chest. "Holy Mother of God!"

"I've told them they should come here. Just for tonight, mind."

She nodded. "Of course. Of course." She looked at him squarely. "How do you know they're in danger?

Liam took a deep breath. "It's complicated, but I promise I'll tell you when they're safe. I can't be wasting any time now as I need to help them carry their belongings."

"But you'll tell me everything when you get back. Won't you?"

Liam nodded. "I will, but please don't be saying anything to Da just yet."

"For the Lord's sake, Liam. How can I keep secrets from your da?"

Liam shot her a look. She'd kept a huge secret from him. For many years.

She flinched, seeming to read his thoughts. "I'll not say to Da until they're here, I promise."

He grabbed a piece of bread from the sideboard and shoved it in his pocket. "The Leavys should be almost ready to leave by now."

***

Mary looked out the window as Liam hobbled, almost ran, down the lane. She put her hands to her heart. So, Sara was right when she found the broken photograph frame lying on the ground. Someone did want rid of them. Dear God, these were awful times they were living through. She crossed herself.

She prepared for her visitors as best she could without disturbing Pat. As she did so an idea came to her about how to help her friend. Finishing her work, she took writing paper from the dresser drawer and sat, pen and ink to hand, going over in her head the words she was about to write. She inked her pen and began writing. Having filled a full page with script, she blotted and signed it before sliding it into an envelope. She'd give the envelope to Sara to take with her. Mary hoped this letter would help the Leavys find suitable accommodation for a few days.

Pat was stirring now. She could hear him moving about upstairs. He'd guess something was up as soon as he saw her face. There was nothing he couldn't tell from her expression, and she wouldn't be able to keep it from him. At the very least, she'd have to tell him that they were to have visitors. But most importantly, she'd have to tell him to keep calm. Uttering a silent prayer, she climbed the stairs to the bedroom.

***

Sara looked at William in horror when he told her they would need to make their lives elsewhere.

"But we've never lived anywhere other than Lisowen," she said, tears rolling down her face, two large bags stuffed with her most precious possessions lying at her feet.

"I know, my love. But we need to be safe." He pulled her close to him and kissed her head. "Everything will work out. I know it will."

After explaining the route she should take through the forest, he held the door open. Richard had the wicker basket in one hand, the teddy peering over the top. His wife turned back, for one last look before she clutched Richard's hand tightly. Her shoulders drooping from the weight of her cloth bags, she trailed Richard behind her as they slowly walked away.

William swallowed hard, coming back into the parlour. Already the house seemed chilled as the fire spluttered from a few lifeless coals. He opened the dresser drawer, rummaged around the back and withdrew a gun which he laid on the table. He called to Old John.

Old John came out from the dining room. A shard of sunlight glinted off the silver barrel.

"I'll not be needing this for I've another to do me." William patted his breast pocket, then pointed to the gun. "Please take it."

"Thank you." Old John put the gun into his bag and took a seat at the table. "I've been cogitating that it's best I stay behind and wait for the police. It's imperative that they stake out the right establishment." He set his bag up on the table. "Then I'll leave them to it."

"If you really think that's wise. I don't want you to put yourself in danger."

"Of that, have no fear." Old John rested back on two legs of the parlour chair. "I can well look after myself."

William was surprised. The old fellow was an oddity, that was for sure, but strangely confident. "Well, I don't exactly know how to thank you and young Liam for coming to warn us."

"No thanks are necessary. The RIC will be here soon enough, and they'll catch the villains."

"Perhaps I should stay here with you?" William rapped the table with his knuckles. "Just in case."

Old John took a few seconds before replying. "Your good wife will be looking for you, worrying herself to distraction, I'd be sure. You should go now."

William nodded his head slowly and swallowed hard. "Thank you again." He shook Old John's hand.

Then, he took one last look around the parlour as the memories came to the fore. This was the room where he'd sat on his grandmother's knee, where she'd told him stories of the Children of Lir. It was the room where his uncle had visited, bringing his fiddle and where Sara had danced, the twins mesmerised by their mother, her hair flowing freely, her head thrown back, laughing.

This was the room where his father had passed away and Sara had wept so sorely when the boys left for war. It was the room too, where people gathered to pay their respects when the boys didn't return.

The walls of this house were steeped in recollections both good and bad, and it was heart-breaking to leave this cottage that had belonged to his family for so many generations. They had been lucky never to have had a landlord rapping at the door, demanding the rent.

But of late, William had been expecting such a day as this might arrive. Ireland wouldn't be ruled by Britain for much longer. Signs that the tide was turning were becoming increasingly evident. And he wouldn't be cowed for his allegiance to the Crown. He had to face reality. His family, and those prepared to speak out against the new Government, would no longer feel welcome in this part of the country.

Sighing, William picked up his suitcase and briefcase and, without turning round, opened the door and trudged away.

***

Old John set his bag on the table and extracted the cap with the scarf attached that he'd so carefully stuffed with sheep wool. Aunt Rose would have been proud of his handiwork, for the stitches were fine and even, and the cap had been stuffed to full capacity. Placing it on his head, he secured the scarf across his face with a large safety pin and stood to look at his reflection in the mirror hanging over the fireplace. Only his eyes were visible. He laughed at the strange figure with the balloon-like head and bull-sized neck staring back at him.

Good, he thought, and went to lock both doors.

***

Liam met up with the Leavys and helped them carry their bags for the last part of their journey. Mrs Leavy, freed from the weight of her bags, still walked with hunched shoulders, her gaze to the ground. Her husband held himself erect, his hat on his head, as though on official business; suitcase in one hand and briefcase in the other.

Richard bounded on in front, obviously excited at the prospect of playing trains at Liam's house. "Mr Carson wants to see your house," he said breathlessly, clutching the wicker basket carrying his teddy to his chest.

"And my mam and da will want to meet Mr Carson," Liam replied, amused at what his father's reaction might be to meeting a teddy called Edward Carson. Any mention of that name in the months before had caused his da to shake his head and mutter under his breath.

When they reached the house, Richard stood by Liam's side as he flung the door open. "Mam, they're here!"

Standing in the parlour were his mam and da; his da by the fire, his mam at the table, setting cups and saucers out.

"Come in, come in," his mother called out, a worried look on her face, beckoning them in with a curved arm.

"Oh, Mary," Sara cried out. "You can't imagine what I'm feeling."

Liam saw his mother go to her friend and pull her close to her chest.

"I know, I know," she whispered. "I'm so sorry."

William stood by the doorway, his hat in one hand. He looked at Liam's father. "So good and kind of you, sir. We don't know how to rightly thank you."

"You're very welcome." Pat said, giving a little cough. "Your family is safe with us."

Chapter Fifty-Five

Dan was in a fierce mood. It was bloody typical of his cousin to choose that weekend to die, so that Dan had to be there at the wake, sombre and sad with the rest of the family. And then Declan had decided to avail himself of the poitín. In no fit state, he was, with his eyes rolling back in his head. Dan would have to do without him. He sidled out the door, pretending to head for the privy. That eejit of a son wasn't fit to be given any responsibility. So be it. Three men should be more than enough to tackle Leavy and his wife and child.

He had everything worked out in his head. Leavy would take him to the buried money, and Dan would make sure the ground was well and truly dug up, for it would make a convenient grave for the Protestant fecker.

Ger and Martin would take the woman and her brat out to the forest. They knew what to do with them.

Dan checked in his pocket for his gun. The other pocket was stuffed with his flashlight and balaclava. Good. He was prepared. He strode out purposefully towards the Leavy house.

The two men were waiting for him, as arranged, at the bottom of the lane leading to the farmhouse. They pulled on their balaclavas when they saw him.

It was midnight and the house was in darkness.

Dan banged hard on the door, his fingers clenched into a fist. "Open up!" he yelled. "Open the fucking door or we'll kick it down.'

He shot at the lock. The door swung open.

With a crooked finger, he beckoned the men to follow him inside, shouting, "Come out from wherever you are, Leavy!"

In the pitch black, Martin tripped over a pail. It clattered across the stone floor, sending pieces of coal flying. "Fuck!" he shouted.

Holding the gun in one hand and his torch in the other, Dan used his thumb to slide the switch on. A thin yellow shaft of light shone out in front of him. The glow of torchlight showed up the table, the chairs, the grandfather clock, the empty fireplace.

He went to the foot of the stairs and called up. "Come down, Leavy! And bring your wife and family!"

No sound.

"Get the fuck downstairs if you value your life!" he shouted, angrily.

Nothing. Where could they be at this time of night? Had some fecker warned them?

"Ger! Martin! Check if the bastards are hiding in the bedroom. I'll guard the door."

As the men ran upstairs, from behind the coat stand, something moved.

"What the–!" Dan startled, shining the light in the direction of the noise.

A man with a monstrously large head, his face obscured, pointed two guns straight at him.

"Jesus Christ!" Dan dropped the torch. It bounced off the stone floor, the light flickering on and off.

A gunshot rang out and Dan fell to the ground, screeching. He clutched his wounded hand, his gun spinning away from his grasp. As he writhed in agony, the torchlight spluttered out.

Struggling to his knees, Dan felt about the floor for his gun. He heard Ger and Martin thundering down the stairs. More shots rang out, and the two men cried out; cursing, banging and scraping their way to the bottom of the stairs.

"The bastard's got my arm," Ger shouted.

He and Martin yelled as they stumbled across the parlour floor, shooting wildly around them.

Dan lay as still as he could. He was in danger of being killed in the crossfire. Shots whizzed overhead. Then he heard footsteps, the door being flung open and Martin and Ger running off.

"Come back and help me, you feckers!" Dan roared but the door banged shut.

This is it, he thought and closed his eyes. He steeled himself for what was to come. Instead, he heard the uneven tread of the shooter moving towards the door, the slam of wood on wood, then silence.

Several minutes passed before Dan felt able to get to his feet. He thrust a dirty handkerchief into his palm to stem the flow of blood. His head was spinning. Who, or what, had just shot at him? For the life of him, he couldn't figure it out. Some beast of a policeman? A fecking mute with a bad eye for shooting? If only he could get his hands on the bastard, he'd throttle him to death.

And would the bastard be waiting for him outside? Or did the fecker think he'd been killed when he'd just been lying still? *That must be it*, he thought, relieved. He'd take the back way out of the house and hide out the night next door, at O'Farrell's farm.

He lurched to the back door and opened it slowly, then moved to the yard door. He listened for the sound of anyone moving about but all seemed quiet. Grasping his wounded hand tightly, he staggered out unto the back lane and climbed gingerly over the fence that led to O'Farrell's land. Clearing another fence, and cursing from the searing pain in his hand, he tramped towards the outhouse.

As he stumbled along, he felt his footstep on something soft. Losing his balance, he slid to the ground. Feckin' cowpat. "Fuck!" he yelled. He sat on the ground, breathing heavily.

The bull was upon him before he realised. Tossed up and into the air, he felt an explosion of pain as something pierced his chest. He screamed and screamed as the bull came at him again.

And again.

***

Old John took deep breaths of night air into his lungs as he walked away from the house. He felt strangely calm. He stuffed the revolvers into his pockets and tugged his wool-stuffed hat and scarf off. He'd be far away before dawn, and tomorrow he'd be on the bus to Dublin. Aunt Rose would be pleased to see him.

Someday, he thought, *when the time would be right, he'd return.*

***

The first bus from Lisowen to Kilkenny train station would leave at seven am. The Leavys were ready to leave shortly after six. Mary had a bag filled with apples and buttered brac for their journey. Liam played trains on the floor with Richard until his father said that they should get going.

"You'll be on a real steam train today, and it'll be a grand adventure for us all." William smiled.

Mary handed Sara the letter she'd penned the day before. She'd already explained where the family should try to reach before nightfall. "You'll be treated the best. Of that, I'm sure."

"Cultra." William ran his hand around the back of his head, his hat in hand. "There'll be buses from Belfast to take us there." He gave Sara's hand a squeeze. "With luck, and God's will, we'll be there by the evening."

Mary saw Sara's head droop, a single tear drop to the floor. She pulled her friend close to her, whispering in her ear. "You'll be back here in Lisowen someday."

Sara's shoulders twitched convulsively as she sobbed on Mary's shoulder.

Mary felt her own eyes smart. She blinked hard but unbidden tears rolled slowly down her face. "Now, no bawling." She swiped her fingers over her cheeks. "We'll see each other soon enough, for we'll both still be in Ireland. Think of those that have gone to America and the like."

"True, true," Sara whispered, her voice breaking.

William and Pat shook hands, William expressing his sincerest thank you and Pat professing that he'd done little, and that Liam was the man to thank.

Liam came down the stairs with a pack of cards, which he handed to Richard. "Happy Families. I used to love this game but it's time for them to have a new owner."

"Thank you." The little boy smiled. "I'll put them in the basket with Mr Carson." He set the cards on top of the teddy's paws. "We'll play this together on the train."

"Indeed, we will, son," William tousled his son's hair before turning to Liam. "And thank you again. As I said to you last night; yourself and Old John have saved us." He put his hand out towards Liam who took it. "You've been incredibly courageous, Liam."

Richard looked up at his father, a puzzled look on his face. "Has Liam been very, very good?

"Yes, son. Liam has been very, very good."

From her doorway, Mary watched the family leave, promising herself that she would hold her emotions tight. "Take good care, now," she called after them.

Sara looked back at her and tried to smile.

Chapter Fifty-Six

For the first time in their married lives, Sara and William awoke in a bed that didn't belong to them. A large bed in a large room. Sara lifted the bed clothes and placed her bare feet on the floor. She felt the warmth of a rug beneath her toes. Moving to the windows, she pulled the heavy curtain back a fraction. Light poured into the room. She draped the heavy end of the curtain over a wing-backed chair and surveyed the room.

The hands on the mantlepiece clock showed ten past nine. In the corner sat a red velvet chaise longue and, to the side, was an intricately-carved oak wardrobe. Richard lay sleeping on a small bed, the tip of his thumb to his lips. Above him, the morning light caused shadows from an elaborate chandelier to dance rainbows on the walls.

William stirred. "What time is it?"

"Long past our usual rising time." Sara looked at her face in the gilt-framed mirror above the basin. Was that really her? A woman with lines radiating out from her eyes and mouth, her hair flecked with grey strands. She blinked at her reflection. She felt sad, waking up in this strange house that wasn't hers. At least she'd slept well, the exhaustion of the journey and the lateness of their arrival contributing to a good night's rest.

William was suddenly behind her, his arms about her waist. "Thank God, we're safe." He kissed her neck before giving her a gentle hug.

After breakfast, they took a stroll in the grounds. She was glad to see Richard playing hide and seek among the shrubs, seemingly oblivious to what had happened. She looked out towards the lough. White gulls tinged with black were wheeling like kites in the air, making their lazy circles over calm water.

"William."

"Yes, my love."

Sara looked up. The clouds looked like smoke from the steam train that had brought them from Kilkenny to Belfast. "Wasn't it so strange arriving here with all our belongings and handing the butler Mary's letter."

"Very strange."

Sara felt fretful, as though her old way of life was lost to her. "What are we to do now?"

William took her by the hand and she felt the warmth of it. "We'll start looking for a house. A house to rent that will suit the three of us."

Coming down the wide steps of the large house, a young woman, her peach dress fluttering in the breeze, called out to them. "Mr and Mrs Leavy!"

William smiled.

"Lady Gilroy!" Sara waved back.

Chapter Fifty-Seven

It had been two weeks to the day since the Leavys had left Lisowen. Two weeks without Sara seated at her parlour table, a cup of tea in hand. Mary sighed as she took two glasses of freshly-made lemonade outside to Pat and Liam.

Her men sat on wooden chairs, their heads bent over an old pair of bellows that had come apart. Pat was holding one end as Liam worked with pliers, his tongue between his teeth.

Pat looked up as she set the lemonade in front of them. "Just the thing for us hardworking men." He reached for his glass and, catching her eye, winked.

She set the other glass down in front of Liam and flicked back her curls. "Is that what you call yourselves?"

Liam and Pat chuckled.

Back inside, Mary pulled some newly-laundered sheets from her basket. Flicking a drop of water on the iron that had been heating on the fire, she leaned across the table, and skated the iron over the fabric, watching the creases disappear. As she ironed, her mind drifted back to the night that the Leavys had stayed with them.

They were gone, with no plans to return. The first letter from Sara had said that one of the schoolteachers was to buy their house. She blinked hard. Did that mean they'd never be back? She folded the ironed sheets and set the iron back on its holder at the hearth.

She felt in her apron pocket for the letters that had arrived that day. Both were postmarked in the north. One she recognised as Sara's handwriting but the other was unfamiliar in its script.

Holding Sara's letter up to the light of the window, she read aloud:

19, Newtownards Parade,
Belfast,
15th September 1920

Dear Mary,

I've so much to tell you and I know that my first letter was too brief, for I do believe I was still in a state of shock. I could only find words to say that we were safe and to express my gratitude to Liam for saving our family's lives. Of course, we are indebted to Old John too, but alas have no way of contacting him. When he next visits Lisowen, please give him our heartfelt thanks.

Now that we are somewhat settled, I can tell you more about what has happened. I have to say that Lady Gilroy was wonderful. She's such a beautiful young woman and I'm so glad to say that she's married a very acceptable young man. Herself and Lord Gilroy could not have been more hospitable.

Lady Gilroy said that she knew what it felt like to be forced out of your home, and she offered to have us stay with them for another week or two. However, William began looking for a house as soon as we arrived and, yesterday, we found the most perfect place to rent off the Newtownards Road. It has running water, no less, and a parlour with a range, a small dining room and two bedrooms. I feel we are somewhat blessed.

Lord Gilroy is influential in one of the schools in Belfast, so William will be back teaching soon and earning a fair wage. It is so much to take in, that my head is in a complete spin. Richard was unsettled at first, but I'm relieved to say is more himself now.

I'm afraid to say that Belfast is not free of trouble either. There was rioting a few weeks ago around the shipyard, and I believe many workers were thrown out. It is all horrible, isn't it? However, William says that our family will be safe here and we should stay in Belfast for now.

Even though William feels Lisowen is not safe for him, I promise to visit someday. As I wrote in my first letter, our house there will be sold. Miss Montgomery, the new headmistress, is to move in later this month. Fancy that! A woman in charge.

I have to say that I feel very sad to see the house sold. That house had been in William's family for so many generations.

Anyway, please think about meeting me in Dublin. We could go to the Shelbourne and enjoy taking tea together, God willing, before Christmas is upon us. My head is bursting with things I want to tell you and I so dreadfully miss our chit-chats.

Meanwhile, I trust that you are well, and that Pat and Liam are also.

I leave you, your very good friend, wishing yourself and your family all that is good and true.

Yours sincerely,

Sara

PS. I've enclosed a little something to thank yourself and Pat for helping us out that night.

Keep it for Dublin.

Mary opened the small brown wage packet and removed a ten-shilling note. She folded the money inside the letter and, stuffing it in her apron pocket, swallowed hard and rubbed her eyes. Then she took the other letter and opened it, searching out the signature at the bottom of the page: William Leavy.

After reading the first few lines, she slid the letter back into the envelope to read properly that evening. It was nice of William to write to her and express his thanks, she thought.

Taking the jug of lemonade and a glass for herself back outside, she topped up Pat's glass. "Sara wrote to me again," she told him.

Pat cleared his throat. "They're all right now, aren't they? The Leavys?"

"They seem to be, according to Sara. William Leavy sent a letter of thanks too."

Liam held out his glass to be re-filled. "I'll miss Mr Leavy. He knew lots of things."

Mary poured herself some lemonade and sipped it. The sour, sweet taste made her mouth water. "About Sara. We want to meet up in Dublin, sometime soon."

"And?" Pat asked.

"Well, do you think you two ejits could manage to cook for yourselves for a day?"

Pat stroked his chin with his finger and thumb. "What do you think, son?"

Liam smiled. "I don't know, Da. I suppose we could try?"

**

As the light faded, Mary lit the oil lamp and stoked the fire. Pat had retired early, and Liam was outside, talking with friends. They were planning on going fishing before school the next day.

She took the letter with the italic script and opened it with her thumb. Smoothing out the creases on the table, she held the letter up to the lamp light.

19, Newtownards Parade,
Belfast.
15 September 1920,

Dear Mary,

I feel sure that Sara has told you all about our current circumstances, so I will not repeat what you already know. Suffice to say that we are settled now, thank the Lord.

I have your son and Old John to thank for saving our lives. I have kept in contact with Miss Montgomery and she tells me that the details of the raid are undetermined, but it is enough to say that the gang were thwarted. She heard that the police moved in under the cover of darkness, that the gang ran away and, in doing so, the blacksmith was gored by a bull. (I am sure you will have heard all this too.) I am afraid that it would be unChristian of me to make comment.

The real reason for this letter, besides expressing my heartfelt thanks, is due to the thinking I have done since coming north. When I look back on the last few years, I am so saddened that my boys did not return from war. Of course, I am full of pride for the sacrifice they made. They were heroes for what they did for their country. What they might have done if they had come home, I will never know.

I saved for their education and now I can only hope that young Richard will avail of the full educational opportunities that will be presented to him.

When I say that I saved for my boys' education, I saved diligently for both Arthur and Samuel. I have now but one son and that is why I would like to be a beneficiary towards Liam's future education. Sara and I would be most proud to be involved in his future. I got to know him a little when he came to me for extra lessons, and I regard him as a fine young man.

I am very much hoping that yourself and Pat will be in agreement to this arrangement. Without Liam's fortitude, I might not be here to write this letter. We hope that when this country returns to normality, we both can come to visit and maintain a fine and cordial friendship.

Yours sincerely,
William Leavy

THE END

Printed in Great Britain
by Amazon